THE LEGEND OF DIABLO

OTHER TITLES BY V. S. MCGRATH

The Devil's Revolver
The Devil's Standoff
The Devil's Pact
The Houseguests (A Devil's Revolver Story)

Writing as Vicki Essex

Her Son's Hero
Back to the Good Fortune Diner
In Her Corner
A Recipe for Reunion
Red Carpet Arrangement
Matinees with Miriam

THE LEGEND OF DIABLO

V. S. MCGRATH

THE DEVIL'S REVOLVER BOOK 4

BRAIN MILL PRESS
GREEN BAY, WISCONSIN

The Legend of Diablo is a work of fiction. Names, places, and incidents either are products of the author's imagination or are used fictitiously. Any resemblance to actual persons, living or dead, or locales is entirely coincidental.

Published in the United States by Brain Mill Press.
Print ISBN 978-1-948559-33-1
EPUB ISBN 978-1-948559-36-2
MOBI ISBN 978-1-948559-34-8
PDF ISBN 978-1-948559-35-5

Cover illustration by Cassandre Bolan.
Cover design by Ranita Haanen.
Print spread by Ampersand Book Design.
Original interior illustrations by Ann O'Connell.

www.devilsrevolver.com

To you, the reader. Giddy up, y'all.

CONTENTS

LAND ACKNOWLEDGMENT STATEMENT

The place I call home and on which I produced this work is the traditional territories of the Haudenosaunee and the Mississaugas of New Credit, and is subject to the Dish with One Spoon wampum. I acknowledge the Indigenous people who have lived and worked this land for over 15,000 years and continue to seek justice today.

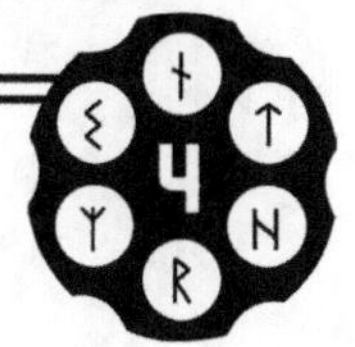

THE LEGEND OF DIABLO

Round and round the circle whirls
Red blood flows through boys and girls
Who so e'er the black thorn pricks
Is the one Diablo picks

NEW SPAIN
1725

The bones, the eye, the corn from ash. The water drawn three times from the bottomless well. The skin of an unborn black gosling. And, of course, the pistola. Javier went over the list of ingredients four times, checking them off as if one might disappear suddenly.

"Are you sure you want to do this?" Fernando kept his eye out for coyotes, soldiers, or anything that might interfere in the ritual. The ring of torches in the middle of the desert would draw all manner of beasts, the worst of them man.

"It's this, or Duarte keeps after me." He ground his teeth. "I'll never join them, Fernando. And I can't let anyone else suffer." He glanced toward the fire. "Is it hot enough, do you think?"

"You're the prodigy. You tell me."

The flames didn't look special, but the fire had been lit with an ember from the funeral pyre of a virgin. The scroll had said the flames would need to be white and black—all he saw was mundane yellow and orange, and they were running out of firewood.

Would it still work? He delved into the filaments of reality with his magical senses, seeking the tenuous connections that would allow him to draw together the forces he needed to build the weapon.

"It's almost time," Fernando warned. "The moon is high."

"I'm ready." Javier checked and rechecked the protection circle, then gestured at his longtime friend to back out of it.

He'd memorized the incantation on the scroll before it had disintegrated. It was seared into his mind like a brand now—one of the things he'd sworn to erase from his memory after he'd made the mage gun. The knowledge was too dangerous in Duarte's hands, which was why Javier had stolen the scroll in the first place. Three men had already died trying to perform this ritual. Few were skilled or powerful enough to cast this spell.

And you are?

Don't think about that, he countered himself fervently. Doubt had no place in magic.

He began the chant, adding each ingredient as he circled the fire. The pistola went in last—it'd been an old piece, a single-shot antique found on a body by the side of the road. The threads told him it had once belonged to a pirate and had traveled far, but it was barely used and too rusted to be reliable.

With luck, Javier wouldn't have to use this weapon, either. Its mere existence should be enough to deter the men pursuing him.

The incantation ended. The spell's ingredients almost entirely smothered the flames now. Had he not built the fire up enough? The gooey eye of a hawk leaked and sizzled, while the bones released greasy black smoke. Plumes of white smoke wafted into the air.

Fernando hovered at the edge of the protection circle, looking forlorn. Javier sagged as despair took hold. All that work, all those months gathering the ingredients—

Then he felt it. The threads of the universe slackened and parted, like a beautiful woman's face peering through overlong bangs. The flames leaped, and then a beam of light shot up from the firepit.

Javier stumbled back as a violet-rimmed portal opened beneath the firepit, the ingredients hovering within the light. The magic emanating from that pinhole in reality made his bones shudder. He heard all the realms singing in a chorus of minor keys, layers upon layers of resonance that threatened to pull him apart. It blasted his ears, filled his head, until his whole body shook, his bones pulsating with power.

"Javier!" Fernando shouted.

He held out his hand to stop him. He couldn't let his friend breach the circle, for his own safety as well as for the spell's sake.

The black-and-white smoke that hung in the air surged and recoiled, spiraling tightly. All of a sudden, it was as though he'd been thrust into a potter's kiln. He hissed as his exposed skin blistered and peeled like flakes of ash. He covered his face as the flame focused down to the power of a tiny sun, all of it centering around the pistol.

In his mind's eye, the threads of the universe tautened once more so that the tapestry of fate was rewoven. The pattern remained, the ropes and bundles strong and tight as always, but something was different about it now. It seemed… shorter?

As the flames receded, he shook his head and blinked past the dark splotches dancing in his eyes. Nothing was left of the ingredients except the pistol, which had melted to become… a lump of metal. Or was it ivory? Or pearl? It shifted through shadows, a braid of energy and matter. And it… sang. Just the barest echo of that fading chorus. He reached into the smoldering embers and picked it up.

Its warm weight was comforting, but also… Javier frowned. The song became a keen. Sadness. Anger. Hurt. Like a curious wolfling caught in a rabbit snare, whimpering for its mother. He stroked it gently, soothing it.

"Javier!"

A flash of light, and then a loud boom rang across the land. A blast of cold air hit him. He looked up. A white streak of light angled downward, a faint bluish glow trailing behind it. It got closer, bigger, and then Javier realized it was not going to stop.

He dove out of the protection circle as the fireball crashed, plowing a deep gouge into the earth and sending a wake of grit over Javier. The torches went out, and darkness engulfed them.

Fernando helped him to his feet. "Are you all right?"

"I'm fine." He glanced toward the crater with a frown, his heart hammering.

"Did it work?" Fernando held up a lantern.

Javier looked at his hand. The lump of twisted metal was still not a gun. And yet…

He closed his eyes. The gun's threads were tangled, twisting, writhing like a knot of rutting snakes in heat. It *was* a gun. It *had* been a gun, and now it had been reformed. Transformed.

He opened his eyes and looked down. The pistola had been restored, the grip made of buttery ivory, the barrel shining. Fernando exclaimed, "You transmogrified it!"

He didn't have a chance to correct him. Something rose from the crater where the firepit had been. No, *someone*.

Javier picked up a rock and whispered an incantation, then threw the stone into the sky so it hovered and cast its brilliant light over them. His knees grew weak; after the ritual, his energy had been sapped. He wouldn't be able to defend them magically.

He raised the mage gun shakily as the being unfurled. No telling what had come through from the other side when he'd bound the demon to the pistola. He hoped El Diablo was willing to meet the challenge…

The creature moaned.

Javier drew back sharply. It was a man. At least, something that appeared to be human. The being's neck was bent at an unnatural right angle to his body, and his shoulder blade jutted up at a sickening slope, but there was no blood. No open wounds spilling his guts across the ground.

The being slammed the heel of his palm against the side of his head, snapping his neck upright, then pulled his shoulder back so the bones popped into place.

"Madre…" Fernando crossed himself, eyes wide. Javier saw why.

The creature was entirely naked, only… there was nothing to show them it was a *he*. That curiously blank space made everything inside him squirm. He'd not been a terribly devout student of the Bible, but he did know what kind of creatures came without manhood or feminine clefts, and hazy memories of those lessons surfaced.

"You… you're an angel…" He lowered the gun. It had to be. Magic needed balance: it made sense that the demon he'd summoned and trapped within the gun had also called down a divine power of equal value. That hadn't been mentioned in the scroll, but it made sense…

The creature looked up as if noticing them for the first time. His eyes were…gods, they were like two large gems, facets sparkling and shifting between the color of the sky and a stormy sea. His long blond lashes fluttered like birds whose wings had suddenly been clipped. "Where am I?"

He'd said it in their language. With their accents, even. His shaking voice had a flutelike quality to it, as if he were speaking through choppy, windswept waves.

"I am not sure this place has a name," Javier said carefully. "But we're three days' ride northwest of the nearest village. We're safe here from the soldiers."

"Soldiers?" The creature—a man, Javier decided, with his soft, deep voice—shook his head, as if having a hard time understanding. He staggered forward, those strange eyes panning the flat, dusty plain bathed in night. He cast his gaze toward the stars, faint beyond the hovering glow stone. His chest rose and fell rapidly, and he collapsed to his knees, moaning.

"Javier, what are you doing?" Fernando whispered as he drew closer.

"I don't think he'll hurt us." He grabbed a flask and blanket from their provisions. "He's a…guardian, sent to protect the power of this gun and keep it out of the hands of evildoers." He didn't want to admit to his friend he didn't know what this being's purpose was, or how he might have messed up the spell. "Get the horses ready. We should leave this place before we attract any more attention."

Dutifully, Fernando hurried away. Javier draped the cover over the naked angel, noticing he had no wings. He thought of the stories of Icarus, the fool who'd flown too close to the sun… No, wait, Icarus hadn't been an angel. Javier frowned. He'd never been a very good student.

He held the flask out. "Easy, friend. We will not harm you."

The man refused the flask. "I… I don't know… Why am I here?" he croaked, shuddering.

That was the question.

Perhaps God is testing me, Javier thought self-consciously. Cold sweat dampened his brow. He kept glancing at the creature's back, expecting to see wings.

"Let's get somewhere safe," Javier urged. "I will do what I can to help you, friend. My name is Javier Punta." He held out his hand. "What do I call you?"

The man considered him warily, but grabbed his hand and pulled himself to his feet. "I am called Abzavine."

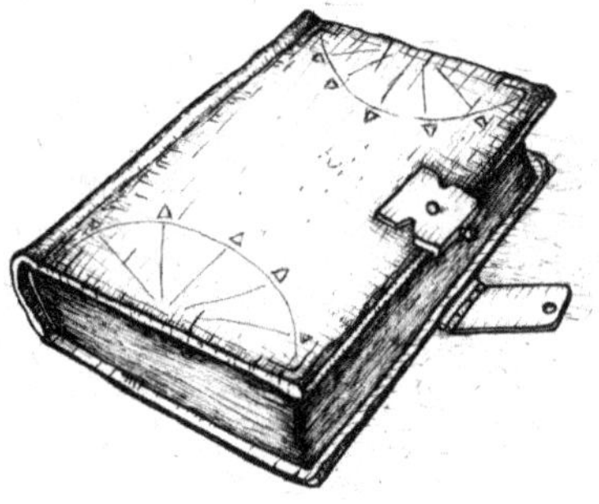

CHAPTER ONE

CHICAGO, APRIL 1899

"The funds just aren't available."

Jane set her jaw. "You know that's not true." She dug her heels in literally, refusing to let the three men past the office door until she'd made her case. Though they towered above her five-foot-six stature, they'd never try to remove her forcibly. "If we're going to catch her—"

"The agency has more urgent cases, Jane." This from Eric, the Pinkerton Agency's chief of sorcerers and her direct boss. "*Paying* cases, I might add. The Blackthorn Rogues are the Division's problem, not ours."

"The Blackthorn Rogues have killed fifty-six men in the past four months," she said. "The Division and local law enforcement don't have the resources to stop them. *We* do."

Eric and Jefferson exchanged the briefest of glances, but they shook their heads. "I'm afraid it's not within our jurisdiction." Jefferson was the agency lawyer, the one responsible for telling them what they could and could not do. Ever since New Orleans, he'd been in a lot more meetings with her.

Jane clenched her fists. "Three years ago, Diablo was the *only* thing all of you cared about."

"Three years ago, we had a paying client whose patronage we depended on to fund our other ongoing investigations. But that's gone now, thanks to the mismanagement of those funds *and* a certain botched operation." Eric huffed.

Jane folded her arms across her chest, heat rising in her. "Thomas Stubbs wasn't my responsibility." She took a step forward, pressing her unblinking gaze upon Eric like a thumb. "As for New Orleans, if you'd given me the resources I'd asked for—"

"Stop this right now," William Pinkerton barked. He'd been silent up to this point, and his sharp tone cut through the room. "Jane, that's enough. I won't have you using your parlor tricks on your fellow agents. Especially not your superiors."

She lifted her stare off Eric, and he relaxed. She cut her uncle a look. William Pinkerton was a fair man, but she didn't dare push her luck. He went on, addressing the men. "Bringing up New Orleans doesn't change what happened. It also doesn't give Jane any credit, despite years of exemplary service." He added that last for her benefit.

"You need to let go of the Rogues, Jane," Jefferson urged. "There's enough work for all of us without having to chase down a gang of common thugs."

"I'd hardly call Hettie Alabama common," Jane snapped. The gang leader had eluded her for over four years now. She hadn't even come face-to-face with the outlaw yet. "There's a reward out for her, right? What is it now? Three thousand dollars?"

"Five thousand," Eric said, "dead or alive."

"A reward like that would be worth the investment. Not to mention the publicity we'd get."

"Jane." William's voice was low, sympathetic, but not warm. "I understand your dedication to this case. I know what catching her would mean to you."

"Do you?" She set her teeth.

"Quentin was a good man and a good agent. They all were," he said more quietly. "I want Hettie Alabama to hang just as much as anyone. But the Pinkerton Detecting Agency is not in the business of vengeance. Leave that to the gunslingers and bounty hunters. Put your feelings aside. Hettie Alabama is too dangerous to go after. We're stretched thin as it is."

"With Division truancy and missing persons cases," she scoffed. "There's a killer on the loose, and you expect me to stand by and let her go?"

"I expect you to do your job." The steel edge of his tone and his unwavering glare were a stark reminder that William Pinkerton had not helped build what amounted to the largest private army in the United States because he had a bleeding heart. "Drop this Blackthorn Rogues business, Jane. That's an order. Eric will assign you something worth your talent."

He started toward the door. At first Jane wouldn't budge, but William kept coming. He was a large man whose girth shouldn't be mistaken as the result of idleness or gluttony. At the last minute, she stepped aside, and the three men barreled past her through the door and down the hall.

Jane cursed and punched the doorframe as she exited. This wasn't just about Quentin, though the Pinkerton agent who'd taken her under his wing deserved far better than he'd gotten. All she wanted was justice and to put a stop to the killings. Over the years, Hettie Alabama had murdered eight of their agents, and dozens more men from the Division and police force. How could her uncle and the others let her get away with that?

She stalked to her office. It was one of the smallest, but it was private, and it was hers, and she'd worked herself to the bone to earn it. She extracted a flask of whiskey from the corner filing cabinet. The liquid scorched down her throat and into her belly, dissipating some of the haze of her anger.

Someone behind her cleared his throat, and she turned.

A man sat in the lone visitor's chair crammed against her desk. He was in his thirties, with sandy hair that needed a trim, and spectacles. No ring, so he was a bachelor. And though the briefcase he clutched on his lap was of good quality, his scuffed shoes and threadbare suit were not.

"Does your employer know you drink on the job?" he asked pointedly. His accent was cultured—English, for certain, but toned down after years spent in America. But she didn't need to take in all those details to know who the man was. She'd only scheduled one meeting today.

"Probably." She returned the flask to the filing cabinet. "But I won't tell if you won't."

He straightened. A ramrod would envy his posture. "See here, miss. I've been waiting for quite some time now, and I haven't even been offered a cup of tea—"

"Would you like one?" she asked.

He blinked, nonplussed. "Pardon?"

"A cup of tea."

"Y-yes, but—"

She stuck her head out the door and yelled, "Margaret!"

The secretary she shared with another agent leaned back in her chair, peering across the hall. "Oh, Jane, I meant to mention, your ten o'clock—"

"So I've discovered. Please bring Professor Gallagher a cup of tea. And coffee for me." She shut the door again and went to the desk.

Professor Gallagher stared at her. "*You're* Agent Pinkerton?"

"Jane Pinkerton," she said cursorily. "Agent will do fine, though."

He shook his head. "I'm sorry… I was given to understand… That is, the letters I received—"

"You assumed they were from my uncle, the esteemed William Pinkerton, head of the Pinkerton Detecting Agency, which was why you left your students at Harvard so quickly." She nodded along, straightening the few items she allowed on her desktop. A ledger, a fountain pen, a magnifying glass, and the glass paperweight Quentin had gifted to her the day she'd received her Pinkerton badge and master sorcerer's shield. The paperweight had a thick blue-gray swirl in it—the eye of the storm they all lived in, Quentin used to say, not unlike the unblinking, never-sleeping eye the Pinkerton Agency's logo was styled after.

She sized up the man sitting across from her. "I assure you I had no intention of misleading you, professor. Everything I wrote in my letter was true. You'll be paid handsomely in exchange for your help with this case." If she could get the money. Without funding approval, though, she'd be paying the good professor out of her own pocket until she could convince Uncle William otherwise.

The man looked skeptical. "With all due respect, Miss Pinkerton—"

"Agent," she corrected, arching an eyebrow at him.

He pursed his lips. "*Agent*… I was hoping I could speak to someone who had more…authority."

"You mean a man."

His cheeks flushed, and he pushed his shoulders back. "Yes, I mean a man. I was expecting to deal with Mr. William Pinkerton—"

"My uncle is far too busy to deal with consultants," she interrupted. "As for your *expectations*, professor, those were yours and yours alone." She could see she was starting to rile him, so she gentled her tone and softened her eyes. "As a man of scholarly magic, science, and intellect, you know very well that assumptions lead to disaster."

He shifted uncomfortably beneath her pointed gaze. "I suppose you're right. It was my error."

"Not an error, just an assumption. But it's your unadulterated insight that I need for my investigation. That, and your expertise on the mage gun known as the Devil's Revolver."

Margaret bustled in with the tea tray laden with biscuits and tea, and coffee for Jane. She placed it on the desk in front of the professor and walked out again. He seemed put off that the secretary hadn't poured for him.

Jane picked up her own cup of black coffee. "I understand you are the foremost expert on Diablo," she said encouragingly. Men did love to listen to themselves talk, and it would put him at ease and provide her a refresher, as well as a moment to enjoy her coffee.

Gallagher didn't disappoint. He sat forward. "Well, I've always been fascinated by the stories of Elias Blackthorn. You see, my father witnessed the Rogues robbing a bank in Virginia. Despite the stories of a black-hearted bandit, this Elias—presumably the one before Jed Crowe—evacuated the women and children from the bank. Then he disintegrated the bank manager's desk to get him to open the safe." The professor's gaze grew distant. "My father told me that story so often… But his version of events didn't line up with the legend of the demon inside taking over the wielder's soul. I suppose I can't resist a romantic tale. That's how I ended up writing my doctoral thesis on mage guns throughout history."

"Yes, I've read it."

He ventured cautiously, "I'd heard rumors that Diablo resurfaced as early as four years ago. There were police reports about an altercation in Barney's Rock a few years back in which at least three men were killed by a single gunshot that glowed green—Diablo's signature mark. And there were stories of a man and a horse cut down by a green light in Hawksville, Montana."

Jane remained silent. She didn't want to tip her hand until the professor agreed to cooperate…and be discreet about it.

"I'd also heard the Pinkerton Agency has been looking for Diablo for quite some time. At one point, I tried to talk to the agent in charge of the file…Thomas Stubbs. But I understand he's been dismissed for mismanagement of agency resources."

"Among other issues." Fellow agents had complained of the man's casual disregard for bystanders and the safety of the general public. Stubbs had taken to assigning the most unscrupulous agents to his details, many of whom had also been sacked. Uncle William had buried the scandal with Stubbs's dismissal.

"I can only imagine. I met him less than a year ago. He was quite hostile toward me. I offered to share what I knew about the gun, but he wasn't interested. Said he knew all he needed to. It seemed to be a rather personal matter to him."

That lined up with what she'd heard about the veteran agent. Stubbs had been so obsessed with Diablo, he'd resorted to lying and stealing from company coffers to fund his search. At least, that was what Eric and Jefferson had reported. The anonymous client who'd originally hired the agency to find the mage gun had pulled their business after learning about Stubbs's overzealous spending. Uncle William had made the whole company tighten its belt and file a lot more paperwork as a result.

"So you've been actively searching for Diablo?" Jane asked him.

"Only in my spare time, and with limited resources. Mostly I resort to letter writing. I'm hoping to get funding for a cross-country trip next summer to visit all the towns Diablo's reportedly made an appearance in."

"And what will you do with your findings?" she asked.

He shrugged. "Publish them, I suppose, but they'll likely be deemed too lowbrow for scholarly interest and too boring for a dime store novel. I'm not the storyteller my father was, unfortunately. I firmly believe, however, that the immortal Elias Blackthorn wasn't the legendary gunslinger or boogeyman the tales make him out to be. I'm convinced their villainy is the gun's doing."

"Never underestimate man's propensity for evil, professor," she said flatly. "We as a species are capable of great cruelty."

"I'm only interested in the truth, not tall tales."

She considered him a long moment and poured his tea. He added three spoonfuls of sugar himself and slurped loudly. "What can you tell me about the Elias Blackthorn who had Diablo before it disappeared?" she asked.

"Jed Crowe? Not as much is known about him, apart from the fact that he was the father of Butch Crowe, who changed the name of the Blackthorn Rogues to the Crowe gang when he took over. Unfortunately, every last member was summarily executed for Weredom in Sonora, so I didn't get a chance to interview any of them." He sighed. "As far as anyone's been able to determine, Butch Crowe never had Diablo. Apparently, the father-son relationship was somewhat fraught, according to a barber they frequented in Texas. The man cut their hair every month. Word is, the elder Crowe wanted his son to have better...but that's neither here nor there."

He waved a hand. "Anyhow, it's said Jed Crowe was typical of the other Eliases—ran his crew with an iron fist. Had a streak of cruelty in him that got wider and wider, especially toward the end of his life. Some think that's what Diablo's blood price is—a bit of the wielder's humanity."

"Not you, though."

"I think the men who've had Diablo weren't all hardened criminals; they became them over time. The mage gun made them arrogant and overconfident in their power. They say the demon in the gun whispers to the wielder. Whether you believe in heaven or hell, *something*—whether it's a creature from another dimension, a ghost, a human soul—is inhabiting that weapon. Some say the demon casts an influence spell on the wielder, making him or her the true slave. Perhaps Diablo has affected Hettie Alabama in a similar fashion." He paused. "I could have told you all of this in a letter. Why did you need me to come all the way to Chicago?"

Jane set her cup down. "I understand you went to the Academy."

Gallagher shifted in his chair. "It was not my most successful venture."

"You flunked out."

"The practical spellcraft eluded me," he bit out.

"You had some interesting theories, though."

"Which I never attempted to realize in any way, shape, or form." He was perched on the edge of his chair now, looking ready to flee.

"You can relax, professor. I'm not going to report you for theoreticals, though they are, in fact, the reason I asked you to come." She leaned forward and dropped her voice. "Do you think you could do what you proposed? Sever the bond between the Devil's Revolver and its wielder?"

His hands trembled as he removed his glasses and polished them with his pocket square. "As I said, I was never any good at the practical side of spellcraft. I only built the theory out of a few old spells I'd read about... old wives' tales and superstitious habits, really."

"You'd be surprised how much magic a superstitious habit can hold," Jane said. "If you believe anything enough, you can reshape reality."

"I'll be honest," he added hesitantly, "that paper was something I wrote on a whim, to see whether the university would accept any cockamamie idea its students threw at it. A progressive institution should foster free thinking, of course, but what I proposed was frankly ridiculous."

"Your teachers seemed to find your ideas interesting enough to pass you."

"I passed because I was outrageous, not because I was right or because I'd defended my theory sufficiently. My professor of Mechaniks thought it had merit, but the man was tippling throughout his lessons. I could have sold him magic beans if it was late enough in the day."

His embarrassment was understandable. His theories had been unprovable by magical standards, and a joke by mundane ones.

And yet he'd gained a teaching post in one of the most prestigious universities in the country, made a name for himself in magical and Mechanikal academia. A man didn't get that far on outrageous theories or a lack of confidence in them.

"Gods, I thought I'd buried that paper," he mumbled. He frowned at her. "How did *you* find it?"

"I'm a detective. It's what I do." She faced him. "Let's be open with each other, professor. I don't believe for a moment you are truly that embarrassed about your ideas. So answer me truthfully: is it possible to separate the mage gun from the wielder?"

He ran a hand through his hair. "Even if I could find all the ingredients and it was actually possible? No. I couldn't perform such a spell on my own. I'm not sure anyone would be willing to perform these rituals. They're not Division-approved, for one."

"As if that's stopped anyone in the past."

"Secondly, some of the spells I proposed combining are dangerous. Illegal, even. I only figured out how to stitch them together because I recognized the common elements from all the disparate cultures—the use of blood, the fasting and the prayer..." His shoulders sagged. "But again, it's theoretical only."

The door shuddered open. It was Margaret. "Agent Pinkerton, you wanted to be notified if the Division was attacked again?"

Jane leaped out of her chair and grabbed her bowler hat and reticule. "Where?"

"A small town in Texas called No Hope."

"Cheerful." She looked to the professor. "Professor Gallagher, I'll cut to the chase. I need to stop the Blackthorn Rogues and haul in their leader. You said you wanted to find the truth. That's all I want as well." And to avenge her mentor. "You want Diablo, I want the wielder."

His eyes widened. "You're hunting Hettie Alabama."

She nodded. "And I need your help to stop her before she kills any more innocent people. Diablo is the source of her power—without it, she's nothing. If you're amenable, I will deputize you now and place you under the standard Pinkerton nondisclosure agreement we give all our contract hires."

"Y-you mean a silence spell." He paled.

"I assure you it won't hurt unless you actually try to tell anyone what you're doing with us..." She added as an afterthought, "Or they put a truthtelling spell on you."

He eyed the door as if ready to bolt back to Harvard.

"If you can figure out how to separate her from the mage gun, we can end her reign of terror. In exchange, you'll receive the stipend you were promised, a portion of the reward money, and you will be given a chance to study the mage gun Diablo at your leisure." She held out her hand. "Do we have a deal?"

CHAPTER TWO

NO HOPE, TEXAS
TWELVE HOURS AGO

"There are still only five men."

"Count them again." The bland order chafed every time it was repeated. Hettie knew that, but she'd also learned not to jump into any situation until she was absolutely certain.

"We should go *now*," Duke Cox growled. The man had been with her for nearly three years, and he still questioned her orders. "We've been sitting on our asses for damn near two hours, and it's hot as hell out here!"

"Hell's a lot hotter, and it's where you'll end up if we're not careful," Hettie said without looking the man's way. "Count 'em again, Tommy."

The younger man peered through his spyglass once more. "Five, Mizzay."

She cut him a narrowed look. Duke cuffed him in the back of the head. "Not *Miss A*, you lunk. You call her Blackthorn when we're out here."

"Sorry, Miss—I mean, Blackthorn." Tommy lowered his chin. "Won't happen again."

She kept her expression cool. "Count 'em out loud, Tommy, so we can be sure."

"One, two, three...four...five." He paused. "No, wait, six. Seven! I see more of 'em now!"

His pitch rose with excitement, terror. "Fifteen! No, twenty!"

"Twenty, eh?" Hettie sighed as she conjured Diablo. "Not as many as I'd hoped." She rolled her neck, and it popped. "Plan's still the same, though. Five or twenty-five, it don't make a difference."

She notched her chin at Tommy. The young sorcerer hastily put his spyglass away, then raised a bright pink conch shell and recited the amplification spell precisely. Hettie's throat expanded as she put her ear and mouth to the shell. "Walker, d'you hear me?"

"There are twenty-three men, including the drivers." His voice was like a whisper carried across the sea. He had a similar conch—amplification spells were messy because, when cast, everyone could hear them. Tommy, however, had crafted this pair of linked talismans so that their conversation would be private. He was extremely talented, though too anxious by half. It was a dangerous combination in someone so young.

"Twenty-three. We only had twenty." She glanced at Tommy again, eyebrow arched. He immediately started recounting.

"They're using hide spells, Hettie. They're anticipating trouble. It's gotta be a trap."

"It's *always* a trap. But we need that canister." She looked at Tommy, his pale forehead beaded with sweat. He would need a hit of juice soon.

"Time to move." She nodded at Duke. The man signaled the others to prepare for the assault.

The men got into place. Hettie stood and stretched just as a shadowy bloom of darkness alighted from the twisted tree above them, landing on the rock pile fence they'd been crouched behind.

"Open for business?"

She waved off the raven familiar. "Let me be, Rok. I'm busy."

"Busy, busy business. That's the name of the game." The spirit bird clicked his beak. *"How many souls will you reap today? Bringer of blood, bringer of death, of war, of pain and ends, bringer of—hrrk!"*

She squeezed the bag of bones in her pocket as if she meant to strangle the bird. "Please shut up, Rok, or I'll grind your beak down for tea."

The bird squawked and promptly settled. "No wonder Uncle drank so much," she grumbled. Why he'd bonded this chattering spirit familiar to her when he'd died was something she still hadn't figured out. Rok could be useful when he chose to be, but mostly, he was just annoying. "Go to it, bird," she commanded.

Rok took off in a cloud of black dust. She watched him wing into the white-hot sky and dissipate in a puff of ash.

No one could see Rok except her. Familiars didn't bond to mundanes, and despite wielding the world's most powerful mage gun, Hettie was as giftless as they came. Eventually she'd stopped trying to convince anyone the raven existed. Even Walker was skeptical. Instead, she used Rok's gifts as needed, and the gang had learned to trust her uncanny instincts.

The intensity of the sun dimmed, though the sky was clear and cloudless. The men stirred uneasily beneath the greenish light of a supernatural eclipse.

Hettie took this as her cue. She walked into the open toward the cluster of buildings that made up No Hope—four sun-baked wood structures including a general store, a saloon, a clerk's office, and a long-shuttered sorcerer's saloon.

She approached the wagon, keeping an eye on the engine and the men guarding it. As she left the perimeter of the gang's hide spell, she spotted more Division agents perched on the roofs, waiting at windows, hiding in the shadows. They'd come with shotguns and pistols, knives and talismans. Not a lot of good they'd do against her and Diablo.

One of the men shouted a warning. Heads snapped up, muzzles swung around.

Some of them didn't wait for the order to fire. They knew the stories. They pulled their triggers before they could even be sure it was her, but those reckless men faltered, and their eager guns jammed. A few bullets peppered the ground around Hettie, kicking up plumes of dust, but she kept walking. A raven's caw echoed over the field. *"Bad luck, bad luck!"* it sang in a throaty hiss of laughter audible only to Hettie's ears. Rok had done his job and cursed those who would harm her.

Hettie signaled her men at the same time she dropped into her time bubble.

She drew her saber, the singing of the blade in the deafening silence making her teeth ache. The sword had come from a Division officer she'd killed almost a year ago—a deviant of a man who'd become well-known for beheading the criminals he pursued, serving as judge, jury, and executioner. She'd given him the honor of Diablo's fire, neither a quick nor painless death by the end. That'd been the last time she'd used the gun to kill. The last time she'd slaked its blood lust.

The saber was cleaner in many respects. While Diablo never missed, it had a mind of its own and could prolong an agonizing death. It had killed when all she'd wanted to do was maim, drinking down another one of her precious years. Her control over it was not absolute. It sometimes thought it knew better than her, and for that reason, she could not always trust it.

The mage gun had taken its toll, its blood price, with interest. She reckoned that with her brittle, gunmetal gray hair, the dark circles under her eyes, and the sun-weathered lines on her face, she looked at least twenty years older than her actual age of twenty-one.

The truth was worse: she didn't know exactly how many years she'd added. She'd once asked Walker when he'd lost count of the number of men he'd killed. He hadn't responded.

She started with the snipers. There were more and more of them with each new attack—as if they thought they were safe perched high above everyone, picking off whoever they could, never having to look their victims in the eye.

Cowards, she thought in disgust, spotting the first man lying on the rooftop. She climbed a ladder to the topmost vantage point and began her grisly work.

The last Walker had seen of Hettie, she'd stepped out of the magic blind and was striding toward the town. At the first volley of fire, she'd vanished, and the distant caw of a raven made his skin prickle.

He always took a second to scan the ground for her crumpled body. Every time they went out and she withdrew into her time bubble, he feared she might rematerialize as a corpse on the doorstep to the swirling hell's gate.

"Madre," Lena whispered, crossing herself. Beneath the truthteller, the horse known as Tisiphone shifted restlessly.

"Trust her." He swallowed back the cold, hard lump that rose in him every time they went on a job. These two words sustained his faith in Hettie, in the knowledge that whatever else it might want, the mage gun his stepfather had created would protect its wielder.

The air bristled as the Division agents realized they had fired at a field of nothing, or perhaps a ghost. Walker knew that feeling well now—the collective intake of breath as their enemies finally grasped exactly who and what they were dealing with.

A blood-curdling scream pierced the air. It was joined by another, and another, until a shrieking chorus echoed around them. Walker spotted the writhing bodies atop the roofs. Hettie was doing her work.

His sorcerer sent up the signal to charge. "Let's ride!"

Walker's team spurred their horses into action, leaping through the perimeter of the magic blind. They yipped and hooted, kicking up a lot of dust and circling the town, corralling the Division men within.

On the southern flank, Duke's group opened fire, raining bullets upon the confused and disoriented soldiers. Caught up trying to reload or unjam their guns, the Division men dove for cover, shouting and seeking orders from their commanders. Walker knew who the officers were on sight: they thrashed on the ground, screaming, blood pooling around their ankles. Their Achilles tendons had been cut.

Hettie appeared above them like a wraith. Her mussed gray hair waved around a sallow mask of blank indifference, the kind of expression Death probably wore as he performed his duties. The captain and his second scrambled to draw their sidearms as the gang closed around them.

Before Walker could even think to shout a warning, Diablo winked into Hettie's hand. Its matte black surface absorbed the sun's scalding glare. She pointed the mage gun at the two men on the ground.

"Captain." Her low deadpan carried, thanks to the amplification spell. Her voice had grown harsh over the past few years, rasping like a snake crawling across shale to shed its skin. "I'd hate to send any more of your men home in caskets, so if you could please tell them to put down their weapons..."

"You're her." He glanced up and around, but his triumph quickly dimmed.

"You're wondering about your snipers." Hettie dumped an armload of rifles in front of the captain. She hadn't been carrying them a blink ago. Little pink bloodied nubs rained down along with them, but it was only when a large hand slapped onto the dirt that Walker realized they were fingers.

"That one tried to fight me." Hettie gestured toward the clerk's office, grimacing. "If you get him some help now, he may yet live."

The second-in-command retched. The captain growled, "You...you little whore—"

Walker took a menacing step toward the man, but he needn't have. "Whore?" Hettie tilted her chin up in thought. "Is that all you have as an insult, Captain Crenshaw? Whore?" He flinched when she addressed him by name. "I know some fine young women and men in the profession. They're smarter than you, at any rate. They don't go gambling away their hard-earned paychecks at the poker tables. What do you suppose your wife, Annabelle, thinks of that?"

Walker frowned. She was putting on a real show today.

The captain pursed his lips. His second-in-command looked equally appalled, though Walker doubted it was the man's gambling habits that'd shocked him.

"Kade," Hettie addressed the second, startling him. "Please relay my orders. Captain Crenshaw's a little tongue-tied at the moment."

"L-lower your weapons. Lower your weapons!" he shouted to the remaining soldiers.

The men slowly obeyed. Duke's boys confiscated their guns and lined them up with their hands over their heads. They made them kneel in the dust as they divested them of all their money, weapons, talismans, and boots. There was always a need for boots. Walker and the others kept their muzzles trained on their prisoners.

"What do we got, Lena?" Hettie called over her shoulder.

"One canister, half full." Lena was in charge of the sorcerers who provided magical protection. "Ammunition, food...ooh, dynamite!"

Hettie nodded. "Load 'em up. And check on Tommy. He's a little peaked."

Walker would have words with Tommy later. The young sorcerer had juiced up before they'd left, but he'd expended his power too quickly. The highs didn't just come from the hit—they came from using the juice, performing magic. He worried the young man was getting hooked.

Hettie paced along the line of prisoners. "Gentlemen," she addressed the Division men, "if you know anything about my reputation, then you know how this goes. Tell me a useful piece of information, and I let you live. Tell me a lie, and you don't."

"H-how are we supposed to know what's useful?" someone asked tremulously. The man next to him knocked him with his elbow.

The kid was fresh out of the Academy, like so many she'd encountered lately—smooth-faced and gangly, his collar and cuffs too starched and too white. Students were being fast-tracked to serve the Division. Hettie tilted her chin. "Well, it depends. There're only a few things my boys and me really want. Money, magic...and my sister." She panned the men. "Now, which of you happens to know where Abigail Alabama is?"

As expected, they were silent. The Division was notorious for keeping its projects secret, even from its own agents. That way, no one person knew *all* of the Division of Sorcery's machinations.

Hettie nodded to Duke, who whistled. His people had rounded up the snipers, their hands bloody. Some were missing more than just their trigger fingers, and one man clutched a stump that had been hastily bandaged.

Hettie took out a wicked-looking curved knife, and the snipers shied away.

"Money, magic, or Abigail Alabama. Information that leads us to one of those things gets you home. And don't try to lie—I've got three truthtellers with their eyes on you. Who wants to start?"

The gang shifted restlessly beneath the scorching sun.

Hettie sighed. Her duster flapped, the leather snapping like a whip in the wind.

Captain Crenshaw gasped as a tiny cut, deep and small like a snakebite, opened up along the side of his neck. Another appeared across his forehead. Blood ran down his face.

He yelped and grabbed the side of his head, smearing blood across his cheek. A piece of his left earlobe was missing. Then a slice appeared on his jawline in the cleft of his chin and through his lower lip. He screamed as blood poured from his face.

Walker kept his eyes fixed on the man as he flailed, yelping with each new cut. The others squirmed as the Division captain was reduced to a fleshy whittling stick by his phantom assailant. It was no poltergeist, though; Hettie was using the time bubble to inflict her torture without being seen.

"Money, magic, or Abby Alabama." Hettie pointed her curved blade at Crenshaw. "Or y'all can watch me shave him down to the bone."

The wounds gaped like tiny, bloody, hungry mouths. Crenshaw spat a wad of crimson. "Don't give this witch a single damned word or I'll shoot you myself!"

Hettie frowned. "Really, captain, that ain't good for morale."

He showed her what he thought of her morale by extending his middle finger. *Bad move*, Walker thought, and sure enough, the captain howled and fell over, clutching a stump where his offending finger had once jutted. Hettie tossed the useless digit into the pile along with the others.

She paced along the lineup, wiping her hands on a handkerchief, and stopped in front of the last man. "What's your name?" she asked.

"Freddie Henricksen." He added, lowering his face, "Ma'am."

Hettie's lips twitched. "Freddie. Tell me something useful and you can get up off your knees and sit in the shade over there."

He licked his lips, keeping his gaze down. "I... I did security for a payroll wagon. Runs every Thursday from Gull Falls."

She smiled. "See, that wasn't so hard, was it?" She nodded, and one of her men grabbed Freddie and led him to the shade of a scraggly tree. "Freddie's going home to his family on his feet and fit to keep earning money. How about the rest of you?"

"I did payroll, too," another man volunteered quickly. "In Jailor's Creek, last Monday of the month."

"Me too!" another man said.

Hettie nodded, and the men were pulled out of the lineup. The secrets rolled out steadily after that. After all, it was just money, and banks were insured.

When half the men had been freed from the lineup, Hettie held up a hand. "Seems we'll have plenty of cash for the next little while. How about magic?" She examined the remaining agents. "You boys know anything about the Fielding expeditions?"

"Y-you said money, magic..."

"Or Abigail Alabama." She nodded. "If any of you has information about her, I'll let you all go at once. Your compatriots were smarter, faster—they have less to lose giving up secrets about payroll wagons." She flashed her teeth in a humorless smile. "Tips on magic or Abby. Whaddya boys have?"

Crenshaw started to growl a warning, but Duke hit him again to shut him up.

Reluctantly, one older man said, "I ran security for a Fielding expedition two weeks ago."

"Uxbridge, you shut your mouth!"

He looked the captain in the eye. "Ain't worth our lives, captain. I've got three girls to feed."

Hettie seized on the information. "Where'd the engine go?"

"Did a short route through Kansas. Went to five towns before we drove the engine and the canister to Junesfield. They were put on a train and transported away."

"Where does it go from there?"

"They don't tell us that."

Hettie checked with Lena, who nodded her assessment. He wasn't lying.

"How many other Fielding expeditions met you in Junesfield?" Walker prompted.

"Haven't I already given you enough?" the Division man asked irately. When Hettie's eyes bore into his, he sighed. "Seven, as far as I could count."

"Thank you, Mr. Uxbridge. Your information has earned you your freedom." He was taken out of the lineup, and she addressed the remaining men. "If any of you can tell me anything about where the canisters are being banked, you can all go free right now. I'll even give you your boots back."

"We don't know anything about that, we swear," one young man blurted. "They don't tell us anything about the Fielding expeditions!"

"I don't suppose they would." Hettie studied the prisoners' smooth, pale faces and came to the same conclusion Walker had a moment ago. "All you greenhorns are too young to be on those expeditions. The Division's only assigning veterans and elite agents to those details. Ain't that right, Uxbridge?"

The older man stared resolutely at the ground as the younger agents peered at him.

Hettie raised her voice so they could all hear her. "Did you know they're *forcing* gifted to bank their magic? That they're stealing powers from old and young alike?" The cold, hard anger pressed into them like the barrel of a gun. "Did you know they're draining them dry?"

"That's League propaganda!" Captain Crenshaw barked. "Those rogue sorcerers are terrorists bent on destabilizing gifted and mundane unity."

"Whereas you're all upstanding citizens dedicated to…what? Taking magic from your fellow man? Ripping children from their families to stock your ranks?" Hettie's death glare panned over the Division men, many of whom were young enough to have gone through exactly that, even if the experience had been wiped from their memories.

"Mr. Uxbridge," Hettie addressed the older Division agent. "Tell us the truth. Did anyone come forward *willingly* to bank their gift?"

The man lowered his chin.

"The League of Sorcerers has been telling the truth, hasn't it? The Division's been rounding up all the gifted. They hold them down while they're kicking and screaming, put those clamps on, and drain 'em dry. And they kill anyone who tries to fight back."

"Lies!" Crenshaw howled.

The men stared, appalled. "Uxbridge?"

Walker knew by the slight compression in the air that the truthtellers were applying a subtle spell on the Division agent. Even though Walker no longer had his stepfather's borrowed magic, he could still sense when spells were being used.

Uxbridge's face grew red, and he scratched at his neck. The flesh cinched in an invisible vise, and the man spluttered and fell to his knees.

Shit! "Undo that silence spell!" Walker shouted.

Lena leaped from the saddle and slipped a rope around the man's neck, speaking an incantation. Uxbridge continued to struggle. "It's binding!" she yelled, and the two other truthtellers joined her, placing their hands over the man's shoulders, chanting in tandem.

Uxbridge jerked. His lips turned blue despite the sorcerers' efforts. He thrashed, scrabbling at his throat as the binding spell silenced him forever. When he stopped twitching, Captain Crenshaw growled, "Traitor deserved it."

A sick feeling swamped Walker, and he glanced over at Hettie.

Her eyes were wide, unblinking and cold. Slowly, she turned toward the captain. "Not every Division enforcer gets a binding silence spell put on him." She pointed at the man's shield—the badge that indicated his rank. "What'd he do to earn it?"

The truthtellers turned to face the captain, whispering their spell in unison, the sound like the shushing of a creek wearing down a river stone.

"Had an attack of conscience," Crenshaw blurted. "The little ones cried too much for his soft heart to take. They had to put the binder on him to keep him from telling the world what was happening." He glared. "Good riddance to him, I say. A dimcan like him was just taking up space. It'll happen to the rest of us, too, if any more of you decide to turn traitor."

"Uxbridge was a fifteen-year vet!" one of the freed soldiers said. "He didn't deserve a binder!"

"And he ain't no dimcan," another snarled. "He was a good man, decent, modest. He didn't flash his power around like you do."

The captain seemed to realize what was happening. "You idiots! Uxbridge is dead because of that witch! She's geised you all to turn against me!"

"I'm mundane," Hettie replied evenly. "You know that. Your men know that. The only reason you keep calling me a witch is because you have a small vocabulary and very little imagination."

She conjured Diablo. "Truth is, there's no word for what I am. Except disappointed."

She raised the mage gun. Walker's grip tightened over the reins and on his sidearm. "You got anything you want to tell me before you meet your maker?"

"Go to hell," he spat.

She shrugged. "Been there twice already."

She pulled the trigger. The captain shrieked as Diablo's fire engulfed him in a brilliant blaze of green. The flame swirled and swallowed him up, then disappeared, leaving only a greasy smudge on the ground.

A sickly greenish glow enveloped Hettie. She set her teeth as the mage gun drank down a year of her life in one long draw. It used to be that she'd scream, long and loud, the kind of cry that tore a man's soul apart. But these days, it was as if all she had was a little cramp. She huffed as Diablo released her, and she straightened, rolling her shoulders back. Dark shadows hung beneath her hollowed eyes, giving her the look of a skull.

"The rest of you are free to go," she said to the Division men. "There's been enough death today." She withdrew a pouch of coins and went to Kade, the second-in-command. "You'll deliver this to Mr. Uxbridge's widow and daughters, along with my deepest regrets and apologies."

Kade was still staring wide-eyed at the spot where his captain had been. He fumbled the sack of coins, seeming surprised at the weight.

She looked over the Division men. "Remember what happened here today. The Division isn't your friend. Once they've taken magic from all the gifted, they'll come for you next. They're not interested in your loyalty, only control of your power, and one day you'll realize how they first took it from you. Listen to what the League of Sorcerers for Free Magic is saying. Don't trust the Division."

The Rogues collected the cart containing the Fielding canister and engine, the Division men's horses, supplies, and loot. Hettie mounted her own stalwart mare, then flicked her gaze toward Walker.

"Let's ride!" he shouted. The Blackthorn Rogues galloped out on a wave of thunder and dust.

NEW SPAIN
1726

Though Javier had never put much stock in the church's teachings, watching Abzavine consecrate the very earth beneath their feet and coax life-giving water from the desert had him rethinking his faith. He decided the angel Abzavine could be nothing but one of God's divine messengers. And the people he brought to the oasis agreed.

They were but thirty-four at first, many of them friends and family, orphans and grieving widows who'd lost loved ones to the violent men who'd harassed them for years. As word of Punta's refuge spread, more people arrived every day. The village was mostly an arrangement of tents, but it would soon be more. He welcomed anyone and everyone needing safety. Respite. A home.

It wasn't as though he could turn anyone away, after all. Javier was partly to blame for their misery. He'd told himself he could not have stopped the beatings and rapes and extortion. He'd told himself he could not have stopped the massacre. Giving himself up to Duarte, leasing his powers to the army and their evil deeds... No, he wouldn't do it. But his sanctimony didn't help him sleep any better at night.

"Looks like we'll have more mouths to feed at supper." Fernando pointed to the specks on the horizon. He glanced back over his shoulder toward the women preparing the evening meal. The beautiful Yani glanced their way in that moment, and she gave a shy wave. Fernando ducked his head, embarrassed. "I'm not sure we'll have enough," he said. He peeked back at Yani and gave a short sigh.

"There will always be enough." Javier said this with certainty, but anxiety swept through him. What if it was Duarte's men? His Vision told him it wasn't. He and Abzavine had spelled the area to make sure only those who knew about it and had the right intentions could come here. Still, one day Duarte might come for Javier, and the mad captain would not hesitate to kill every last person here.

Javier's grip tightened over the mage gun. Never again. He would not allow anything else to happen to these people. They had suffered enough because of him.

"I want to build a wall," he said.

Fernando glanced up. "A wall?"

"To surround the village." He nodded toward the cluster of homes around the well. "We need protection."

Fernando rubbed his jaw. "All right, but what would we build it with? The land may sprout good corn, but it will be years before we have enough trees for timber."

"It's said the old masters across the sea raised the stone straight out of the earth to help build their Great Wall to protect their kingdom. They pulled up the firmament itself, like roots from the soil." He scanned the land around the village. "I'm sure I can do something like that here."

"A wall won't stop refugees from coming," Fernando pointed out skeptically. "That is why you built this place, no?"

"I'm not trying to keep *all* people out. Just the *wrong* people. I want to feel safe."

Fernando sighed the way he often did when his friend got ideas. Javier was the one with the prodigious gift and the mage gun—it wasn't as if Fernando could stop him.

Javier approached Abzavine for guidance on the wall spell. The angel had taken to perching on a nearby butte, watching and protecting the villagers, or more specifically, Javier and the demon-possessed gun holstered at his side. He wore clothes and shoes like any other man yet always seemed naked to Javier somehow. He rarely came down to the village. He needed no sustenance, from what Javier could tell. He simply kept vigil up on his tower.

The angel already seemed to know what he was going to ask as he climbed the steep path. "You're thinking of defenses."

"I'm thinking of the future. We need to protect the village in case the army comes out here looking for us." *For me* was what he'd meant, but he didn't want to sound too self-important. "You've said you will not intercede should they try to hurt the others, and I understand that. What I'm asking for is the means to protect myself and these people, should the need arise."

"You have the gun." Abzavine nodded at his hip.

Javier grimaced. "I will not use Diablo unless I have to. I am a peaceful man."

"A peaceful man with a gun."

Javier chose not to read too much into his casual observation. "What we need is a wall. One that might withstand attacks both mundane and magical."

The angel considered his request with a tilt of the chin. "Walls are for keeping unwanted elements out... and animals in."

Sometimes Abzavine reminded Javier of a precocious child trying simple concepts on as if they were dress-up clothes. But then, what would a divine being from heaven know of warfare and suffering? "Yes, that is exactly what we need."

The angel's eyes became like murky pools, glazed and unfocused, as if he were staring into a deep well. "It is something we can do," he said after a moment's consideration. But then his gaze glided up to Javier's face. "What will you do if the army *does* breach your wall?"

"For all our sakes, we will have to make sure it can't be breached," Javier replied grimly.

"For *your* sake," Abzavine amended. Though it didn't sound like a correction as much as it did a portent.

CHAPTER THREE

"Are you certain?" Jane scrutinized the young lieutenant, Kade Fewings, as he shuffled on stocking feet in the dust. He couldn't seem to meet her eye and merely nodded at the ground.

"It was her, for sure. The outlaw Hettie Alabama. She went and killed both Uxbridge and the captain."

Jane let her stare rest on Kade, then slowly lifted it off him to inspect the charred spot on the ground where Captain Crenshaw's greasy ashes stirred in the wind. "Your captain was clearly a victim of her infamous mage gun. Tell me again how she killed Mr. Uxbridge?"

He grimaced to where the Division man's body was being loaded onto a cart. "Uh…strangled him. Just…strangled him."

"Why didn't she shoot him, like she did with Captain Crenshaw?"

Kade swallowed. "I…I don't rightly know. That woman's crazy. She's a bloodthirsty criminal. A murderous witch—"

"There's no need for invectives, Mr. Fewings." She lowered her voice. "I'm asking you candidly what *you* saw, or what you think you saw, not what the Division would have you write in your report."

He glanced around nervously. "I…I don't know what you mean, Miss Pinkerton—"

"Agent," she corrected automatically.

"—but it's just as I said. She and those bandits attacked our expedition. They took everything and killed two of our finest. Then she went and cursed the others with a silence spell so they couldn't tell anyone what they'd seen."

The Division men sitting against the wall of the saloon looked dejected, angry, indignant. And she couldn't get a word out of them. Not without killing them.

How convenient.

"And you managed to escape from this particular curse?" she asked blandly.

Kade fumbled for the talisman in his pocket. "I earned my anti-influence charm a month back," he said with nervous pride. He held out the piece of feldspar for her to inspect. The charm was the Division's ultimate badge of loyalty. "It kept me safe from their curse."

Jane handed it back. "Thank you, Lieutenant Fewings. Those are all my questions for now. I'm sure you need to attend to your men and their…morale."

He hurried away, shoulders hunched. Jane knew she made men nervous with her stare, though she didn't apply truthtelling spells or any other influence magic on anyone the way Uncle thought she did. She'd simply found silence and unflinching eye contact were far more effective tools for her trade.

"I didn't know the Rogues used silence spells on their victims," Professor Gallagher said. It annoyed Jane that while she was the one who wore the Pinkerton master sorcerer's badge, the professor's mere presence as a man lent her more authority to ask questions. Just one more reason she needed to keep him around, since no other agent was likely to accompany her on this personal investigation.

"They don't. Bullets are always cheaper than geises. They wouldn't waste magic on a Division troop like this." She glanced back at the soldiers as she and the professor walked a short distance away. "There's definitely a silence spell on them—that's not unusual for men working under the Division. But if I were a betting woman, I'd say that Lieutenant Fewings followed Division protocol and silenced his men *after* their encounter with the Blackthorn Rogues."

"Why? What could have happened that they'd possibly have to hide?"

"The Division is a rabbit warren of secrets, Professor. And they guard them with the lives of their people." She walked the perimeter of the tiny town, the professor at her heels.

"I may not be a high-caliber sorcerer, but even I can tell that lieutenant couldn't have performed so many silence spells at once."

"His sorcery ranking certainly doesn't indicate it. But considering their cargo, he doesn't need to be."

"You think he juiced? I thought the Blackthorn Rogues took the canister."

"Juicing can hold for weeks with conservative use. He could easily have juiced before arriving here." She glanced around. "In fact, I'd say he did so on purpose. This wasn't a Fielding expedition stop. It was a trap. There are far too many soldiers for this to be anything else. Still, he'd need more magic than I could detect on him."

"So he could've juiced off the engine."

"My understanding is that the expedition engines are one-way: they don't have leads out to ensure that the men traveling with the canisters don't try to juice themselves or otherwise steal from the Division. If this were a trap, the smart thing would have been to juice all the soldiers here to fight the Rogues. Unfortunately, the Division is more greedy and suspicious than it is smart."

She scanned the area around the town, looking for what, she wasn't sure. Scrubby, tough grasses clawed their way up from crumbly, parched dirt; a snake skin waved from a branch where it had caught; a flower that had been crushed underfoot reached toward the sky as if seeking one final kiss from the sun—

There. Something glinted in the weeds.

She found the shards of glass within a hard stone's throw from the edge of town. The spherical shape of it suggested it hadn't come from a whiskey bottle or a broken window pane. She picked it up. A thin brass band inscribed with some mixture of protection and binding spells jingled around it. Even broken, though, Jane felt a slight, sickly pull from it.

"What is that?" Gallagher asked warily.

"I think it's a Fielding canister."

"So small?" His eyes widened. "Did the gang use a spell to shrink it?"

She cut him an arch look. "Don't be ridiculous." She inspected the rest of the glass pieces. "It was only a matter of time before the process was miniaturized." Whole, the bottle would be about as big as her fist.

"Do you think that belongs to the Blackthorn Rogues?" he asked.

"They wouldn't leave something we could use to track them lying around." She gathered the pieces into a handkerchief and scratched a protection circle in the dirt. She sat down within it and laid the glass shards in front of her, then spat in the circle and exhaled a hot breath over the flask. She murmured a short spell. Her Vision lit up, and she followed the faint trail of power indicating the flask's path in the past few hours. Sure enough, it led toward the Division men.

"This belonged to Fewings," she concluded, wiping the protection circle away. A faint headache pounded at her temples. "It's likely he juiced to perform that silence spell, then threw this flask as far away as possible."

"But what about this attack would the Division want to keep a secret?" Gallagher asked, confused. "Didn't *they* ask us here to investigate?"

Technically, no, but Gallagher didn't need to know that. She glanced back toward the knot of agents. "I have a feeling if we tried to interrogate the lieutenant further, we'd have more bodies on our hands."

"So you're not even going to ask him about it?"

She stared hard at the glass bottle. "I'm not convinced this is directly related to Hettie Alabama or that it'll help us find her, and we have to stay focused on the case. Besides, when it comes to the Division, there are some questions you learn not to ask."

Even so, all this effort to silence the entire troop smacked of more than the Division's usual paranoia. Something strange was afoot.

"Blackthorn's Hell" was the name of the Rogues' base of operations wherever they camped, but in the past few months the ghost town they'd moved into had become home. Drained of magic and ore and bypassed by the rail lines and telegraph, the nameless town had been abandoned for decades before Hettie and her crew arrived. The buildings were dilapidated and dusty, but most of the walls and roofs were intact and provided the shelter they needed. While many of the Rogues had homes, and in some cases families, those who had nowhere else to go lived in Blackthorn's Hell.

Hettie remained in the saddle until the men had unloaded the Fielding canister into the old hostler's barn with the others. Once the juicers got their share of magic in a civilized and orderly fashion, she dismounted and handed the reins to a young man who'd appointed himself lead hostler. With over two hundred men in her employ, people who carved roles for themselves in her outfit were valued.

Walker waited for her, scowling, hands on his hips. She stifled a weary sigh, walked past him with barely a glance, and headed straight for her quarters, located in one of the rooms of the defunct saloon.

"You gonna tell me what happened out there?" His boot steps shook the ground at her heels.

"What's to tell?" Her voice was rusty, her throat dry from the long ride. "We had a good day."

"Since when is two dead and a fistful of trigger fingers a *good day*?" They entered the saloon, which the gang only ever used for meetings. She marched up the stairs, exhaustion settling into her bones.

"Did any of ours get hurt?" she asked blandly.

He hesitated. "No."

"Then it was a good day."

In her room, she pulled off her duster and hat, then tugged off her gloves. Blood crusted under her nails.

She sat to pull her boots off. Walker glowered as she continued to ignore the angry questions in his face.

He began, "I can understand you being mad at Crenshaw—"

"He was a Division dog."

"—but you didn't have to kill him. He wasn't worth a year of your life."

She cut him a look, irritated. "You don't get to make that decision. Not for me."

Walker set his jaw. "What about the snipers?"

"What about them?" She pulled off her blood-spattered boots and tossed them into the corner of the room. "Would you have preferred I slit their throats? You knew the plan. If I hadn't taken their fingers along with their guns, you'd all be dead right now. I couldn't take chances."

"Did Diablo tell you that?"

His tone grated on her. "What, you suddenly don't trust him? Or is it *me* you don't trust?"

Walker's broad shoulders sagged. "Of course I trust you." His voice softened. "Whatever you do, I'll always trust you. But what happened today… We've talked about this. You can't keep adding years to your body—to your life. And I don't mean just the men you kill. Every minute you're in that time bubble counts on your life. How much extra time did you put on yourself finding out about Crenshaw's habits?"

More time than she probably should have, but the Division captain's attitude had grated on her. Not that it was any of Walker's business. "What's the matter? Don't like older women?" She stripped her short jacket and vest off. "Or do you miss the pretty young thing I was four years ago?"

"This isn't about that, and you know it. You only have so much time on this earth, and…" He pursed his lips. "It's not like you to be so reckless, Hettie."

Dammit, she hated it when Walker got soft on her. "I did what had to be done to protect the people I care about. What I did wasn't reckless; it was necessary. If you can't stomach it, I'll make Duke my second, and you can go preach to the masses."

"Stop." He stepped closer, not touching her, not doing anything but pinning her with the hard, cold blue of his eyes. "Stop trying to push me away. I know you're hurting, and not just from Diablo's curse."

Hettie clung to the fury banked beneath her cold demeanor. Some days it was the only thing keeping her from crumbling again. "I'm fine."

"You're not. You've been riding hard and burning the candle at both ends and in the middle, from what I can see. Worst of all, I don't even know when you're doing it. You could hare off to God knows where, getting yourself in all kinds of trouble—"

She dropped into the time bubble, then ran for the chamber pot and heaved, emptying what little she'd had in her stomach. The day had been too much already, and she didn't need Walker of all people lecturing her about her choices.

When her breathing evened out, she glared over her shoulder. He could say whatever he wanted about Diablo's abilities, but he gave her plenty of opportunity to calm down without anyone watching.

"Guilty, guilty, guilty!" Rok resolved on the chair back in a cloud of ash.

She spat the foulness out of her mouth. "What do you want, birdbrain?"

"The tab comes due when you do," he reminded. *"Pay the piper at the toll bridge."*

"Yeah, yeah." The damned bird was always hounding her about what she owed for the favors he granted. Whatever her bill was, it didn't matter: she was bound for hell. What more could they possibly take from her? She whipped her balled-up socks at him, and he squawked indignantly before flapping away in a puff of dust.

She emptied the chamber pot and scrubbed her face and teeth. She glanced into the dull mirror, checking her pale, haggard complexion, the fine lines around her hard eyes and frowning mouth. Only when her tears had dried did she reposition herself in front of Walker and drop the time bubble.

"—and be back before I can even blink." He exhaled and forked a hand through his hair. "I can't protect you when you do that."

"It's not your protection I need." She stepped up to him so her chest brushed against his. He inhaled sharply. "Now are you going to get naked, or do I have to do it for you?"

His scowl crumpled, betraying his powerlessness. He gripped her shoulders and kissed her deeply, softly, fiercely, until a new kind of ache grew inside her. She wrapped her arms around his neck and pulled him close, kneading the firm muscles of his back.

Frantic with the need to touch him, to feel something other than the nauseating emptiness inside her, she tore at his clothes, popping the buttons off his shirt front and running her fingers over his scarred chest. He let her, his rough hands curving around her hips.

Walker had always been a tender and considerate lover. From the very first time, after he'd nursed her out of a state of wretched grief, he'd taken things slowly, eased her into a part of adulthood she hadn't given much consideration. And for a short while, that had distracted her.

He'd asked her to marry him after that first time. She'd said no, knowing he'd only done so because honor demanded it. Deflowering her was hardly the worst of his crimes, after all, and there'd been no baby. If he'd been disappointed by her answer... well, that was neither here nor there.

Afterward, he lay in her bed with one arm draped over his eyes, snoring lightly. Hettie watched the rise and fall of his scarred chest. The burns and bullet wounds, some of them recent, mapped out so many stories. It was only then that she noticed the silence, and she conjured Diablo. The sly little devil had dropped them into the time bubble, stealing a moment out of time for her and Walker.

She couldn't find the heart to admonish the demon in the mage gun—he meant well. But it was disconcerting when Diablo exercised its own free will.

She dressed, letting Walker sleep, and headed down into the saloon, reveling in the silence of the time bubble as she poured herself a whiskey. She spent what time she could in the solitude of her silent, frozen world, thinking, planning, researching, sometimes traveling. She was probably adding at least ten to twelve hours on a regular basis. Not that it mattered much to her—ever since Abby had been taken, she hadn't been able to sleep for more than a few hours at a time.

"Did you have a good rest?" Rok perched above the smashed bar mirror, his query snide. Hettie ignored him as she sipped her drink.

"As many of those as you drink, you can't shut me up. Jeremiah never seemed to get that."

"It's not for *you*." She slugged back the last finger of whiskey, letting the burn trickle down her throat and into her gut. Sometimes that bite was the only thing that relieved the cold, hard lump growing in the depths of her soul like a tumor.

Rok cackled and ruffled his smoky feathers. *"Sip of courage, sip of courage. How much bravery can you drink?"* A desiccated hiss flickered past his snipping black beak.

Hettie put the bottle and glass back and wiped her mouth, steeling herself for the talk with her men. She dropped the time bubble when she'd practiced her words and anticipated every objection she could think of, then headed to the big house.

Her people were still riding high on their triumphant return, celebrating their victory. One of the men played a merry jig on a fiddle. Others clapped along and drank. One of the newly juiced sorcerers was showing off, juggling three glow stones while changing them from red to blue to yellow, green, purple, brown…

"Waste of magic is what that is," she said flatly.

The fiddle squeaked and stopped abruptly. The juggler fumbled the stones, and they clattered to the ground. He gathered them up quickly and muttered an apology. Everyone looked down at their boot tips.

"Don't mind her. She's just jealous 'cuz she's mundane as a mule." Duke Cox sauntered toward her, whiskey bottle in hand. "Gracing us with your presence, then?"

She kept her feet planted, staring Duke down the way she would a mangy dog. "Tomorrow, I want you to assemble a team and ride out to Gull Falls, find out what you can about that payroll. Send a posse to Jailor's Creek, too."

His expression fell. "Can't you give us a rest? This campaign took weeks to plan."

"You got somewhere else to be? We didn't pull in half as much as I thought we would in No Hope, and if I recall correctly, the men like to get paid."

He glowered and lowered his voice. "I didn't make you leader so you could push us around and make us do all the work."

"You're right. You didn't make me leader at all. I took over because you couldn't get anyone to go along with your dumb-ass schemes." She conjured Diablo in front of his face. "Need me to remind you how motivating I can be?"

Duke's lip lifted in a silent snarl, though his eyes never left the bloodred trigger thorn. The men around him had gone quiet. "Gull Falls and Jailor's Creek. Fine. What about you?"

"I'll be heading to Junesfield. Alone."

"What about Walker? He going with you?"

There was no man she trusted more at her back, but someone had to keep an eye on Duke and the others. "Easier if it's just me." Besides, holding the time bubble with more than one person was harder. "Take care of the men while I'm gone," she told him. "I don't want to hear about any fights or any misbehavior they'll regret." She panned the room with her warning look. The more eager, loyal men nodded solemnly. Duke, despite his paranoia and pettiness, nodded along. He was a soldier, though not a great one. For all his posturing, he liked being told what to do—more than anything, he craved approval.

She went to talk to Lena and the other sorcerers who lived in the abandoned schoolhouse. She and Walker had recruited the truthteller out of a town near the border. She'd been a late-blooming gifted, her minor abilities suddenly flaring to life at age seventeen, and like so many gifted these days, she'd fled rather than go to the Academy.

When Hettie walked in, Lena was talking lowly with Tommy, who looked despondent. "It was an honest mistake," Lena assured him, "but honest mistakes get people killed out here. Next time, breathe. Take it slow. Better to be right than fast, and careful rather than dead. Understand?"

Tommy nodded. Hettie waited for him to go before stepping out of the shadows. "He's still green," she said.

"He's eager to please. He looks up to you." She smiled crookedly. "But he's learned his lesson. I'll work with him more on his Vision."

Hettie nodded. "Did y'all make it through the day okay?"

"We're fine. Las Furias were very good. Hardly fought us."

"They know better than to misbehave on a mission." The three sister mares she'd brought with her from Mexico had proven their value ten times over. She was glad she'd reclaimed them from the Favreaus' Yuma household. "Duke will be splitting the crew into two teams to wait out those payroll wagons. I want you to go with him, keep an eye on the sorcerers, and make sure they don't overjuice. I'm heading to Junesfield. I'll be back as soon as I can."

"You're still looking for Abby." It wasn't a question.

"All these Fielding canisters gotta be headed somewhere. Wherever the Division is depositing them has to be where they're keeping Fielding, if he's still alive. Abby'll be there, too."

"Is that what the League's been telling you?" Lena asked archly.

To Lena, the League of Sorcerers for Free Magic could not be trusted. When she was a child, the League had burned her father's salon to the ground and killed him when he'd tried to stop them. She couldn't condone those who purported to fight for the rights of the gifted when they attacked Division-sanctioned sorcerers.

Hettie didn't have the same qualms. Not when Abby's life was at stake.

According to her League contact—aka Sophie Favreau, who had been secretly funding them for years—the Division had been marshalling its forces, though for what purpose, no one could say. Since the government didn't seem worried, no one else was either, but the League was adamant the Division was on the cusp of something sinister.

When Sophie had presented the League with Hettie's story about her sister, they'd taken up her cause, helping in the search for Abby the same way they helped the hundreds of others whose gifted loved ones had gone missing. They funneled any information they could to Hettie through Sophie. In return, one day, Hettie had promised to help them.

"I haven't had a lead in weeks," she said. "I have to go. Be certain."

"The League could be manipulating you. Giving you false hope."

"For Abby's sake, they'd better not." She notched her chin up. "I'm trusting you to care for the sorcerers. Duke'll make sure everyone gets their juice, but you're the one I trust with their lives."

Lena studied her. "You say you're coming back... but you're not sure you believe it. What is it you think you'll find where you're going?"

"I was hoping y'all could tell me."

"Vision doesn't work that way," Lena said regrettably.

Hettie sighed. If it were that easy, she would've found Abby by now. "You know how it is. I don't know what'll turn up, so I don't know when I'll be back."

Lena embraced her, leaning her forehead against hers. "Vaya con Dios," she whispered.

Hettie doubted God went anywhere with her. But she accepted what comfort Lena offered.

She ordered one of her men to saddle a fresh horse and stock her with provisions, then went to the Fielding canister for a hit. Six men guarded the stockpile at all times. They'd amassed three partially filled canisters and one working Fielding engine, which Horace had retrofitted with leads out to juice. The portable prototype they'd stolen three years ago was still squirreled away for safekeeping.

The Mechanik in charge of the machine quickly attached her to the engine. "Single shot?"

"Double." She had no idea what she was going up against.

He turned the dial to the spot marked two, then threw a few levers and hit some buttons. That the design of the engines had evolved over time made Hettie suspect Alastair Fielding had been rescued at Swedenborg and was once again in the Division's employ. Some days she regretted not shooting him dead when she'd had the chance.

The iridescent glow of magic lit up the leads and clamps attached to her forearms. A cold, shivery trickle suffused her veins, dripping into her heart and mind, opening her senses, filling her until she wanted to soar up into the sky.

She reminded herself it was for everyone's good—the juice helped her extend Diablo's abilities for much longer periods. The expansive sensation of the stolen magic sliding into her was simply a pleasant side effect of the transfer. A necessary evil. She wasn't hooked.

By the time she was ready to go, she found Walker saddled and dressed for a long journey, holding the reins of her horse along with his magicked mare, Lilith.

"No," she told him preemptively.

"Not your call to make." He folded his arms over his chest. "You think you can up and leave whenever you like and not even tell me?"

"I could just bubble out of here, y'know."

"But you didn't."

She huffed. Walker knew her too well.

"I take it you're not going by remote Zoom, then," he said.

"After No Hope, the Division will be looking for any strong magic signatures, and I don't want them tracking us here. Besides, the sorcerers need their rest, and I don't want to juice them any more than is absolutely necessary."

He eyed her critically. "*You* juiced."

"Don't start." She took the reins and adjusted the saddle.

"I don't like what it's doing to you." It had taken him years to shake off the hunger for magic, and it continued to be a struggle. He'd lived nearly half his life holding Javier Punta's power, then given it up. He wouldn't even go near the canisters if he didn't have to.

"You worry about yourself. I'm fine."

They said nothing more as they saddled up. She wasn't about to admit to him how relieved she was for his company. Still, she wished he wouldn't treat her as if she needed constant minding. She could take care of herself. She was the only one who could.

NEW SPAIN
1736

The village was surrounded.

From the highest rooftop, using his Vision, Javier could see everything beyond the walls. The neatly arranged army formed a patchwork quilt of regimented soldiers around Villa del Punta. Battle spells bounced against the magic barrier, but every strike made him flinch, like a pellet stinging his skin. He could hold the protection spell almost indefinitely—even in his sleep. Abzavine had seen to it that the bond was permanent. But Duarte's men had dug in for a long campaign. They'd cut off all access in and out of the area and were bombarding the village day and night.

"Javier."

Yani stood below him in the church tower. He climbed down. "What are you doing here? It's not safe. Certainly not in your condition." The baby would be here any day now.

"The council has gathered. They are planning a counterattack. You have to stop them."

Javier snapped, "You should not be meddling in the men's affairs, wife."

Her eyes blazed with anger. "That is right. I *am* your wife. And this is *your* child. But if you allow the men to open the gates, you may see the end of us…of all of this."

But if they didn't do anything, the people would eventually starve, or be driven mad with fear by the long, amplified diatribes meant to demoralize them. Descriptions of what would be done to the men, women, and children of the "illegal" town were softened with empty promises of how anyone who surrendered would be treated well. It had already been six days, and his people were starting to grow desperate.

He went down the stairs, helping Yani along, though she slapped his hands away when he tried to curve an arm around her thick waist. As they reached the ground level, Fernando looked up. His lips pursed tightly, and he looked away again.

"Go back to the other women," Javier told Yani sternly. "Do not interfere with me again."

She left in a huff.

"We cannot continue like this," Fernando said as Javier joined them. "We need to launch a counterattack."

"What about Abzavine?" one of the men demanded. "Where is our guardian angel? If he is so powerful and benevolent, why hasn't he interceded?"

Javier clenched his fists. "He has sworn an oath to protect El Diablo only. He cannot interfere in mortal affairs."

"He will not have anything left to protect if he doesn't come down from his mountain and help us." Fernando gripped the edge of the table. "Any day now, their cannons will arrive, and then nothing will stop them from breaking down the door."

"The terrain is too rough to transport cannons and cannonballs," Javier reasoned. Of course, he couldn't be certain the army wouldn't have figured out how to do just that.

Fernando huffed. "Javier, the barrier is tied to your life. All it would take is a stray bullet or an assassin's knife. If you're hurt, we will be defenseless. If you want to save us, you need to show Duarte and everyone else you are not a sorcerer to be trifled with. You must use El Diablo."

Javier set his jaw. "I cannot. After that first time…" He didn't like to think about it. He'd fired the weapon in fear and anger, killing a soldier who'd wandered from his troop and gotten lost. Javier had mistaken him for a scout—a spy—and had dispatched him with too much haste.

And he'd paid the price. Oh, how he'd paid. The mage gun had torn a year off his life, swallowed a piece of his soul like a mouthful of sweet water after a long drought. The agony of it had him vowing to never use the thing again. And yet El Diablo's bloodlust had only just awoken. She whispered to him even in dreams, singing a seductive siren's song of death and destruction.

Fernando's nostrils flared. "What good is this symbol of your power if you refuse to use it? I did not help you gather all those... those infernal *materials* for the spell so that you could stand by and do nothing!"

His friend's voice burned like acid. Javier didn't want to admit his weakness to the others. He hadn't told anyone about the blood price: the truth was, he was ashamed of his creation. This weapon was an abomination. Hubris bound in wood and iron and dark magic. He should have known that building the mage gun would have consequences.

Even now, the demon within yearned to prove itself, to show off its abilities, daring him to test its powers against the men threatening his home, his friends and family.

He'd never anticipated how insistent that little voice could be.

A loud boom shook the air, and Javier collapsed to his knees, the air knocked from his lungs. It felt as though his whole skeleton had been rattled. He stared up at the council wide-eyed. "That was no battle spell."

Everyone ran outside.

Fire spread across a swath of the houses, their roofs collapsed. Women and children screamed and ran, while others hurriedly formed bucket lines to put the flames out.

"Cannons?"

"No." Fernando pointed at the wall. A large chunk of it had been knocked over, and the perfect V of the collapsed portion framed a catapult set among the troops.

"How did we not see that?" Fernando growled, his annoyance clearly aimed at his magically gifted friend.

"They must have been building it under a hide spell." That was surely why the sorcerers had been bombarding them continuously—to distract him from any other subtle magic activity. He cursed. Cannons and cannon fodder were difficult to move, but a medieval siege engine could be transported in pieces and reconstructed on the field.

A shout went up, and the arm suddenly flung a second flaming payload. Javier planted his feet and stabbed his fingers into the ground, drawing power up from the earth.

The fireball crashed against the barrier, its flaming core of pitch-soaked iron scraps penetrating and slamming into another row of houses. Javier reeled back and landed hard in the dirt, head spinning. He felt like he'd been kicked by a mule.

"Javier!" Fernando was at his side in an instant. "Are you all right?"

He shook off the ache singing in his skull. Screams rang out around him. He touched his brow, and his shaking fingers came away wet with blood.

Release me, Diablo whispered. *Unleash me.*

He clenched his teeth. His friend was right: Duarte and everyone else who sought to control him had to learn he was not a sorcerer to be trifled with. But there were hundreds of soldiers out there—how could he stop them all without paying the blood price?

"I need to root myself, shore up the barrier, while the men take out that catapult before it does any more damage."

"The moment we open the gates, the army will rush in."

He looked at the V in the wall. "We have to stop that catapult," he whispered again, holding his breath.

Javier waited, counting on his friend's hesitancy to save his life. Javier did not want to be the one to hand him his death. But…

Fernando made a frustrated noise. "If you will not do what is needed, then give Diablo to me and I will lead the charge!"

Javier swallowed. "Fernando…you don't understand…"

"You need to protect Yani," he said angrily. "You promised not to run away again."

"I'm not."

"Hiding here is just as bad. You made Diablo to protect us, but it cannot fire itself. Killing is not work for sorcerers like you. It's for soldiers like me." He held his hand out. "If you won't wield the devil's own revolver, then let me do it for you."

The relief that only cowards could feel in surrender slid through him as he slipped the mage gun into his friend's hand. "End this," he said. As it left his palm, a tingling crept up his arm. And then the weight of it left him, the voice that whispered and hummed suddenly silent.

Fernando's eyes went wide. His grip spasmed over Diablo. The weapon molded to his hand and, like a flower, blossomed and transformed. The barrel doubled and lengthened, the grip curved. It had become a different gun, one that suited Fernando.

"Dios." His friend marveled at the newly formed weapon.

Another blast of battle magic rocked the town, and Javier braced himself.

"Go," Javier directed. "I will hold the barrier and cover you as best as I can."

He watched his best friend go, taking his little devil with him. Shame funneled through him; he should have told Fernando about the blood price, about the dangers of using the mage gun. He had to take it back before Fernando used it and found out how he'd been betrayed.

But before he could call out to him, another blast from the catapult crashed through the wall, and Javier was knocked backward.

When he came to, the catapult was a pile of ash, the army had been decimated...and his friend was gone.

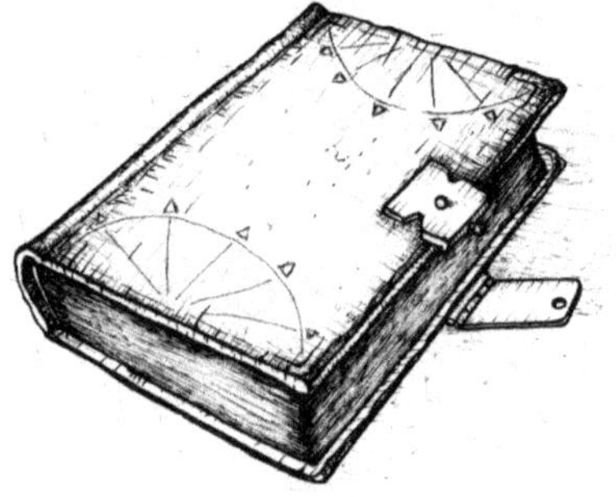

CHAPTER FOUR

Junesfield was a small, industrious lumber town in Kansas. The place was tidy, the roads magically reinforced to keep them from getting muddy—an expensive spell for a lumber town—and the buildings were brightly painted and well-kept. The railroad had been a blessing for the economy and was probably the reason why the Division had chosen Junesfield as a central hub for the Fielding canisters—the town was central to many of the smaller hamlets and villages in the county.

Just outside town, beyond the decorative timber archway, piles of discarded scraps and beams nailed together in rough rows of crosses lay along the path. Inside the time bubble, Hettie and Walker dismounted and walked their horses around them.

"Barricades," Walker observed. "They used them during the war to stop cavalry charges. Look." He pointed toward a row of men. "They're digging a trench, too."

"They expecting a fight?"

"Anything worth protecting gets proportional defenses. We must be on the right track."

They navigated around the stock-still tableau of people loading and unloading carts, children running through the streets, neighbors waving at each other. It reminded Hettie of Newhaven. She wondered about the townspeople back in that place she'd once called home. Wondered about her friend Will Samson, the sorcerer Henry Bale, the healer Miss Yellowhawk who'd helped save her life...

She clamped down on the homesickness welling up inside her.

"Go check the warehouses," Hettie directed Walker. "I'll search the rest of the buildings."

Walker frowned. "I thought we couldn't be too far apart in the bubble."

"The juice helps. Just go."

She made her way through every shop and saloon, picking up a few essential supplies along the way. The canisters were too big to hide. That strange sucking feeling they radiated couldn't be easily concealed from a gifted populace, and they wouldn't keep a lot of the canisters together where they might affect other spells.

She checked every building and found nothing. Absently, she fingered the little bag of raven bones in her pocket. Rok's smoky form flapped down to rest on her shoulder.

"You called?" the demon familiar rasped.

"Do you sense any Fielding canisters in town?"

The raven snipped his beak in the air. *"No canisters here."*

Hettie's spirits dropped. *"But,"* Rok interjected, *"there are traces of magic everywhere."*

"From what?"

"Don't know."

"The canisters?"

"Don't know."

Odd. The raven familiar knew everything. And he wasn't prone to lying. "Maybe the sorcerers in town are juiced. Show me the gifted."

Rok took off and circled the town overhead, his ashy wings raining down a fine shower of soot. As the particles landed on the gifted, they lit up like sunlight glowing through a new spring leaf.

Hettie noted the faces, inspected the men for any signs they were with the Division. They usually displayed their badges prominently when they were on official business, but that she couldn't spot their shields meant little.

She counted seventeen gifted, most of them older folks. Not many for a Division town. Of course, any children with the gift would've been sent to the Academy…or else they had run away. So the ambient magic Rok was detecting wasn't likely from juicing.

Two men in particular caught her attention. They stood close together, heads bent, one man's eyes locked on the building across the way, every taut line of their bodies telegraphing anxiety.

She could drop out of time, maybe try to listen in on their conversation, but she didn't know where Walker was, and she couldn't leave him exposed.

She found him just as he was exiting one of the warehouses near the train station. "No canisters or engines here. But I found something else." He beckoned her inside and pointed toward one corner where several men were unloading crates from a wagon. One had been cracked open, and she peered in with a frown.

"Guns?"

"And ammunition. Enough to equip an army." He pointed. "There's more in there."

"Army's not stationed around these parts. So what are they stockpiling for?"

"Maybe *us*. After No Hope, could be they're loading the Fielding expeditions for bear. Seems excessive, even for the Division."

"Nothing's excessive for them." There had to be at least ten crates of guns in here. She supposed she could destroy them, but then they'd know something was wrong, and she could lose her only lead to Abby. "Maybe they planted the idea of Junesfield in that Uxbridge fella in No Hope. Maybe they're laying another trap for us."

"Nothing about our outfit's told them we're that stupid or reckless," Walker countered. "We're as successful as we are because we're careful."

"So let's pretend this isn't for us. What would they arm themselves against?"

"The League? The Mundane Movement?"

"The Division hasn't fired on their own citizens…yet. Or if they have, they wouldn't be making quite this much of a show of it." She gestured around. "This might be a Division town, but look at these people. Look at their faces. They're not living in fear, even with this many guns passing through and all those barricades going up. Either they don't know what's coming, or they think they're invincible."

"Or they're under some kind of influence spell." Walker folded his arms. "We can't be certain unless we check it out in real time. You have the anti-influence charm Lena made?"

She pulled out the talisman from around her neck. "Never go anywhere without it."

They found a spot where no one would notice two rough-looking types popping up out of thin air, and Hettie dropped the time bubble. The town roared to life, the hustle and bustle an assault on her ears after hours of silence. Carts clattered through the street, men shouted, and everyone moved with purpose.

Hettie nodded toward the two anxious-looking men. "I wanna follow those two."

Walker nodded. "All right. I'll hit the saloon, see what I can find out. Meet back here in an hour."

Hettie tugged the brim of her hat down and surreptitiously made her way to a stall close to the men, who continued their low conversation in the middle of the thoroughfare. She caught a snippet as she passed.

"…not enough. We need more men to dig trenches. We're totally exposed out here, and when they bring in the next canisters…"

Hettie forced herself to keep moving. So the Fielding canisters *were* coming through here. She and Walker must have just missed a shipment.

She pretended to browse the stall's wares, straining to eavesdrop. The man at the stall held out a bottle. "Best garlic ale in the county," he said with a smile. "Drink this, rub it on your skin, and it'll keep the vamps away."

"Vamps?" Hettie startled. "You mean vampires?"

"Among other creatures." His smile brightened as he hooked a potential customer. "Vampires, Weres… even those things I hear are roaming all over the country south of the Wall. Choopookaburra."

"Chupacabra," she corrected, opening the bottle and taking a whiff. Not so much medicinal as cheap gin mixed with garlic, herbs, and some other green things he'd probably pulled off the side of the road.

The two Division men came closer, still engrossed in their heated conversation. Wanting to keep up the pretense of being a casual shopper, Hettie rubbed some of the ale on her skin and sniffed it. It reminded her of Uncle after a week without a bath.

"Why not have a sip?" The man poured a thimbleful into a shot glass and pushed it toward her. "It'll warm you through. All natural, no magic spells or potions, I guarantee."

"Guarantee! Guarantee!" Rok squawked from the top of the stall's sign. *"Thief and liar guaranteed!"*

Hettie set her teeth and sipped the stuff. It burned on contact, the powerful funk reeking of months-old unwashed laundry. "That'll keep *something* away all right," she coughed.

"Don't you know it. It's a recipe from my grandmammy's days, back before the last vamps were staked and burned. Seems like we need it more and more, what with all the attacks."

"What attacks?"

"You haven't heard?" He gave a bleak and incredulous chuckle. "Word is, the vamps have returned. There were a couple of attacks on those Fielding expeditions. They come here, you know, to unload, get those canisters shipped off." He nodded toward the train station. "'Course, no one's supposed to talk about it. But I've been chatting up the men who ride security with the engines—boys, really. They're graduating them earlier and earlier from the Academy these days."

"Do you know where they take the canisters?" she asked, trying hard not to sound too eager.

He chuckled. "Ain't nobody who knows that, except maybe the officers. But you know the Division. They play their cards close to their chest." He lowered his voice. "Hell, ain't nobody in Junesfield's supposed to even know the canisters are coming through here. Kind of obvious, what with all the agents and security and those barricades like we're expecting General Lee to come charging in. You can never have too much protection, though." He shook the bottle in a prompt.

Hettie bought one, keeping an eye on the Division men as they paced toward the building they'd been nodding at. Of course, he might be telling tall tales to sell his snake oil, but there was often a grain of truth to be found among such stories. "Tell me about these attacks. Where'd they take place?"

"Been all over, from what the papers are saying. First couple were in New Mexico, near where Swedenborg used to be." He lowered his voice. "They say that's where the vamps crawled out of hell. Straight out of the ground, like maggots through a corpse."

Hettie's skin lifted with goose bumps. "Where else?"

"Somewhere in Louisiana, near New Orleans, some small town a few hours away… What was it called? It had a funny name… Pigeonhole?"

"Quail's Hollow?" she croaked.

He snapped his fingers. "That'd be the one." He shook his head. "Heard that whole town was torn apart. Division had to go down there and raze the place, make sure the 'blood hunger' didn't spread." He snorted. "That's the problem with these scientist types. They think vampires were just sick folks that needed medicine, but my grandmammy knew better. Infernal demons need exorcising…"

Hettie barely heard him through the rush of blood in her ears. She started toward the saloon.

"Wait up!" The man grabbed her wrist. Diablo jumped into her palm, and she pushed the muzzle into the man's face. "Whoa there, partner! Didn't mean anything by it." He held up the bottle of garlic ale she'd left behind and laughed nervously. "Helluva quick draw you got there." He eyed the Devil's Revolver charily. "Nice piece, too."

Hettie snatched her hand out of his grip and hastily stuffed the mage gun back into her holster. She swiped the bottle from him, then whirled away.

She found Walker chatting up a woman at the bar. She was a willowy thing, golden-haired and fair. The rouge on her cheeks and tint on her lips glinted as she laughed and stroked Walker's arm.

Hettie ignored the flare of heat in her chest and marched up to him. The woman glanced up curiously, her smile broadening. "This your friend? Y'know, I have a friend who could join us. Or maybe you'd like it to be the three of us together?"

Hettie pushed her hat up to look the woman in the eye. "I don't share."

The woman went pale, the words stopping in her slender throat. She left them stiffly, crossing the room with rapid, stumbling steps.

"You didn't need to scare her off." Walker tossed back his drink. "She was just warming up to me, getting ready to tell me about the Division presence in town."

"Never mind that. I got what we need. Let's go."

Across the room, the saloon girl anxiously relayed something to a large man, glancing at Hettie and Walker fearfully. The man looked their way, eyes narrowed, and Hettie knew she'd been made. "Dammit." She grabbed Walker's wrist.

"Hold it right there!" The big man drew his sidearm. "You with the scar!"

Walker slipped in front of Hettie, hiding her behind his bulk. "Easy there, hoss. I'm sorry, I didn't mean to show any disrespect for your employee." He tossed a few bills onto the counter. "I'll be on my way. No need for trouble." He backed toward the door, and Hettie inched along behind him.

The big man whistled. Four men drew on them, including the bartender, who pulled a shotgun out. Walker and Hettie stopped dead in their tracks.

"You're *her*." The big man sidled around Walker, eyeing Hettie up and down. "You're the heathen witch Hettie Alabama."

She sighed. "Why does everyone keep calling me that?" A cold weight settled in her stomach, and she pushed it down deeper so that she was rooted, boots to earth.

"Reward for her's over three thousand dollars by now," one of the armed men said, licking his lips. Around them, saloon patrons edged out of the crossfire, ducking low behind their stools. "Dead or alive."

"Actually, it's five thousand." Hettie stepped out around Walker. She met the eyes of every man there. "This ain't gonna end well for you boys." She glanced around the room. "And it'd be a pity to shoot this place up. I like the chandelier."

"I can buy ten more when I turn you in." The big boss lumbered toward her. "Now get on your knees like a good girl."

She sucked in air between her teeth and exhaled. "Walker, d'you fancy any of the whiskeys on the shelves?" she asked over her shoulder.

"Got my eye on a couple, yeah."

"All right. I'll do my best to save them."

ᛉ

They walked out less than a minute later—about ten in Hettie's bubble time—with all the saloon's cash, three bottles of top-shelf whiskey in Walker's bag, and some new bloodstains on the cuffs of her shirt. The bounty hunter dumped an armload of guns into the nearest water-filled trough while Hettie checked the blade of her curved dagger, making sure it was spotless before sheathing it. The syrup world engulfed them in thick silence once more, except for the screaming men she'd left behind. Their weight in her bubble would be released once they were outside of Junesfield, and then she'd reform the time bubble so it was just her and Walker.

The bounty hunter ground his jaw as they mounted up.

"*Now* what's got your goat?" she asked when his stilted silence dragged on.

"If you don't know, I don't want to say."

"You sulking that you didn't get a go at that saloon girl?"

"Is *that* what you think?" His disbelief morphed into anger.

She barely lifted her shoulder, the numbness inside spreading icy fingers through her core. She'd made it clear he had no obligation to her—what more did he want?

Walker cut his mount in front of hers, eyes flashing. "I just watched you cut the ankles of five men without batting an eyelash."

"I could've killed them outright, you know." Which she might have done to keep them quiet, except that Walker had been there, and she hadn't wanted him to witness that.

"And I'm supposed to be grateful you didn't?"

"I don't need you to be anything. You're a gunslinger, Walker. How many men have *you* killed?"

He ground his jaw. "We're not talking about *me*."

"Exactly my point. You keep holding me to some impossible standard when I have just as much to lose as you do. Maybe even more. I have to do what I have to do to find Abby and to keep everyone I care about safe." Even if it was from her own monstrosity. She drew herself up. "You were the one who wanted to come along. I wouldn't even have had to do all that if you hadn't followed me."

He scoffed. "Not killing people shouldn't be a burden."

Everything inside Hettie flexed, like a taffy being pulled in every direction, thinning to the point of snapping. She wanted to apologize and ask for his forgiveness. Another part of her wanted him to just go away and leave her alone. Still another quietly whispered that he'd be better off without her…and she'd be better off without him.

She could drop him out of the time bubble, get back to Blackthorn's Hell, and move the gang before he returned. But she knew he'd find her. He always did.

"What did you learn?" he asked sullenly after a time.

She told him haltingly about the so-called "vampire" attacks on the Fielding expedition, and about Swedenborg and Quail's Hollow.

"Quail's Hollow? That town where you bamboozled the folks out of their magic?"

"It was Horace's idea." She'd gone along with it, though, so she could hardly blame the hostler. "We need to go there. I can't trust the word of some snake oil peddler. I need to see what kind of damage was done. What that engine of Fielding's did."

"If the Division burned the town to the ground, there won't be anything to see." He rode alongside her. "What're you really worrying about?"

She was silent for a long moment. "We need to go see Sophie."

"I don't think that's a good idea."

"We used that engine on her. We should check on her, see if there's anything we need to do for her."

"We're putting her at risk every time we go to her."

"If you wanna head back to the hideout, take a train. I'll pay your way."

"You can't get rid of me that easily," he bit out, tugging his hat lower over his eyes and glaring hard down the road. "You wanna go see Sophie? Let's go see Sophie."

EXCERPTS FROM THE DIARY OF FERNANDO RICO

COURTESY OF THE WOLVERTON GRAY BERKELEY COLLECTION

He is still coming.

I can't see him. I don't think I want to see him, but I know he's there. El Diablo tells me, every minute of the day, to run, run far away, as far as I can from the angel of death. I have not slept for weeks. I am not even sure I know how long it has been since I left Villa del Punta, since I took out Duarte and scattered his men. It feels like one long, unending nightmare.

I feel like an old man. I *am* an old man. Older than I should be. Did Javier know this would happen? I would curse him if I did not

My horse went lame two days ago. I traded her for a mule. This wretched beast is too slow for El Diablo's liking. She nags me worse than any wife—faster, faster. Never stopping. Never slowing.

I know the angel is closing in. He came to me in dreams, demanding I return the gun. His eyes glowed like flames. He was angry. He brandished his own hellfire, but then Diablo saved me, woke me up, told me to run toward the sea…

I am here now. I am building a raft that will carry me away from the land, away from *him*, out where he cannot track me. I must make it strong—I cannot swim. God willing, the tides will carry me back to shore somewhere far away from here.

God help me, I need forgiveness. I should never have left Villa del Punta. I don't even know if they're still alive…

No, it is better this way. I am a coward and traitor. And *they* were weak and stupid. It was a fool's dream to think the army would let us be. Now I am alone. El Diablo is the only thing I can rely on…

Oh, Javier, can you ever forgive me?

He is coming again. I must work faster.

CHAPTER FIVE

"I'm surprised the Pinkerton Agency hasn't put more people on this case."

Jane looked up from her newspaper. Professor Gallagher had been silent most of the train ride to Junesfield, as Jane was not much for small talk. It seemed all that silence had given him too much time to think. "How's that now?" she asked.

"I assumed with the remote Zoom to No Hope, and now this train ride, it's obviously an important case." He leaned forward. "You need more assistants—other agents under you who could follow up on these leads."

"It's not as high on the Pinkerton's priorities as you might think," she responded. "We're a private firm, don't forget. We earn more bringing in Academy truants than we do bringing in criminals. I'm on my own with this case because I'm efficient and use the resources I'm allotted judiciously. And I prefer to handle the investigation myself. Rest assured, you and I are the only ones needed on this case." She hoped that answer was enough to assuage his curiosity. She nodded to his notes on the undoing spell. "How's that coming along?"

He sighed. "I remember the spell. I know it by heart. But I'm telling you, the practical nature of it—"

"The components of the spell should be easy enough to find, no?"

"Depends on how easy you think virgin's blood and ash from the funeral pyre of a murderer are to find," he said. "Not to mention this, uh, Marriage Trap plant." He shook his head. "All that aside, this spell has never been tested. I daresay I'm not sure it would even work—it was meant as a hypothetical for demonically imbued items."

"I wouldn't have invited you all the way to Chicago if I didn't believe in you, Professor Gallagher." Jane's forced confidence was all she could offer him. "Think of it this way—once we've acquired everything we need, you'll finally be able to prove your theory one way or another."

"You understand we'd need to have Diablo within the protection circle for us to be able to perform the spell?" He gestured at the scribbles in his notebook.

"One step at a time, professor. We can make inquiries into your shopping list on our travels."

An hour later, they disembarked in Junesfield and met with the local sheriff. "I don't remember calling the Pinks with regards to this matter," he said, eyeing them up and down.

"We're investigating a related case." She nodded. "Is that the file?"

"Not a whole lot to tell." The sheriff slid the folder toward Gallagher, but Jane snatched it up first. "I got called to the saloon and found these five writhing on the ground with their ankles cut. I thought there'd been some kind of accident, but they say it was Hettie Alabama."

"But she was nowhere in sight?"

"Thought maybe they'd all drunk some bad moonshine, but one of the girls confirmed it. Hettie Alabama and a big fella in black."

Jane read the report and memorized the victims' names. "I'd like to interview these men, please."

"You go right ahead." The sheriff made a vague gesture. "I won't stop you."

Or help them, apparently.

Over the course of the day, they interviewed each of the men. The story was the same all around: they'd recognized and tried to apprehend the wanted criminal, but then she'd disappeared into thin air, and before they knew what was happening, they'd been cut down and she was gone.

"This isn't the first time Hettie Alabama's been reported vanishing in front of people." Jane stood on the porch of the saloon after their final interview.

"Perhaps she juiced and learned to perform some kind of hide spell?" Gallagher suggested.

"I doubt it. The saloon has a null spell over it, probably to protect the girls from influence magic and to prevent folks from skipping out on their tabs. A master sorcerer would've had a hard time maintaining any kind of enchantment. A mundane like Hettie Alabama wouldn't have stood a chance."

"But you think Diablo has something to do with it. That it gave her the power to do all that to those men."

She nodded. "Did you spot anything that might've indicated it was the Devil's Revolver?"

He shook his head. "Diablo's powers are vast and not well documented. There are stories of everything it's done, but they're just that—stories."

"I suppose there's nothing in those stories about the mage gun turning the wielder invisible."

He shook his head, then reconsidered. "There is one possibility. It's based on the story of Elias and the Mad Bull."

"The one where he shoots the rampaging bull from around a corner?"

"It's one of the few most everyone knows about because a preacher who was there wrote it down. There's a line in that story that's never made a lot of sense to people: 'From 'round the corner made he a dark stroke, and as if smoke and lightning played Pyathagoras's mathematics, Elias smote the bull.'"

"I always took that to mean he fired through the building, maybe through a window," Jane said.

"That's not the part that confuses people. It's the ''round the corner made he a dark stroke' that doesn't make sense. In a few other versions, there's some allusion to something else happening. It's described in one account as a flash of light. In another, it's like a smear across a wet canvas."

"That's not disappearing, though."

"No. But it does describe something that is moving fast. There are plenty of talismans and spells that can make a man work faster."

"But not so fast they can blur," she said skeptically.

Gallagher spread his hands. "All I'm proposing is a theory—that Diablo has given its wielder abilities that make some of the legends associated with it true."

She pondered that as they made their way to the hotel, where they'd stay before heading back to Chicago the next morning.

Over dinner in the hotel's dining room, Jane and her cohort were approached by two men.

"Are you Agent Pinkerton with the Pinkerton Detecting Agency?" A rail-thin, mustachioed man stooped toward Gallagher, eyeing him cautiously.

Jane put her napkin aside and cleared her throat. "I'm Jane Pinkerton."

The men startled, as if only just noticing she was there. They cringed away from her flat, unblinking stare. "I do beg your pardon...um...*Miss* Pinkerton."

"Agent. What can I do for you gentlemen?"

She waited a beat as they exchanged looks, and she sighed inwardly. "Whatever it is you've interrupted my meal for, I'd appreciate a quick explanation. My food's getting cold."

"O-of course, Miss...*Agent* Pinkerton." The other man, younger and portlier with baby-smooth cheeks, snatched his hat off his head. "I'm Hans Voorhees, and this is my associate, Arnold Holtz. We're the liaisons to the Division of Sorcery for this area. We'd heard representatives from the esteemed Pinkerton agency were in town—a relative to Mr. William Pinkerton himself, no less. We wanted to discuss hiring your team to deal with some, uh, matters of security."

"*Magical* security," the man added, eyeing Jane's master's bars over her Pinkerton shield.

They must have been desperate if they were willing to approach her rather than ask whatever group of sorcerers were in the village. "I'm only in Junesfield as part of an investigation into a different matter. I'm afraid I don't have the time or resources for a second caseload."

"We'll pay you," blurted the thin man. Then, more urgently and in a whisper, "Off the books."

Gallagher raised an eyebrow. Jane tilted her chin. "You have my interest."

They sat at the table and bent close. "We have a situation with an employee of ours. We think he was attacked on the road, only…he doesn't seem to remember what happened. That's why we need a master sorcerer. Can you plumb a man's thoughts?"

"It's not my specialty, but I have been trained."

The Division liaisons looked at each other, carrying on some silent conversation. "That will have to do. If you're amenable to an agreement and will submit to a silence spell…"

She sat back with a snort. "I will submit to no influence spell administered by the Division," she bit out. "I'm a vetted agent of business working for the Pinkerton Agency. That should be guarantee of silence enough. Besides," she added with a sniff, "my paycheck is my bond." She panned her gaze left and right, making sure the men felt the full weight of it.

"W-we didn't mean to offend, only it's standard procedure…" He trailed off and swallowed, averting his eyes. "But we're willing to disregard that for now. If you'll please join us at the sorcerer's salon after you've eaten, you can…ah, begin you work."

"Is this strictly aboveboard?" Gallagher asked when the men had left and Jane tucked back into her meal.

"Strictly? No." She cut into the overdone pot roast. "As long as we don't put it on the books. You won't tell anyone, will you?" She winked.

"I'm hardly in a position to." He rubbed his throat and glanced about nervously. "But I've got a bad feeling about those two."

"They work for the Division—our genteel magical overlords. No one has any reason to trust them, especially if they're offering to pay you under the table."

"Then why on Earth did you accept the job?"

"Where's your academic curiosity, professor?" She bit into a piece of undercooked potato and frowned. "Besides, if it were that dire a secret, they wouldn't have approached us out here in public. They would've simply kidnapped me. Or you, I suppose, if they had no idea who I was."

He compressed his lips. "You're awfully nonchalant about that."

She waved. "I'm not worried about those two. If you're concerned about your own welfare, you can go back to your room."

"I'm not letting you go off unescorted with two strange men," he said, affronted.

The corners of her lips twitched. She didn't think he would.

ᛉ

They finished their meal and met Holtz and Voorhees at the sorcerer's salon. The public workshop for sorcerers was like many in other towns—clean, both in the mundane and magical sense, with a collection of spellbooks neatly shelved in the main room and an attendant who kept talismans and ingredients for various potions and other concoctions in locked cabinets behind the counter. The large spell room in the back was ringed by a number of protection spells. This salon also had three smaller cells for people looking for magically sterile spaces to try new spells or develop talismans.

Most salons were partially owned and subsidized by the Division of Sorcery. Salons provided local gifted with Division-produced ingredients and materials for spells and talismans, vetted spellbooks, and other resources. The salons were also tasked with disseminating magic regulation, and they hosted elders and masters when all the children who'd come of age were tested for the gift.

Academy graduates had opened salons all over the country, spreading the Division's reach far and wide. It wasn't an easy life with the Division breathing down your neck all the time, but it was better than working as an agent, a fate imposed on nearly every gifted born these days.

Holtz and Voorhees greeted them tersely. "The man we need you to plumb is…somewhat disturbed," Holtz said. "We've tried for days to get something out of him, but he only babbles in riddles."

"What can you tell me about him?"

Holtz handed over a dossier, and Jane flipped it open. Douglas Carlyle, age twenty-two. Single. Born in Arkansas. Graduated from the Academy and hired as an enforcer. Specialties: protection. Nothing there was surprising. "So what happened to him?"

"All we know for certain is that he was sent ahead of the rest of the group. On his way here, something happened to him, and he's... well..." He flapped his hands uselessly.

"And what is this group on their way here for?"

"They're transporting supplies. For the salon."

The catch in Voorhees's voice told her he was lying, but then she doubted anything either of these men said was the whole truth. She handed back the dossier. "Where is he?"

"Room three. We thought a quiet environment might help him relax some."

Meaning they'd locked him up for his own protection.

"Agent Pinkerton," Gallagher said quietly, "you shouldn't go in there alone."

"Of course I won't. You'll come with me."

"I— I will?"

"You've a PhD, don't you? You can examine him for trauma."

"I'm not *that* kind of doctor."

"You are today." She strode out of the room and went to spell room three. The heavy wood door was bolted from the outside, and a small pane of glass covered by a sliding panel allowed people to peek in to make sure whatever was happening within wasn't of an illicit nature.

A dim, brownish glow stone lit the interior. Douglas Carlyle sat unmoving in the corner of the bare room, knees drawn up, eyes staring straight ahead. He was an unextraordinary young man of medium build, with dark hair sticking up in all directions from running his hands through it repeatedly, his chin sporting patchy, overgrown stubble. Little set him apart from any other soldier or enforcer Jane had encountered in her twenty-nine years of life. It was the look in his eyes, though, that caught her attention—bleak and hunted.

Jane breathed out and touched her Vision talisman to help her focus. She couldn't see anything hovering around him—no ghosts or miasmas that might indicate a curse or haunting. "How long has he been like this?"

"Two days now. He hasn't slept much, either, as far as we can tell. And he won't eat."

Jane unbolted the door and stepped in. Gallagher was right behind her.

"Mr. Carlyle? Douglas Carlyle?"

He shuddered and met her eye. He didn't flinch, didn't blink. He stared right through her. "My name is Jane Pinkerton. I'm a master sorcerer with the Pinkerton Detecting Agency. I'm here to help you."

"Master?" His voice creaked from disuse. He scrambled to his knees. "Master. Master. Master." He reached out and clawed at her skirts. Jane stepped back as Gallagher moved in front of her and shoved the man away. Carlyle moaned and cowered in his corner, muttering, "Master. Master. Master."

"You didn't need to do that," she snapped at the professor, pushing him aside.

"He was accosting you!"

"The man's clearly terrified and is looking for help." She knelt to Carlyle's level. "Can you tell me anything about what happened?" she asked him.

But Carlyle was back to staring again, like a rabbit watching the darkness for the wolf that stalked him, too afraid to move and give himself away.

Jane sighed. So she'd have to plumb his thoughts.

She asked Gallagher to close the door while she prepared herself. She withdrew her talismans and laid them on a piece of silk. A phial of thrice-boiled water. An evil eye charm made of blue glass. A piece of quartz. She brought the bundle under the man's nose, letting him breathe over it.

"The four elements method," Gallagher remarked interestedly. "I didn't think many sorcerers still used those rituals."

"I'm trying to concentrate," she bit out, and the professor shut up. She'd prefer if he waited outside, but she doubted he'd leave her alone with Carlyle.

She began her incantation. She didn't want to touch the Division man's hands in case he reacted poorly, which made the spell more difficult, but Jane hadn't been at the top of her class at the Academy for nothing. Slowly, she opened her eyes, meeting his gaze unblinkingly, letting the world around her blur.

Darkness clouded her sight. She was sharing his vision now. It was nighttime in his mind, an impenetrable blackness enveloping him entirely.

She made out the faintest scuffle, but that might simply have been Gallagher in the background. He breathed loud enough to stir the dead.

The rustle of leaves caught her attention. She focused, trying to see past and through what Carlyle was experiencing. He wasn't fighting her, which was unusual for a Division agent. They were all trained to resist mental probing of any kind. Right now, all his walls were down, and the darkness was blotting out other thoughts and memories. He was trapped in this moment.

Show me what came before this, she thought at him. *Show me what you saw.*

She met resistance as his mind clenched against the idea.

Please. I'm trying to help you.

The gentlest probe from her had the doors to his mind swinging wide. And then she was there. The world was a collection of smears of light and color, like an impressionist painting. All around her, she could hear gunfire, shouts, and a sound like... a growl? Wolves? Weres?

A bloodcurdling scream rent the air. The sharp smell of blood and shit filled her nostrils.

"Run, Douglas! Get help!" The voice became desperate, and it gave a cry, then a gurgle: *"Get the masters!"*

"Masters. Masters. Masters." Carlyle said it close to her ear. "M-m-masters. Help."

A scuffling sound, and the light smears darkened and blended back into the night. The screams and gunfire faded, and then all she could hear was Carlyle's heavy breathing.

Except something was following him.

Sweat beaded on her upper lip. Something was after her. It moved fast, stealthily. She scrambled through the dark, blindly groping along the wet ground, trying desperately to hear above the pounding of her heart. The path at her heels slipped away like a tunnel swallowing itself in her wake. She tripped and plowed into the ground, then scrabbled for her gun as the thing rushed out of the darkness at her—

"Agent Pinkerton!"

Jane gasped, spine arching as she surfaced from Carlyle's memories. The Division man was lying on his side in fetal position. Gallagher held her on his lap.

"Dammit." She pushed out of his hold. "Why'd you interrupt me? I was close to finding out what happened!"

"You're bleeding."

Her fingers came away from her upper lip wet. She snatched the handkerchief he proffered and pinched her nose. "I may not have done well at the Academy," he admonished, "but I do know when a plumbing has gone too far. You were getting lost in the vision."

She grimaced over at the agent. "Carlyle's closed to me. The plumbing activated his mental defenses. I won't be able to plumb his mind again."

"You would have been no good to anyone if you'd lost your mind in his twisted thoughts." He let out a breath. "What did you see?"

"Enough. And not nearly enough." She snatched the door open and marched out.

Holtz and Voorhees met her with eager, expectant faces. "Gentlemen, I can't begin to tell you what you face, only that it was enough of a challenge that the captain of the expedition ordered Mr. Carlyle to run. Something attacked your men and has likely killed them all. Whatever it was stalked Mr. Carlyle here."

"That's all you have?" Holtz's eyebrows lowered. "What attacked the others? And what about Carlyle?"

"I'm afraid there's nothing I can do for him. He may need to be sent to an asylum. His mind is too dark to fathom." She shook her head.

"We were expecting results, Miss Pinkerton," Voorhees said a little too forcefully. "We are not satisfied by this outcome."

She squared her shoulders so she faced them both head-on, widening her eyes so they received the full weight of her disdain. "I suppose you're going to tell me that you'll only pay me half of what you promised." She lifted her chin. "Then I suppose you'll threaten to report me to my employers for misconduct. And then you'll make some unkind remark about my gender and other members of my sex."

Holtz sputtered, "See here, Miss—"

She took two menacing steps forward until she was only a handspan away. Holtz and Voorhees stepped back. "You think you can browbeat me into accepting your terms and trying to fulfill them with some other favor you now wish me to do. Gentlemen, I will save you the effort. I will take full payment for my services. You will not harass me further, and I will not report *your* indiscretions to the Division."

"We don't know what you mean," Voorhees said shiftily.

"Mr. Carlyle's memories have been wiped. Poorly, I might add. There aren't many sorcerers who can do this, but Division agents of a certain level can." She nodded toward the man's shield. "*You* did this, only you did it wrong—the council would have your badges for such shoddy spellcraft. You didn't need me to read his mind to find out what happened—you already knew. You've put barricades around the town in preparation for an attack. You just wanted to make sure no one else could read his mind and find out what he knew." She leaned toward Holtz until he recoiled. "So what will it be? Assault on a Pinkerton daughter, or payment and my bond of silence?"

"How can we trust you?" Holtz bit out. "You're a woman."

She turned her glare on him. "I know how to keep secrets. And I will keep yours, if only because I have no wish to be involved in whatever it is you're up to here. Your incompetence unnerves me."

Her insults could've provoked them to further outrage, but they didn't. Fear had them in its cold grip. The men looked at each other as if weighing their options. Behind her she could sense Gallagher flexing as if ready to fight... or, more likely, flee.

Don't be stupid, she projected through her hardened gaze. *Don't make things more unpleasant than they have to be.*

They didn't. Grudgingly, Voorhees extracted an envelope, opening it and checking its contents before thrusting it toward her. She didn't bother to count the bills as she stuffed it into her reticule.

"Good evening, gentlemen," she said as she departed. "Pray our paths do not cross again."

"What just happened?" Professor Gallagher followed her out as she headed straight for the hotel.

"They tried to wipe Carlyle's memory, make him forget whatever it was he saw. I imagine they wanted to make sure no one could get out of him what I did." She rubbed her throbbing temples. Her nose had started bleeding again, and she dabbed at it with Gallagher's handkerchief.

"That doesn't make any sense..." They walked into her room together, a silent acknowledgment that hers would be safer from the Eye and eavesdropping. "If the Division is so invested in silence, why didn't they just kill Carlyle?"

"Killing isn't as easy as the penny dreadfuls make it out to be," she said. "You saw those men. They had about as much gumption between them as a bowl of thin gruel. Besides, sorcerers are few and far between now, and the investment in getting the gifted to the Academy is growing by the day. They were probably instructed to maintain as much cover as possible, and only to kill if necessary."

"That's a lot of suppositions."

"The Division likes their secrets." She sat back and stared out the window. "First the silence spell in No Hope, now this memory wipe. That's a lot of magic to be putting in keeping agents quiet—unprecedented, really. There has to be a connection."

"The Blackthorn Rogues?" Gallagher offered.

"Perhaps. Their members could have juiced up, gone Were. It definitely wasn't men that killed those Division troops."

"That would align with the stories of the Crowe gang," the professor said, a note of skepticism in his tone. "But my understanding was that the Weres from the Crowe gang were all killed in Sonora."

"They were. And it isn't easy to find a warlock who can turn that many Weres. I hate to admit it, but I'm having a hard time pinning this on Hettie Alabama." As many bodies as they'd left behind, there was a certain surgical precision with which they'd struck. This campaign made no sense.

Moreover, she couldn't suss out why the Division would hide *this* attack from anyone. The newspapers had stories aplenty, sensational though they were. No one could deny the attacks were happening.

Which meant the Division was trying to hide something specific about *what* was attacking their people and what they had attacked. Because Carlyle had seen *something* worth wiping.

If it had been vampires, she might have caught a glimmer of that. She'd never met a vamp before, but supernaturals like Weres and vampires gave off a particular aura, especially in visions. She'd seen nothing like that plumbing Carlyle's mind.

She talked it out. "Carlyle's memory may not have been intact, but his fear was real. Memory wiping can remove the facts and the events, but not always the emotions. That takes a lot more skill, and these two bungled it entirely."

"Can... can *you* wipe memories?"

"Any high-level sorcerer with the know-how can. Few sorcerers would want to, though. Memories are difficult to handle. Those memories don't get erased, after all. They get transferred." She tapped her temple. "Usually to whoever is doing the wiping. I don't fancy remembering things that never happened to me. Too confusing."

"If Holtz and Voorheers wiped Carlyle's memory like you said..."

"It'd explain why they're so scared." She nodded. "They likely had to perform the spell together. It's a complicated one. It'd mean they'd each have a piece of those memories. And in my experience, things are much scarier when you *don't* have the whole picture."

Gallagher paced, then went to look out the window. "What are the Division's interests in Junesfield?"

She shrugged. "Aside from the salon and the rail line? Not much. Basically, it's an arterial town. Gets supplies where they need to go to all the other villages and towns in the area."

"Maybe it's the other way around." He said it slowly. "Maybe it's funneling resources to someplace. Or redistributing resources."

"It's a rail line. That goes without saying."

"No, I mean, Junesfield is, what, a timber town? Mining?"

"The mines are drying up, but I suppose there's some industry left."

"But not that much. I've visited enough mining and lumber towns to know what makes it viable. This place has a healthy population. Lots of families, lots of young people. No one here is sick that I can see. Everyone's well-fed. And there's a shiny new fire pump parked outside the church."

"You think they're getting their income from something other than timber."

He nodded. "Here's the thing. The Fielding expeditions travel all over the country, but no one seems to know where they go to deposit the magic they're collecting. They stopped publishing that a few months after the League of Sorcerers for Free Magic started protesting the expeditions at every stop."

"You think Junesfield is a magic depot?"

"A transfer point, maybe, on their journey to take the engine canisters to their final destination."

"Which could be anywhere on the rail line." Jane considered this carefully. "It makes sense. Voorhees and Holtz weren't exactly forthcoming about what Mr. Carlyle was doing on his mission. And I didn't buy that he was just shipping supplies. If it was a Fielding expedition, that would give us a link to No Hope. Maybe the Division's trying to keep the final destination for the canisters a secret."

"That still leaves the question of what attacked Carlyle and his team. If something followed him to Junesfield, all these people could be in danger."

Jane exhaled slowly. Mysterious violent attacks. Secret Division plots. It was far more than Jane had bargained for.

What would Quentin do?

Focus on the case. You can't go chasing every rabbit down every hole. If you do, you'll find yourself buried six feet under.

"We can't worry about this," she said determinedly. "We have to focus on finding Hettie Alabama. We know she was here—which means she'll be back."

"You're not concerned about these attacks?" Gallagher's face screwed up. "What about the connection to No Hope?"

"We know she hits Fielding canisters. That's as strong a connection as we need. Meanwhile, the only attack we should concern ourselves with is the one coming from the Blackthorn Rogues." She flattened his disapproving scowl with a glare of her own. "Until I have Hettie Alabama behind bars, I can't let anything else distract me."

VIRGINIA
DECEMBER 1765

"Goddamned vampires." Captain Elias Blackthorn surveyed the bodies on the cart, wrinkling his nose. He supposed he should be glad for the bitter winter frost—the smell and the flies were so much worse in the summer. "I thought we'd taken care of this problem, lieutenant."

"I'm sorry, sir. You know what winter is like for the locals. I can only imagine how desperate the covens get around this time of year."

"Are you empathizing with those abominations, lieutenant?"

"N-no, sir," he said quickly. "I'm just saying—"

"They're a scourge on this land and need to be wiped out." He ripped the covering away from one body, spotting the telltale puncture wounds. "Make sure the bodies are staked and burned. I don't want them clawing their way out of the ground while we're asleep."

He headed for the command center. If the Crown hadn't signed that treaty with the covens to stop the hunts, he would have sent his men to roust the remaining clans from their lairs. King George's particular fascination with the bloodsuckers had never sat well with Elias. Then again, the longer he served in this place, the less love he had for the man sitting on his throne across the sea.

He entered the building, grateful to be out of the relentlessly icy wind.

"Captain." A young soldier saluted him smartly. Elias grimaced inwardly—the soldier was barely a boy, though he detected a trace of the gift on him. He should be in school learning the magical arts, not running errands in the barracks, but such was the life of many young men who needed to find a way to feed their families, as Elias had. "There're two men in the fort with a... a body for you."

"Another?" he said wearily.

"Not one of ours. A Spaniard. They found him floating in the water, but he has something on him no one wanted to touch in case it was cursed."

"'In case'?"

"A couple of sorcerers said they couldn't quite tell what it was. They told the men to bring it to the nearest master."

He followed the young soldier out to where two men in thick leather and hide clothing rested by the fire. They were trappers, mountain men who made their own fortunes and carved their destinies in the land itself. Blackthorn admired such men. They stood slowly as he approached.

"They tell us you're the sorcerer to see 'round these parts." The man's thick accent hovered between French and something he couldn't quite put his finger on. An Arcadian, perhaps.

"I have my master's level from Halderbrook. What can I do for you gentlemen?"

"Figured you might be interested in this." The man stooped over his sled, piled high with furs, and pulled the top sheet of canvas off.

Elias held his nose. The body beneath was in quite a state, the flesh bulbous and sagging off his frame like spoiled, not-quite-cooked egg whites. The skin on his face was translucent blue and showed the dead black veins beneath. His open mouth was a garden of rotted teeth. The cold had kept some of the corpse intact, but not much.

"There." The trapper pointed grimly.

Clutched against the corpse's breast, as if he'd died clinging to it, was a lump of twisted metal, something that might have once been a pistol but was now as degraded and misshapen as its owner.

Elias wasn't sure why he hadn't felt it before—later, he'd marvel that the call of the mage gun hadn't entirely overwhelmed him.

He reached down hesitantly, sensing the magic radiating off the thing. Cursed or enchanted? He couldn't tell unless he examined it more closely.

The corpse held tight to the object. Elias made a face as he pried the fingers off.

The moment his skin made contact with the cool metal, a shivery feeling skated through him, like a million tiny snakes wriggling into his pores. He nearly dropped the thing as it warmed, and then he suddenly couldn't drop it at all.

In a panic, he began an incantation for protection—a catch-all spell that would spare his men if the thing were some kind of magical trap. But then, as if his soul were being jerked upward, he felt a heightening sensation, and he gasped.

"Captain Blackthorn!" The young soldier was at his side, steadying him. "Are you all right?"

"I..." He shook his head. The hunk of metal in his hand had changed. It had become a pistol, finer than some of the weapons he'd seen on generals' belts. He marveled at the shape and balanced weight of it, the fine filigree details on the barrel and grip, the trigger's seductive curve. And it...spoke to him. Not in a literal way, but deep down, as if it were reassuring him that now they had each other, he could do what he wanted...

"Captain...?"

"I'm fine." He hastily stuffed the gun in his belt—he'd been pawing it like a pup at a teat. He addressed the trappers. "Thank you for bringing this to me. I'll see that you're both paid for your troubles, and fed and housed until your departure."

"One more thing." One of the trappers produced a side bag and opened it. Inside was a leather-bound journal in an oilskin. "We found this on him. Neither one of us can read all that well. I don't think it's in English. I imagine it has some interesting things to say, though."

The book was wet in many places, the pages close to pulping. Opening the journal carefully, he quickly recognized the script. Spanish. Blackthorn spoke a number of languages fluently, Spanish among them. "Thank you. Private, see to it that this man is given a proper burial. I won't have the Spanish accusing us of savagery."

"Yes, sir." The soldier hurried off.

Elias didn't read the journal until he was safely ensconced in his quarters later that evening. Something warned him not to show the weapon around too much. That deep-seated paranoia only grew as he worked to translate the journal.

As he read, Elias felt drawn to the man, so similar in breeding—Fernando had been a soldier, an educated officer who'd abandoned his post after witnessing the mass murder of women and children in New Spain, joining his friend Javier in his quest to protect the innocent. The ink had run in places, so he didn't have a complete story, but he inferred that the two had built a new town together, Villa del Punta, and had made the mage gun to help protect them. And for some reason, Fernando had taken the gun called El Diablo and simply…left.

By the last page, the words were nearly illegible, written in the shaking hand of a dying man pleading to the heavens, to his people and his country and Javier for forgiveness. He mentioned something about an avenging angel stalking him before he took to the seas in the hope of evading his pursuer. After that, the words turned to scribbles.

It was clear these were the ravings of a sick man, and yet the tale, incomplete though it was, circled through Elias's thoughts like a leaf caught in an eddy. He held the beautiful mage gun, inspecting it as intimately as a new lover, coaxing it to give up its story, fill in the blanks smeared throughout Fernando's journal.

Finally, it did, in dreams.

And then came the seeking eyes, fixing on him like a beacon.

By week's end, Elias had abandoned his post and disappeared into the wilderness…along with the journal and the mage gun.

CHAPTER SIX

Sophie's modest cottage was tucked away in a remote corner of Texas, not so far from civilization that she couldn't reach help if she needed it, but not so close that she was constantly visited by nosy neighbors. It was a pretty stone cabin with a large vegetable plot to one side and a chicken coop on the other. A couple of goats roamed the grounds, keeping well away from the garden, probably because it had been spelled with some common protection charms. They bleated balefully at Hettie and Walker's approach, and Hettie got the impression they were there as guardians more than for the milk they provided.

The Favreaus owned properties all over the country, but this safe house was Sophie's alone, bought anonymously through a third party. Hettie had learned that the heiress had been making investments and buying real estate long before her fallout with her father. A good thing, too—Atherton Favreau had publicly disowned his only child after she'd escaped from Swedenborg and become a wanted fugitive working with the League of Sorcerers.

Hettie had often wondered if this was the kind of life she would like to live—a quiet place to grow things and be alone, but not too alone. She imagined Sophie must hate it.

"Don't trip on the barrier spell this time,"Walker warned her. "I don't want to be riding around looking for where you got punted to."

She curled her lip. "You'd think she'd know the difference between friends and threats by now."

"Considering it's you, I'm not sure anyone knows the difference," he deadpanned.

Hettie stopped at the gate. If she knew Jemma, Sophie's bodyguard would already be stationed somewhere with a rifle pointed at her chest. "How flies the raven?" she shouted.

There was a long pause before the response came from a source unseen: "Toward the moonrise, never ceasing."

"It should walk, then." She waited. The barrier crackled, the power of it relaxing enough for Hettie and Walker to pass. Magic shimmered over her skin, as if they'd walked through a bubble and the film of soap had swept them clean.

The door opened. "You're still alive," Jemma observed. She wore her knives on the outside now, bristling like the spines on a porcupine. She was otherwise unchanged, despite the three years of running and hiding from the law. The bodyguard's constant state of alertness had always been a part of her, Hettie supposed.

"I'm hearty stock." They clasped forearms and hugged cursorily—the embrace of soldiers at war. Walker doffed his hat and greeted her with a respectful half bow, and Jemma gave him a crooked smile.

"You're still running with this outlaw, Mr. Woodroffe?"

"Wouldn't be anywhere else."

"Shame. Just remember, if you're ever looking to be a man of leisure, Miss Sophie will set you up."

Hettie repressed a scowl; she knew it was only a half-joke. Sophie had made it clear that Walker would be welcome to replace Marcus as her head of security, though since her standing had been greatly diminished, the invitation implied a much different position in her household. One that Jemma was apparently all right with.

Hettie presented Jemma with one of the bottles of fine whiskey they'd pilfered from the saloon in Junesfield. "A gift."

Jemma accepted it and notched her chin toward the cottage. "She's inside. Wipe your feet—she just swept."

The cottage was neat and sparsely appointed, nothing like the lavishly decorated Favreau mansion in New Orleans where Sophie's grandmother, Patrice Favreau, the Soothsayer of the South, had resided. Sophie sat in a chair by the window, staring through the lace curtains.

Unlike Jemma, Sophie had not fared well. Three years of constantly looking over her shoulder, all while maintaining her glamor to keep them hidden, had taken its toll. She was still beautiful, but tired, her golden curls limp, her complexion pale, her eyes lacking luster. She looked too thin, but aside from that, if anything were wrong with her because of the Fielding engine, Hettie couldn't tell.

Of course, it had been three years ago, and all of Sophie's magic had been restored to her at once. Hettie would never forget how the engine had changed Sophie when her powers had been siphoned off. The madness had settled in quickly, and she'd pulled a gun on her friends. How much of that was the engine or her stress at the time, Hettie couldn't say. Sophie could be dramatic. But she wasn't attacking Hettie for Diablo's magic now, so that was something.

Hettie removed her hat. "Sophie."

The sorcerer didn't say anything at first. She was eyeing them as if they might be a writhing mass of snakes stuffed into human-shaped sacks. Jemma went to her quickly. "It's all right. It's Miss Hettie and Mr. Woodroffe."

Sophie's white-knuckled grip on the Derringer loosened beneath the folds of her skirts. She slipped the gun into a pocket and stood slowly. "Forgive me. It's been a difficult week."

"Trouble?" Walker asked.

"The League staged a protest in front of town hall near Houston on Tuesday. The Division and the Pinkertons were there, and they beat and locked up many of my friends." She pursed her lips. "I'm afraid of what might be happening to them now. I haven't been able to make any connections via interpolation."

"I tried to discourage her," Jemma murmured to them. "But she won't listen to me."

"You can't risk the Division finding you here," Walker said. "I know how helpless you feel, but the best thing you can do for them is stay away. If the Division gets you, they'll get the leaders of the League."

"I've been careful," Sophie said with a sniff. "I'm not naive."

Hettie studied her carefully. "You been juicing?"

She shook her head fervently. "No. I've been clean for months now." She bit her lip. "The League frowns on it. And I... I can't risk it anymore." She glanced toward her bodyguard, friend, and lover. Worry and a tiny smile of pride lit Jemma's face.

"That's mighty brave of you, Miss Sophie," Walker said, though Hettie felt his words arrowing through her. "I know how hard it is to get off the stuff."

"You didn't come all this way to pay a social visit." Sophie gestured them to sit as she poured tea.

"What? You don't think I enjoy small talk? I can gossip." Hettie sat and picked up the tea and saucer daintily. "I've all manner of tales about my men's flatulence and nighttime habits..."

Jemma barked out a laugh, and Sophie shook her head, smiling. "Your civilized conversation could use some work, Hettie."

"Ain't nothin' civilized about what we do. It's what happens when you hang around a bunch of stinking men too long. I've got Lena and a few others, but I miss being around more women. I even miss the dresses sometimes." She sobered. "Any word about your grandmother?" *Or Abby?* That last thought was a given, but Hettie didn't want to sound too insensitive.

Sophie didn't meet her eye. "No. But I won't stop looking."

Hettie's and Jemma's gazes connected. They'd lost hope that Patrice was still alive. It had been nearly a year since Hettie had stopped feeling the driving impulse to search out the cause of the soothsayer's blackout. And yet Sophie's quest continued.

They had dinner together—Jemma had roasted a chicken, and Sophie plucked vegetables from the garden and made a dish all by herself!—because these rare visits to old friends demanded such social niceties, but also because Hettie really had missed Sophie and Jemma. Catching up, comparing silly tales about the goats and the men, made it almost feel like they lived a normal life. A happy one. Pretending like this was just a friendly visit made Hettie forget the scab Abby's absence had left, one which she'd picked at nonstop for three years. She imagined it was the same for Sophie and her grandmother.

But then they had to get back to business.

"Here." Hettie handed over the list of Fielding expeditions she'd been compiling from the past few jobs. "Looks like the Division has been stepping up their campaign."

They cleared the dining table, and Sophie unrolled a large map of the country. A series of X's had been marked upon the map, and she started noting the new information, writing down the names and dates and anything else of use in tiny, neat print.

"We were just in Junesfield," Hettie said. "Supposedly the expeditions offload there, and the canisters get shipped out on trains. But when we arrived there wasn't any sign of them, and no one knows where they go."

"The town had a whole lot of guns, though," Walker put in. "And they're set up like they're getting ready for war."

"Perhaps they're preparing for *you*." Sophie sent Hettie a narrow look. "You're something of a mythic gunslinger among the League."

"A little legend never hurt my reputation," she countered with a half smile. "Thing is, I don't think all this to-do's for us. There've been a bunch of attacks on Fielding expeditions. It's been in the papers. People are saying it's vampires, but I think it might be man-things."

"You can't be serious," Sophie said. "I've read those stories, too. At most, they're Division propaganda to keep travelers off the roads so they can move the engines more swiftly."

Hettie turned to Jemma. "Remember Quail's Hollow? That's where some of the earliest attacks were. There, and in New Mexico, near Swedenborg."

Jemma paled. "You saying *we* made some of those man-things?"

"If we did, they're gone now. We took a detour before coming here. The town's been burned to nothing. No one in the area knows what happened, though they're saying it was a wildfire that swept the area. Not a single survivor left. We couldn't even find a mass grave."

"And we looked," Walker said grimly.

"But... you used Fielding's engine on *me*," Sophie said faintly.

"I don't know anything for certain. Maybe the Fielding expeditions went through Quail's Hollow after we were there. Maybe the engine we used on you was different somehow; Horace took it apart enough times that something could've changed. Plus, we put all your magic back in you right away. We don't know anything about longer-term effects. But it's been three years—if you haven't turned man-thing by now, I don't think you will."

Sophie's shoulders relaxed some. "So what about Quail's Hollow?"

"Maybe there really was a fire. Maybe it's all tall tales. But after Swedenborg... after seeing those Level Zero prisoners, and hearing about these attacks now, I can't ignore what might be out there."

"Magic-starved madmen on a rampage," Walker murmured to himself. "I can believe it. Getting off the juice is..." He trailed off, glancing mournfully at Hettie. "I'd be preparing the town for battle, too, if I knew a mindless magic-hungry mob was coming."

Sophie exhaled. "I'll talk to the League. Chances are they're aware of this already; they have people tracking magic anomalies. Either way, there's little we can do about this. Frankly, whatever's attacking the Division, it's to our advantage. They're slowing the expeditions." She lifted her chin. "Those troops deserve what they get for the crimes they've committed."

Hettie grimaced at Sophie's bloodlust, though she was hardly one to judge. Since their escape from Swedenborg, they'd each been fighting their own private wars for the ones they loved. She nodded toward the dozens of X's on the map. "So what's it looking like?"

"The expeditions are still avoiding the larger cities, but they're starting to hit the big towns now." She pointed at a line connecting a bunch of X's through Nebraska. "That's a train of engines hitting all the same stops over and over again. They're draining them dry."

"Division's getting bolder," Walker growled.

"Well, with the president supporting the Fielding campaign, sorcerers have no one to turn to for protection or help, despite the egregious abuse of their constitutional rights." Sophie gripped the edge of the table. "Our people have done all they can to spread the word to the gifted to keep away from the expeditions."

"The League is sheltering anyone fleeing from the Division," Jemma added. "They're being hunted and rounded up like animals."

"Still no sign of where the canisters are heading?" Hettie asked.

Sophie shook her head. "My guess is they're remote Zooming them away, though I can't imagine how they're stabilizing the Zoom tunnels with those engines passing through."

"Abby could do it," Hettie said quietly.

"Or a group of juiced sorcerers could," Walker said, though not unkindly. "We don't have proof either way."

Hettie scrunched up her face, willing the X's sprinkled like so much confetti across the map to resolve into an arrow pointing the way to Abby. She knew Sophie was hoping for the same for her grandmother.

"What's your next move?" Jemma asked.

"We need to keep an eye on Junesfield, see when the next canisters arrive. If a Fielding expedition comes in, then we'll know we're in the right place."

"The League would certainly be interested in what's happening there," Sophie said. "I could send word out—"

"It's too dangerous. Junesfield's a Division town; it's chock-full of agents looking for rogue sorcerers."

"Well you can't go there yourself, and that motley crew of yours isn't exactly inconspicuous. What are you proposing?"

Hettie grinned. "That we call up some old friends."

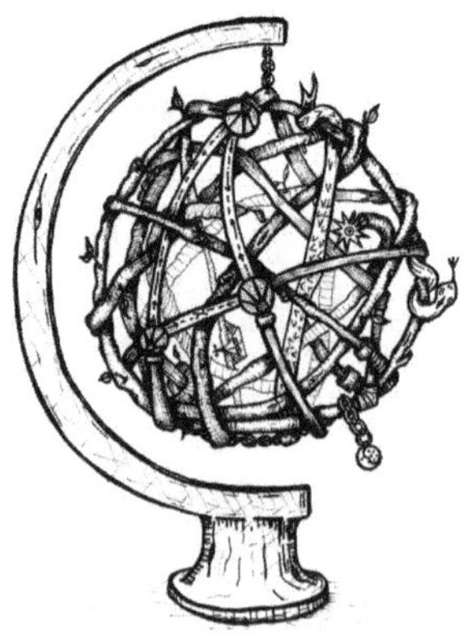

CHAPTER SEVEN

Horace Washington had done well for himself in the years after Swedenborg. The business contacts he'd reestablished and made along his journeys with Hettie and her crew had helped him build a new life, though it was not quite the empire he'd once had.

With a small gift from Sophie—a reward for aiding her escape from the sorcerer's prison—he'd set up in a town called Feeney's Elbow as a hostler, a sometime Mechanik, a tradesman who wasn't afraid of work, and a delight to the people who came to him with all kinds of problems, from broken clocks to broken legs. He procured all sorts of items for the townspeople. His shop grew, and now it was a general store, though no one called it that in deference to Mr. MacKinnon's more traditional dry goods store. No, Horace was just a hostler who ran a "side business," and the townsfolk in Feeney's Elbow were comfortable with that. That they might go to Horace first for better prices and service was a secret they all kept close.

Hettie and Walker rode in under the bubble, skirting the statues in the street. They found Horace in his "shop"—a barn where he tended his horses, with the back few stalls reserved for his wares and staples. He was in the middle of polishing a brass lamp. No one else was there, so Hettie shut the door for privacy and released the time bubble.

"...she's comin' round. Polish that lamp, she's a-comin' round. Sweep out the cobwebs, she's a-comin' round. Oh lord, the devil, she's a-comin' round..." Horace's work song reverberated through the rafters, rumbling in Hettie's core. He stopped, sensing he was no longer alone.

He turned. His smile broadened, though a flicker of trepidation passed over his face. "Speaking of. I wasn't sure when I'd see you next."

"You're seeing me now." They hugged, and he slapped her back avuncularly.

"Woodroffe. How're you faring?" the businessman asked over her shoulder.

"Same as usual."

"That bad, huh?" He grinned at them both and gestured. "You wanna see her?"

Hettie's chest ached. "How is she?"

"For a girl her age..." His smile faltered. "I'm doing the best I can."

He brought Hettie around the back to where several large outdoor stalls abutted the barn. The farthest one in the row was stuffed with clean straw, and it was roped off as if the creature within were a museum piece. Then again, maybe she was. She'd run with not one but two of history's Elias Blackthorns.

"Jezebel," Hettie called softly as she tiptoed under the rope. The big gray-white mare lifted her chin, gave a huff. She pushed to her feet slowly, her steps heavy and unsure. She sniffed the air, nose raised, inching forward unsteadily.

Tears welled in Hettie's eyes as she reached out and stroked Jezebel's velvet-soft muzzle. The old horse snuffled her hand and lowered her chin to rest against Hettie's shoulder. She blew out a hot breath over her neck.

"She's almost completely blind now," Horace said. "And ornery as hell about it."

"She never was very patient, even when she could see." Hettie took the apple Horace held out to her. Her father's horse lipped up the treat greedily, then submitted to being brushed. Tears burned in Hettie's throat, and she swallowed past a lump. "Is she in pain?"

"No," Horace said gently. "She's comfortable as can be. Getting fat and living a life of leisure, grand old dame that she is."

"How long…?" She couldn't finish her sentence.

"I'm afraid God doesn't give us His schedule. For all I know, she could outlive us all. But…" He sighed. "There's only one more ride in her. One pasture left to go to."

"We'll give you two some privacy," Walker said.

The men left her alone with her father's horse. Hettie brushed out her mane until it glowed, then braided a few strands the way she used to with Abby's hair. "I hope you're happy here. I'm so sorry I can't keep you at Blackthorn's Hell myself…" She swallowed thickly. "It's not as nice there, anyhow."

The old mare nudged Hettie's hand and blew out a breath. Forgiveness. Her legs began to tremble, and then she knelt and lay back onto the straw with a heavy sigh. Hettie cleaned the already pristine stall as much as she could, then touched their foreheads together and kissed Jezebel good-bye.

She dropped briefly into the time bubble to recompose herself. Her back ached as she stood. Hettie had never imagined her own body giving out the way Jezebel's was, but that had been her own doing—the blood price and the time bubble chipping away at her day by day.

She rejoined Walker and Horace inside. The hostler poured her a shot of whiskey, which she downed gratefully. "I got this from a client as a gift. Been saving it for a special occasion."

"Business has been good, then?"

"Getting by all right, thanks to Marcus."

"Where is he?" Sophie's former head of security had joined Horace in business, lending him some amount of credibility, security, and respect.

"He'll be back soon. He's out patching a roof." He glanced down at his hands. "For a man missing half of his life, he's built himself a new one handily. I don't suppose you've found his effects?"

"Neither his book nor his mage guns have turned up. I'm assuming Luna and Claire are in the hands of the Division."

Horace wiped a hand down his face. "I can't imagine what it must be like... or why he'd ever enter that devil's bargain with those mage guns of his. What is a man but the sum of his experiences?"

"Love will make you do strange things," Walker said. "And that man loved Sophie."

"Makes me wonder who else he might have loved before he got those guns." Horace slugged back the finger of whiskey and put the glass down. "So what can I do for you two?"

"We need eyes in Junesfield," Hettie said. "Someone not connected to either the League or to me."

"We're not connected?" He feigned shock. "Miss Hettie, I'm offended."

"You have aliases and respectability," Walker said, "and more connections than either of us."

Horace smiled. "Not that I'd ever cop to that." More brightly, in what Hettie thought of as his shop voice, he added, "I'm just Horace Washington, mister. I like to help."

"We'll pay you for your time, of course." Hettie drew out a pouch heavy with coins and set it between them on the table. "This is business."

Horace smiled. He never insulted their intentions or intelligence by refusing payment. "Business it is. What's the story?"

It took them a while to tell him about the Fielding expeditions and the stockpile of guns and barricades.

"You planning a job?" Horace raised an eyebrow. "Junesfield's a town full of families."

"This is a fact-finding mission only. I just want to know where the canisters are going." She'd worry about raiding the town only after they'd established for certain it was a depot.

He nodded in understanding. "All right. I'll go to Junesfield myself and send you a message through the usual channels when I hear something."

They haggled over reimbursement. Hettie knew the risks of being associated with her, and she wanted to pay the man accordingly. Marcus returned as they argued. He'd shaved his beard since she'd last seen him. He looked older somehow. "Why is the door—" He stopped and grinned. "Miss Hettie."

They went through another round of hugs and pleasantries, shared another drink and small talk. Horace brought him up to speed. “What say you, Mr. Wellington? Up for the trip?”

Marcus scrubbed his jaw. “Well, I’m not letting you go on your own. I’ll call Jimmy O’Leary. He’s a trustworthy hand, good head on his shoulders. He can take care of Jezebel and the other horses here, deal with the everyday.”

“Thank you, gentlemen. I’m afraid I can’t stay much longer, and I don’t want to monopolize any more of your time.” She and Walker stood. “Please get to Junesfield as soon as possible and keep me updated.” She counted out another wad of bills from her billfold. “This is for train fare and telegraph, plus wages for your worker.”

“You’re a generous patron, Miss Hettie.” Horace graciously pocketed the money. “I do hope we find what you’re looking for.”

“So do I.” She hugged them both, and Walker shook hands with the men. She tipped her hat. “Safe travels.”

“Good hunting.”

Hettie took Walker’s hand and dropped into the time bubble.

From Horace’s point of view, his friends were there, and then they weren’t, like ghostly dust motes in the fading sunlight. The barn door was open once more as if it had never been closed. He rubbed his eyes, a feeling of dread welling up in him.

“What do you think she’s up to?” Marcus stood still as a cat watching the space their friends had occupied seconds ago. He rubbed his knuckles restlessly.

Horace huffed. “Same thing she’s always been up to. Chasing death and vengeance.”

“And you’re okay with helping her out?”

“Better us than some untrustworthy no-account. We owe our lives to Miss Hettie. For all the wrong she’s done… for all the bad, she’s still good, and better than most. Grief’ll make people do things they wouldn’t otherwise do.”

“Shouldn’t we be trying to help her move on?”

"Trying to get her to give up on her sister would be like trying to convince the devil to give up his crown. Even in hell, you've gotta cling to something." He sighed. "C'mon. We've got a train to catch."

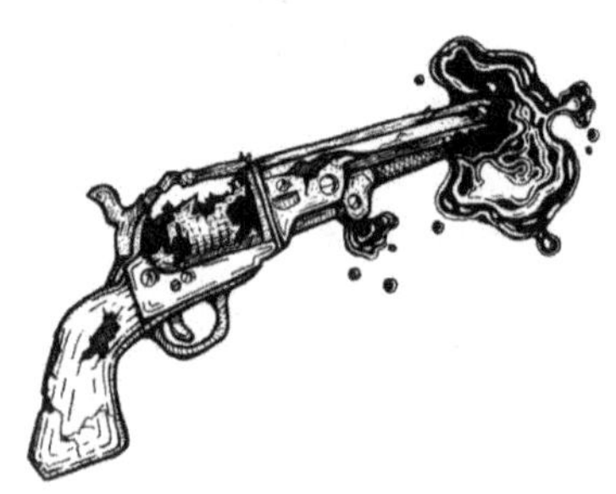

MASSACHUSETTS 1780

Elias had encountered only one other vampire in his life. It was back in England, long after the coven wars had decimated the vampire stock. He'd found the wretched creature huddling beneath the straw in the darkest corner of the barn during one of the hottest summer days he'd ever lived through. Being nine at the time, he'd thought it prudent to dispatch the abomination himself instead of calling his father, who was busy with the tenants.

The pitifully thin vampire had been asleep, weakened by hunger and probably on the run from the mobs and hunters bent on annihilating their kind. Elias had stuck the creature through with a pitchfork, straight through the heart as the elders had taught.

That first stab had to be strong and true to break through the breastplate. Once Elias had pierced that tough shell, the prongs of the pitchfork had sunk into the creature neatly. Elias stood on the fork, pinning the writhing vamp. Couldn't have it crawling around bleeding all over the farm and fouling the earth, after all.

He watched the thing die, stripped the many layers of clothing off him, then dragged the body out into the sun, where its pale flesh sizzled and flayed away in sheets like the pages of a book thrown into a bonfire.

His father and mother had been proud of him. Vermin were not to be tolerated, after all.

Thirty-five years later, he'd changed his mind about their kind.

He hadn't known the first time he'd met her she was a vampire, of course. All he'd seen was a group of men dragging a woman in widow's weeds off her horse as he'd been traveling through the woods. Glimpsing her finery, they probably thought her a spy for the redcoats. He hadn't intended to get involved, having shucked his duty to the Crown a long time ago, but Diablo, being an apparently noble demon, had insisted. *It* had saved the woman and slaked its thirst for death in one brilliant burst of power.

As Elias lay recovering from the mage gun's hefty blood price—four years, dammit—he decided it couldn't be all bad if the woman was wealthy and rewarded him for his bravery, but she'd fled, fast as fire on tinder, streaking away through the trees, probably terrified by the gun's sure aim and his gut-wrenching screams.

Two months later, he met her again while he lay dying. She knelt by his side in that dark street outside the tavern, a froth of black lace haloing her like smoke, her lilac scent drifting around her like a cloud. Soft, pale hands slipped over his, clutching the wound in his gut. She smiled down at him. "I remember you," she said. Something about her voice reminded him of moonlight.

He must have passed out, because in the next moment he found himself on a settee in a plush room. The woman bent over him, the widow's weeds gone to reveal a pale, unblemished visage. A dark curl had escaped her carefully coiffed bun and brushed against her cheek. Her red cupid's bow lips pursed in consternation. Blood soaked her up to her elbows as she tried to stanch his wound.

Her green eyes glinted with hard light. "You're dying," she said matter-of-factly. "I'm afraid I have no magic or medicines to stop that from happening now. You will soon start on the path to the gates, and from there..." She trailed off.

Elias's lip trembled. He stared up at the ceiling, thinking he might have preferred to see the sky instead.

Then she leaned toward him. "It doesn't have to be this way."

She told him she was one of the progenitors, the original vampire species, born with their gift and curse, immune to human disease or aging, nearly immortal, stronger than ten men, with gifts that surpassed even the greatest of sorcerers'. Elias wanted to flinch away, but he didn't have the strength. Every heartbeat pumped another gout of blood onto the floor, brought him one step closer to death's door. He thought about that vampire he'd killed in the barn as a child and prayed she could not scent that death on him.

"I am indebted to you," the vampire said. "You saved me from those hunters when you had no cause to…and paid a hefty price." She touched his cheek. "I can't save you. But I can *change* you."

"I won't go vampire." He'd done many terrible things in his lifetime, including stealing the mage gun that drove him to the edges of the world…and away from *him*.

"I won't turn you. That is a half-life, a difficult life, and my stepchildren can be fickle. But I can bind you to me."

"Bind…?" He was shivering hard now as pain dug its sharp claws into his flesh.

"It is old magic. A spell lost to time, except among our kind. I can stretch out the life and time you have left." She sounded nearly desperate making her case. "Please, let me help you."

Elias hadn't wanted to say yes. Neither did he want to die. He knew then he was a coward, first for abandoning his post when he'd read about the avenging angel and sensed it coming—now for abandoning humanity altogether.

His body was suddenly racked by agony as the wound split his gut and poured stomach acid into his abdomen. He gave a hoarse cry, thrashing his head in the semblance of a nod, a sound of surrender gurgling up his throat.

The progenitor seized his wrists and pinned him down as if he were a child. She moved like a wraith, a wisp of shadow tying him to the bedposts so he lay spread-eagle and…naked. She'd stripped him of his clothes in the blink of an eye.

What she did to him next was not something he liked to dwell on. He hadn't thought his body could react so viscerally, so basely, to the weaving of the spell, the way she'd drawn his life force to the surface of his skin. When she'd touched him, he'd tried to cling to the world he knew, to the man he'd been—even to the bullet wound killing him. But then the bonding had happened, and suddenly he was no longer just himself, but also partly her, a creature of the night, of dark desires and a hunger that couldn't be quenched by food and drink and sex alone.

And then came the darkness, a sleep so deep and pure it might as well have been death.

The bullet wound was gone when he woke up two days later, and so was the vampire. The innkeeper told him the widow Mrs. Underwood had paid for the room till the end of the month while he convalesced. Elias hadn't even known her name.

Had it all been a fever dream? He found the mage gun on his bedside table, untouched. He picked it up, heard the hum of smug satisfaction. As if it had gotten what it wanted, and now…

He listened. *He* was gone. The creature who'd pursued him could no longer follow. Elias felt his sudden freedom from scrutiny draped over him like a mantle of invisibility, if such a thing existed; like a rabbit pursued through the muck till it was so thoroughly crusted it couldn't be scented anymore.

He gave a sharp laugh of relief, of bleak joy. It was over. Whatever Progenitor Underwood had done to him had muted Diablo's call to the guardian who pursued it.

With a new lease on life, he went to shave. He accidentally nicked his chin with the straight razor…

And the cut healed immediately.

Everything inside Elias curdled. The woman had said he hadn't been turned…

But then… He drew the blade down his cheek, and the wound sealed up almost instantly.

If he wasn't a vampire… *what was he?*

CHAPTER EIGHT

When Hettie and Walker returned to Blackthorn's Hell, Duke and the others were still out hunting the payroll wagons.

"Still?" Walker huffed. Walker seemed to forget sometimes that the time bubble had shortened their time away from the hideout.

"It takes as long as it takes," Hettie said, waving him off.

He glowered. "You need to keep Duke in check. That man's liable to mutiny."

"As long as the money's good and the food, whiskey, and juice are flowing, the men won't have any reason to change horses. Duke joined with us, remember, not the other way around. Man might be good at busting heads, but he can't lead a charge. Besides," she said more mildly, "Lena's with him. The men'll listen to her more than him on account of her magic."

"You don't think that's a bone of contention he'd pick his teeth with?"

"Malcontents will always find something to be angry about. If he really cared about what the gifted had over him, he wouldn't be seen in the company of juicers."

Walker sighed. She knew he thought she'd become complacent about her role as the head of the Blackthorn Rogues. She did care about their welfare, despite what Walker thought—a happy crew was a productive and obedient one. But the day-to-day drudgery of making sure everyone was paid and fed and not at each other's throats was not what she'd signed up for. She had to be everything for these men and women: charismatic, ruthless, fearsome, ambitious—a force to be reckoned with. It was exhausting. The only reason she'd taken up her position in the first place was to have extra hands in the search for Abby.

Walker, meanwhile, was a born politician. The moment they'd set up in Blackthorn's Hell, he'd decided they needed to conduct themselves like a real town. He'd organized the distribution of supplies and pay, disciplined the rowdier members, and exorcised the ones who couldn't be controlled.

When Duke had realized his men were following Walker over him, Duke had picked a fight with Walker and lost. He'd been stewing ever since.

The men's power struggle didn't mean a lot to Hettie. Everyone there was afraid of *her* and of Diablo's power, and ultimately, that was all that mattered. Her doppelganger, Mizzay, had had a hair-trigger temper and a cruel mage gun to express her displeasure. Hettie, meanwhile, had the memory of a wronged woman, the patience to outlast a mountain, and the means to take one down in the blink of an eye. To cross Hettie was to risk utter annihilation.

She only cared about one thing, and that was finding Abby. More than three years of fruitless searching didn't mean her sister was dead. She was out there somewhere. And Hettie was closer than ever to discovering where.

A few days later, the men who'd gone to rob the payroll wagons returned. Duke rode ahead of the last group to arrive, smoking a fat cigar and showing off a new hat. He tossed her a heavy sack of coins, which she caught neatly. "The information was good. *Very* good."

She tucked the money away without counting it. Duke wouldn't cheat her out of her cut. If he ever intended on betraying her, it wouldn't be over a few dollars.

She surveyed the men, who looked tired but happy to have finished the job. "Make sure everyone gets rested. I'm going to need them again soon."

Duke's face fell. "We just got back—"

"Not right away. But soon. We'll meet tomorrow morning to discuss it."

He grumbled as he went off. He'd probably been expecting more praise, but Hettie was not his mother. Maybe she should've given it to him just to keep the peace, though.

She signaled a grim-faced Lena to follow her.

"How did things *really* go?" she asked Lena.

"Niles and McGuiness were shot dead. Kendall and Franklin got flesh wounds. Doc's fixing them up now."

Hettie set her teeth and cursed. "The take?"

"Good. I didn't see any skimmed from the top. But…" She hesitated.

"What's wrong?" She hesitated. "Tommy?"

"He's fine." She waved. "He was careful this time. Listened to everything I told him. Kept him in the back of the lineup, casting low-level protection."

"That's good." A small knot in her chest loosened. She worried about young Tommy. The kid was too eager to prove himself. He'd get himself killed.

"The thing is…it was too easy."

"Maybe you're underestimating yourself."

"We outnumbered the security crews three to one, and they were all enforcers. Barely a ranking sorcerer among them."

Hettie thought hard. "Did you sense anything wrong with the money? Any counterfeit bills? Any geised loot or tracking spells?"

"None of that. The take was clean."

"Maybe they're getting careless. Or maybe they're concentrating their forces on protecting something more valuable than money. Not even a Pinkerton among the wagons?" The Pinkertons were well-known for providing security to payrolls.

"I guess the Division has them focused on rounding up truant sorcerers." Lena's lip curled. Rumor was the detecting agency had cut a deal to exempt their own sorcerers from mandatory power banking.

"If there's anything hinky about this take, I reckon it's just mismanagement of the Division's resources. They couldn't have prepared for an attack that quickly after No Hope," Hettie said.

They went into the schoolhouse. Over a cup of strong coffee, Hettie briefed Lena about her trip but didn't mention her visit to Sophie. She told her she'd sent scouts ahead to Junesfield and would hear from them soon.

"So you're planning on hitting Junesfield, even though they're preparing for war?"

"We're thinking it must be these attacks they're worried about. Which, if it's man-things, only reinforces my belief that the Fielding canisters are going through the town."

Lena had heard Hettie's stories about the man-things at Swedenborg. She worried her lower lip. "I know what it'd mean if you could figure out where all the canisters were going." She left Abby's name unsaid. "But we have a good life right now. The Division can't find us. We're well-fed. If we're not careful, all of this…all of *us*…"

"No one will be forced to come along. And I wouldn't hold it against you if you didn't." Hettie lifted her chin. "But I could really use you, Lena. All of you."

Lena hesitated. Hettie knew she'd pushed the sorcerer to do some awful things, but without Hettie the Rogues wouldn't exist, and Blackthorn's Hell wouldn't be the refuge so many of them needed.

The truthteller sighed. "I have my reservations," she said. "But I trust you. I'm in."

Hettie got the first telegram from Horace and Marcus a couple of days later. She read it to the meeting of her lieutenants—Duke, Walker, Lena, and their most powerful sorcerers.

Dear Mother stop
Business is good stop
Supplies arriving daily stop
Five broken wagon wheels stop
150 dollars for repairs stop
Delayed a fortnight stop
Your loving sons stop

Excitement built in Hettie's gut. Five canisters due in two weeks. Junesfield was definitely a hub, meaning the train taking them out of there would be heading toward the Division's central depot.

"A hundred and fifty men." Walker wiped a hand down his face. "That's an awful lot of soldiers."

"We'll call in all our people," Hettie said confidently. "The take'll be a good one."

"Five engine canisters will set our people up for a while," Lena agreed.

"Not to mention whatever loot the men take from town," Duke added. At everyone else's grim looks, he growled, "Oh, don't be such bleedin' hearts. This is a rich town. You said no raping, we don't rape. You said no unnecessary killing, we maim instead. But no looting?" He made a *feh* sound. "What kind of sissy outfit have you turned us into?"

"The kind that keeps y'all alive," Hettie snapped. "You wanna loot? Go ahead and try. Just don't expect us to remote Zoom you to Doc's bedside if you get a belly full of lead. The citizenry is armed to the teeth."

Walker grimaced at the telegram. "Two weeks ain't enough time to get everyone to Junesfield."

"We'll remote Zoom in. It'll give the sorcerers time to rest and juice before we have to pull out again." Hettie pressed her palms over the roughly sketched map of the town spread across the table. "We'll hit the town when all the canisters arrive. Just like in No Hope, we'll have a team to the west entrance, one circling the town from the south, and another watching the northeast approach." Excitement vibrated through her, her sense of purpose renewed for the first time in months. "This has to be the train to the central magic depot."

Walker exhaled. "Okay, say we take the train. We can't kill *any* soldiers. One of them has to know where the canisters are actually going. And we're not going to be able to truth it out of him with these Division silence spells."

"Wouldn't the engineer know?" Hettie asked.

"The engineer just drives the train. He's most likely taking his directions from whoever's in charge."

"I might have a solution," Lena said. "I've been developing a blanket spell to ungeis the Division men. With the help of a few other sorcerers and some juice, I think we might be able to loosen the ties that are keeping their lips sealed. Enough at least to interrogate a few and keep the ones who might know something from dying outright."

"You can do that?"

"Contract spells—and silence spells—are only as ironclad as the caster is strong and the participant is willing. I get the sense these boys didn't sign up with the Division willingly or submit to the silence spells without some duress."

"Whoever's in charge will likely be a company man, though," Walker said. "A veteran. A true believer."

"Stands to reason they'd be the only ones who'd know where to take the canisters," Hettie agreed.

"If the blanket spell works, we'll be able to spot the ones suffering the most under interrogation and break the silence spell before it kills them." Lena's confidence heartened Hettie. Lena didn't have the stamina Uncle had had, but she was smarter and more resourceful than most Division-trained sorcerers Hettie had known. She might even have rivaled Uncle for ingenuity and creative spellcraft.

Walker stared at the map, tapping his finger on the train tracks alongside the mountain town. "It doesn't make sense. The Fielding expeditions are heavily guarded. There are a hundred and fifty soldiers in Junesfield now. How could all those men *not* know where they're headed? Memory wipe?"

Lena shook her head. "It'd take too long and be too difficult. You'd need a lot of high-level sorcerers, for one, and that's not something the Division has in spades right now."

"Well, they can't just be letting these trains travel unguarded."

"Maybe that's exactly what they're doing." Walker circled the table. "They only need to protect the canisters from people like us for as far is it'd be dangerous to leave them unguarded."

"You mean, closer to cities," Duke said.

"Assuming that's where they're headed." Walker nodded. "You get the train to a big town, bigger than Junesfield, and it'd be a lot harder to hit with local law enforcement thereabouts."

"Not to mention the dampening effects a metal-laden city has on battle spells," Lena added.

When Hettie realized she'd been silent for a few beats too long, she dropped into her time bubble and gave herself the luxury of time to think. Only when she'd looked at all the angles and thought out all the possible drawbacks did she jump back into time. "We can't make any assumptions about where these canisters or these soldiers are heading. All we can do is hit the town hard and make it count. Walker, Duke, make sure the men don't kill the older or more powerful sorcerers. They'll be the most likely to know where the canisters are headed. Lena, do what you can with the blanket spell. Pick your sorcerers and whoever else you need for this yourself. You can have an engine and a canister to do with as you wish."

"What about you?" Lena asked as Hettie started for the door.

"I'm gonna do what I always do."

Walker mumbled, "I was afraid you'd say that."

By the end of the week, the Rogues left Blackthorn's Hell in teams via remote Zoom to various positions throughout the misty pine forests around Junesfield.

Over the following week, Hettie traveled in the quiet of the bubble to check on the arrival of the canisters and on the encampments where her men awaited further orders. They were restless and bored; some itched to do violence. Others just wanted to be back in the comfort and safety of Blackthorn's Hell, or out on the town, or with their families. She spent a little time assuring them the take would be worthwhile, her sudden appearance among them a stark reminder of Diablo's power.

When she was satisfied no one was going to turn traitor—which was always a possibility with the bounty on her head rising—she'd rejoin the others at the main camp. Walker scowled whenever she popped out of thin air. She might only disappear for what appeared to him to be an hour or two, but he knew she was living her own lonely life outside of time.

"You can't keep haring off on your own like this," Walker said in the privacy of their shared tent one evening.

"I do what I need to do."

He brushed her gunmetal-gray hair away from her face. "You sleeping at all?"

"Don't need to."

"Is it the nightmares?"

She cut him a look. Did he really have to ask? She'd literally been through hell and back twice; killed men with her bare hands; ended dozens of lives with Diablo; and, worst of all, watched her sister surrender to the forces Hettie had sworn to destroy.

One night, she'd dreamed Butch Crowe had joined the Division alongside Thomas Stubbs, and together they'd torn Abby into pieces. In the throes of her nightmares, she'd nearly blown Walker's head off.

After that, she'd been careful about falling asleep around him. She couldn't afford to hurt anyone else she cared about. "I ain't tired."

"You're still human."

"You so sure about that?"

He kissed her deeply to prove it. Hettie submitted to his touch, his fingers warm on her cold skin. He broke off and leaned his forehead against hers. "Sometimes I'm *not* sure. But that doesn't mean I don't love you."

Every time he said it was like listening to another drop of water splashing down into a deep, dark, cold well she'd never be able to drink from. *Plish.* "We should sleep," she said, and she turned over and shut her eyes.

The next morning, they got some bad news.

"The northeast team reported three of their men missing. They were supposed to be on watch but didn't show up for breakfast."

"Who's missing?" Hettie asked.

"Adam Pranica. Benjamin Harrison." The man sighed. "And young Tommy."

Hettie flinched.

"Damned deserters," Duke spat. "They can't have gotten far. We need to take 'em out. We can't risk 'em blowing the whistle on us before we hit town."

"No. I'll go after them. You meet up with the south team, get them in line."

"They have at least six hours on us. We should hit the town *now* before they can warn anybody."

"I won't blow this because we got itchy. Anyhow, I'd rather give Tommy and the others the benefit of the doubt, see what they have to say for themselves." She glanced out into the woods, thick with mist. "Maybe they just got lost."

"Or maybe they're having an attack of conscience, hitting a town like Junesfield. Tommy was always soft, and Adam and Ben were lazy. You don't think some of us have thought this was the perfect time to turn you in with a whole company of soldiers just waiting for us?"

Hettie met Duke's eye coldly. "That something *you* been thinking about?"

The look on his face clearly said yes. Diablo leaped into her hand, weighty with the need to do violence, but she didn't draw on him.

When he didn't say anything more, Hettie holstered the mage gun. "I'm going to look for my men. I'll be back before you know it."

"I'll go with you." Walker said. "You'll need a tracker."

She didn't, and almost told him no, but in the time bubble it didn't matter—they would, in fact, be back before anything needed to be done.

They set out toward the hills where the northeast group was camped, out of sight of the town's largest lumber mill and work camp.

"What do you think, Walker?" she asked over her shoulder. "Would Ben and Adam turn traitor?"

"They're not that ambitious, far as I know. A little bit embarrassed about what they're doing with their lives, maybe, but I can't read anyone's minds. Fact is, I think it's more likely they got bored waiting out here in the damp and went to find a saloon or a whorehouse." He paused. "You didn't ask about Tommy."

"I want him to speak for himself." She thought she'd treated him well. But then, she didn't know what else he'd faced among the older, rougher men. Perhaps he'd been scared about this job.

As they rode up the trails, a flurry of sooty dust motes congealed together, resolving into a form soaring on silent wings next to Hettie. *"Lost your sheep, Little Bo Peep?"* Rok cackled. *"Rok knows where to find them."*

She set her jaw. Walker couldn't see Rok, but he'd caught her talking to the familiar now and again, and it seemed to unnerve him. As much as he knew about magic, there were some things he didn't understand, and the demon servant Jeremiah Bassett had somehow bound to her on his death was one of them. It wouldn't assuage the bounty hunter's fears to let on that Rok came to her even in Diablo's time bubble. Still, Rok had his uses. Uncle had always been good at finding things. Now she knew how he'd done it. "Show me," she murmured.

The raven angled up above the tree line, going roughly northwest until he was circling a heavily wooded area at the rocky base of the hills. When the route became too clogged with boulders and undergrowth for the horses to get by, they dismounted and followed the rockfall down into the gully.

"You smell that?" Walker wrinkled his nose.

She did. It was unmistakable: blood and offal and a foulness wrought in a gruesome death.

They found what was left of the men dashed along the bottom. Their flesh was mottled with bruises. Their innards were strewn about like morbid streamers, and blood stained everything. Hettie held back her gorge, pulling the bandana around her neck up to cover the stench. "That's Ben and Adam all right." She scanned the area. "No Tommy."

Walker squinted up at the hill. "This doesn't make any sense. There's nowhere they could've fallen from that would've done this much damage."

"Maybe some animals got them." It didn't sound convincing even in her own ears. This carnage was inhuman.

Surely Tommy couldn't have inflicted such savagery upon the two men. He was a sorcerer, so technically he had the potential, but he hadn't completed his training at the Academy. The way the men's bodies were damaged would've required a high-level spell, too.

He couldn't have accidentally cast this spell in fear. Spellcraft required skill and singular concentration and a hearty amount of ritual, talismans, and materials. Hettie knew that much about magic. Abby had performed all kinds of magical feats with barely a thought, but her sister's indigo powers were a mystery, and Tommy was nothing like her as far as Hettie knew.

"They were dragged." She pointed at the bloodied trails. "Tommy couldn't have done them both like this." Neither Adam nor Ben were small men.

"A pretty long way for wolves or anything else to carry 'em, too." Walker stepped over the tracks and followed them some distance from the bodies. He put his hands on his hips and stared at the ground. "Huh."

"What is it?"

"Not sure exactly. It looks like it should've been a protection circle. But it's done in blood here."

"Blood magic?"

He knelt, touched the ground. His finger came up dark, and he sniffed it. "Yep."

Hettie turned the men over, searching their pockets. They were still flush with cash and a few bullets, but their weapons were gone. If Tommy had done this, why hadn't he taken the money? Maybe he'd been too scared to think.

Or maybe someone else had done this.

She pocketed their effects. "We'll have to bury 'em. Can't have their ghosts following us back to Blackthorn's Hell."

They dug two shallow graves in the soft loam and laid the bodies in. Walker said, "I suppose someone should say something." And when Hettie didn't volunteer, he huffed.

"Lord in Heaven," he began a little unsteadily, "take these two into Your care. They weren't too bad. Did what they thought they had to..." He cleared his throat. "Guess that's all we can do in this life."

They shoveled dirt over the bodies. She thought about the plot beneath the tree on the hill at her family's ranch where Paul, Ma, and Pa were all buried. Uncle would've been buried there, too, if it hadn't been for the Division. Who knew where they'd put him? She hated the thought of him as a ghost, wandering the land, seeking absolution or closure or justice... Then again, the old coot's checkered past likely hadn't earned him a pass through the pearly gates. Being a ghost might be a blessing.

When she died, there wouldn't be a body to bury. The hell gate would open to claim her and Diablo.

"Burn, burn, burn!" Rok cawed from a branch, shaking out his feathers.

"Shut up," she muttered. Walker looked up, nonplussed, and she waved him off. "Just thinking out loud."

When the job was done, they continued through the woods. Still no sign of Tommy. The trail went cold as they emerged near a wide, well-worn path cutting along the hills. Looking back, she could almost spot the thin trail of campfire smoke from the main camp in the distance, barely visible through the thick blanket of fog.

"Tommy must've run," Walker said. "Or else he's in the woods somewhere..."

Being eaten by maggots was the unsaid sentiment. "We should keep looking."

"We've been at this for hours. Maybe you don't need sleep, but I do, and we should both go back to make sure everyone is on point."

"They won't miss us. I can keep going."

"Hettie." The patience in that single word flexed and creaked like a bent reed on the verge of snapping. She knew Walker would follow her even if he was bone-tired and half starved. He wouldn't let her go after Tommy alone. He said, "Tommy's a smart kid. Wherever he is, he'll be fine. But we need to get back."

He was right. They needed to focus on Junesfield. On Abby. Tommy would have to wait.

CHAPTER NINE

"Aren't you going to have dinner?"

Jane watched the hills. The bay of a wolf was answered, strangely, by the yipping of a coyote. Her skin crawled. A cold, uncanny mist had sunk into Junesfield. Townsfolk out for their evening constitutionals marveled at the clouds swirling around their feet until a uniformed man scuttled them off the road, waving people indoors.

She reached out with her Vision but sensed no spells, curses, or other magic draping the town in that cloying sense of dread. "I'm not really hungry."

Gallagher sighed. In some misguided attempt to impress her, he'd insisted on demonstrating his skills as a chef by making them a dinner of steak and kidney pie. "Something doesn't feel right," she said, moving away from the window.

"How's that?" He poured the wine, and Jane picked up her glass and took a swig. Tart and mossy, but too new. She was certain someone had added something to try to make it taste older but had only ended up with moldy grape juice.

"When I was young…when my gift first manifested…I used to know what days were good days and what days were bad days at the orphanage."

"Orphanage?"

"Oh, I suppose you don't know the whole story. I was shunted from place to place till I ended up in the Academy. Robert Pinkerton adopted me straight out of the dormitory. Long story short." She waved her hand. "Anyhow, I used to know deep down what days I had to keep quiet to avoid a beating."

"How horrid. I'm sorry."

"It's nothing for you to be sorry about." She rubbed her shoulder absently, the phantom sting of the cane still a sharp reminder of her childhood. "The point is, since those days, I've always felt a kind of...hum inside me. A tremor in my bones when something bad was coming. Right now I'm feeling that feeling like an earthquake."

Furrows appeared between his eyebrows. "Perhaps you simply need something to eat. Some wine to relax. A good night's sleep. All this waiting for Hettie Alabama and her gang can't be good for one's nerves."

She downed the remaining contents of her wineglass, choking down the moldy flavor. "It's not the waiting that's getting to me." She gestured out the window. "All these soldiers, the defenses around the town... What are they for?" A group of men passed under the window, their rifles clattering against their backs. "Where are they headed? Junesfield is big, but not big enough to support a company this large. They only just arrived...but they look ready to leave at any moment."

"Perhaps they suspect the Alabama gang is coming."

"But they haven't evacuated the women and children. You'd think if they're actually here to protect the people, they'd do exactly that." She shook her head. "Something's coming. Something..." She stared out the window, eyes wide as she focused on the town's perimeter. The hairs on her nape lifted as she sensed movement, a *presence*, like a living shadow creeping among the trees.

Jane crossed the room, snatching up her reticule and drawing her Colt revolver. She checked the load as she headed down the stairs and into the street, then jammed the gun back into her bag as she left the hotel.

The professor caught up to her. "Agent Pinkerton, where are you going?"

"For a constitutional." She looped her arm through his and tugged him on, tilting her chin toward the soldiers rushing ahead of her. "We should see what the hurry is all about."

Gallagher was so discombobulated he nearly stumbled over the drunk lying in the street. The man shook a fist at him, slurring obscenities before collapsing back on the road.

They were stopped moments later by a Division soldier. His badge read Mendel. "Sorry, sir, ma'am. You should head indoors. The streets are closed to pedestrians right now. We've had to institute a curfew."

"Surely that can't be." Jane fluttered her eyelashes. "Mr. Jones here was going to show me the property he intended to buy for my dressmaking business when we are married."

"Indeed." Gallagher fell into the role quickly. "What's all the ruckus about here, young man?" His voice held all the authority of a teacher disciplining a student for tardiness.

"We're getting a shipment in," Mendel said somewhat apologetically. "You know what these canisters are like."

"Canisters?" Jane perked up. "You mean a Fielding expedition is arriving?"

The young soldier looked a little less sure. Jane had to clamp down on the urge to use a truthtelling spell on him.

She tried a different tact. "I'm new in town. Mr. Jones is trying to convince me to settle here in Junesfield. But you see, if I do marry him, I'll be bringing my elderly mother, who's a sorcerer. If there are issues with magic… I mean, if she might be affected…"

The young man relented. "Well, uh, miss, the short answer to your question is yes, Fielding canisters do roll through town now and again for transport on the train, but it usually happens at night. I'm surprised no one in town has mentioned it to you. It's the worst-kept secret around." He chuckled drily.

"Is that why all of you boys are here?" Jane asked. "To guard the canister?"

"I can't share that with you. But we'll be out of here tonight if all goes to plan." He glanced back nervously. "Now, I have to insist—"

A blood-curdling scream rent the air. Jane spun around.

The drunkard who the professor had nearly tripped on struggled in the arms of a man nuzzling his shoulder. Jane thought she was seeing things, but no, it was a man—a vampire?—biting another man.

The drunk thrashed, blood gushing from his neck. Jane pulled her Colt from her reticule, took aim, and fired just over the attacker's head. He released him, and the drunk scrambled away, clutching his wound.

The man, if that was what he was, lurched and sniffed, maw dripping gore. His empty eyes zeroed in on Jane, and he lifted his head as if scenting prey. He snarled and bounded toward her, arms outstretched.

Jane pulled back the hammer on her gun, shouting, "Stop! By order of the Pinkertons—"

He kept coming.

She fired. The bullet found its mark in the creature's shoulder, but it didn't stop. She cocked the gun again, but Gallagher placed himself in front of Jane just as she aimed for the creature's heart.

"Get out of my way!" she shouted. But the professor stood frozen in place. The creature was only a few feet away—

"Get down!" She was shoved to the ground along with Gallagher as a barrage of gunfire rang out. The creature jerked and fell, riddled with bullet holes and oozing thick, dark blood. Its eyes stared emptily, hungrily at her.

"Are you all right, miss?" A handsome older man with reddish hair helped them both to their feet.

"I— I thank you, sir."

His kind eyes turned glacial as he berated the soldiers. "Trigger-happy idiots! You could've shot the lady!" He glared at the men crowded around the dead thing in the street. His refined English accent didn't match the rumpled, plain clothes he wore, Jane thought. And his high-level gift was clear. He bent to collect the spilled items from her reticule.

Mendel hurried over, his face pale. "I'm so sorry, miss—"

"It's all right. We're safe thanks to mister…?"

Jane's redheaded savior handed over her reticule, including the Pinkerton badge. "Your things," he said tightly, then hurried away.

Of course someone with his gift would be nervous around a Pinkerton. They'd been rounding up truants for the Division, after all. Mendel stared at the badge. "You're a Pink sorcerer?"

"Yes." She scanned the crowd, but the redhead had vanished. "As is my companion." She gestured at Gallagher, who looked shaken but unharmed. "What was wrong with that man? Did he go Were?" Or worse—had he gone vampire?

"I'm not sure I can say…" Which meant he wasn't sure he could tell her. His face set in decision. "But if you're a master sorcerer for the Pinkertons, we could use your help. Come with me. You'll be safer behind the lines by the train anyway."

"Safe from what?" Gallagher asked, but the man didn't say anything more.

He herded them toward the train station. Soldiers rushed toward the barricaded perimeter surrounding the town, but more of them crowded around the train, armed and restless as they watched the hills.

Suddenly Jane's limbs grew weak and shaky, as if a flu had overtaken her. A faint bluish light tinged the air, rising like a moon of ill omen. Gallagher gasped.

A Fielding canister was being lifted by a crane onto one of five empty train beds, ropes dangling from the net like so many loose threads. The cylindrical glass tank was shrouded by a thick, thorny webbing of iron. It was far cruder and uglier than the drawings of the earliest designs Jane had seen in the newspapers. As the canister settled onto the flatbed car, sluggish soldiers gingerly wrapped it in a padded blanket for transportation.

Mendel spoke to an older man with a captain's shield. He hurried over and extended a hand toward Gallagher. "I'm Captain Nichols. Private Mendel tells me you're with the Pinkertons. That you're sorcerers."

"We are." Jane inserted herself in front of the professor. "I'm Agent Jane Pinkerton. Professor Gallagher is working with me as a consultant on a case. What's going on here, captain?"

"We're here to facilitate the transfer of five Fielding canisters. A barrier spell was supposed to be erected, but our Division liaisons have disappeared."

"Let me guess. Holtz and Voorhees?" At the captain's grimace, she said, "We've had dealings with them."

"They were supposed to secure the shipment and help us deal with the attack."

"Attack? Is it the Blackthorn Rogues?" Jane asked.

"If only. This is strictly classified information, though I can't see how or why the Division wants this kept under wraps. Our enemies tonight are some kind of abomination we haven't encountered before. You've probably heard the stories of attacks on the road. Well, these monsters have been stalking the expeditions, and now they're headed here. That's why the town is on a curfew tonight. Whatever those things are, there are more of them on the way. We've been ordered to wait for the other canisters before we can leave town, but we're going to need some help from a master sorcerer."

Jane noted the man hadn't been affected by any kind of silence spell. A trusted officer, then, and one who'd reached his limit. "Battle magic isn't my forte," she said. "My specialty is detection, Vision, that kind of thing. I can perform some limited protection magic…"

He shook his head. "The problem is that these things are attracted to magic. They go after the gifted first." Another barrage of gunfire erupted, this time to the east side of town. Captain Nichols cursed. "Whatever you can do to help us stave off the attack until we load the train would be appreciated. We need to get these canisters away from populated areas. The train is our only hope."

He started to leave, but she grabbed his arm. "Captain, I don't understand. Your company is here to protect the town, isn't it?"

His look hardened. "Our orders come from the Division through the president. We're only here to guard the train."

"And leave the people defenseless as the canisters are shipped off?"

"The people have been ordered to stay indoors. We have our mission, and we have to see this train off safely. With any luck…these things will follow it out of here." He hurried off, shouting commands to his men.

"What are we going to do?" Gallagher asked.

Jane didn't have an immediate answer, or even a quippy comeback.

All she could think was she should have gone home to Chicago while she'd had the chance.

CHAPTER TEN

Hettie woke up to the distant rumble of thunder.

She hadn't thought she'd been sleeping—usually, she lay staring into the darkness, waiting for Walker to fall asleep before getting up to do something more productive. But then her eyes had snapped open. A heaviness filled the air, and her head throbbed as she sat up. Walker was not there.

She found him standing outside the tent, staring into the dark across the tops of the trees poking up through the unfathomable shadows below. Only the faintest sliver of moon was visible, as if a thumbnail had punctured the inky sky. The rumbling continued, but it was more like a series of low pops outside.

"What is that?" She strained to hear.

Others were crawling out of the tents now, guns drawn in trepidation. The air was cold, and a faint acrid scent touched their noses. Somewhere in the woods, an animal yipped and yowled.

"Junesfield is under attack," Walker said sharply.

Everyone looked to Hettie. "By who? I didn't give any orders—"

Unless it was her own people. What if it was Duke? He'd been itchy to hit the town after Tommy and the others had disappeared. Hettie swore. "Everyone, get your asses in gear!" Fire and damnation, she was not about to let that train get away!

ᛉ

It took far too long to rally the teams. Eventually, the ready signals went up: a flurry of red fireflies, spiraling up through the air like tiny demons racing out of hell.

Hettie spurred her horse forward, and the others filed after her, gathering speed as they sprinted down the hill and across the fields surrounding the mountain town.

The lower-level sorcerers threw glow stones into the air. Hettie could see the barricades and trenches ahead... but they were empty. Confused, Hettie reached for her time bubble—

It didn't come.

Panic seized her. She hadn't been hobbled like this in years. Only the warlock Zavi had been able to stifle Diablo's powers...

The smell of death hit her then, putrid and gag-inducing. The horses whinnied fearfully as the town loomed ahead. Several of the buildings were on fire. People were staggering and screaming in the streets.

"What the—" Walker was cut off as a figure popped up from the grass ahead of him, startling his horse. Hettie's skin prickled as it *looked* at her with ruined eyes, its slack, rotting jaw dripping with blood...

Her heart squelched. *"Man-things!"*

Walker's horse danced away from the creature stumbling toward it. The ruined man latched on to Walker's leg and dragged him off his horse.

Hettie drew her saber from its sheath and swerved her horse to intercept. She leaped from the saddle, landed on the man-thing's back, and hacked at its neck. Putrid gore sprayed her, but the creature kept clawing at Walker. He finally managed to thrust the thing back with one boot, and Hettie swung and sliced its head clean off.

"Hell's bells..." Walker staggered to his feet, swiping the creature's blood from his eyes. All around them the other teams were riding through, circling and firing their weapons to create panic and confusion. It was hardly necessary; Junesfield was already in chaos. Man-things ran and hobbled through the streets, chasing those caught outdoors, clawing at barred doors or smashing windows and climbing through. Hettie watched in horror as one woman-thing tackled a full-grown man and sank her teeth into his neck, tearing out his throat. When his struggles subsided, she started ripping at his clothes.

"Hettie!"

She was so engrossed by the awful sight she hadn't noticed the man-thing shambling toward her. He was slow because one of his feet had been mangled. As he reached for her, the boom of a shotgun rang out, and the creature reeled back, a pulpy hole blown through the side of his head.

Hettie looked toward the source of the shot—Lena rode up. "The train is here!"

"Where are the soldiers?" And why weren't they defending the townsfolk?

"At the station. They're fending off these things!" Her face was pale. "There are dozens of them, Hettie. Hundreds. And they don't feel pain."

And she couldn't use Diablo on them without losing a year of her life for each one she killed. She reached for the time bubble again, but it wouldn't come. "Something's blocking Diablo from working." She opened her hand but couldn't conjure the mage gun. She cursed.

"What do we do?" The plan had hinged on Hettie being able to dispatch the most dangerous elements in her time bubble. They hadn't counted on null spells, which Diablo could normally breach, or mindless man-things on the rampage.

She ground her teeth. "If there are canisters on that train, the plan's still the same."

"We can't fight all those things *and* the Division," Walker argued.

"Point the men toward the train. They'll have to pick off the man-things, then close around the soldiers."

"Couldn't we just let them pick each other off?"

"We do that, we might lose whoever knows about the final destination."

Lena nodded stiffly and drew out a handful of talismans from around her neck. She recited an incantation, activating her amplification spell that linked all the Blackthorns, then broadcast Hettie's orders.

Hettie mounted up and rode toward the station, dispatching the man-things in the streets with her saber. Walker rode next to her, emptying his pistols into one creature. Only a shot to the heart or head seemed to put it down quickly.

"I don't get it." Walker paused to reload. "I thought these man-things were drained sorcerers turned feral. There aren't *this* many sorcerers in the county that aren't Division."

Hettie had thought the same. "Maybe they traveled from Swedenborg. We don't know for sure what happened to all the inmates there." She checked in with her teams. "Duke, what's your situation?

"My situation's in the shithole." He grunted, and a loud barrage of gunfire rang out. "These things are everywhere. I've already lost Biggs and Burns. The station's overrun—soldiers' hands are full trying to keep those things away. There are three canisters on the train now. We should cut our losses, take what we can, and git."

"Stick to the plan," she shouted. "Help the soldiers. Put the man-things down. I'll be there soon with the others."

"Dammit, Blackthorn... we're dying out here!"

"Stick to the plan." His invectives soon trailed off as he focused on the fight. The men trusted her—they would fight until she told them otherwise.

Her last lead to Abby was on that train.

"Hettie?"

She looked around, realizing she knew that voice. "Horace?"

"And Marcus." The Englishman's voice was strained.

"We're pinned down in the hotel," Horace said. "These things are coming through the windows!"

"There are women and children in here!" Marcus shouted. "They're going after the gifted!"

They're going after Marcus. He was a high-level sorcerer, after all.

"Hang on. I'm on my way." She nodded to Lena, who cut off the amplification spell. "I'll get them out of there. The rest of you get to the train and don't let it leave till you know where it's going."

"Hettie—"

"Just do it!" She wheeled her horse around and headed for the hotel.

"Head for the train station! Take out as many of those man-things as you can, but don't hurt the soldiers!"

Jane's skin broke out in goose bumps. That amplified voice had been a woman's—was it Hettie Alabama's?

She could eavesdrop on any amplified conversations being relayed. She'd opened her ears to listen to the army's chatter, but she'd caught the Blackthorns' instead.

"They're coming." Jane's tremulous whisper sounded as if it had come from a different woman. Hettie Alabama was here. The woman who'd killed her mentor was finally within her reach.

"Jane!" Gallagher hauled her back. She'd absently stepped out of the perimeter the soldiers had created around them. She shook herself as the professor clutched her. "What are you doing?"

"She's out there. Hettie Alabama."

"We're not going to wade through these…these *things* to find her."

They couldn't rightfully be called human, though they had once been, clearly. They were in all states of dishevelment and damage, and completely oblivious to it. They shuffled with the blank expressions of men come from the horrors of the battlefield, their shocked gazes distant and unblinking. A pass with her senses told her some of them had once been gifted but had been drained of their magic, much in the way juicers were. The others… She shuddered. They felt like blank spaces. Mundane and alive, but not quite there, like the reverse of a phantom. Soulless. A shadow made flesh, carrying their emptiness around them.

They gave off the same sucking void feeling as the canisters.

The creatures crowded around the empty flatcar she stood on. More surrounded the Fielding engine that had just arrived, protected by men who beat the creatures with the butts of their empty rifles. Somehow in the midst of the chaos the canister was lifted off the cart by a crane. It swung precariously out of reach above the ground. Slavering men and women threw themselves and anything that might get that magic-filled tank down. Some lobbed rocks and sticks that bounced harmlessly off the side. One creature climbed on top of a stack crates and uselessly launched himself at the canister. He crashed to the ground, landing on his neck with a sick snap.

"Zombi," Professor Gallagher muttered. Jane looked at him questioningly. "There's a Haitian tradition of reanimating the dead," he babbled nervously. "A kind of sorcerer—a necromancer of a type—can bring dead flesh back to life to do his bidding, though the vessels have no spirit of their own."

"I don't think they're dead," Jane said. "You can see the way they're exerting themselves. They're panting. The dead don't breathe. And they bleed"—she pointed at a man riddled with bullet holes—"they just don't feel it till it's too late." Bodies too ruined to go on were starting to pile up in the streets. Even so, there were too many of these zombie creatures to stop.

"Either way, if we don't do something soon, we're going to be next."

Hettie rode up to the hotel. Man-things clawed at the doors and beat the windows. One creature clambered up the porch overhang. Hettie aimed her horse at it and sliced a foot off, spraying blood over herself. The man-thing kept going. Before she could draw Diablo and take out its legs, it had smashed through a pane of glass and scrambled inside. Screams, and then gunshots, erupted within.

She had to get these things away from the civilians. She sheathed the saber and drew Diablo, firing into the air. "Hey!"

The man-things turned toward her. Their eyes were like blank voids threatening to suck her in. The blaze of a nearby building fire illuminated their torn and muddied clothes and the scars on their arms and faces. Some of them had wounds that had gone gangrenous, but they didn't seem to notice. They were impervious to pain, mindless with their insatiable hunger for magic.

She blasted several glowing green holes at their feet. The display of power only whipped them into a further slaver. They detached from the hotel front and started toward her.

The horse danced back, and Hettie guided the terrified mare into the middle of the street. Other man-things had heard Diablo's call. She was reminded of the chupacabra, the demon spawn who'd also been attracted to the infernal power of the Devil's Revolver. She could use that.

"C'mon, ya varmints!" She fired into the air, then spurred the horse into a quick trot down the main street, glancing backward.

They scrambled after her like limping, starving coyotes, with Hettie as their Pied Piper. But where would she take them? She couldn't lead them to the train, even though that was where the firepower was. That would be heaping more problems on her people.

Rok burst into a cloud of ash high above her, cawing as he angled up toward the sky. She gazed into the dark shape of the hills.

Of course. She rode toward the mountain path just fast enough to keep the man-things following, firing Diablo intermittently to keep them focused on her. The time bubble still wouldn't come, even outside of town limits—not a null spell, then. "Rok, why isn't Diablo working?"

"No magic where no magic lives," he said almost worriedly. *"Their hunger will never be sated."* He stayed high above the throng, she noticed, not even wheeling above the man-things bunching up behind her.

When she could see Junesfield from high up on the road, she searched for what she needed and eventually came to a drop-off. Rok disappeared once more, safe, she presumed, in whatever otherworld he existed in when he wasn't at her side.

The stream of man-things climbed the slope. She dismounted and slapped the horse's rump, letting the terrified creature bolt. Then she drew her saber.

The man-things crested the hill. Their empty eyes and clutching, ruined hands tracked Diablo. One of the creatures rushed her, and she chopped at his neck, the blade sticking as it hit bone. She kicked him off, the grip of her sword slick with blood.

The man-things closed around her, and she backed toward the edge of the drop-off.

It's all you now, she said to the mage gun. Diablo didn't respond.

She exhaled and pulled the trigger, pointing it skyward. A hell-green beam engulfed the weapon, lighting up the trees and hills around them. The man-things wailed, a perverse sound like a moan of grief and ecstasy all at once. They surged toward Hettie.

She felt her heel hit the crumbling edge of the ground. The man things were twenty feet away. Ten feet. With all her might, she lobbed Diablo from the precipice and stepped off.

The saber clattered away as her arms and hands scraped down along the rough cliff face, finding and losing purchase inch after crumbling inch. Her fingers finally dug in and locked as she found a sturdy handhold.

Dirt rained down on her as the first man-things leaped after the mage gun. The bodies streamed over the cliff, a stampede of men and women diving to their deaths after a false promise, a certain doom.

At first there was only the silence of airborne bodies. The cliff was at least five stories up, and it shouldn't have taken so long for them to fall. She'd never forget the stench of those bodies—almonds, old blood, urine, feces—as she clung for life. That arc of rotting humanity flowed just feet behind her like a waterfall of death and decay.

Then their bodies hit the ground with sickening thuds and snaps, the jagged rockfall crunching and grinding beneath a rapidly growing reef of protruding bones. Flesh slapped flesh, wet and loud, as they piled on top of each other. The smell worsened as their diseased innards were exposed. Hettie gagged but didn't let go. Her arms screamed, her fingers were numb, but she did not want to meet her own doom in that pile of death.

Finally the flow of bodies stopped. Below, a woman-thing buried waist deep on top of the pile struggled, only she was digging… down. To get to Diablo. To get to the source of magic she desperately craved. Hettie's saber was lost under all those corpses, too.

Hettie hauled herself up over the edge, clawing across the ground away from the grisly scene. Then she turned over and vomited. The smell was too much.

"H-Hettie?"

She peered up blearily. "Tommy?" She pushed onto her hands and knees.

The young man was shaking violently. He was filthy, a cut on his leg and upper arm crusted with blood. His face was heavily battered, too. "I-I-I n-n-need…"

She reached out, at once relieved. "You'll be okay, Tommy. The others aren't far. We'll get you to a doctor." Whatever her hurts were, she ignored them. "Who did this to you? Was it Ben and Adam?"

He shook his head, teeth chattering. "They… th-they took m-my magic…"

Her skin prickled. "Who took it?"

"Those… things…" He pointed toward the cliff and gave a ragged sob. "I'm s-so c-cold." He kept coming toward her, though. "You're warm. Y-you're… light."

Everything inside Hettie recoiled. She'd heard those words before from Walker when he'd been coming down from the juice. She backed away. "I'm going to help you, Tommy. Sit down right here. I'll go get my horse—"

"No!" He lunged, and his hands closed around her throat.

CHAPTER ELEVEN

The zombies were closing in. Jane had already watched two soldiers get dragged screaming into the horde. She would not let that happen to anyone else. She fingered the charm dangling at her wrist, but now was not the time for it... It was an absolute last resort.

"How can you Pinkertons not know any battle magic?" Captain Nichols asked irritably, firing his sidearm into the throng to little effect.

"Those spells are difficult to cast even under ideal conditions." She gestured at the chaos around her. "I'd need a sterile, silent environment and at least three more high-level sorcerers to assist me to counter an attack of this size. And I don't see any of your men slinging hexes."

"They're mostly mundanes and new recruits," he admitted gruffly. "More soldier than sorcerer."

Great. Jane thought hard.

"Do you have dynamite?" Jane asked the captain. Even if these zombies were people, she couldn't be noble if she were a corpse.

"We can't risk damaging the canisters," the captain said sternly.

"Is that why your men aren't shooting at the creatures around the cart?"

He met her eye dead-on. "A stray bullet could prove catastrophic."

Jane huffed. "We'll just have to get them farther from the canisters, then."

A cluster of the zombies scrabbled for something on the ground—a fallen glow stone. That gave her an idea.

She gathered some bricks sitting on the flatbed car, drew a protection circle on the wood in chalk, and placed them in the center. Making glow stones was a simple trick, one of the first spells they learned in the Academy advanced classes. She spoke the enchantment out loud, precisely, so that she could hear herself over the gunfire and screams. In seconds the bricks glowed orange-gold. Not the best glow stones she'd ever produced, but sufficient for their purposes.

"Throw these as far from the train as you can." She passed them to the captain and Gallagher. "If I'm right, those things should cluster around them, and you can pick them off."

They did as she instructed, and sure enough, a few of the zombies broke off and dove for the glow stones. One male grabbed a broken half brick and proceeded to swallow it. Three other creatures tackled him, tearing his jaw off to pry the glow stone out, but then they jerked and collapsed to a twitching heap as they were perforated with bullets.

"We're going to run out of ammunition before that last expedition arrives." The captain glanced up at the canister hovering above the adjacent flatbed car as men struggled to maneuver it in place while fighting off the zombies.

More of the creatures emerged on the other side of the tracks, and the soldiers closed around the train and its precious cargo. They were penned in on all sides. "We can't hold them off," Jane said. "This train needs to leave now!"

Gunfire erupted around them. Jane ducked as a bullet whizzed past her ear, and Gallagher dropped to the ground next to her.

"Thank the gods!" But then a new fear crept into Nichols's face as a band of horsemen, twenty or more strong, galloped toward the train station, mowing down their attackers. A man in black spurred his mount straight through a knot of zombies, swinging the butt of his rifle and bashing the creatures' skulls.

Jane recognized him. It was the mercenary Walker Woodroffe, believed to be Hettie Alabama's second. His broad silhouette had shown up on a number of wanted posters, though his head wasn't fetching nearly as much as his commander's.

Where Walker Woodroffe was, so too would be the outlaw Hettie Alabama.

ᛉ

Hettie's vision grayed as Tommy's fingers squeezed her throat. She kicked weakly, her thrashing sapping her strength. She called for Diablo, but it wouldn't come. The mage gun was silent, buried beneath the mountain of death below her.

Tommy's grip loosened abruptly, and Hettie collapsed to the ground, gasping. A figure struck lightning quick, bashing the Tommy man-thing back, kicking his feet out from beneath him, pushing him toward the edge. Hettie couldn't see very well, but she heard the click of a hammer being pulled back. Hettie tried to croak out a protest—

A gunshot cracked the air. Tommy fell down dead, his brains splattered behind him.

Something inside Hettie wrenched. She cried out, her throat raw and tight. Every muscle screamed with pins and needles as she tried to regain her hazy vision.

The stranger was barely a shadow against the night. The sliver of moon was high now, hanging over his shoulder as if it were winking. He hurried to her side.

He reached for her throat. She batted at his hand weakly, thinking maybe he was trying to end her himself, but then a warm white light filled her vision. Coolness flowed over her, permeating her flesh, driving away the pain and replacing it with a serenity that finally gave her a chance to inhale and let out a broken sob for Tommy's death.

"I didn't think us meeting again would be a reason to cry," the stranger said wryly, pulling her into a sitting position.

He wasn't a stranger, of course. Hettie flung her arms around his shoulders and hugged him tight.

"Ling." She cried into his shoulder, suddenly feeling not quite so alone for the first time in three long years.

Jane scanned the horsemen's faces even as she checked the load on her pistol, but the riders were moving too fast for her to make out the distinct plume-shaped scar Hettie Alabama was known for. Soon the soldiers would exhaust their ammunition and be at the mercy of the Blackthorn Rogues.

Jane gripped her gun. If they were taken prisoner, she'd hide among the Division troops, wait to face Hettie Alabama, and shoot her dead. No one would suspect her; she could cast a glamor, make herself invisible in plain sight. She would get justice for poor Quentin and all the other people Hettie had killed—

"No! Stop!" Captain Nichols waved his arms frantically. The Rogues were firing on the zombies closest to the canister. Soldiers dove out of the way of the bullets wildly ricocheting off the cart.

A teeth-aching *ping* resonated through Jane like a bell across a lake. The air stilled with a sudden intake of breath. Hovering just inches above the flatbed, the glass canister crackled and rocked in its rope harness.

The sickly sucking sensation emanating from the canister expanded, making Jane's stomach turn. Gallagher grabbed her wrist, his body tensing. She couldn't tear her eyes away as the glass spider-webbed and the magic inside started seeping through.

The zombies moaned.

"Retreat!" Captain Nichols shouted. "Run, run, *run*!"

Jane found herself whisked off her feet as Gallagher half carried her away from the train. The soldiers turned and fled at top speed, and the zombies clambered onto the flatbed car and embraced the dangling canister like newborn kittens suckling at their mother's teats.

A wave of power seared her back. Gallagher wrapped himself around her. In that split second, she fingered the charm at her wrist and stabbed the sharp tooth through her thumb, speaking the three easy syllables Quentin had taught her.

A flash of light engulfed her—

Hettie was bowled over by a slobbering, stinking mass of fur and muscle. She laughed and struggled to sit up as Cymon tackled her to the ground, whimpering and woofing in joy.

The dog paused and suddenly looked toward the town. He cowered, whining.

A boom echoed through the trees, and Hettie shot to her feet. "The town. My people are there for the train."

"Hettie, wai—"

A blue-white flash filled the sky, the town, the trees, and beyond, washing everything in white, blinding them.

Then came the wave. Hettie stumbled back, but Ling caught her and shielded her with his body. Her skin rippled with sparks, fizzling out, igniting something inside her like a match to lamp oil. Suddenly, she could hear Diablo calling to her.

Help me, he shouted.

Hettie reflexively opened her palm, and the mage gun leaped into her hand, filling her mind with relief and gratitude like a small child excitedly recalling the horrors of a day at school. Her palms glowed gold the way they had when she'd first come back from hell after saving Abby. But the gun wasn't the one calling to her.

Help me, Hettie.

"Abby?" It came out on a strangled gasp, echoed in her sister's faint plea.

Help me.

She stumbled forward. Ling grabbed her, held her close. He was saying something urgently to her, to reassure her, but she didn't hear him.

Help me.

"Abby!" Her sister was alive! "Where are you?"

There was no response. The white burn across her vision was fading, and darkness returned, along with an eerie silence.

When she could see again, the town looked like nothing more than a smear in the dark. Walker... Lena... Her heart crawled into her stomach. "What just happened?"

"A canister exploded." Ling was trembling. His hands glowed an intense white. He closed his fists and exhaled as the magic subsided. "It must have failed and leaked magic."

"What does that mean?"

"You've seen juicers. The town is flooded, and anyone who was near that canister is either juiced up or dead. We need to go." When she didn't move, he said, "Hettie, listen to me. Your sister is alive. We were in San Francisco when she used her power—"

"I know. She came to me. Saved me, but the Division got her." She could hear the remorse creeping into her voice, but now was not the time to examine her guilt. "I heard her just now. She's calling out to me."

Ling went on, "I've been trying to find out where she ended up, where the Division might have taken her. I came to Junesfield following one of my leads. I'm guessing you were doing the same. Come, we need to leave this place."

"I can't just leave. My people are down there." Her voice broke. "Walker's down there."

Ling's expression tightened. He said nothing more as he brought his horse around and they mounted. Cymon trotted faithfully next to them, his tail drooping as they neared the ruined town.

Fires burned. Bodies lay in the road. A few people wandered through the streets, eyes wide and watery. Hettie came upon one woman frantically drawing a protection circle in the dirt before dropping into it in fetal position, whispering an incantation.

"She's cocooning," Ling explained, his voice hard. "It happens sometimes to gifted who've overjuiced. They feel like all the magic is about to burst out of their skin, so they draw a protection circle around themselves to keep it in."

All the horses were dead, their eyes burned out and smoking. A scattering of man-things lay in the road, mere husks of flesh now, as if their corpses had been out in the sun for months. Among them were other bodies, eye sockets charred, their faces slack as if they'd glimpsed something remarkable at the moment of death. Somewhere a baby cried.

"Gods," she whispered. "What happened?"

"When the canister exploded, the magic inside killed any mundane it came across."

"I don't understand. How can magic do that? Shouldn't the mundane just be juiced?"

"All I can think is that the concentration of magic in these canisters, or else the way the magic has been transformed, has somehow made it deadly to mundanes. The only person who might be able to explain it would be whoever created these particular Fielding engines."

The certainty with which he said it made her stomach sink. "You've seen this before."

Ling's expression was grave. "There was an accident in Oregon. A canister had fallen off the mountain path and shattered just outside of a town. It killed all the mundane Division troops and the livestock below for a mile."

Her heart took a dip as fear consumed her. She ran toward the train station, shouting Walker's name.

Man-thing husks littered the ground like deadwood. Division troops lay prone, some twitching, others dead, that same look of wonder burned into their waxen faces. She came upon the first of her men, the mundanes who'd been with the gang since her doppelganger had run the outfit. Loyal to Hettie Alabama, no matter who she was.

All dead. Heaped together with horses and man-things and soldiers alike.

"Walker!" Her voice broke as she searched frantically among the bodies, seeking that broad, dark frame. Every shoulder angled up from the ground marked another dead, and her throat tightened with each body she turned over. She'd sent them here. She'd sent them to their doom—

"Hettie." Lena limped toward them, walking Tisiphone. A large form was draped over her saddle.

Hettie's breath stopped in her lungs. Tears flooded her eyes.

"He's alive," Lena hurried to say. "We were behind the train engine when the canister burst. The metal shielded us from the worst of the blast." She eased down onto a crate, shaking. Ling approached, and Lena tensed, her hand going to her holstered weapon.

"It's all right," Hettie said. "He's an old friend."

Walker gave a low groan. Hettie had never heard a sweeter sound.

Ling helped Walker off the horse and laid him on the ground. His eyelids were swollen and red, and tears leaked from them. "He should be dead," Ling murmured, glancing back at the train and the bodies around it. "The magic he borrowed from Javier Punta must have left its mark. He was a vessel for so long, he was able to absorb the magic that did hit him."

"My deflection barrier might've helped," Lena said.

Ling nodded. His palms flooded with light, and he placed them over Walker's forehead and eyes. Lena crossed herself and muttered something as she looked away from Ling's ether magic. Hettie found it strange that a high-level sorcerer like Lena would be so superstitious.

Walker gave a deep sigh as Ling's healing magic faded. "He may be blind for a while," Ling said. "I can't fix that—the damage is too extensive. I can ease his pain, though."

"No need to put yourself out on my account, Mr. Tsang," the bounty hunter grumbled. Ling took his hands away and stood.

Hettie stifled the urge to wrap her arms around Walker. "What can you see?" she asked instead.

"Nothing, really. Shadows. Light." He held his head. "My skull feels like it's going to explode."

Lena pursed her lips. "You've been steeped in magic, Walker."

He stiffened. "You mean…I'm juiced?"

"It appears so. You got lucky. Every other mundane in the street is dead." Ling said it with the remoteness of a plague doctor. "The magic will fade faster if you use it."

"No. Half the high was using the magic." He clasped his hands tightly together as if he might conjure a flame then and there. "What about my eyes? How long am I going to be like this?"

"I can't be certain. But you should keep them covered, let them heal."

He cursed and got to his feet. Hettie went to help him, but he pushed her off; whether he knew it was her or not, she couldn't say. "What's it look like around us?"

"Like hell." Though Hettie could safely say this was a spring fairground compared to her experience of the place she had a standing reservation in. "Our people are down. The horses are all dead."

"Except the magicked ones." Lena gestured at Tisi. "Gifted and magic had a certain resistance to this…bomb."

Bomb. That was what Zavi had set off at Swedenborg, only it had done the reverse—taken the prisoners' powers, exploding them, and killing off the sorcerers, or so she'd been led to believe. The thing was, she'd never found any bodies at the prison in New Mexico, and no sign of any mass graves. Had the inmates turned into these man-things?

That had been three years ago, though. Surely they hadn't been wandering the land that long?

"Did you find Horace and Marcus?" Walker asked.

Oh, gods, she'd forgotten about them! She took off running to the hotel.

Smoke filled the air. The upper floors of the building were ablaze, and people ran out the front doors, coughing. It seemed the building had sheltered the guests from the wave of magic, probably thanks to the ornamental sheet metal used all over the siding. "Horace! Marcus!" She stared into the flaming windows above.

"Miss Hettie." Horace was already outside in the alley, bent over a man on the ground, his shirt soaked in blood.

Marcus.

Horace gripped his neck, blood pulsing through his fingers. Ling pushed past her and quickly put a pad of linen over the wound, taking Horace's place.

Hettie knelt next to the sorcerer. "It's all right, Marcus. You're all right now."

"That thing got inside, went for a lady. Marcus tried to fight it off, and it bit him. Shook him like a ragdoll till I shot him." Horace's voice trembled. "Vampire?"

Hettie shook her head. "Worse."

Ling's palms glowed as he started healing the man. A strange look filled Marcus's eyes. Bleak, desperate. He licked his lips and stuttered, "C-c-cold."

"I'll get him some blankets." Horace hurried away.

"Hettie…" Marcus reached out to her. "That thing… It did something to me."

"You'll be all right, Marcus."

"N-no. It…it took m-my…" He pursed his lips, shame staining his pale cheeks. "My magic."

"I can't stop the bleeding," Ling said, confounded. "It's like I'm pouring water into a bucket full of holes. There's . . . there's nothing in him I can grasp to close the wound."

"But you've healed mundanes."

"My power hooks into the qi, the powers that come from within. I'm telling you . . ." He lowered his voice. "There's nothing in Marcus. He's been drunk dry."

"I'm c-cold." Blood matted the man's ginger hair.

Hettie set her jaw. "Then we'll do it the old-fashioned way."

Horace returned with a fine blanket that smelled of smoke, pilfered from the lower levels of the burning hotel. "We need a doctor," she said.

"Town doc's dead," Horace said grimly. "Saw him back there in the street."

Hettie huffed. "I'll do it myself. Needle, thread, hot water—"

"No." Marcus clamped a hand over hers. Blood spurted from the wound, trickling from the corner of his mouth. "That thing took my magic and now . . . I can feel it. What they're feeling. The . . . hunger." He closed his eyes. "I don't want to become one of those things."

"Don't you worry about that." She had to close that wound, stop the bleeding. She drew Diablo—

Marcus's eyes widened, and he thrashed, reaching for the gun. He got his palm over the wheel, his flesh sizzling at the cursed revolver's touch, but he wouldn't let go.

"Marcus, stop!" Horace pried him off the mage gun and wrestled him back, but it wasn't much of a fight. The bandage around Marcus's neck had fallen away. The blood wasn't pouring from the wound quite so enthusiastically now.

Hettie looked helplessly up at Ling. He gave a barely there shake of his head, his expression bleak. Then she realized what he was saying.

Her muscles tensed, as if that tightening could hold her friend together. "Marcus, you listen to me. Everything's gonna be fine . . ."

Marcus's eyes widened. "I . . . I remember . . ." He smiled, staring up at the sky as if it were alive and bursting with new stars. Then his brow wrinkled. The smile faded. Tears welled up, and he exhaled shakily. "Tell . . . her . . . I'm . . . sorry . . ."

His spine relaxed. His eyes turned empty.

Horace wrapped his arms tight around the man's shoulders and started to cry.

A numbness swept through Hettie. She barely registered Lena and Walker's arrival as she folded Marcus's hand over his chest.

"His internal injuries were too great," Ling explained softly. "A rib had punctured his lung, and his trachea was nearly crushed. Even if I could have stopped the bleeding and healed those injuries, I have no idea how the magic drain would've affected him."

"So that man-thing did drain him of his magic somehow?" She looked to Horace.

"I saw it happen. Just like a vampire…" He gazed down at Marcus. "He died the way he always wanted to—protecting the innocent. He was a good man. A good friend."

The roof of the hotel collapsed in a shrieking crash of timbers. Hettie gazed around, as if only just then noticing the destruction around her. This was *all* her fault.

All of this to find Abby…and she hadn't been able to do that.

"Dammit." Hettie kicked the dirt. A tiny, unsatisfying clod dislodged from her toe. It was only the beginning of her building rage. "Dammit. *Dammit!*"

Everyone was silent, holding their breath as if they expected something more. Why were they all looking at her for answers? She clearly didn't have any.

Walker said, "We should round up whoever's left. Take what we can and get out while the getting's good."

"Why?" Hettie growled. "This was my last chance at finding Abby. What good will running away do me now?"

"All's not lost, Miss Hettie." Ling laid a hand on her shoulder. "I was trying to tell you before: this train wasn't my only lead."

Hope unfurled inside her, and she gripped his hand, grasping at anything he had to offer. "Where is she?"

"I don't know that, but I heard about a former Division agent gone rogue. He was supposedly in charge of one of the first Fielding expeditions. He disappeared somewhere in Montana after abandoning his post."

"It'd take a traitor to know one," Walker said.

Ling cut him a look the bounty hunter couldn't see. "I don't need you to remind me of my past actions, as I'm sure you wouldn't want to be reminded of yours, Mr. Woodroffe. I came here to pay my debt, to do as I first promised and to find and protect Abby."

"I guess we're going to Montana, then," Hettie said.

"Now?" Walker stepped forward unsteadily, his hard gaze a little off center. "You can't just leave the gang like this."

"He's right," Lena said. "We need to regroup, gather whoever's left, and go back to Blackthorn's Hell."

"I came to find Abby," Hettie snapped. "That was the only reason I agreed to lead the Blackthorn Rogues in the first place. Instead I've been playing outlaw with a bunch of hooligan boys, and look where it got them!" She gestured around. "Dead! All of them, dead!" The hot tears threatened to pour from her then, but she held their acrid burn back, letting them sear her throat. She deserved all the pain in the world for getting Tommy and the others killed.

The stunned silence was punctuated by the wailing baby. "This isn't your fault, Hettie," Walker said softly.

"Then whose? Huh?" She hissed out a breath. "I won't give up on Abby. I can't. I heard her just now. The juice got in me and I heard her calling out, clear as bell." She hadn't even heard her in the water, and Hettie had endured plenty of dunkings, holding her breath till her lungs gave out, straining for the voice of her sister. "She's out there. I'm going to find her."

Walker's eyes grew sad. "Don't look at me like that," Hettie warned. "Don't you dare even think what you're thinking. She ain't dead, Walker. You wouldn't have been with me all this time if you thought so."

"You're so sure about that." The plainly spoken statement drove an icicle a little deeper into Hettie's heart, pinning her resolve that much more securely.

"Hettie, you can't just leave. The Blackthorn Rogues are *your* outfit."

What was Walker not getting about her decision? "The Alabama gang was Duke's. If he's not dead…" She pressed her lips together. Even that thought stung. "He can have whatever's left of the gang. Or you can kill him and run it yourself. I don't give two figs. Far as I'm concerned, the Blackthorn Rogues are through."

"So that's it? You're just gonna abandon us and run?"

"I'm running to the only thing that matters. The only thing that's *ever* mattered to me." Diablo leaped into her fist, though she kept it pointed at the ground. "Any of you wanna to try to stop me?"

Silence. Good. She needed her energy to get away from the smell of death, the howls of the maddened, and that screaming baby.

"Hettie." Walker's voice was low, pleading. "You can't go alone."

"I'll be with her." Ling said it with quiet conviction.

Walker ignored him. "Just wait a couple of days. My sight will get better—"

"Or it won't get better at all." Hettie surveyed his ice-blue eyes. The bleak helplessness she saw there twisted her innards into knots, made her feel like a heartless monster. But her sister was out there, and Ling was going to help find her.

Her mind was made up. "I'm sorry, Walker. You'll only slow me down."

"Hettie, don't leave—"

She dropped into the time bubble. Giving Walker one last lingering look, she turned and touched Ling's arm, then took Cymon by the collar. The big brown dog shook himself, head twitching this way and that as he took in his silent surroundings. He gave a short whine and stuck close to Hettie, tail tucked between his legs.

"We're going to need horses and supplies," she said to Ling. "Montana's a long ride from here."

He looked all around them, grimacing. He didn't seem to need an explanation of her new powers. "Don't you want to say a proper good-bye?"

She didn't respond.

CHAPTER TWELVE

Jane groaned, her skin crawling, her breath coming in short gasps as a winged worm of happiness flirted through her, extending her senses, tickling her mind's eye and bringing it to tears. She gave a short laugh as a bubble of pink magic drifted up from her lips like a plume of smoke. It had been one of the little tricks she used to do when she'd first discovered her gift in the orphanage—blowing little colored bubbles for the younger children to giggle at.

Only then did she realize she was being smothered by a rather heavy blanket. Too heavy for this time of year. She pushed at it, feeling its firm bulk between her legs.

The deep moan atop her had her shooting straight up, dumping the fleshy blanket off.

It was Professor Gallagher. Jane ran through the jumble of memories crowding her brain, then remembered what had happened—light, and activating the protection charm Quentin had made for her—

She stared at her hands, awash in sparks and color. She'd been juiced; she knew because she'd dabbled in recreational juicing at the Academy. It had rarely gone well for her.

Her gaze went to the train, to the bodies in the streets and all around her. Her mind processed the sight, but instead of a scream, a giggle bubbled up through her, followed by a series of green and blue spheres wobbling from her mouth.

"Agent Pinkerton?" The professor was staring at her from his spot on the ground. "Are you all right?"

"Bever netter." She hiccuped. "Oh, dear."

Gallagher gently coaxed her toward him. "Perhaps you should sit."

"I'm Jane," she said, grinning, though what she was smiling about, she had no idea. "And you're... you're Hamish, aren't you? Professor Hamish Gallagher." She enunciated the words carefully, aware of the shapes her lips were making and the bubbles lifting off her skin. "Hamish Gallagher. Hamish Gallagher. Hamish Gallagher."

"It's a ridiculous name," he acknowledged, scratching a circle on the ground with a piece of charcoal. "I'm fully aware."

"Rightly so. You sound like some kind of breakfast dish. Hamish Gallagher. Like a pile of ground pork and oranges topped with a fried egg and whipped cream. Oh, dear, I seem to be hungry." She let him lead her into the protection circle, and she plopped down, her skirts pooling around her prettily.

"As am I. It's the magic. We've both been affected. Not as bad as these poor mundanes, though." Jane looked at the corpses, that odd feeling boiling up inside her once more. A stream of pink bubbles floated up from her mouth on a hiccup. "Your protection charm saved us both, but I'm afraid you took the brunt of the blast." He hesitated. "Thank you for saving me."

He sealed the circle and carefully recited an incantation. Jane didn't like people doing magic on her—she didn't trust other people's spells and hadn't since her Academy days. But then that strange feeling lifted from her, and the colors and bubbles dissipated.

Dawn stole into the sky, casting the trees against dark blues and grays. About a third of the town was engulfed in flames, but the shiny new fire pump sat uselessly in the streets. Apparently no one still alive knew how to use it.

Jane's heart sank, the high of the juice gone. She stared all around her at the death and destruction.

The air turned frigid, and a dime of darkness appeared above them. Gallagher pulled her back as a remote Zoom tunnel irised open, filling the air with flurries and staining the ground with frost. Jane frantically looked for her gun, but it had been lost somewhere…

William Pinkerton stepped through the remote Zoom with six other armed agents flanking him. Jane swallowed drily. Her uncle rarely left the office these days, and his glower told her he hadn't done so happily. He looked around cursorily, and then his eyes landed on her and Professor Gallagher.

"By the Almighty…" He advanced, his bulk shadowing the fires around him. Every last trace of the giggles left her. "What are you doing out here?"

"How did you find me?"

"Do you really think I'd let my own niece work for me without having some way of tracking her?" He held up an amulet, a stone wrapped with strands of that peculiar shade of auburn Jane called her own. "I felt the explosion, Jane. A canister ruptured here, didn't it?"

"You know?"

"Junesfield? Yes, I've heard some stories about the Division presence here. The question is, why are *you* here? I thought Eric had given you a case in New York."

She wasn't about to feed him a story—her uncle didn't need magic to know when someone was lying. So she told him the truth.

"The Blackthorn Rogues raided the town. Hettie Alabama might still be here," she said. "We have to find her."

"We're not doing anything of the sort. I told you to drop this investigation."

"I'm not after Diablo—"

"No, you're after revenge. Quentin would be appalled by your behavior."

"Mr. Pinkerton." Gallagher stepped forward. "I assure you, Agent Pinkerton did nothing—"

"Who the hell are you?" William sized him up, surprised to be approached by the bald-faced academic.

"Professor Hamish Gallagher, sir. Agent Pinkerton hired me to consult on the case to find the outlaw Hettie Alabama."

"I didn't authorize this. Jane, what have you promised this poor man?" He turned angry eyes on her. Jane shrank under his thunderous gaze.

"I'm an expert on the Devil's Revolver, sir. I was made to understand the Pinkerton Agency would be paying me for my services in exchange for help tracking down the Blackthorn Rogues and the mage gun known as Diablo." He sounded uncertain now, his gaze sweeping toward Jane in a plea.

William Pinkerton let out a long, put-upon sigh. "I'm afraid you were misled, Mr. Gallagher. Jane doesn't have the authority to hire consultants, nor the personal budget. She's a junior detective and is only supposed to be working under Eric's direction, despite what she might have told you." He cut her a look. "He's quite upset with you."

The look on the professor's face would've created a storm of rainbow bubbles from Jane's mouth if she was still juiced. She wished she were. Gallagher's expression grew pained, then angry as he faced her. "You lied to me."

"I didn't. You would have been paid if we'd caught her." She quickly added, "And we can still catch her. The gang is in town right now. I saw her lieutenant, Walker Woodroffe—Hettie Alabama has got to be close by!"

"No. I refuse to be pulled into this, Jane. The Zoom will only be open a few more minutes. You're coming back to Chicago with me right now."

"Don't you even want to know what happened here?" Jane demanded. "Look around, Uncle! There are dozens, if not hundreds, of people dead here, and the Division and Hettie Alabama are responsible! They've committed an act of unspeakable mass murder!"

"A terrible tragedy, clearly—one I hope you had nothing to do with." He eyed her as if he wasn't sure. "But this is the Division's problem to solve. The Pinkerton Detecting Agency has no ties to this business whatsoever, and if you know what's best, you'll make sure it stays that way and pretend you never saw any of this. Do you understand?"

"Uncle—"

"Not another word! I made you a junior detective because your father would've wasted your talents in New York filing papers for him. I can see now that my trust was misplaced. You will go back with us now and accept your punishment."

Jane set her teeth, dug her heels in ready to fight. But her uncle grabbed her arm and yanked her through the Zoom tunnel. Gallagher and the other agents followed.

She looked over her shoulder. For a fleeting moment, she thought she saw a woman in black staring back.

With a rush of cold, the aperture winked closed.

MISSOURI
1840

"Pa...there's someone here to see you."

Elias scowled, though he could barely see Junior through his hazy vision. "I told you, no damned priests." He'd had enough of Reverend What's-His-Name's visits since that damned bull had gored him. Over a hundred years on this earth, and *this* was how he was going to go...by infection from a pointy horn. The indignity of it all would be funny except he'd lost his sense of humor around the time his wife had died.

"Not a priest... A...a...woman?" Junior glanced behind him nervously.

Despite his torpor and the shaking of his muscles, Elias was at once alert. "You let her in?"

"She said she's an old friend."

Junior had never been all that bright, and he was far too trusting. But if his visitor was who he thought, there would have been no stopping her. "Come here, son." Elias reached under his pillow and pulled out the gun. Junior shied back. "I said come here."

His boy shuffled nearer. Elias closed his eyes, gripping the mage gun. *Watch over him as you've watched over me. Keep him safe.*

"This is for you." It slid from his palm with a sound like a sigh. A heavy velvet cloak seemed to slip off his shoulders. Elias Jr.'s eyes widened. The revolver shifted form in his hands, became... smaller, as if to accommodate the boy's grip.

"Pa, that's your special gun. I can't take it."

"You have to. It's my legacy—our family's legacy. One day I hope you'll pass it on to your son. But it's sacred, all right? You've got to protect it. Keep it close. Don't hand it over to anyone, not unless you mean to let them keep it, understand? It'll protect you. One day... you'll understand. And keep it away from our guest. Whatever you do, don't let her see it."

Elias's heart broke as fear entered his son's eyes. It was the same fear Elias had lived with from the moment he'd become... whatever he was, living this abominably long life. The boy wrapped the weapon in a piece of linen and put it under his shirt, and Elias told him to wear his mantle coat over it. It was too large on his tiny frame, but it was loaded with protection charms and had some coins sewn into the lining.

He touched his son's face—so like his mother's—regretting his lies, his secrets. "Show my guest in, then go to town for me, won't you?" He hacked up a wad of blood. "Get me... get me some apples."

"They're not in season, Pa. And what'll be left of the harvest will be shriveled..."

"I've faith in you, son. Don't come back till you find me the ripest, juiciest red apple you can find, all right? Go to the next town over if you have to."

"Yes, Pa." Bless the boy, he was barely twelve, on his way to becoming a man, and Elias would not be there to guide him. But at least the boy would have Diablo.

"Before you go, bring the lamp here." He indicated the lantern. "I might do some reading."

His son hesitated. He knew his father couldn't see very well. "Pa... are you sure...?"

"Get me that apple. Red as blood, you hear?"

Junior brought the lantern, then left the room, taking Elias's heart with him. A moment later, the widow progenitor Underwood stepped in.

"So you've given up already?" She stood over him, disappointment carved on her beautiful, icy visage, unchanged after all this time. "You wouldn't be dying unless you truly meant to."

Elias sat back against his pillows. "Sixty years on top of what I already had was enough. Watching all your friends and family die around you isn't pretty."

"You get used to it," she said quietly.

An old fury, a wound that had festered worse than the bull's gore, burned in his gut. "You said I wouldn't be turned."

"You weren't. Did you ever have the blood hunger?"

"No. But that doesn't explain what I've become." He wanted to know why she'd left him as she had, with so many questions, floundering and alone. He'd thought she'd meant to…keep him. "Why did you just leave me like that?"

"I don't have an explanation, exactly. I'd had every intention of staying, but…when we bonded, something happened. I've only recently discovered what it is." Her green eyes glowed with intensity. "Your mage gun has powers similar to my own. The spell that bound us exchanged some of our abilities in a…pact. A devil's bargain. That demon is a sneaky one." She huffed. "It's rather hard to explain to a mortal. All I can tell you is that when the bind was complete, I had to run. I knew *he* was coming for me."

Elias's memory stretched thin as he reached into the distant past. "The guardian."

"That cursed demon in the gun stole some of my powers and knotted the bond to me. Once you fell asleep and I felt his presence, I ran." She set her teeth, the points of her canines dimpling her lower lip. Her scowl deepened. "I've run from many things in my life. I've had a lifetime of avoiding and dispatching mobs and hunters and those who would harm me. But I have never known a force as persistent as Abzavine."

Elias's skin broke out in goose bumps. "So he has a name."

"One you should forget. I did my best to thwart him, but he…" She shuddered. "He will not stop until he has your mage gun. He called it—"

"Diablo." Elias closed his eyes. "And I don't have it anymore."

Progenitor Underwood studied him. "You really don't, do you? What happened to it?"

"It's gone. You don't need to worry about it."

"But I do." Shadows darkened her face. "He's furious with me for the way I've betrayed him. He'll find me soon. The link between us hasn't been severed. The only way I can save myself now is to present him that which he desires most."

Elias watched her, gave a chuckle. "Deals with the devil don't tend to go well."

"He is worse than any demon I've known. He's a...a monster." She gripped his hands. "Listen to me, Elias Blackthorn. When the mage gun stole my powers, it also took my curse. When I die, my spirit will be forcibly returned to the realm of progenitors—the unending torment you call hell. If you do not wish to be forever trapped there, you must relinquish the gun before you die."

Elias set his jaw. "I don't have it."

"But you know who does. Tell me so I can relieve them of that burden."

When he didn't respond, her pale face warped into an ugly mask of anger. *"Tell me!"*

Elias gave a spumy cough, and she backed away in disgust. As she did, he tugged at a loose thread in the coverlet. He rasped, "Come closer. I'll whisper his name to you."

The vampire's face softened, and she leaned down, her perfumed bosom brushing against his chest.

Elias yanked the thread hard to pull it loose. He spoke a quick incantation as it fell over the progenitor, and she stiffened as the spell tied her down against him.

Her eyes flared wide. "You think your little parlor trick can keep me trapped?"

Elias smirked. "No." He grabbed the lantern his son had put by his bedside, cinched one arm around the woman's narrow waist, then smashed the lantern against her back.

The oil sluiced across them both and immediately caught flame. Underwood shrieked, and Elias hugged her tighter, thinking of his son dawdling through the market, looking for an apple he'd never find.

Sweet boy. He prayed Diablo would protect him, prayed his son would forgive his father's sins, and for the burden he'd placed upon him.

He gripped the vampire with all his strength as the blankets and bedclothes went up in smoke. His flesh boiled away, but he didn't feel pain. Just a sense of freedom…and utter sadness.

I'm sorry, Elias, he thought, when his viselike grip around the vampire's waist crushed around an empty bodice, a dress full of ashes. And then he, too, was ash.

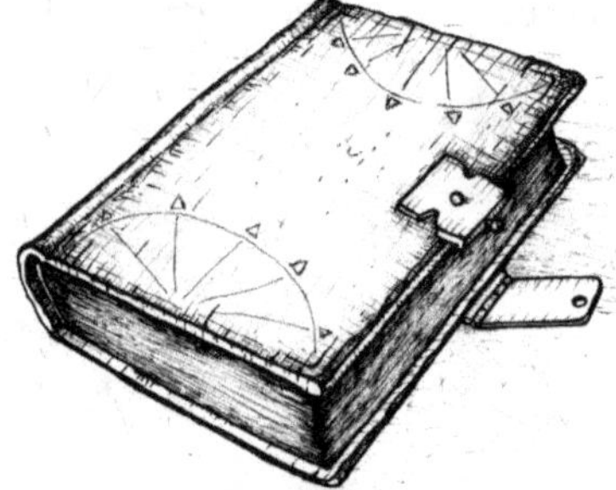

CHAPTER THIRTEEN

MONTANA

Ling was a steady travel companion. With days of riding to fill, Cymon loping happily at their sides, Hettie told her story at her pace. The more she told him, the more she wanted to tell him. Ling was a good listener, and it felt good to unburden herself to someone from her old life. Someone who knew her sister's habits, who'd known the ranch and her parents.

In turn, he recounted his time with Abby in San Francisco. She loved hearing all the details about the training she'd undergone with the sorcerer Ling called Auntie Wu. He went into minute detail, seeming to know Hettie wanted to hear about the food they'd eaten, the state of the beds and rooms they'd inhabited. Abby had sounded comfortable. Happy, even.

Then Ling recounted the strange events that had led him to discover the Division's experiments on kidnapped Chinese sorcerers, and the "hog" engine that had sunk in San Francisco Harbor. He told her about how, in their most desperate hour, Abby had somehow transported him and all the captives to the other side of the world. And he told her about the journey back across the ocean to find her.

"But…how did you get back into the States? Isn't there a ban on Chinese immigrants?"

"Getting into the country isn't difficult if you have the money and the resources," he said grimly. "Ah-Gu funded my trip and got me the appropriate papers. Technically I'm a representative working for her business interests here."

"You could have stayed in China."

"My duty to Abigail and to you remains unfulfilled," he said simply. "And now that your uncle is dead… your father would not want to see you alone."

"I don't need protecting," she said gruffly.

"Nevertheless, I am here." He sat straighter. "The fates have guided me to you. With luck, they will guide us to Abby as well."

She wasn't sure she liked either the fates or luck, considering all they'd put her through. "How'd you even know where to start looking for Abby?"

"She'd sent us to the place we all felt safest—home. Following her unusual logic, I believed that she was heading to find you. I tracked your last known whereabouts to New Mexico, but the trail ended there."

"So you saw Swedenborg."

"What was left of it." He nodded grimly. "Abby's indigo power was everywhere, even after all those months. She put up quite a fight before they managed to subdue her. I followed the trail for miles. They'd taken her east to what used to be a Division stronghold. They remote Zoomed from there. I managed to track down and interrogate one of the Zoom sorcerers, and he told me they'd traveled to Kentucky, but that wasn't their final stop. I've been crisscrossing the country, following that lead for the past two years, but Abby's indigo trail has faded. That's why we're headed to Montana."

"This man we're looking for," she prompted. "How'd you hear about him?"

"Dugald Smedley was never an inconspicuous agent," Ling admitted distastefully. "A bit of a blowhard with a penchant for gambling. In my early days at the Division, everyone seemed to know him. His father was a decorated senior agent on his way to joining the council of elders. Smedley leveraged that to bully others into doing his work for him, using his name and his charm to dazzle the instructors. His talent was in influence magic, too, which made him doubly dangerous. Eventually people caught on to his manipulations, trusted him less, started protecting themselves against his power." Ling pursed his lips. "Not that that stopped him from rising in the ranks. His father got him his post, of course."

"Never underestimate nepotism. So how'd you know to follow the Fielding expeditions to find Abby?"

"I told you about the hog. This Division project has many applications, but I believe they're concentrating the magic supply to feed Abby's indigo abilities. She took in the powers of dozens of sorcerers as if they were nothing more than a piece of taffy, and then she opened a remote Zoom portal to the other side of the world without breaking a sweat. With powers like that, I believe the Division must be leveraging her. They could be feeding her the power from these canisters to do whatever they want her to."

"Why not feed her blood? Wouldn't that be just as good?"

"I don't think you understand the extent of her powers," Ling said. "Blood can fuel her regular magic, yes, but her indigo abilities far exceed any known magic in this realm. The pure essence of magic, or whatever is being siphoned off the sorcerers, seems to be much more potent and reliable. If just a small taste can get her to do all the things she did in San Francisco, there's no telling what they can achieve with more." He gazed at the horizon. "Rumor is, Smedley supposedly abandoned his post after his last canister delivery. He's wanted by Division truancy agents. I think he saw something he shouldn't have and ran."

"Do you think he knows where Abby is?"

"At the very least, I'm certain he knows where the canisters are headed. That's the best lead we'll have on Abby."

They stopped in every town and way station they came upon, asking about Dugald Smedley. Unfortunately Hettie didn't know what the man looked like except by Ling's description: a white man with dark hair, fat around the face, with muttonchops and a particular affinity for flashy talismans. Being a sorcerer well-versed in influence magic, he could have cast a glamor to change his appearance, but Ling seemed confident he'd be able to pick the man out of a crowd.

One morning, Cymon sniffed the air and his tail wagged hard. He took off into the grass, a dark streak bounding fast across the plains.

"Cy, wait!" Hettie took off after him, cursing the dog. They didn't always ride under the time bubble, but closer to towns they did, and since she hadn't juiced for days, the bubble stretched thin the farther he went. He left a trail through time like a flowing river, his path cutting a swath of swaying green through the time-frozen world.

"Cymon!" Hettie's horse crested a hill. The time bubble suddenly popped, and the wind rushed through her ears and stung her eyes, bringing tears.

Her skin prickled as she took in the scene spread out below. A ramshackle house. A ruin of a silo and barn, overgrown with weeds and wildflowers. And there, perched above it, the old tree where her family was buried.

The ranch.

Home.

Cymon barked happily as he sniffed the ground, remarking familiar territory with gusto. Hettie approached a little more warily.

"Gods." Ling breathed. "I can't believe I didn't recognize where we were. I know you told me it'd burned down, but… I'm so sorry, Hettie."

Silently she spurred her horse forward, steeling herself to face the past.

Without the ability to love her parents, the ranch offered little in the way of nostalgia except for what her memories of Paul and Abby and even Uncle provided. The rubble still had not been cleared, and the roof of the house had leaked and caved in. Long grasses overran just about everything, including the hummock that had once been the woodpile—the scene of her near death.

She gazed at the dilapidated house, wondering if there was still anything left inside worth salvaging.

Ling let her go in alone. Predictably, the house had been ransacked in the years she'd been away. Very little was left. Clothing, cookware, furniture—anything that wasn't nailed down had been taken away. Even the potbellied stove had been ripped out. There were even places where the polished floorboards had been pried up, leaving gaping holes all through her childhood home.

Instead of anger, a curious sense of acceptance filled her. This was no longer her life—it never had been, really, considering her father had built the place on a foundation of lies.

Maybe she should finish the job. Burn the house to the ground and whatever sham of a legacy it stood for and spite the scavengers in the process. She wondered what the people of Newhaven might have learned about Pa and his past as the outlaw Elias Blackthorn in the time since she'd been gone. She wondered what they thought about her taking her father's place.

Diablo suddenly jumped in her hand, yanking her arm around with such speed she nearly pulled the trigger. *What are—?*

A shadow flickered in and out of her vision, just at the corner of her eye. The hairs on Hettie's neck rose. Had a ghost taken up residence? Was Paul or someone else reaching out to her to berate her, to haunt her for neglecting the house, her sister…

No one was there.

"Ling?" she called out. No answer.

"Rok?" she croaked.

The raven resolved, inky black in the gloom. *"Home, home, never come home,"* he squawked, then gave a laugh. *"Little girl can't come home again."*

She ignored him. "Was that you just now?"

"No, no. Just shadows of the past."

The floorboards above her creaked in what had once been her room. She knew every inch of this house, and now she could recall the distinct sound of every footstep across the worn wood. Ma's soft step as she went to make breakfast. Pa's heavy boots clomping up the stairs after a long, hard day. Even Paul's clumsier steps—he'd had big feet.

Abby's footsteps were too soft to ever be heard, though. A ghost through the world…

The creak came again.

Hettie quietly removed her boots, drew her bowie knife, and climbed the stairs, avoiding the fourth and seventh steps, which had always groaned underfoot. She switched her knife to her other hand and summoned Diablo. Whoever was in here was sure to be armed, and if it was kill and lose a year of her life or be killed instantly, she wasn't taking that chance.

She crouched down. "Whoever's in my room better jump out the window," she said loudly. She dropped into her time bubble and opened the door.

The man had his back pressed to the farthest wall, eyes canted toward the window. He had a revolver in his hands, gripping it too tight. The hammer hadn't even been pulled back. Hettie studied him a second and released a sigh before holstering her weapons and plucking the revolver from the man's hands.

He slipped into her time bubble, jumping away when he found her standing next to him, his own hands empty.

"Will Samson." Hettie greeted blandly. "Been a while."

Will's eyes widened. The blacksmith's son who'd lent her a dollar on that fateful day of the shooting contest had grown up some over the past four years. He sported a short, dark blond beard, and he was broader and more muscled now. He wore a deputy marshal's badge on his vest, but he smelled of smoke from his father's blacksmithing business. "H-Hettie?"

She shoved his gun in her belt. "What're you doing in my house?"

He searched her face, blinking hard. "I-is it really you? What happened?"

With her lined face and gunmetal-gray hair, she reckoned she must look older than his ma. "Depends. Are you asking in the name of the law?" She nodded at his badge.

"I'm only a deputy," he said defensively. "I come out here now and again to make sure the place isn't being ransacked."

"And to make sure the notorious outlaw Hettie Alabama hasn't come home to roost, I s'pose." She hitched up her gun belt. "Considering the state of things, I'd have to conclude you're failing at your duties, deputy."

His Adam's apple bobbed. "I don't believe the stories for a second, Hettie," he hurried to say. "The Division has to be lying about everything you've done."

"What're they saying that you don't believe?"

"Murder, robbery, arson, kidnapping, rustling…" He scoffed, albeit nervously. "I don't know that there's a single charge they haven't put on you."

She sighed and folded her arms. No sense lying to him, even if it meant she'd lose his respect and whatever was left of their friendship. At least she'd spare him from the danger of associating with her. "I'm afraid it's all true, Will. Every word."

He paled. "Oh."

"Whatever you think of me, though, I don't hold it against you. I've done some bad things, not because I wanted to, but because I was forced to. But I won't do 'em to you…unless you give me cause to." She wondered why Diablo had been so protective of her when Will could barely swat a fly without feeling bad. "Must be why Cymon didn't bark. He recognized your scent."

She walked out of her old room, and Will followed. "Truth is, Will, I'm not all that interested in criminal enterprises. I'm looking for Abby."

"Abby?" He blinked. "I thought… Didn't she…?"

"It's a long story. I found her with the Crowe gang, but then the Division took her from me three years ago, and all we've got for a lead is a name. We're in these parts looking for a man called Dugald Smedley. Fat around the face, muttonchops…"

"The gambler."

Hettie's heart leaped. "You know him?"

Will grimaced. "He plays cards at the saloon in Newhaven, day in and day out. He's been in the middle of a few fistfights now, whether he wins or loses. Gets out of it every time, the slimy charmer."

"He's a sorcerer who specializes in influence," Hettie told him. "He's probably casting a spell on folks around him."

Will went quiet, his face drawn. "What?" she asked.

"You don't know?"

"Know what?"

"Two years ago, the Division rolled through. They were testing a device in the old mines…and something happened." He bit his lip. "The magic's gone from Newhaven. All of it."

Hettie found Ling, and Will told them the story. A Division team had come to town with what everyone had thought was a Fielding engine, but instead of lining up the sorcerers to "bank" their magic, they'd traveled to the long-depleted mines.

No one thought much of it at the time; the Fielding expeditions hadn't been as suspect back then. Only recently, when sorcerers started being arrested or detained and rumors of accidents started spreading, had people become more resistant to the mandatory banking of magic. Hettie wondered how people would react when they learned about the man-things.

"One day we had magic," Will said. "Then, at night, something happened. The ground shook. It rippled like a wave on a blanket, shaking us all topsy-turvy. And then we heard folks screaming. The gifted, all of them on the ground, flopping like fish. And there was light coming out of them, and out of the ground, as if they'd been full of flames all along. There was a big cloud of pure light everywhere for a long time, but maybe it was just a few minutes. I don't know." He shook his head. "The light just kind of hovered there. And slowly it was heading back to the mines, flowing like a river downstream. After a bit, it was all gone, and it was dark again. Everyone went to bed with magic, and the next morning, it was all gone." He hung his head.

"Did anyone go to the mines to see what had happened?"

"We couldn't get close. Marshal sent a posse out there, and Division enforcers turned 'em back. The sorcerers were getting mighty antsy, so the marshal requested help from the cavalry. They wouldn't help. Their orders came straight from Washington to facilitate the Division's banking efforts. By the time we did finally get out there with a mob, they were gone."

Grover Cleveland had always been agnostic when it came to his stance on sorcery. No mundane president would alienate either the pro- or the anti-magic demographic. With the rise of the Mundane Movement after Swedenborg's downfall, however, the tide had changed. William McKinley had run on a platform that heartily endorsed the protection of the gifted from harassment and violence, and supported Division autonomy to achieve peace and stability for the gifted. Once elected, the president had given the Division even more power over magical affairs. Ironically, that self-governance had come at a high cost to the sorcerers they were supposed to protect.

"Sounds like the Division," Hettie said. "How are the sorcerers?"

"That's the worst part. They all went mad. Ran out of town, first toward the mines and then..." He shrugged. "They left families behind. Children. Just ran into the woods and the fields and never looked back."

"I don't understand." Ling looked around, and then, for good measure, opened up a glowing palm. "Magic doesn't just leave a place. My magic comes from me—my qi. Every tradition and belief has different origins for their magic. It doesn't just go *missing*."

"Well, that's the thing, Mr. Tsang. The Alabama ranch is just outside of what we call the dead zone. Just beyond the Gunnersons', no magic works."

"None?"

"See for yourself."

They did. Ling, Hettie, and Will rode out past the Gunnersons'. The couple's ranch had been abandoned, too, and likewise ransacked. "Poor Mr. and Mrs. Gunnerson were killed by one of those sorcerers gone mad," Will explained regretfully. "Bashed their skulls in like pumpkins."

Hettie's stomach churned. The horses faltered, and Cymon stopped dead in his tracks and whined.

"This'd be it." Will pointed at the series of stakes tied with black ribbons marking out a rough border that curved around the town. "No magic from this point on."

"Has any sorcerer crossed in and lost their powers permanently?" Ling asked.

"No. They simply can't use magic within the dead zone."

"Like a null spell?" Hettie asked.

"No. This is different." Ling closed his eyes, swiping a hand over his face. He gazed past the border, eyes wide. "It's like there's nothing there. As if the world just... ends on this side."

Cold trickled down Hettie's spine. "Maybe you should stay out of Newhaven," she said. "In case this dead zone takes your magic, too."

"It won't," Will assured. "Henry Bale, the sorcerer's salon owner? He wasn't in town that night. When he got back to Newhaven, he found the place in chaos, and his powers wouldn't work. He closed the salon and left town—the marshal had me escort him. Once he was outside the border, he got his magic back. He helped mark most of the null zone before he left."

"Where'd he go?"

"Not sure." He scratched his nose. "Got the feeling he didn't want to be around to answer to the Division, neither."

Hettie looked at Diablo. If there was no magic past this point, she'd be going in without the mage gun's fantastic power. Of course, she still had the gun itself, and her knives. But no time bubble. No easy exit.

And everyone in Newhaven would know her.

She didn't have much choice, though.

She spurred the horse forward, and Ling followed. She felt nothing at first. Not even a tingle.

She looked to Ling, who seemed equally confused. He opened a palm and stared; narrowed his eyes and focused. His breath quickened as he touched the talismans at his neck, whispered incantations, one after another, panic increasing.

Hettie tried summoning Diablo, talking to it, using the time bubble. Nothing happened.

"Step back across the border," Will said, half amused and half sad. "You'll be fine on the other side of the line."

Ling did so. He snapped his fingers and a spark lit between them. He sighed in relief.

"Well, I guess we'll have to manage." Hettie readjusted her gun belt and looked to Will. "Deputy, I'm afraid I'm going to have to keep your gun."

"What?"

"Sorry, Will. It's for your own good, really. You know I could've outdrawn you, and I can see the ring on your finger, which means you've got a wife to support. Congratulations, by the way."

"I got married last year," he said faintly. "And Deborah's six months along."

"Congratulations doubly then." She pulled her gun on him but kept it hanging loosely at her side. "Now, I can't ask you to turn your back on your duty and ignore the fact that I'm here. A man's gotta feed his family, and frankly the bounty on my head is too much of a temptation, even for you." She squinted at the horizon. "I won't kill you, on account of our past friendship. I'll even leave you all your limbs. But your gun's coming with me. And your horse."

Will moaned. "Aw, Hettie! Do you hafta?"

"Yup. I'll leave your effects at your father's place when we're done." She'd leave a small present for the new baby in his saddlebag, too. "But for now, for your safety, sit tight here. In fact, stay the night. Pa used to keep a flask of whiskey in the cellar on top of the highest shelf. It might still be there. Tell the marshal you got drunk, lost your gun, and fell off your horse."

Will grumbled and dismounted, and Hettie tied the reins to her saddle horn. She tipped her hat. "Sorry again, Will." She clucked her tongue, and the horse started forward.

"Think he would've done like you asked if he'd known your gun wasn't loaded?" Ling asked as they rode away.

She drew Diablo from its holster. "Remember the day we found this? I loaded it with .357s from my rifle." She snapped the wheel open, displaying the filled chambers. "As many times as I've cocked the hammer and pulled the trigger, they've never been used."

Ling grimaced. "Let's hope it stays that way."

CHAPTER FOURTEEN

Newhaven had definitely seen better days.

The sorcerer's salon was closed, of course. From what she could tell, some derelicts had moved in to make it a one-dollar whiskey joint and card hall. Many shop windows and shelves were empty. The Chinese laundry was shuttered. The tannery where the shooting contest that had started Hettie on her misadventure had been shut down, too. The Robsons must've moved on.

She looked for friendly faces among the townsfolk but found none. People hurried through the streets, heads down, faces grim. If they paid her any mind, they gave her a wide berth as she and Ling hitched their horses outside the saloon.

"Better make this quick," she said. "I don't need anyone recognizing me."

Cymon sat on the porch to watch the horses. Ling and Hettie pushed through the swinging doors. The place was quiet, the piano in the corner silent in the midafternoon. A couple of barflies dozed in chairs. Only one table was occupied by a group of five poker players.

Ling nodded toward the soft-jowled man facing the door. The dark, curly bristles of his muttonchops looked like sheepskin glued to his face. He had small, beady eyes, and his hair was greased back.

He wore a fine-looking gray suit, though the elbows were frayed and worn, probably from the way he leaned against the table.

"Are we playing cards or not, gentlemen?" His twang sounded like an affect to Hettie's ear. As if he were a more cultured man playing at sounding the yokel. Or perhaps it was the other way around.

One by one, the men folded. Smedley grinned as he put a pair of queens down and gathered his winnings with a sweep of his arm.

Hettie made her way to the bar, turning her back on the card players but watching them through the reflection on the long, cracked mirror above the shelves of whiskey.

"We can't confront him here," Ling murmured. "Not without magic. We should wait till their game is done."

Behind the bar, a woman in a fine dress languidly made her way toward them and leaned up against the counter. "What'll you be hav—" Her eyes widened. "Oh. Oh!"

Hettie's hand went to her gun as recognition fluttered over the woman's face. But then Hettie realized she knew the woman, too. Her face was smoother, fuller, and her once-limp hair was now artfully arranged, but Hettie did not miss those sharp eyes. "You... you're..."

"Missy Parsons. From Hawksville." Her smile broadened. "Hettie Alabama. As I live and breathe."

Ling's gaze darted around nervously.

Hettie dropped her chin and tugged her hat down. "I'm sure you have that wrong..."

"Hush now." Missy quickly got to pouring them each a drink. "This one's on me." She leaned in. "I ain't givin' you up to the feds or anyone else."

Hettie relaxed. "I thought you came to Newhaven for a new life." She took in their surroundings with a glance. It was a step up from the inn where she'd found her, but...

"I ain't whoring anymore, if that's what you're wondering. When I first came, I got a job as a shop assistant, but then the Division drained all the magic out of here, and things took a turn. Job market ain't what it was." She sighed. "At least for now, I'm a hostess. Wages are a bit better, and I'm not on my back all day. But it seems Newhaven's the new Hawksville." Her gaze grew distant, and her expression clouded. "Seems I can't catch a break. Maybe I was born to this life. Maybe it's all the Lord has for me."

Guilt lodged in Hettie's craw. It wasn't her fault Missy's fortunes hadn't turned, but she felt responsible nonetheless.

"Did you ever find your sister?" Missy asked.

"It's a long story. Short end of it is, we're still looking." She sipped her drink, letting the whiskey burn its way down. "You know the fancy man in the gray suit?" She notched her head to indicate the card game.

"Who, Dugald? Just about everyone here knows that cardsharp." Her narrowed gaze canted toward him. "Handsy and a lousy tipper. Gets into the occasional fistfight, sore winner that he is, but he pays his bills and hasn't caused any real trouble so far. You're not bringing it to him, are you?"

"Not if he's cooperative. We need to arrange an interview with him," Hettie said.

"About what?"

"Nothing of major concern. We just need to ask him a few questions, then we'll leave town. No muss, no fuss."

Missy shook her head. "Paying customers are harder and harder to come by these days. His tab keeps me off my back. I can't jeopardize that."

Hettie unfolded a wad of bills from her inside pocket. The woman's eyes went wide. Hettie deliberately counted a few out, then a few more, and put them on the counter. "We're just two businesspeople looking to get a transaction completed. Maybe you could put us up in a room for the evening, send up some dinner, and then extend an invitation to Mr. Smedley to join us?"

Missy smirked and slid the bills toward her. "Miss Hettie, I do believe you're flirting with me."

"I've a hearty respect for working girls. Think Dugald does, too?"

"Can she be trusted not to turn you in?" Ling asked once they were ensconced in the room. It smelled musty, but the sheets seemed clean enough. What else happened in this room was not something Hettie wanted to think about.

"She said she wouldn't; I'm inclined to believe her."

"But she's a whore."

"And I'm a murderer." She met his eye. "You don't know this, but she helped us in Hawksville. She could've turned us over to the mob back then, but she didn't."

"You didn't have a bounty on your head then."

He was being cautious, of course, but Hettie was certain Missy wouldn't call the authorities on her. "Some things are worth more than money. Missy gets that. How're you feeling? With no magic, I mean?"

"It's…strange. Quiet." He shook his head. "I seldom reach for my magic, but knowing that I don't have it, that it's not there when I might need it…"

"Minor inconvenience?"

"It's more than that. It's a bit hard to describe. Magic has always been a part of who I am. It's determined where I stand in the world. I know I'll still have magic once I leave this dead zone. But to suddenly not have it…to be essentially mundane…"

Hettie chuckled. "Welcome to the club."

He gave her a critical look. "With Diablo, you're just as gifted as I am. Maybe more so. Don't deny that your bond has changed you, Miss Hettie."

"At least I ain't itching to cast a spell."

"Aren't you?" He glanced down at her hands. She hadn't noticed, but she'd been scratching at her palms, and they were raw and red. She stilled them immediately and flexed her fists.

"I'm just antsy about Smedley," she snapped.

While they waited, they ate dinner and got a chance to wash up and rest. Dugald Smedley didn't leave his card game until well after midnight.

The doorknob rattled as someone jangled the keys in the lock. Hettie and Ling flanked the door while Missy dragged a stumbling Smedley in. He reeked of sweat and whiskey.

"I knew you couldn't resist my charms," the cardsharp said, unbuckling his pants. "Ain't a woman around who can say no to Dugald Smedley."

"I'd beg to differ." Hettie cocked Diablo, the hammer pulling back loudly as she pointed it at the man's heart.

He spun around, trying to pull up his pants from around his knees. "Wh-what is this?"

"Mind you don't make a mess," Missy said as she closed the door behind her.

Dugald swallowed visibly. "Listen, I've got money. Plenty of it. You want money? I've got a billfold in my jacket pocket—"

"Thank you, Mr. Smedley, I'll help myself. But that's not what we're here for."

Ling kicked a chair into the backs of his knees, making him sit down hard. He kept one hand on his shoulder and pressed the blade of a knife against his jawline. "Don't call out," Hettie said. "Don't scream. Otherwise, my associate will silence you."

"What do you want?"

"You were an agent for the Division in charge of a series of Fielding expeditions in the west before you abandoned your post. Isn't that right?"

"I don't know what you're talking—" He yelped as Ling's blade nicked him. "That hurts!"

"It'll do more than hurt if you don't answer our questions," Ling hissed. "Are you or aren't you Dugald Smedley of Haskleytown, Virginia?"

"Please, don't take me back there. You have no idea the things they did..." Sweat beaded on his upper lip.

"We're not Division truancy agents," she assured him. "We're not even bounty hunters. Though I understand there's a reward for information leading to your whereabouts."

"Whatever they're offering, I can double it. I can't go back there. They'll drain my magic, wipe my mind, turn me into an idiot and lock me up in an asylum—"

"Worry about what *we* can do to you first," Ling uttered lowly. "Tell us where the canisters from the Fielding expeditions end up."

"I...I don't know!"

Ling scraped the knife edge down Smedley's throat and the man gave a strangled cry, which Ling muffled with his hand. "You had to know where the collected magic was being funneled. What do you have to lose by telling us? You're in a magic dead zone. No silence spell can kill you here."

He made a frustrated noise. "I don't know because they never told us where the depot was. Everything got channeled through different locations to remote Zoom sites, and they only told us where those locations were a few days before the scheduled drop. They move the drop sites every few weeks!"

"What about Junesfield? Canisters were being delivered to the train there…"

"That's just one joint on a many-legged delivery system. I'm telling you, there's no way to know where the next remote Zoom opens unless you're an officer."

"Which you were." Dugald flinched as he met her eye. "So how do we find out where the next Zoom opens?"

"There's no way! The location comes through interpolation. They'd need to connect to you directly, have a piece of you to find you. They're not just broadcasting the location of the depot out into the open."

Hettie's grip tightened on the gun. If she shot him, there'd be no consequences—magically, anyhow. She wanted to do violence on this craven man. She couldn't be certain he was telling the truth, of course, and part of her wanted to drag him outside of the dead zone and get Ling to do a truthtelling spell on him just to be sure. But the fear in Smedley's eyes told her he had nothing to hide. No reason to invite torture when he had nothing to share and no loyalty to anyone but himself.

Ling asked calmly, "Tell us what made you leave the Division. What did you see?"

Dugald licked his lips. "Can't you buy me a drink first? It's a long story."

"Make it shorter."

Smedley huffed. "When we first started, our mission was to encourage sorcerers in all the small towns to bank their magic. It was all voluntary, and they determined what amount they wanted to bank. It was tedious. There were bank slips and receipts, a lot of paperwork…"

"But…?"

"We got orders that it was mandatory for every sorcerer to bank at least half. Then we got orders to take it all. We got reinforcements, and we were told to take every sorcerer and line them up for a full drain. We were to tell folks it was to inoculate them against a plague only sorcerers were getting. People were saying it got the soothsayers first. Now it was affecting everyone else."

"I never heard anything about a plague," Hettie growled, though of course she knew about the soothsayers' blackout.

"The Division's good at spinning yarns. Some folks knew about the soothsayers already. Then there were the stories of attacks by some kind of creature on the road targeting sorcerers. Those little backwater towns I visited were scared right enough, and the dimcans went willingly. Others, not so much."

"So you hunted 'em down like dogs."

"I didn't say I was proud of what I did. I was doing my duty. Taking orders."

"But then something changed," Ling prompted.

Dugald's shoulders shook. "On my last run, the sorcerers we drained caught up to us a couple of nights after we left town. We were prepared for an angry mob, but not..." He closed his eyes. "They killed all my men. Tore them limb from limb like they were animals. I ran and didn't look back."

Hettie swallowed thickly. "What happened to the engine?"

"Oregon," Ling interjected on a shaky breath. "That was the accident in Oregon. The one that exploded above the town and killed everyone."

"It didn't explode," the former agent said. "The Division just made it look that way. Those...things cracked it open with their bare hands, releasing the magic. When the cleanup crew came, they made it look like an explosion. They didn't want anyone to know about those drained people who'd attacked them."

"None of this helps me," Hettie said impatiently. She cocked her gun and put it to Dugald's head. "You've got ten seconds to tell me something useful about how to find the Fielding depot. Ten..."

"I've already told you, I have no way to know!"

"Nine...eight..."

"Take me outside the dead zone and use a truthtelling spell. I'm not lying!"

"Seven...six...five..."

"Hettie..."

Dugald's whole body shook, and sweat gathered at his temples. "Th-there's nothing I can do! I'm MIA! Dead, for all they know! I can't go back!"

"Four, three, two..." She dug the barrel of the gun against the base of his skull. She hoped his fleshy neck was enough to muffle the gunshot.

"All right! Don't shoot!" he screamed. "I...I can reestablish contact with the Division. Intercept the interpolation."

Hettie kept the gun pressed into his nape. "How?"

Dugald huffed. "I came to Newhaven because of the dead zone. No magic works here, so they wouldn't be able to find me. I found a way to block out the Division's Eyes and Ears. I had to juice up pretty heavily to get me all the way to Montana without them Seeing me. I break that spell and I'll hear them again. But I'd need to be closer to one of their outposts. They have talismans that help locate and transmit interpolation. There's one in Kilraven's Peak. Take me there, and I can tell you where the next depot drop will be."

Hettie's heart filled with hope, but then Ling gestured her aside.

"This is a terrible plan," he said quietly. "Kilraven's Peak is a day's ride away, and well out of the dead zone. We take him out of Newhaven and he'll have his magic back. He could use his influence powers on us, if he isn't already leading us into a trap."

"It's always a trap," Hettie said, "but it's all we've got to go on."

"He can't be the only Division agent who knows something. We could try to find someone else to at least corroborate his story. This is just walking into the lion's den."

"I can't just hope another lead will show up. Abby's alive, and she's out there, waiting for me." She let out a breath. "Three years, Ling, with the Division doing gods know what to her. I have nightmares about it, but before I heard her I could at least pretend it was just my imagination, leave myself room for doubt. I could...*hope* she was dead." The admission filled her mouth with a bitter tang. "But she's not. She's being held captive, and she's probably being tortured. I have to save her."

Ling bit his lip. "I'm as committed to this cause as you are," he said, "but we need to proceed with caution. We know little about this man and the lengths he might go to to escape."

"We can assume he'd go to every length," she assured him. "Which means we will, too."

ᛉ

They left for Kilraven's Peak before dawn. According to Dugald, the Division outpost lay among the cluster of hills that had never been of much use to anyone except the snakes and outlaws who sometimes hid among the jagged piles of sedimentary rock jutting up from the land. Legend said a couple of high-level sorcerers had dueled out here over the honor of a woman named Verity Kilraven, churning up the ground in their epic battle. It was Verity herself who'd stopped the fight, using all her power in one spell to stop the two men she loved from killing each other and sacrificing herself in the process. Love made people do strange things, Hettie supposed.

As the horses plodded along the trail, Hettie watched the trees. They were taking a huge risk, marching into the Division's clutches on a known liar's say-so.

She scratched at her palms and kicked her horse into a trot, eager to get out of the dead zone. She'd feel safer when she had Diablo's powers back.

"What will we do if he tries to give us away at the site?" Ling indicated Dugald, riding ahead of them. His hands were tied in front of him, and a rope attached to Hettie's saddle horn kept the man tethered to her. "A single shout and we'll be exposed."

"He'd get a bullet in the back before he got one peep out." This she said loud enough for the gambler to hear.

"The way I see it," Dugald said over his shoulder, "you'd put a bullet in me if I led you wrong. You'd put a bullet in me if I were lying. You'd put a bullet in me if you decided I wasn't worth trusting and you had to keep me quiet. Can't risk me reporting the infamous Hettie Alabama to the authorities, am I right?"

"I don't see how going straight to a Division outpost is improving your situation," Ling responded.

"Dead if I do, dead if I don't," Dugald replied. "I like living and breathing, thank you very much, and I'd like to keep doing so for as long as possible. Now, once I intercept the Division interpolation, they might notice and send people—or geises—after us. *You're* going to have to keep me alive and safe long enough for me to lead you where you want to go. Long enough even that I might convince you to let me go."

"You're *that* confident of this plan?" Hettie deadpanned.

"I'm a born gambler," he said, flashing a humorless grin. "Confidence is all I have when I'm down to my last dollar."

Outside the dead zone, Ling cast protection spells on himself and Hettie in case Smedley thought to use his influence powers. Hettie clamped a pair of iron manacles on the gambler to null his magic until they reached their destination. She kept a pair handy for exactly this kind of situation.

At the edge of the ridge, Hettie peered through her spyglass at the jagged hills, spotting movement clustered around a campsite.

"That's the Division all right," Ling confirmed. "The flags indicate it's a communications outpost."

"That's a lot of soldiers for a communications outpost," Hettie remarked.

"Nothing's ever what it seems." Dugald pointed. "I need to be as close as possible without being noticed, preferably above the camp. We can circle around the long way and make our way up to that plateau."

The trek took another three hours; they had to be careful not to attract notice. They clambered over slick, moss-covered rocks that protruded like snaggleteeth. A rabbit darted out of a hole, scaring Hettie into summoning Diablo. It bounded away, wiggling into yet another cranny.

In due course they arrived on a plateau high above the camp, affording them a perfect view and good cover. From here Hettie could see what she hadn't been able to spot before: train tracks.

The rails gleamed in the sunlight, curving alongside the camp and ending in the middle of nowhere like an unfinished thought. There was no station, no platform. Not even a bumper. The gravel berm simply tapered off, the rails jutting out impotently.

"When did they build those?" she asked, handing Ling the spyglass. He lay on the ground next to her as he observed the camp.

"They're new, I can say that much." He shot a look at Dugald. "You didn't mention the tracks."

"What do I know of railways? They build them everywhere. Why would this be important?"

"Because there's nowhere to go from here."

"Maybe they were put in to deliver supplies more easily."

"The road isn't that hard, and what would they need to ship out here that couldn't come by wagon?

A shout went up. The Division soldiers drew, whirling their rifles around. Dugald dropped to the ground like a stone. At first Hettie was afraid they'd been spotted, and Diablo jumped into her hand. But the soldiers swung away from them, westward.

A woman was limping toward them, hugging her elbows. Her dress was ragged and dirty. Her straggly hair hung around a too-pale face. A soldier holding a pistol shouted at her, his voice faint and incoherent from where Hettie was. The woman kept moving toward him. If she was saying anything, Hettie couldn't hear her.

The man tracked her with his sidearm, still shouting at her. But she kept going, still hobbling, not paying the soldiers any mind. They watched her as if waiting for an order to fire—but if there was one coming, the commanding officer wasn't giving it.

She was just ten feet away from the men now, reaching out her hands in supplication. The man with the pistol shouted. The gun cracked, the sound reaching Hettie a fraction of a second after the flash and puff of smoke exploded from the barrel. The woman jerked but didn't stop.

A shout, and the air was suddenly filled with gunfire. It echoed against the stone, sounding just like someone emptying a jar of nails onto a hardwood floor. The woman's body jerked left and right, falling to her knees as the bullets tore through her.

Finally, the woman fell facedown to the dirt and didn't move. One of the soldiers prodded the corpse. A pair of men carried it away on a stretcher, a dark stain left where she'd lain, and disappeared behind the rock formations around the hills.

Man-thing. Hettie's throat tightened. What was it doing out here on its own?

No, not on its own. Hettie bit her lip. There would be more nearby. More coming…

"Was that…?" Ling asked.

"We need to get out of here." There was no telling where the man-things were or how many of them. Hettie had no intention of finding out. She turned to Smedley. "You going to do your thing?"

He jangled the manacles. "Just say the word." He didn't look any more eager to stick around.

"Remember," she warned, brandishing Diablo. "One wrong move…"

"You'll put a bullet in me, yeah, yeah. I don't exactly want to get stuck out here, you know. Especially if any of those things are in the area."

He drew a protection circle on the ground in charcoal and asked Ling for a few ingredients for his spell—salt, sand, some kind of leaf, all of which Ling readily provided from a well-stocked catalog gifted to him by his patron.

Hettie had once thought to juice and learn some spells herself so she could defend herself against magical attack. But despite having done a lot of reading on magic, memorizing the ingredients, incantations, and minutiae that made up the intricacies of each and every spell was beyond her. She'd been wary of trying even the simplest of spellcraft. Too much could go wrong—Lena and the others had warned her of that. Now she only juiced to extend Diablo's powers.

"All right," Dugald said. "I'm going to begin. You"—he nodded to Ling—"are going to need to keep a close watch for interference from the Division once I make contact. I'm putting my ass at risk here. I might as well be dancing naked on the hilltop."

"How long will this take?" Hettie asked.

"Could be hours. It's not as if they broadcast interpolation constantly. It happens randomly. Daily. We could be here all week."

Hettie chewed the inside of her cheek. She didn't want to be anywhere near this place if man-things were about.

They didn't have much choice, though. Night fell, and Dugald remained seated in his circle, eyes closed. Ling had said the man had definitely performed some kind of communication spell and was in a meditative state, his mind open to receiving messages.

As the night dragged on, the cold seeped into her bones—they couldn't light a fire with the Division so close by—and Hettie grew restless sitting on her bedroll. She got up stiffly.

"I need to do my business," she said to Ling. She doubted the sorcerer would try anything with Ling watching.

"Don't go too far." Ling picked up his rifle and rested with his back against the cliff face.

She walked around the ridge, a little farther than she'd intended to go. She'd been wary all evening, on the lookout for man-things, expecting a horde of them to come shambling toward her up the path. That alertness was costing her. She was exhausted. More so than usual.

A metallic creaking noise made Hettie look around, searching for the night creature who sang that strange song. Movement near the camp had her crouching down. She pulled out the spyglass. Torches emerged from the tents as several soldiers hurried out to meet…a train. Not a locomotive engine, but two handcars towing a Fielding canister that, even beneath a canvas tarp, glowed eerily in the dark. The men pumping the handcars hopped off, and there was a flurry of activity as more soldiers emerged.

She couldn't tell exactly what was happening. Despite the torches, the people were just smudges in the dark. They arranged themselves at the end of the rails and didn't move for a long time.

A gust of wind drifted beneath her nose. She caught a strange, familiar scent—the first snowfall, icy and dry. No, not snow—

A pulse of power rippled over Hettie's skin as a remote Zoom spiraled open below, right at the end of the rail. The soldiers had removed the canister from the little platform and placed it on a wooden wagon, and now it was being pushed through to…to the depot!

This wasn't just a communications outpost. It was a direct line to wherever they were keeping her sister!

Hettie's heart hammered. That Zoom wouldn't stay open forever. She had to get her horse, race down there. She might make it through before it closed—

She spun around and slammed into a solid wall of flesh, falling back to the ground in a daze.

"Ling—"

It wasn't Ling. It was—

The butt of a rifle filled her vision as blackness took her.

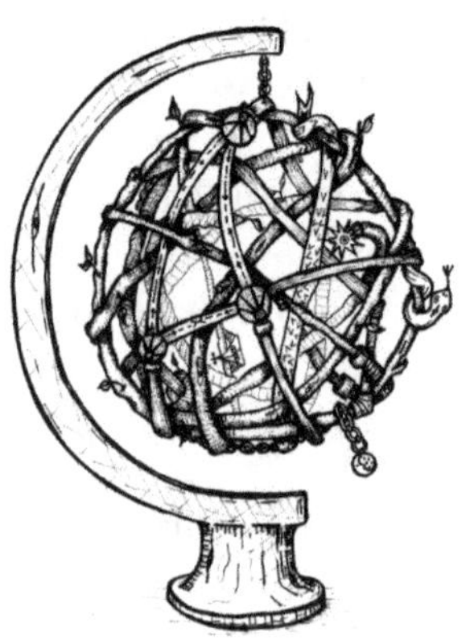

CHAPTER FIFTEEN

The knock on Jane's office door had her pen slipping, smudging the ink across the paperwork. She swore as she dabbed at the blot, making the mess worse. "Who is it?" she barked.

Hamish Gallagher stuck his head in, his face an unreadable mask. "If you have a moment, Agent Pinkerton?"

"You're still here?" She sat back, schooling the regret and other questionable emotions flitting through her at the professor's appearance. She hadn't seen him since returning to Chicago more than two weeks ago. "I thought you would've gone back to Boston by now."

"Mr. Pinkerton—your uncle, that is—had me consulting on a side case." He glanced at the visitor's chair, piled high with reports, and decided to remain standing. "I suppose he felt bad that I'd been dragged all the way out here for…nothing."

"I suppose you're here for an apology." She laced her fingers together and cleared her throat. "I admit I misled you. Though I swear I would have paid you with the reward money had we caught Hettie Alabama, or else from my own purse—"

He put up a hand. "Your uncle already explained your motivations. I'm sorry you lost your mentor. I understand now why you did what you did."

Jane released a pent-up breath. "Nonetheless, I lied to you. Put you in danger. Wasted your time."

He smiled lopsidedly. "I'd hardly call what happened a waste of my time. I met you, after all."

She ignored his compliment. "My penance." She gestured at the paperwork forming her prison. "For trying to do what's right, no less. Uncle William still refuses to discuss what happened. What we saw."

"I haven't had a decent night's sleep since then," Gallagher admitted, looking down at his fidgeting hands. "But no one wants to talk about Junesfield. Except you, I guess. I'm planning to write a letter to Congress to expose these horrible misdeeds—"

"Wait… My uncle let you keep your memory?" she asked, nonplussed. "No silence spell? No bribes or threats to keep you quiet?"

"I should hope not. It would be—"

"Standard operating procedure. You heard him. The Pinkertons don't get involved in Division affairs." She couldn't imagine William Pinkerton simply eschewing standard procedure.

Jane got up from her desk and paced, the sheaves of paper flapping in her wake. She considered Gallagher carefully, trying to puzzle out why her uncle would exempt him from the agency's strict code of silence. The professor wasn't entirely reputable, she supposed. He had a teaching job, but no tenure. He'd flunked out of the Academy. He'd only just made it through his university studies. And he taught in the field of Mechaniks, a questionable if not controversial subject in itself.

He was so mediocre, no one would ever take him seriously. Just as no one had ever taken his theoretical spell to separate the mage gun Diablo from its wielder seriously.

"This makes no sense. My uncle wouldn't have forgotten something so important if he were looking to bury this."

"Well, I'm not an official member of the Pinkerton Agency. I don't have any ties or contracts or anything that binds me legally or magically. Well, except to you."

Of course. The agency had a number of lucrative contracts with the Division—it couldn't be involved in any investigations that looked too closely at their works. Not officially.

But why leave Hamish Gallagher alone? What did he know that he needed to...

Jane inhaled sharply. "Your spell. Your theory for separating Diablo from the wielder. Do you still remember it? No one took it from you?"

"Yes...but what—"

She ran out of her office and down the hall.

"I'd rather not have my memory wiped, thank you," Gallagher called after her. "Uh, Agent Pinkerton?"

But Jane was already rounding the corner to her uncle's office. His secretary rose to stop her, but Jane pushed in without knocking.

"Uncle William," she declared, "I quit."

William Pinkerton looked up from his paperwork, his face set in stern lines. "Do you, now?"

"I no longer wish to work for the Pinkerton Agency, and...and renounce the privilege and protections afforded to me by this badge." That last part stuck in her throat. She took the shield from her belt and placed it on his desk carefully.

Her uncle held her gaze a moment longer. "Is this what I get, then, after everything I've done for you? I'll not hear the end of it from your father, you know."

"Uncle William, with all due respect, I have to do what's right, and I can't do it if you and Father insist on keeping me tethered to the agency."

"It's for your own protection."

"I know. And I appreciate it. But this case...finding Quentin's killer—"

"This isn't the Wild West anymore, Jane. We're men of the law, for all that's worth. We have to abide by the rules, even if the stakes are personal. This is the way civilized people behave."

"What happened in Junesfield was far from civilized—"

The flash in his eyes silenced her immediately. He canted his head to one side, then stood to inspect a portrait of his father, Allan Pinkerton, founder of the agency, hanging on the wall.

"My father used to say that finishing the job was the most important thing. The agency grew as fast as it did because he was ruthless, and he believed in the fights he took on, even if he ended up on the wrong side of history." He glanced at her. "Are you really ready to do what's right over what's necessary? Or do you only *think* you know what's right?"

"I have to do this, Uncle. Quentin..." She swallowed as emotions she'd spent a lifetime learning to suppress bubbled to the surface. "He was everything to me."

His shoulders sagged. He sighed and moved back behind his desk. "I didn't want to hear that. I'd hoped this Hamish Gallagher might have... well." He went on shuffling his paperwork. "Very well. I accept your resignation. You know your way out."

"I'm keeping the gun. It's mine."

"Mm-hmm. Mind you don't shoot yourself in the foot with it."

She waited a moment longer, hoping for something more, some words of wisdom or even just a good-bye handshake. When none was forthcoming, she turned around.

"Jane," he called, and she stopped. He met her eye. "I don't have to tell you just how dangerous Hettie Alabama and the Division are. And if you're no longer employed by our agency, you're subject to the Division's mandatory banking rules, meaning you'll be required to report to the nearest Fielding outpost. I'm not saying you should disobey that edict. But whatever trouble you do get yourself into, I can't help you."

She swallowed thickly. "I know."

"See Margaret on the way out. She'll give you your last paycheck and your... severance."

Jane left her uncle's office feeling strangely light and at odds with herself. What had she just done? No badge, no agency behind her... She was on her own now.

Gallagher caught up to her. "Jane, what happened?"

Not on her own. She grabbed his hand and dragged him along with her.

"Are you still interested in finding the Devil's Revolver, professor?"

He blinked. "Diablo? But I thought your uncle said..."

"I've resigned my position. I'm free from the agency's rules. Now I can do as I wish. If you're amenable to my terms..."

"You have terms?"

"A fifty percent share of the reward and everything I promised you before with respect to the mage gun, if you help me capture the outlaw Hettie Alabama."

"But what about the Division? And those zombie things…"

"They're all linked," Jane said fervently. "I just know they are. It's no coincidence Hettie Alabama was involved in the kidnapping of Alastair Fielding alongside Sophie Favreau. No coincidence Hettie Alabama was at Swedenborg and now Junesfield. She has been systematically raiding Fielding expeditions for a reason, and where those canisters are, the zombies follow. We're going to find out exactly how Hettie Alabama is involved in all this. And we're going to end her once and for all."

When Hettie's feet touched down in the place in-between, she shuddered. She didn't know exactly how she knew, but the place was empty, desolate, though part of her felt as if it should be full to the brim with people.

Instead she stood in a thick fog, the air cool on her skin, like a dead man's breath trickling down her neck.

"Is anybody out there?" she called. No response came.

Around her there was a shushing noise, like a great, heavy sigh. The rasp of wings taking flight surrounded her, and yet she could see nothing.

Her heart hammered, and she closed her eyes for what felt like a very long time, long enough that she might even have fallen asleep, if such a thing were possible in this place. Every time she'd appeared here, it had been for a purpose. She'd found someone to speak to, whether it was Patrice or Diablo or Javier…any of those faces would be welcome.

Still no one greeted her.

Her throat thickened, stifling a sob. "Rok?" she croaked out. She'd even welcome the demon familiar's yammering if it would break up that rush of wings.

A lone caw startled her, and she whipped around, searching the slate-gray skies for the bird. It was answered by another harsh rasp, and another, until the air was suddenly filled with angry raven cries, all of them berating and judging her.

"You're a disgrace to your family name."

"You'll never rest, you despicable criminal."

"The place you're going is far worse than hell."

"You've killed sons and fathers. You've taken lives worth much more than your own."

"This is far less than you deserve."

Hettie stiffened, willing the tears of hopelessness back behind narrowed eyes. "Ain't nothing you can say I don't already know," she bit out. "But if you think you're so brave casting judgment from the shadows, why don't you come out and face me?"

The rush of wings tapered off, and the cawing died out. Hettie almost wished they'd come back instead of leaving her in wretched silence.

She started walking, having little else to do. The road in-between had to lead somewhere, but without a guide, it wasn't as if she knew where to go…

Diablo resolved in her hand, and Hettie jumped. It hadn't even occurred to her to summon the mage gun. It ticked in her palm, tugging her arm like a hound on a leash.

She veered around, following the gun's lead. In less than five steps, a door appeared. Plain wood with a brass doorknob, just like…

Just like the door to Abby's room back on the ranch.

Her breath stuttered. "Abby!" She grabbed the doorknob and turned it—

A force like a fist slammed into her face, knocking her straight out of the in-between, as if the fog-filled world were just in the other room and Hettie had stumbled through the doorway. She sat up gasping, coughing, her lungs feeling as if they were full of cobwebs. Her limbs were tangled beneath the bedsheets, and she struggled to throw them off, ensnared like a tiger under a net—

"My goodness!" a prim voice exclaimed. "Miss Hettie, it's all right, you're safe. Breathe, breathe…"

Diablo jumped into her hand as Hettie threw herself to the side, tumbling out of bed and crashing to the floor, banging her elbow hard. Bed? She pushed to her feet—yes, a bed with a canopy and fine white sheets with lacy eyelets. She swung her arm around, seeking her target, her head spinning, aching…

"Wooh…" She'd meant to say, *Who are you?* but it had come out slurred.

"I know it's hard to understand what's happened," the voice soothed, pleading, "but try to calm down and breathe. You've been asleep for a long time and haven't had anything to eat or drink. You're weak from the journey and the illness."

Illness? She searched her hazy memory. Flashes of a nightmare assaulted her. Monsters…creatures like men who hungered for magic…a ghost bird leading her through the fog…a pit full of snakes and blood…fire…

"Easy, easy." The spinning eased as she was helped onto the edge of the bed. Hettie felt so weak she could barely protest. "You need to lie down. I'll ring for some broth."

Hettie blinked up at the woman. She had brown hair with threads of silver all through it, and her eyes were a flat, pale blue, the pupils like the hole in a bead. She smiled, showing tiny teeth. For some reason Hettie thought of the mannequin heads milliners used to model their hats. "Who're you?"

"I'm Ophelia. Your lady's maid…" Her face fell. "You don't remember me?"

"Maid?" She shook her head, her thoughts cloudy. "I…I never had a…" Her temples throbbed, and she winced.

"Oh, dear. The fever must have affected your mind." Ophelia reached out but hesitated. "If you wouldn't mind putting the gun down…"

Hettie stared at the revolver in her grip. Diablo. She knew it was hers, knew it was a mage gun, knew its curse. Her understanding of it was firm. But when she tried to remember how she'd bonded to it…

Pain lanced through her skull.

"No one here will hurt you," Ophelia assured her quietly. "Please. Put the gun away and lie back. If anyone here meant you harm, you wouldn't have woken up."

That seemed to make sense. She set Diablo on the occasional table next to her.

Ophelia tugged on a bellpull. In a few short minutes, a different maid came with a tray of warm broth, a glass of milk, and a little bread with butter. Hettie sipped the broth cautiously, found herself ravenous, and gulped it down in seconds. Ophelia smiled gently.

"I'm so glad you're back," she said, tears roughening her voice. "I was so worried..."

Hettie felt a twinge of guilt, though she certainly couldn't be responsible for her illness. "How long have I been sick?" she asked thickly.

Ophelia clasped her hands. "Nearly two weeks now."

Two weeks? Hettie shot up at that proclamation, but her limbs were feeling heavy. "I...I can't be here. I need to... to..."

Need to what? She'd been headed somewhere...or had been looking for something... Someone? The impulse was seared in her mind like a brand, throbbed at the base of her spine, yet she couldn't discern what it was...

"What you need to do is lie down. You'll be no good to anyone if you fall back into your coma."

Hettie shook her head, even as Ophelia helped her into the feather-down bed. She sank into its cloudlike softness but fought the encroaching slumber.

"What happened to me?" she managed through puffy lips.

"Hush. We can talk more about it in the morning." The woman pulled the blankets up under her chin. Hettie snuggled down, a deep sense of safety and well-being permeating her.

Diablo popped into her hand. She pushed it under her pillow just as her eyelids drooped.

The dream began almost immediately. All around her, the world seemed to be shrouded in gray, with more and more tarps being dragged by phantoms over formless shapes, a grand house being closed up by its own ghosts.

When she next awoke, the heavy curtains had been drawn back, letting in the golden sunshine. Ophelia wasn't there, but a simple dress had been laid out for Hettie, along with slippers, undergarments, and a pitcher of warm water to wash with.

Slowly, Hettie got cleaned and dressed, her head throbbing and every muscle aching. At the same time, she felt strangely light, as if she'd been carrying a heavy burden for a long time and had been finally freed of it.

Diablo leaped into her hand. She scoffed. "You're needy, aren't you?" She wasn't sure why she'd said it out loud, as if she were admonishing a puppy dog. The mage gun sat mute in her hand, and for a flash, she thought it was *glaring* at her.

She laughed. She must have had quite a fever if she was thinking such fanciful thoughts.

She pushed out of her room, following the polished wood floor of the hallway and the heavenly scent of bacon and coffee down to the dining room. She passed a maid carrying an armful of linens, and the young woman stepped aside and greeted her demurely. Hettie had no idea what her name was. She wasn't even sure she ought to. But she nodded and moved on.

Everything here felt familiar and yet...alien, somehow. As if she'd come home after a long time away, but all the walls had moved and the rooms had been redecorated.

She scanned the paintings of serious men and women, recognized none of them, felt nothing toward them. She studied the wallpaper, a lattice pattern of vines and geometric shapes that seemed to shift like fronds in the wind. She felt as though she were walking through a hedge maze.

The dining room was bathed in light, though the windows were all barred. Brilliant white glow stones set in sconces lined the walls, casting their luminescence so not a single corner was in darkness. A manservant in a crisp uniform silently set a cup of coffee at the table and pulled out her chair. Then he went to the sideboard and collected a plate of eggs and bacon and toast for her before resuming his place by the door.

"Thank you, Gerard." It came out automatically. How did she know his name? She barely recognized him.

"You're welcome, Miss Hettie. It's...good to have you back."

She smiled. She didn't want to let on what she didn't know, so she applied herself to her food.

She put a bite of eggs into her mouth and flinched. Real silver. Why did that feel so odd? Surely she'd eaten with silverware before if this was her household. It was her home, wasn't it?

Hettie swept aside the odd thoughts and ate her breakfast. Gerard brought her a second plate without comment, though she got the distinct impression he was a little put off by her appetite.

"Where's Ophelia?" she asked.

"It's her day off, Miss Hettie," he replied, and added, "I believe she spends her day at the market."

That sounded right to Hettie, though how she could feel that way without knowing anything about the woman seemed strange. She glanced at the seat to her right, the head of the table, realizing it was empty. Who was supposed to occupy it, she wasn't sure, but there was an excitement inside her, buzzing beneath her skin as she stared at that empty seat.

Diablo leaped into her hand again, and a nervous laugh burst from her lips. "Silly thing!"

Gerard tensed at Diablo's appearance, and she put it in her lap. "My apologies. He's being very naughty today."

The doors opened, and a man stepped through. Hettie had the strangest urge to leap to her feet—not in ceremony but because…because…

Diablo whipped her arm up, and she squeaked.

"Ah, I see your reflexes are back. Good, good." The man's eyes twinkled as he poured his own coffee from the carafe. "I'm glad to see you up and about, Hettie."

She stared. She didn't know this man, though everything inside her told her she should. She studied the fine lines bracketing apple cheeks, the carefully coiffed white hair slicked back from his aristocratic face, the neatly trimmed white beard streaked with gray. His white linen suit was immaculate, and his leather shoes, also white, were polished to a glossy shine. He glowed beneath the overhead stone light and the rays slanting in through the bars and mullions. Most startling, though, as he sat down directly in a ray of sunlight, was the color of his eyes—sky blue with an outer ring of violet.

Her arm was still raised, Diablo pointed his way, weighing her down. She scowled at the mage gun. *What is wrong with you?* This man couldn't possibly mean to harm her. People who wanted to hurt her didn't feed her and clothe her and treat her to lavish breakfasts.

The man's face creased. "I guess you don't remember who I am," he said sadly. He gestured her to sit, and she did. Diablo stuck fast to her palm and wouldn't be set aside.

The man chuckled. "Stubborn thing, isn't it? Stubborn as you." He cut up his bacon. "I still remember the day you brought that thing home. Dug it up out of the creek bed and just couldn't help yourself. I'd told you any number of times how you shouldn't touch anything around here that I didn't tell you was okay to touch." He gave her a pointed look. "You remember that rule, don't you?"

She did. All the way to her bones. *Look, but don't touch.* She was certain it would be in the Bible if she cracked it open.

"Who are you?" she finally asked, scratching her palm.

He chuckled, though his eyes were sad. "Hettie, it's me, Pappy. I'm your grandfather."

CHAPTER SIXTEEN

"Pappy." Hettie rolled the word over in her mind, tasting it, unsure what she was sensing.

"Your pa's father," he clarified. "Sometimes you call me Grandpa Berkeley, but I like Pappy better."

She scanned the old man's features again and superimposed her father's face in her mind. Maybe there was some resemblance, but didn't all men start to look alike after a certain age?

"You don't remember me." "Pappy" sighed, putting his coffee cup down. "Your illness was worse than I'd expected."

Hettie's head throbbed, but she didn't say anything. "I just want to be...reminded." She wasn't sure why, but every nerve inside her screamed caution. "It feels like it's all on the tip of my tongue—like I've just woken up from a dream. Please, tell me...where am I?"

"This is your home. We're in Jasper, Kansas. You came to live with me after...after your parents were killed."

Something twinged at the base of her skull. Fire. Smoke. The screams of the pigs trapped in their pen by the blazing barn. Hettie shut her eyes, smelling the acrid tang of burning flesh, then blood and cordite and...lilies.

She gasped. "They were...they were shot."

"Outlaws came to your home, killed your family, but you survived. The marshal found you lying in a creek, nearly dead.

Doctors and healers brought you back from the brink, but you were in a sorry state for months. Raving and delusional." He leaned forward. "A fugue state, they called it. They wanted to have you committed to the asylum, but I refused. You're the last of my kin, Hettie."

She rubbed her temples. "So… I've been here how long?"

"Nearly four years. You came out of your fugue after about a year. You got better. You've been living here, helping me with my projects. Then you got sick. I thought I might lose you this time…" Tears wavered in his eyes, making the blue and violet wobble like the surface of a pan of water reflecting the sky.

He gave a tremulous smile. "But you're better now, and you'll get stronger. Your memories will return in time, too. You just need rest and good food and maybe a turn in the garden. You'd like that, wouldn't you?"

She supposed she would, though everything still felt… wrong, somehow. Like new boots she hadn't broken in.

They finished their meal, and then Pappy took her by the arm and led her through the house. Every door she passed felt familiar, as if she'd been here in a dream.

There were two wings to the house. Most everyone lived in the north wing; the south, Pappy told her, was where his collection resided.

"What do you collect?" she asked.

"A bit of this and that. I suppose the folks around these parts might call me eccentric for my tastes, but what good is money if you can't enjoy it?" When he saw she wasn't satisfied by his answer, he chuckled. "You loved studying and cataloging my items. But it's a lot to see, and I don't want to overwhelm you right away. We'll get to that later."

They emerged into the perfectly kept garden of full, colorful blooms and meticulously sculpted topiaries. Hettie marveled at the bushes trimmed to look like a pair of dancers. She glanced away when a brightly colored bird caught her attention, and when she looked back, she could've sworn the dancers had shifted positions.

"Did they… Am I…?"

"It's an enchanted shrub," Pappy said with a chuckle. "If it looks like it's moving, it's because it is. This whole garden is enchanted.

You think I have the time to prune these things?" He guided her farther along the path.

Above them a raven cawed. Hettie stared up, the huge, inky-black wings spread across the sky. It gave a loud shriek, and for a second Hettie thought it was calling her name.

Berkeley picked up a rock, then whipped it at the bird. The raven screamed and flapped away in a hail of feathers.

"I detest ravens," Berkeley said. "They steal items from the house all the time. It's why I had the windows barred. Wily things figured out how to unlatch the windows and were getting in."

The bird circled back around. Berkeley growled and cupped his hands. A blaze of power filled his palms, and he lobbed it toward the raven. The bird screeched as it exploded in a puff of red mist and black feathers.

"You're a sorcerer," Hettie said slowly, suddenly uneasy. It was only then that she noticed the large star sapphire brooch pinned to his cravat, the runes embroidered on his sleeves, the careful stitching around his collar forming perfect piping—places sorcerers were known to keep their talismans. He wasn't just well dressed: he was armed to the teeth with magicked charms.

"I'm a grandmaster for the Division. Did I not mention that?" He waved his hand around, and a big onyx stone ring winked from his thumb. "How do you think I can afford the upkeep of this place?"

A grandmaster. The Division had only designated a few sorcerers with that title. It meant that he had no specialty, that he was proficient in all the various forms of magic... including influence magic.

Hettie fought a wave of nausea and trepidation. "Can you tell me... more about you?" she asked. It wasn't a stretch for her to sound timid and unsure.

He smiled thoughtfully. "You call me Pappy, though it took you quite some time to do so after you came here. But my name's Wolverton Gray Berkeley the third. I was married to Hannah Mary King... your, er, grandmother. She's since passed."

She studied him. "You hesitated."

His face grew red, and he glanced away. "You never were very tactful. You get that from your father." He cleared his throat. "I hesitated because Hannah is not your biological grandmother. I had an...indiscretion with a woman in town, and she had your daddy. I brought the boy here to raise as mine and Hannah's, but Jack—your father—well, he was more like his momma than me, I guess, so he took off when he was thirteen. Took on a new name—a couple, actually. Disappeared off the face of the earth till the Pinkertons helped me track him down."

The Pinkerton name made her bristle, though she couldn't say why. She'd never encountered one, apart from reading about them in the papers.

"I've been answering a lot of your questions," Berkeley said. "Let me ask you a few of my own. What's the last thing you remember before waking up here?"

Hettie thought back, her head throbbing. "Not a lot. I kind of remember the night my parents died..." It seemed peculiar that she didn't feel sorry about it. She stared down at the gun stuck fast to her palm. "I don't rightly recall how I got Diablo."

"Ah, but you remember the mage gun's name. That's good, that's good."

"Why would *that* be good?" she asked. "I can't remember anything else."

"You really *don't* remember much, do you? And to think I paid for all those lessons with those experts and sorcerers..." He sighed. "Names are power, Hettie. The moment you bonded with Diablo and knew its name, you had control over it. You didn't let it rule you. The Devil's Revolver is just the name the legends gave it. El Diablo is the name its maker gave it. Its true name, however, is known only to the wielder—you. That's what allows you to relinquish it to others."

"But...I don't know its true name." Hettie searched her memory for any clue. She had only ever called it Diablo...hadn't she?

"You've likely never spoken it aloud. You may not even have heard it. The only reason I say this is important is because being bonded to this weapon puts you in as much danger as it does everyone else. Diablo is a big dog on a short leash. It's so busy snapping at everyone around it, it hasn't yet realized it could turn around and kill its master."

She'd heard these words before. A shiver slid down Hettie's spine.

"Not to worry." He folded her hands in his. "As long as you listen to me and do as I say, we will regain your memories and reestablish your dominion over Diablo. I won't let anything happen to you, my dear."

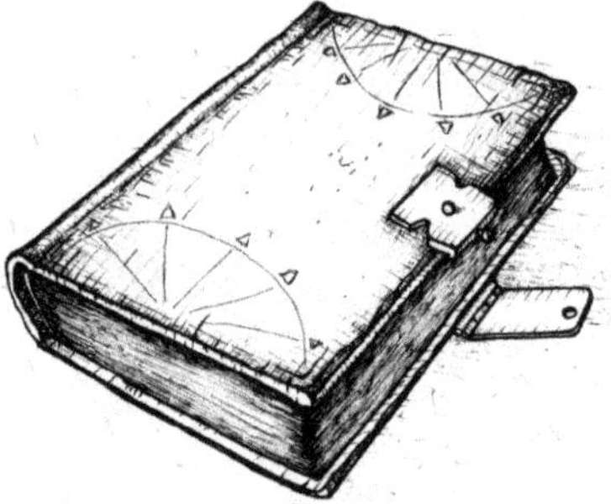

OREGON
1871

Jack Farham reined his horse in hard, kicking up a cloud of dust as it wheeled to a stop. "Get Doc!" he shouted. He slid off, careful not to jostle Jed. Two of the others helped ease the man off the horse's rump, and the poor gelding trotted away, its hind end wet with blood.

"What happened?" one of the men asked, pale.

"Sheriff was at the bank making a deposit. The idiot pulled on Jed—we didn't even see him." He ground his teeth.

"What about the take?" the other asked.

Jack shot him a glare that shut them all up. "Keep an eye out for Butch. We got separated at the bridge—he was trying to draw the deputies away." He hoped his friend was all right.

Doc got their leader to his tent, but as fast as his hands worked to stanch the wound, the stench of shit and the blood pooling around him indicated Jed wasn't long for this world. "Nothing I can do for him," Doc said grimly. "It's the end of Elias."

Jack hated that moniker. As much fear and awe as the name Elias Blackthorn inspired, those in the gang treated it like a title—a crown to be passed from one outlaw to the next. There'd been at least four Eliases he knew of, their reigns short. Soon there'd be a new Elias. And in his need to inspire more fear, to maintain that legacy of violence and horror, the new leader of the Blackthorn Rogues would begin a rampage to outshine all the Eliases before him.

That was how it always was, or so the story went. Jack wasn't sure he wanted to stick around for that. The Rogues under Jed Crowe were practical, sharp, striking with precision and efficiency. Jed could be cruel, but no worse than any other criminal he'd encountered. Jack both feared and admired Jed; he was the closest thing to a father he'd ever known.

"Jack..."

He briskly went to the man's side. "You're all right, Jed. We're back at camp."

"No. I'm dying, Jack. And if I do... The hell gate. It's gotta be you."

Dammit, where was Butch? The man needed to be here for his father. "Save your strength. Butch'll be back soon." He surreptitiously glanced at the blood-soaked bandages, holding his gorge against the foul odor wafting from the bullet wound in his abdomen. Damn sheriff couldn't aim to kill even at five feet.

"There's no time. Listen"—Jed gripped his wrist—"I know my son...he can't take on this burden. It'll destroy him."

"What're you talking about?"

Jed closed his eyes, his breathing labored. "He thinks leading the Rogues will be about hurting as many people as possible. I can't give him Diablo to do that with."

"But...he's your son."

Jed went on as if he hadn't heard him. "I never wanted this life for him. I just wanted him to be safe..." Tears leaked from his eyes. "I should never have left his momma. He needed a softer touch than me..." A deep, watery cough racked his chest. Jack poured whiskey from his flask into Jed's mouth, and he subsided.

"I done him wrong, Jack. Beat him and berated him. Thought it'd make him a man. A better man than me. I done him wrong."

"Don't talk like that, Jed. Butch'll be back soon. You'll make it all right with him, and then you can rest."

"Won't be no rest for me." He gripped his hand. "Diablo won't hurt you. It's been saying...telling me, you're the next Elias."

A spike of fear drove an icy wedge into his heart. "Jed, no."

"It's gotta be this way. You'll understand, I promise. But you need to know some things about Diablo..." He coughed wetly, groaning as blood spurted from the wound, trickled from the corner of his mouth. "There's a...a guardian. I don't know how to describe it to you. Diablo's running from something, some*one*, and it doesn't want to be found. Every time you fire it, *he* will notice and try to find you. The nightmares..." He shuddered. "You gotta keep it safe. Don't bleedin' fire it unless you have to. The power's in *not* using it."

The old man was raving. "You should be telling Butch—"

"I'm telling *you*. Promise me, Jack. Promise me, or I swear I will haunt you and yours till your bloodline runs dry."

"This'll hurt Butch. You said you don't want to hurt him. The gang should be his."

"The gang doesn't matter. Diablo does. I've got a reckoning ahead of me, and I need to know this, at least, might square things with Saint Peter...or the devil. Promise me you'll keep Diablo from Butch. I can't die peaceably unless I have your word." It came out strained, and the man arched and writhed.

Jack swallowed. "All right, all right. You have my word." He gripped his hand tight.

Jed's face went red as he fought whatever demon came to claim him in his final moments. He gave one last sob and pushed the mage gun into Jack's hands. "It's yours now."

"No, Jed, wait—"

As Jed's sticky blood made contact, power tingled across Jack's skin, and he fumbled the mage gun—the symbol the Blackthorn Rogues had followed for countless years. The ivory grip was buttery and warm, the glossy black finish winking in the lantern light. The gun set a million tiny hooks into his skin, catching like a stubborn burr.

"Diablo's yours..." Jed's eyes turned to the sky, and he gave a strangled cry, as if the demons hunting him had finally snared his black soul. A final exhale gurgled from his stiffening lips, and he was gone.

Pain welled up inside Jack, and he let out a single sob, dragging his sleeve over his damp face.

He sat back and bent his head and did his best to say a prayer for the man, even though God had forsaken them all long ago. He wasn't sure how long he knelt there, whispering his promises, before Butch ducked into the tent. "Pa?"

Jack stood slowly. Butch's eyes went from his father's body to the gun in Jack's hand. Jack stuck the revolver into his waistband. "I'm sorry, Butch. He's gone."

The starburst scar on the young man's weathered face bunched and creased, upheaval clear in the landscape of his emotions. Jack had never seen Butch cry—he'd once proudly told him his father had burned the tears out of him when he'd given him that anti-influence mark on his face. But Jack knew grief when he saw it, and though his friend didn't shed a single tear, he was hurting.

He eyed Jack steadily. "Is that Diablo?"

Jack put one hand over the grip protectively. "Yeah."

Butch's lips turned down. "That's mine, you know. Everything he's left behind rightfully belongs to me."

"I know." And yet Jed's words clung to Jack. Jed had been adamant about preserving his son's…honor? Integrity? Soul? None of those words fit whatever Jed had meant. And deep down, like the whisper of life shushing beneath the water, Jack knew he had to follow Jed's last wishes. "But he gave Diablo to me."

Butch's face contorted with something between disbelief and anger. "Why would he do that?"

"He didn't want to burden you with it, Butch. He made me take it to keep it out of your hands."

"Do you even want it?" The young man's eyes narrowed. "We've been friends forever, Jack. I think of you as a brother. And I know for a fact that you don't have the balls to lead."

Jack ignored his friend's insult. "You're right, I don't." He firmed his grip over the gun. "But Jed made me promise on his death."

"He's telling the truth." Doc emerged from around the side of the tent. "I heard it all, Butch. Your daddy made Jack the new Elias. Pretty sure he's bound by a blood oath."

Butch bore his teeth. "You turning against me, too, Doc? Maybe you *let* Pa die so y'all could have a change in leadership."

Gray-haired Doc pulled his shoulders back and leaned in, his voice low and deadly. "You wanna threaten me, Butch, you keep on just like that. I've patched the whole lot of you up more times than y'all are worth. The men know you can't beat and intimidate a bullet wound into healing…or that mage gun into changing hands. Jack's the wielder now. *He's* the new Elias. That's all there is to it."

Butch's lips lifted in a growl. No one would question Doc's word over Butch's. Not if they valued their limbs and teeth.

"I don't want to fight, Butch," Jack said.

Butch spread his hands. "Then give Diablo to me. What good will that gun do you, huh?"

"Ain't about me. It's about the gang." That was a damned lie, and he knew it. But that wild look in Butch's eye put some fear into Jack, and he felt the mage gun thrum in warning, too.

Butch rested his balled fists against his hips and huffed. "All right then, boss man. You gonna lead?" He set his teeth. "What d'you wanna do?"

He'd capitulated far too quickly. Butch might not be ready to shoot his best friend on the spot for Diablo, but he held a grudge like no one's business. There were plenty of ways he could convince Jack to give up the gun without killing him and opening the hell gate.

Jack formulated a plan quickly. "First things first. We stow the loot. Get everyone patched up. Then we're gonna shoot the sonofabitch sheriff that done your pa in. We show everyone Elias Blackthorn can't be killed. And we take that town for all it's worth."

Of course, that was not what happened. Jack made the plans, and after a few days' rest, the gang went back to the town where Jed Crowe was shot. But as the rampage began, Jack wheeled his horse around, picked up the pack of supplies he'd hidden in the woods the night before, and took off, riding fast and far, turning his back on the only people he'd ever called family, chased by a promise he'd made to a dying legend.

CHAPTER SEVENTEEN

Hettie's convalescence was slow. Every morning, she had breakfast with Berkeley—she was having a hard time thinking of him as "Pappy"—and then she'd take a walk with him around the garden before he left her to work for the day, locked away in his study or otherwise out of the house.

Ophelia hovered whenever she was in her room, and Hettie became hyperaware of the woman's presence. Sometimes the maid would prompt her about certain memories, asking if she recalled anything about her past life or her family. She didn't. It grated until Hettie found herself avoiding the maid whenever she could. Perhaps she was worried about her position. If Hettie didn't remember her old life, would Ophelia lose her job? She couldn't imagine why.

In the afternoons, Hettie explored the mansion. There were four floors, the topmost of which housed the numerous but rarely seen servants. They haunted the house, dusting and cleaning and washing and cooking almost entirely out of sight. Dozens of staff to serve the grandest house Hettie had ever seen...and still the place felt barren.

After a week, she'd explored every room except for the mansion's south wing, which was shut tight, the doors locked and, if Hettie wasn't mistaken, enchanted with the faintest of repulsion spells to keep people from entering.

Hettie hadn't even been sure at first why she'd passed the double doors so many times without trying the handles. It had taken Diablo jumping into her hand and guiding her to the threshold to even make her wonder why that whole side of the house was off-limits. She supposed she could have blown the door right off its hinges to find out, but she didn't think her host would approve.

"Pappy" didn't say much about the collection in the south wing, only that "she didn't need to worry about what was in there just now." Hettie wasn't satisfied with the answer but found she didn't want to argue.

Instead he told her about the house, her life, her parents. Apparently he and Hettie had only met once, the day her brother, Paul, was buried. Berkeley had made the trip out to the ranch via remote Zoom to pay his respects to his son and his new family.

"I thought you said he ran away. How'd you know where he was?"

"I never lost sight of him. I'm fortunate I have the resources I have to keep an eye on my kinfolk. I even sent anonymous gifts of money to him when you and Paul were born." He pursed his lips. "He wouldn't accept them. Seemed to know they were from me."

"He never told us that."

"I'm sure there was a lot your father kept from you. You were a sensitive child. The day they buried their son, your parents received quite a stream of folks from Newhaven coming to pay their respects. And you, you poor thing—you were, what, eleven? You wouldn't leave your room, wouldn't eat. Took your papa holding you down and sticking a spoonful of gruel into your mouth to make sure you didn't follow Paul."

Hettie looked away, ashamed. She remembered *that*, though it had been years since she'd broached that darkest corner of her life. The guilt had sunk her into an abyss, and when she wasn't sobbing into her pillow, she'd lain lifeless, holding her breath and staring at the ceiling, wishing her family would find her and bury her next to the brother whose death she'd caused.

She'd begged Paul to take her with him on his ride around the fence. He was supposed to be doing his chores, but she'd wanted to go, too, so he'd put her in front of him on his pony and off they'd gone.

If it hadn't been for her, the horse thief would have just had Paul to deal with. He wouldn't have targeted Hettie, and Paul wouldn't have blindly rushed him to defend her.

Paul would have seen the knife first, known his life wasn't worth a pony. He would have surrendered the mount and walked back to the house. He would still be alive…

Berkeley passed her a handkerchief. "I'm sorry…I know it still pains you to think about."

She dabbed her eyes. "I don't understand how I can remember *him* so well but nothing else." She thought of Paul's smiling eyes and lopsided grin, the little gifts he used to make her. The way they used to play Blackthorn Rogues. The day she'd found an injured rabbit and he'd helped her nurse it back to health, only to have it snatched up by a hawk the moment they'd released it back into the field.

"The mind is a mystery the best doctors, scientists, and sorcerers have yet to fully comprehend. We can't force your recovery," Berkeley told her gently.

Which was not to say they didn't try. Ophelia eagerly showed her the closet full of dresses she owned—simple, well-tailored gowns that suited Hettie's tastes. Ophelia told her about the servants who lived and worked in Berkeley Manor, the family estate her father had once been in line to inherit. She told her about books Hettie had enjoyed—romances, mostly—and showed her the needlepoint she'd completed.

Hettie remembered none of it. She thought she ought to know her own handiwork—surely hours of cross-stitch would have engraved something into her mind?—but all the embroidered pillows and cross-stitched handkerchiefs were unfamiliar.

"Well…I suppose perhaps it's a blessing there are some things you didn't remember," Ophelia said. "You were rather upset when Mr. Woodroffe married."

"Woodroffe?" Her head throbbed.

"Walker Woodroffe. He's one of your grandfather's business associates. He used to come around here quite often. You'd taken quite a shine to him—not that you ever admitted to it, but we all knew. I think he might have liked you, too, even if he was a little too old for you in my opinion." The maid regarded her with a touch of pity. "If you'd only admitted your feelings, Mr. Berkeley would have blessed the union. But I think your coldness drove Mr. Woodroffe away."

Hettie found herself rubbing the hollow center of her chest absently. Walker Woodroffe. It felt…familiar. Achingly so. And yet any tentative connection she might have had faded as she reached uselessly to recall the man's face.

Ophelia was watching her closely. "You still don't remember." She let out a breath and shook her head. "It's for the best, I suppose. No need to add heartache to your condition."

Every evening before bed, Ophelia brought her a broth tea with strong-smelling herbs in it. "You must keep drinking this to regain your strength," she said when Hettie turned it down. "You're still weak."

"I feel fine. I just have a headache."

"Memory is a delicate thing, and you can't afford to lose what you have remembered—or at least learned—so far. Your grandfather had some healers make it especially for you. It cost him quite a lot."

Hettie relented. She didn't want to seem ungrateful, or waste her grandfather's money, though he seemed to have quite a healthy bank account. So every night, with some griping, she downed the horrid concoction in one go.

Her dreams were strange and amorphous, as if the vividness of those visions had been muted and covered with billowing gray tarps. She couldn't see, hear, or sense anything beyond a blurry fuzziness.

One night she heard the distant caw of a raven. She chased the sound through her hazy dream world, calling out, only her voice was gone, muted no matter how much she screamed.

She surfaced in the morning groggy and lethargic. Her headache clung stubbornly, pounding an insistent rhythm against her temples. It had been over two weeks, and she was feeling no better than when she'd first awoken.

"Good morning!" Ophelia chirped as she drew the curtains. The sun cut through Hettie's eyelids and stabbed her brain.

"God's balls, shut those blasted things," Hettie snapped, and the nursemaid gasped.

"Miss Hettie! Where on earth did you learn to curse like that?"

Hettie stared. Hadn't she always spoken like this? She grumbled an apology and let Ophelia fuss over her.

Ophelia sat her down and combed her hair, complaining in the kindest way possible about Hettie's thick, unruly mop before pinning it up. Hettie submitted to her ministrations, but she noticed something strange that she hadn't remarked on before.

"Why isn't there a mirror in here?" she asked.

Ophelia's hands faltered. "Why would you need one? I do your hair and choose your dresses."

"Not that I don't appreciate it"—though Hettie preferred her maid not to hover—"but there are times I'd rather like to inspect myself."

"To be honest," Ophelia said haltingly, "you've always been rather...practical and, um...critical of your own looks. You eschewed all mirrors because you said you didn't cotton to vanity. So your grandfather had them removed. After everything you'd been through, he didn't want to cause you any more stress." She leaned down and smiled. "I can ask Mr. Berkeley to have the mirrors brought back into the house."

Hettie nodded absently. Not wanting mirrors around didn't exactly feel like her, though she could imagine saying something to that effect as an excuse to avoid looking at herself. She reached up and touched her face, feeling the smooth, slightly dull sensation along her right cheek, and she paused. A scar. Yes, she did vaguely remember that. From the night she'd almost died—

A starburst of mottled flesh flashed in her mind. She shut her eyes and shuddered.

Berkeley was at the breakfast table when she joined him. "How did you sleep?"

He asked the same thing every morning. She didn't know what else to tell him other than "Fine." In fact she felt surly, stifled, and sore, and she was beginning to resent her grandfather's patience, which made no sense to her.

Berkeley seemed to notice her mood. "It will take time to recover. When you came out of your fugue state, it was very similar." He grimaced. "But I know you'll get better soon. You're making marvelous progress."

"Do you think… That is, would it be all right if perhaps I go to the town to reacquaint myself?" The restlessness that had suffused her limbs grew daily. The mansion was large, but its opulence closed in on her like a plush mouth filled with gold teeth. "Maybe a tour of the area will jog my memory."

"Good heavens, no." Berkeley looked aghast. "You're not ready for that. You may feel strong here, but that's because I have powerful magics enchanting this house. Wellness charms and spells to keep the elements at bay. Spells for maintaining your strength, and mine for that matter. Beyond the gates, the climate is much less hospitable. As fair as Kansas is, I do like to keep the weather over Berkeley Manor mild. It was for Hannah's nerves, you know, and… well, I suppose I've grown accustomed to it myself. Truth is, we hardly ever need to leave."

Something struggled inside her like a butterfly trapped between two loosely clasped palms. Diablo jumped into her hand, and she stuffed it in the folds of her skirt.

"You're upset," he noted calmly. "Why?"

"I'm not upset." A scream was clawing its way up her throat, though she couldn't understand why. She kept her hand firmly around Diablo. "I think I'm… surprised. I know about magic, but I didn't know the gift ran in my family that strongly. Through you."

"Well, your father was gifted, though he refused to go to the Academy. He never was one for study."

Hettie searched for something to say. Every time Berkeley mentioned her father, it felt like just another drop of rain in a vast, wide ocean, indistinguishable from the rest. It was as though he were telling her the story of some other person, someone she didn't know. He might as well have been a stranger, she supposed. Jack Berkeley, Jack Farham, John Alabama…

Elias Blackthorn.

Her skin bristled as the name skated through her. She'd heard it whispered in her mind straight from the mage gun clasped in her white-knuckled grip. Elias Blackthorn, the legendary outlaw who couldn't die. A boogeyman from a child's song. Suddenly, she *could* connect with the man who was her father… But Pa had never been an outlaw, had he?

She stared at the gun in her lap. Diablo was the weapon Elias had been known to wield. It was putting notions in her head. Pa had never been more than a simple rancher, farmer…

Pain spiked through her temples, throbbing, aching, and she shut her eyes against the assault. She reached blindly for her teacup, not wanting Berkeley to see her struggle. She didn't want him sending her back to bed.

"Come." Berkeley's voice cleared the barb catching in her brain. "I can see you need something to occupy your hands. It's time we took the next step. Plus, I think it's important you see for yourself that I've nothing to hide from you."

"You think I don't trust you?" she asked.

His smirk reminded her of Pa's. "You have too much of your father in you. And don't think I didn't notice your reaction when I said you couldn't go to town. I remember saying no to you once about riding one of my unbroken horses, and you refused to listen to me. You went and took Blackie out anyhow."

A wave of pressure throbbed through her head. Blackie. The big black stallion had been a handful. He'd nearly bucked her right off and then…then…

The memory evaporated, and Hettie bit back a curse. It was all *there*, hidden in a thick, shifting fog.

Her grandfather led her through the house to the south wing. He unlocked the double doors with a key from a set attached to his belt. "You used to spend a lot of time reading and studying in here. Perhaps once you see my collection you'll remember something of your old life."

A mustiness assailed her nostrils—slightly sweet, but also sharp with the tang of engine oil, overlaid with the murkiness of decay. Berkeley murmured an incantation, and the glow-stone-filled braziers and sconces flared to life.

The long main hall was lined with display cabinets containing all kinds of bric-a-brac—books, statues, figurines of men and women in a variety of styles and poses. She stopped in front of a cabinet filled with nothing but helmets.

"*Supposedly* enchanted armor. Of course, metal is already magic-proof," Berkeley said, nodding at one bone-and-leather helm. "I've yet to figure out if the magic in the others is actually intentional or if the creatures they were made of happened to be born or raised on a magical node." He guided her on eagerly. "But the hallway displays aren't nearly as interesting as what's in my workshop."

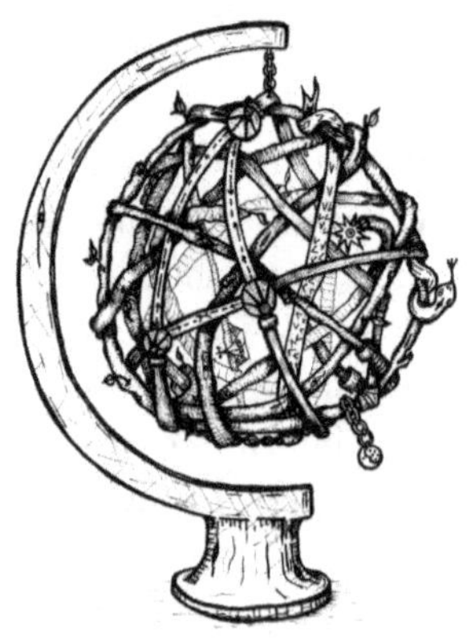

CHAPTER EIGHTEEN

Berkeley took another key from his ring and unlocked the room at the far end of the hall. The molding around the double doors was carved with runes, the doors themselves painted with a number of spells Hettie recognized as wards against the Eye.

As soon as she stepped through, she felt the space around her closing in. The gallery was filled with row upon row of shelves and cabinets, some open, some locked, every single one piled high with books, talismans, and more.

Two shelves were devoted entirely to the bones of various animals. At least she hoped they were all just animals. Another held jars of murky liquid containing preserved specimens—two-headed frogs and snakes, lizards with rainbow scales, small mammals that looked like crosses between rats and fish. Berkeley was as excited as a young boy showing off his toys as he pointed out all his favorite things.

Plants overflowed from the shelves closest to the heavily barred windows. Long green tendrils reached and grasped for her as they walked past, clinging to her hair and clothes. She batted them away and nearly stumbled into a huge potted succulent, deep purple with spiny ridges tipped in red. It bloomed as she bumped it, opening like a cavernous mouth, the sticky exposed pulp glistening and fragrant.

The scent burned in her nostrils, but there was something familiar about it. Something that reminded her of…

"Whoa, now." Berkeley yanked her back. "That's not a plant you want to go sniffing. That's how it gets you. You lean in for a whiff…" He grabbed a nearby branch and brushed the pink pulp with the leaves. The succulent's meaty petals slammed wetly shut, snapping the branch. Hettie recoiled. "The nectar it produces is used in a number of complicated spells. It's also great for catching rats. Unfortunately, it got one of the maids. Digested her for a few days before we found her and could get her out. We call it the Marriage Trap, though I think the colloquial name is the Whore's Mouth."

Hettie grimaced. "Should it be sitting out like this, being so dangerous?"

"Why do you think I have all these keys? You're the only other person I've allowed in here since poor Sophie's demise."

Golden ringlets flashed in her mind. Hettie's head throbbed hard.

"You remember her?" Berkeley asked carefully. "I'm sorry…Sophie was your maid for a while. You didn't get along all the time, but when she was killed…" He shook his head. "You mourned her like she was family."

Sophie. Yes, that sounded…right? She had some impression of a certain haughtiness.

Berkeley urged her on through the library of oddities. She passed a case containing a number of metal objects—daggers, spoons, an oil lamp. Thoroughly mundane-looking everyday items.

"Enchanted metal," Berkeley explained. "That spoon belonged to an aristocratic Scottish sorcerer from the twelfth century who made it to detect poison in his food. That lamp there was said to have once imprisoned a djinn. That pack of needles? Spelled to never pierce living flesh, though they could pierce through diamonds as if they were butter." His eyes sparkled. "These are the rarest of my collection. The spells that can affect metal have mostly been lost to time. It's said only blood magic can truly achieve the enchantments, but I've yet to come across any texts to describe the procedures.

I've heard the spells crumble whatever they're written on once they've been performed."

Close to the metal collection, a little brass bird in a small metal cage ruffled its bladelike feathers and started to chirp and sing a tinny song. Next to it, a Mechanikal automaton nearly twice Hettie's size sat silent in a chair. Its blank bucket head swiveled to peer at her with large bubble-lensed eyes. Hettie jumped back, startled. But the metal man simply returned to its taciturn contemplation, staring straight ahead.

"Don't mind him," Berkeley chuckled. "He looks frightening, but he's quite docile. He was intended to be a dockside laborer, imbued with the soul of a young longshoreman whose legs had been crushed in an accident. Alas, while the spell worked, he was considered an abomination. A mob tried to destroy him. I brought him here for his protection." He glanced back to where the automaton sat. "Poor soul. I doubt he would've consented to the procedure had he known he wouldn't be able to speak or enjoy life as he'd known it. Now he spends most of his days staring at the walls. Doesn't have a whole lot else he can do, though I suppose he's a good listener."

She looked back up at the automaton, who she couldn't help but think was eavesdropping. Its blank face and glass orb eyes didn't give away anything. "So you collect Mechanikal wonders as well as magical ones?"

"Only a few select pieces." He pointed to the ceiling. Hettie craned her neck up to take in the enormous serpentine beast circling the room, the sections of its empty metal carapace gleaming in the light of the glow stones. "One of the first Mechanikal flying machines," he explained. "Or what should be a flying machine. Tannin was one of the earliest metal imbuements in the history of Mechaniks, intended to prove man was meant to fly...with the help of machine and magic. Seems science will fill that role more readily than sorcery now, though. Not that I mind." A crooked smile hitched his lips up. "At one time, old Tannin here terrorized the Louisiana bayou for six weeks."

"And then?"

"Well, the magic just gave out. Souls, too. You can't expect to hold a wild creature's essence captive all that long, especially two natural enemies like a gator and crane."

"Is that how Mechaniks works? Imbuement?"

"It's more complicated than that, but I'm no Mechanik. Mechaniks is the study of the intersection between magic and science, which is why it's not really taken seriously by either realm. I guess Alastair Fielding showed them. Now the whole field is blowing up with people looking to cash in on the Fielding engine's success."

That did sound familiar. But then, everyone these days knew about Alastair Fielding.

Farther on, Hettie came upon a pair of guns resting on a silk pillow beneath a glass case.

They were old single-shot weapons, like dueling pistols, finely wrought with beautiful etchings on the gilded surfaces. Her breath caught—she *knew* these weapons.

Diablo leaped into her palm, ticking in her hand.

As she continued to stare at the pistols, Berkeley chuckled. "You were rather taken with those, though I doubt Diablo would let you handle them. They are remarkably crafted, enchantment aside. I acquired these a few weeks before you fell ill. Haven't had the stones to try them out myself, though."

"They're mage guns," Hettie concluded.

"The only pair I own... aside from Diablo, I mean."

Hettie kept her eyes on the case, though something inside her squirmed. This man did not own Diablo. *She* did. The Devil's Revolver was *hers*, and a part of her wanted to remind him of that.

Diablo ticked in her hand again, and she looked in the direction it indicated. Just beyond the glass case hung an oval mirror, its surface covered with a heavy piece of velvet. Hettie reached for it, hoping to have a peek at her face.

"Don't touch that!" Berkeley grabbed her wrist and yanked her back. Fury snarled his features. "You must *never* uncover that mirror."

"Why not?" She shook off his grip.

Berkeley gave a frustrated sigh. "It's enchanted to show you the most wicked side of yourself. Great men have killed themselves after seeing the truth of their natures. One glance could drive you mad."

Hettie frowned. "Why would anyone enchant an object to do *that?*"

He let out a breath. "Not all enchanted items do what they were intended to do. Spellcraft is part science, part faith. With God's hand in the mix, there's no telling what you'll end up with." He nodded toward the mirror, scowling. "I bought this to keep it out of the public eye—some horrible sideshow barker had been taking it around towns, touting it as a way to reveal the truth. He said it used to be a rich woman's vanity mirror, one that drove her to kill her own daughter for being more beautiful than she."

"That almost sounds like Snow White," Hettie said skeptically.

"The greatest stories have roots in truth."

"If it's so dangerous, why not smash it?"

He looked as if she'd proposed he cut off his own hand. "Every piece in my collection is precious. Unique. The spellcraft used to make such items is incomparable. The Marriage Trap, the mirror, even Diablo…these are dangerous objects, yes, but they must be preserved as a record of magical history."

"Because of the magic drain?"

His chuckle seemed forced. "There's no magic drain." She thought he'd say more, but Berkeley only looped her arm through his, trapping her firmly against his side. "Come, there's more to see!"

He took her up and down the rows of shelves, showing off more of his prized possessions and magical curios.

In one case lay a long wood staff broken into five pieces. Only the section second from the top was missing. She placed her hand over the glass where the missing piece was, feeling a sense of kinship with the staff—incomplete, broken, trapped in a pretty box.

"Saint Merlin's staff," Berkeley said with hushed reverence. "I've never been able to find the final piece. It went missing somewhere in Spain in the early 1700s. Supposedly, if the staff is ever restored, it will point the way to Excalibur."

"Another fairy tale?" Hettie arched an eyebrow.

"You always were a skeptical one. Once you start working with me again, you'll start to believe. That's how magic works, you know. Faith. Conviction. A single-minded pursuit to change the world through your gift." He sighed. "It's a shame you weren't born gifted. With your stubbornness, I believe you would've been an extraordinary sorcerer."

She wasn't sure how to take that comment.

"Come. I saved the best for last."

He unlocked another set of doors at the far end of the gallery. The room beyond it would've been a ballroom in any other manor house. A series of circles in different colors, concentric and interlocking, covered the floor—protection spells to keep magic contained. The perimeter was lined with talismans, braids of twine and hair looped around and around the walls. Except for that, the room was empty, the floor polished to a high gloss.

More runes were painted on the southern wall. They made up the spell for a remote Zoom aperture, though how Hettie knew *that,* she wasn't sure.

From a large, locked cabinet, Berkeley wheeled out a sculpture of some kind, about as tall as him and covered by a canvas tarp. He drew back the covering, revealing a large crystal. "My Zoom icon! Remote Zoom technology made for single sorcerers to wield."

It was like the hunks of quartz that gave the Zoom Unions access to the natural Zooms, only this one had been cut and polished into a perfect egg. The crystal sat in a cage of gold filigree, and beneath it rested a hexagonal box of glass nestled in a netting of fine gold filaments.

The whole contraption radiated an ill feeling, a draw that made Diablo cringe in her mind. "Is…is that a Fielding engine?"

"A canister only, but in miniature. Remarkable, isn't it? You'll get accustomed to the sensation." Berkeley rubbed his hands together. "This is the jewel of my collection, quite literally. Inside that"—he gestured at the canister—"is a flawless quartz orb, and inside that a hundred-carat diamond, mined straight from the heart of Africa. It cost me a lot to finance that expedition, and then I had Alastair Fielding himself design it. This icon has enough power to get us all the way across the country. It took a dozen sorcerers to construct, and another dozen to fuel it." He grinned. "These Fielding engines have been a tremendous blessing to my work. Look." He pulled a round flask from a cabinet, the glass encased in a series of rune-stamped rings. "This was my idea: miniature canisters so a sorcerer can juice on the go. One sip, and a drained sorcerer is revived. The Division was quite pleased with this contribution."

Hettie's palms itched, and she licked her lips. She was on the verge of asking to try a sip from the flask, but she shoved the impulse away. "What... exactly... do you do for the Division?"

Berkeley waved a hand. "This and that. A grandmaster sits on the council of elders, and together we decide how to handle magical affairs. Just like a government, we have cabinets and ministers who deal with specific issues facing the gifted. I'm the grandmaster of magical resources and conservation. I work on projects to help preserve magical traditions and foster magical growth."

"So you must be involved in solving the magic drain."

His expression rippled with displeasure, but he laughed it off once more. "I told you, there's no magic drain. Look around you. If there were a magic drain, Berkeley Manor wouldn't be standing. My great-grandmother rooted the building's foundation in magic. Placed the house on a plot of land no mundane architect was willing to build on. The house has stood for generations."

"But... magic isn't sticking the way it used to." The words echoed from a time and place that seemed as remote as a dream, and she'd spoken them as if someone had fed her the line.

Berkeley regarded her steadily. "It seems some of your memory is returning." His lips quirked. "We've had this discussion a number of times, and you're bent on believing the worst. I keep telling you, magic is not draining from the world—it's simply shifting, as it has throughout history. The sorcerers who can still make it work are the natural inheritors of the gifted legacy. It's nature taking its course, with the strongest and most capable rising to the top, like cream."

"But what about the soothsayers?" The words burst from her lips, and suddenly Hettie remembered something.

Roses. Violet-ringed eyes and the crinkle of a gentle smile. She closed her eyes as a flood of sensation overwhelmed her. Every nerve in her body clenched tight.

"The soothsayers' blackout," she said. "I remember. All the soothsayers everywhere can't scry the future anymore. They've fallen into comas…" Her temples throbbed, and the ground beneath her shifted.

"You've overexerted yourself." Berkeley put an arm around her and started leading her out. "You're misremembering things. There was no blackout—"

She pushed him off. "There is. I remember it." She was suddenly jittery and pacing. "I…I need to find out what's causing it. I'm supposed to…supposed to…"

Berkeley's jaw flexed. "My dear, I'm sorry." He raised a hand and spoke a word.

CHAPTER NINETEEN

Hettie's eyes opened. She was in her bedroom. Pain throbbed through her whole body, and her head felt as if it were stuffed with cotton. She sat up slowly, trying to recall what had happened. She had a vague impression of a big space with…shelves? Like a library, maybe. Her dreams of late had been strange…

Diablo popped into her grip and ticked.

She stared at it, heart hammering. The mage gun was the only thing that felt real and clear to her, and now she knew it was trying to tell her…

"Something's not right." The croaked words came out with more certainty than she felt.

She got stiffly out of bed. She was wearing a nightgown. How long had she been asleep? She thought back but couldn't remember getting dressed, what her last meal was…nothing.

She stood. The floor wobbled beneath her, and for a moment her vision exploded with black stars. When she could see again, she was leaned up against the wall in a narrow corridor. How had she gotten there?

She stumbled down a set of stairs, her feet carrying her through the dark as if by muscle memory. On the lower level, raised voices floated down the hall. Hettie went to a door and pressed her ear against the wood to listen.

"You should keep her locked up." The man's voice was gruff and strangely familiar. Hettie bit her lips as she strained to hear. "…more damage than you think."

"The spell's worked fine…flashbacks…can't anticipate… blasted mage gun." Berkeley. She'd know his voice anywhere.

"I'm more concerned about the inserted memories." It was Ophelia. "They won't stick. Her mind is resistant…as anticipated."

"That's *your* problem to deal with," Berkeley snapped. "I don't pay you to make excuses." The argument became hard to discern, and then came the sound of a side door opening and closing.

The men's voices grew closer. "Typical memory wipe's not gonna cut it with her. She's got a piece of her soul missing, thanks to Bassett. With Diablo in the mix, we can't rely on regular influence magic to control her. We ought to put her down."

Hettie's fingers contracted around Diablo as it doubled in weight.

"I will not lose Diablo to the hell gate, not after all these years. I've paid a small fortune to get my hands on the Devil's Revolver," Berkeley hissed. "Money *you* pissed away."

"Money the Pinkerton Agency pissed away, not me. I was a convenient scapegoat for their reckless spending. Fact is, I got way more done as an independent agent than I did with the Pinkertons. Otherwise you wouldn't have hired me." He paused. "The witch is a liability. You oughta get rid of her."

"She's the wielder. Unless you know of a way to separate the two without the hell gate opening—"

"I told you, convince her to relinquish it."

"I don't need her to relinquish it. That mage gun is cursed, and I won't risk it getting into another's hands. Control the wielder, and you control Diablo." Berkeley sighed. "We'll need to wipe her memory again. Make her forget the past week or so. Start fresh."

"You keep on like that, you'll damage her mind, not to mention that poor woman you're making a vessel for her memories."

"Ophelia was the most qualified memorist I could buy. She'll do as she's told."

"And you call me ruthless?" the gruff-voiced man scoffed. "Way I see it, the wielder doesn't need to be smart to be Diablo's keeper. If it were me, I'd jam an ice pick in her head and nail her feet to the floor."

The voices were growing louder. The doors suddenly opened—

Hettie sat up in bed, the dream fading.

"Whu…" She grabbed her throbbing head. What was happening? These dreams were… No, she remembered…she remembered Berkeley and that man talking about…

If her memories were being wiped and replaced, she couldn't trust anything she knew. She needed to keep track of everything she learned day by day. She didn't know a lot about this kind of influence magic, but she knew enough that she had to take precautions.

She staggered to the desk in the corner and found a small stack of crisp white paper for letter writing. Quickly, she scribbled down a note.

Where could she hide it? If they wiped her memory regularly, she'd need someplace obvious where she'd look, but not so obvious that Ophelia or Berkeley or any of the servants poking around would find it. Of course, if she hid it too well, *she* might never find it.

Then she realized the only place she could hide it. She rolled the piece of paper up and took Diablo out. She just hoped she didn't fire the thing before she found—

The piece of paper jammed on something. Hettie stopped. Carefully, she slipped her finger into the barrel and pulled out another slip of paper, barely bigger than a cigarette.

She unrolled it with shaking hands. There, on the same paper from the desk, was another note.

They're taking your memories. Don't trust anyone.

The room spun. Hettie hastily stuffed the note back into the mage gun's barrel, then folded her new note and slipped it beneath her mattress.

Another note awaited her there in her hasty handwriting.

Pee Wee in the south wing is your friend. He will help.

She stared. Who—or what—was Pee Wee?

A tremor crawled up Hettie's spine, climbing up through her rib cage and rattling her lungs.

The south wing. She knew of it; had she been there before? Yes, she must have.

She started for the door—

ᛉ

Hettie opened her eyes. Her head throbbed.

She tried to sit up, but her arms and legs were held spread-eagle against the bed. Manacles around her wrists and ankles were attached to chains tied to the bedposts. A scream scraped along her parched throat as she thrashed.

Diablo popped into her hand. The manacle around her wrist sloughed off, leaving a flaming puddle of slag on the fine mattress.

She shot the chain off her left manacle and the ones around her legs, then leaped out of bed. She locked the door and pulled a chair in front of it. Right now, all she knew was that she was a prisoner, and the least she could do was slow down whoever her captor was from entering this room. She stuffed down her panic, heart hammering and sweat gathering in her palms, drawing in long breaths to keep the dizziness at bay.

She spied something out of the corner of her eye; she wouldn't have noticed except that the headboard had shifted in her thrashing, and this room was normally immaculate. That she knew that and not how she'd arrived in this place sent shivers through her.

She wedged her shoulder between the wall and the back of the bed and inched the heavy four-poster away, then braced her legs against the lattice wallpaper and heaved the furniture another foot back.

The message was written in blood.

They're wiping your memory. Don't trust Berkeley. Go to the south wing. Find Pee Wee.

The doorknob rattled. "Dammit! Not again!"

"She was chained down! How does she keep escaping?" It was Berkeley. Her…grandfather?

She wanted to call out to him, but she looked back at the wall. That wasn't her handwriting. She didn't recognize it. Who was trying to warn her?

The door rocked as the men outside bashed away at it, the chair holding it shut creaking on thin, tapered legs.

Diablo's weight doubled in her hand. The mage gun's instincts couldn't be denied—she was in mortal danger. If she stayed in this room, those men would wipe her mind and scrub her brain of everything she'd just learned. But if she killed them, how would she get her memories back? They might be the only two who could restore them.

She checked the windows. None of them opened, and they were barred from the outside. She could blast through with Diablo, but then what? She was at least three stories up.

And then she noticed an enormous raven perched on the sill, staring at her. It flapped its midnight wings and met her eye steadily.

Hettie swallowed. She raised the mage gun and fired out the window.

The green beam cut a swath through the room and blew the glass and lattice out in a deadly sparkling shower of molten glass and metal. The raven had taken off before it could be blasted into smithereens, but instead of flying away it soared into the room and alighted on top of the armoire.

The door clattered loudly. They were almost through.

The raven cawed.

Hettie dove into the armoire and closed the door, burying herself behind her many gowns and clutching the silent Diablo.

The bedroom door burst open noisily. "The window!"

"She must've jumped out," the gruff voice said.

"It's a three-story drop," Berkeley said. "How could she possibly have gotten down?"

"You're forgetting Diablo's other power. She could be long gone from this place… C'mon…" The voices faded down the hall. Hettie waited a full ten heartbeats before she dared to move. Carefully, she extricated herself from the armoire.

The raven hissed above her, and she startled. "They didn't see you?"

The bird blinked at her, then gave another caw.

"They don't hear you, either?" She shook her head. Why was she talking to the bird? Or pretending to understand him? Her head throbbed. No, no, she wasn't pretending, unless she'd finally gone mad… And that was exactly what was happening, wasn't it? This place was her home. She'd lived here since…since…

She squeezed her eyes shut, trying to drown out the rush between her ears.

The big black bird gave a loud caw, then hopped down onto the floor and looked at her expectantly. It took flight, its huge wings rustling and flapping down the hallway until it reached the passage to the south wing.

Hettie huffed. "I don't have time to find shiny objects for you to play with," she said impatiently.

The raven clicked its beak, snipping at the air.

She bit the inside of her cheek and aimed Diablo at the door. "I do this, they'll know I'm still inside."

The bird gave a shrug.

Hettie couldn't hide forever. Those men would find her—she was certain of that.

She aimed for the lock and pulled the trigger. A brief burst, and the lock was now a smoking hole.

She hurried in and, as an afterthought, fired Diablo at the ceiling. Flaming plaster rained down and piled up in front of the doors. That would give anyone coming through pause.

She ran into the gallery after the raven. It flapped its way into the workshop and perched atop the glass case containing the brace of mage guns.

"I can't take those. I won't be able to use them." She brandished Diablo. "Remember?"

The bird leaped into the air and cawed, circling the room, ducking and diving through the sections of the Mechanikal flying beast above.

The little metal bird started chirping in alarm. Hettie tried to hush it, but the thing hopped around its cage, its flapping blade-wings sounding like tiny knives being sharpened.

A loud thud behind Hettie had her whirling around to find the Mechanikal automaton looming above her, staring her down with his glassy orb eyes.

"Stay away!" she cried.

The metal man held his arms out slowly, palms open in…surrender? Slowly, joints creaking with disuse, he opened a panel on his torso, just under his armpit. From it, he extracted a small notebook, which he held out.

"For...for me?"

The machine stared at her silently.

She took the book and opened it with shaking hands. The handwriting was familiar but messy, written hastily.

There were several separate entries over a few pages.

You are Hettie Alabama.
Berkeley has been wiping your memory.

The words looked less and less hastily scrawled with each entry.

Pee Wee is your friend. He has been keeping your book safe.
Go look in the mirror of truth.
Ophelia is holding your memories.

She looked up at the automaton. "Pee Wee?"

The Mechanikal man gave a halting salute.

The final entry was written boldly and underlined with deep red blood.

Find Abby.
Berkeley knows where she is.

Abby. Her sister.

Her heart hurt, and her head throbbed. Of course. How could she forget about Abby? The weeks...no, years of searching for her. The Division had her. And Berkeley knew where she was. But how had she learned that?

The mirror of truth would give her the answers.

She ran to the corner where the mirror hung, fingers trembling as she removed the cords keeping the velvet cover in place. Pee Wee lumbered up behind her, expectant.

The cover dropped to the floor.

Hettie scrambled away from the woman who appeared before her. Her brown hair was threaded with silver. The apron around her midsection was stained with blood. Hettie fumbled for Diablo, and the woman imitated her clumsy movements. Only…

No. No, this couldn't be right—

Hettie touched her smooth, round face, squinting at the flat, pale blue eyes that were like beads.

"Ophelia."

She turned around sharply and reeled back.

The woman across the room was in a dark day dress, her gunmetal-gray hair scraped back from her face. A feather-shaped scar left a shiny pink impression on the right side of her face.

"Mizzay," Hettie breathed.

CHAPTER TWENTY

Hettie summoned Diablo—but the mage gun didn't come.

"I'm not Mizzay. She's been dead four years." The woman's voice was raw and low. It was *her* voice—Hettie's voice. "You know who I am."

"You're using glamor." Uncertainty was mixed with her panic.

"Ophelia, listen to me. We don't have a lot of time. You have my memories—the memories of Hettie Alabama. It took a while, but I figured it out. *We* figured it out. Pee Wee helped us." She indicated the automaton. "Berkeley's been using you as a vessel to store my memories. Every time he wiped me fresh, he put a little more of me in you."

"Stay away from me!" Hettie tried again to summon Diablo, tried to drop into the time bubble. Why wasn't it working?

"You're looking for this?" The woman held up the Devil's Revolver.

Something inside Hettie broke. She stared at the woman. No, it couldn't be true. She'd been holding the gun a moment ago—

Hadn't she? She remembered firing it at the window. But how had she gotten here? She couldn't remember running down the corridor, though she supposed she must have. And the doors—she'd…she'd…

"But I remember Abby and Walker and Ling..." She forked her fingers through her hair, massaging her temples. Did they know she was alive? Where were they?

"You *think* you remember everything, but you don't. You're not even sure how you got here." The scarred woman's voice was low and calm.

"I was in my room and... Stubbs and Berkeley broke in, but I hid. There was a raven that led me here..." Hettie's head felt swollen, her throat and chest tight. "This is some illusion magic. Influence or glamor. If I have your memories, how do you know you're missing them?"

"It's hard to explain. Like I said, I've been piecing it together slowly, leaving myself notes..." She held up a second book identical to the one Pee Wee had given her. "I... *we've* been here awhile." She tossed it to her. To the automaton, she said, "Guard the door. Don't let anyone in."

Pee Wee lumbered jerkily out, joints creaking, body plates clanking.

Hettie almost didn't want to open the book, but she did. The thing was filled with notes, many more than her own book, and while she couldn't make sense of them, she recognized the handwriting. It was hers, all done in neat pencil, along with tiny sketches of pieces of the collection. There were pieces of notepaper in there, too. "Short story is, my hold on Diablo is connected to my soul, but a piece of it is missing, which is partly why Berkeley's spells aren't working like they should. Memories keeping rushing back to fill the gap, like water in a hole. But he keeps bailing my brain out, dumping it all in you."

Hettie shook her throbbing head. "This is insane."

"I thought I was going mad myself. All you need to know is Berkeley's trying to control us. He wants to keep me and Diablo here. And he won't take control of it himself because of the curse."

"If all that's true, why haven't you just run away from here? Used Diablo's time bubble and gone off?"

"Because of this." She rolled up her sleeve to reveal an angry scabbing scar on the inside of her upper arm. In crude, sharp strokes, someone had carved the words SAVE ABBY into her flesh.

Hettie felt sick as the woman rolled her sleeve back. "I don't know who she is or why she's important. But *you* do."

Hettie's lungs shrank. "She's my sister. The Division took her."

The scarred woman clenched her jaw and looked away. "I'm sorry to hear that. But…if she's with the Division, isn't she better off?"

Good God, she really didn't remember anything about the Division. "Abby's special. She has these abilities. They call her an indigo child. They're torturing her, doing tests…" Hettie squeezed her eyes shut against the sudden flood of emotions. "I have to save her. She's the only family I have left."

The woman's scar rippled like a feather caught in the eddies of her emotions. "Taking on the Division is suicide."

"That's never stopped me before."

The woman considered her. "You mean *me*. You still think you're me?"

"I don't think— *I am* Hettie Alabama!"

"You're the maid, Ophelia. You're a memorist—you have a gift for taking on other people's memories. You've taken on most of mine, which is why you think you're me. It's likely we've had this conversation a dozen times before." The woman let out a huff. "Look, we don't have time for this. I've got Berkeley and Stubbs locked up tight, but they won't stay that way for long. I need you to give me back my memories and use the remote Zoom to get us outta here. Berkeley's icon can only be activated by a sorcerer."

"I'm not a—"

The woman grabbed her by the collar and hauled her close. "Your name is Ophelia Jones. You *are* a sorcerer, a master-level one. You have the gift, and if you want to save Abby, you need to use that gift to open the Zoom."

Hettie trembled. Nose to nose, she could see every scar she'd garnered over the years: the thick layers of freckles; the bend of her nose, broken at least twice in her lifetime; the lines around her mouth and eyes; the way her jowls were just starting to sag. And her eyes, so like her father's, were as hard, dark, and fixed as the point of a gun.

"But…where would we go?"

"Here." She grabbed the book from Hettie's hands and opened it to a page. "I've no idea where it goes, though." She handed her a burlap sack. "But first I need to grab a few things."

"Are you mad? We don't have time to loot—"

"This is the world's greatest collection of magical artifacts. Berkeley thought he was controlling me, thought I'd become a docile miss helping him with his work. I was a good student. Too good." She smashed the glass case containing the brace of mage guns, and Hettie realized she knew exactly who they'd belonged to.

"Those are Marcus's guns."

"Luna and Claire, the Pistols of Lethe." The woman who looked like Hettie picked up the pillow they rested on, slipped one gun into the sack, and tossed Hettie the other. Instinctively, Hettie caught it, though a shot of surprise punched through her at the cool weight of it. "Keep this on you just in case."

She gripped the weapon firmly, waiting. It didn't burn her hand. Which meant the woman was telling the truth.

Hettie closed her eyes, her gut trembling. *Abby. Just think of Abby.* That was what made her the real Hettie. Her love for her sister.

She stuffed the mage gun into her pocket while her doppelganger snatched a few other items off the shelves, tossing them at Hettie. She didn't question her further—just caught them and bagged them, keeping her mind in the present to stave off the madness. Watching herself move through the room, tearing it apart, felt like some kind of nightmare. She'd never realized how intense she was.

The woman rooted through the shelves of bones, cursing under her breath. "Where is it?"

"Where's what?"

She glanced up as if startled, then shook her head. "No, never mind. There's no more time."

"How long have you—have *we* been here?" Hettie asked faintly.

"I can't be sure. You have most of my memories now. But by my accounting, at least three months."

The breath left Hettie in one go. Three months. Her friends must've thought her dead. And Abby…

Tears flooded her eyes. Was her sister even alive? Had she been calling for her all this time, getting no response? Losing hope?

The outlaw dragged Hettie into the large spell room and threw open the cabinet with the remote Zoom icon. "I know how this works, but I don't have the gift to activate it."

"But you think I... Ophelia does?"

She pinned her with a look Hettie could feel in the marrow of her bones. "I know she's in there, buried under us. She needs to come up for air, break through long enough to speak that incantation." She pointed at the runes on the wall.

A distant banging and shouts came down the hall. Pee Wee's armor clanked and screeched. Something crashed loudly in the corridor, followed by a wave of magic. The woman who looked like Hettie cursed and pulled a brass-tipped staff from the holder in the icon's base. "You speak the incantation, and when the aperture starts to appear, jam this into the hole in the crystal."

"How can you be sure that's how it works?"

"I've watched Berkeley do it more than once now. It's powered by the Fielding canister beneath."

Hettie's mind raced, her breath coming in fast pants. "But... I don't know how!"

The woman snarled and grabbed her by the collar. She pushed Diablo against her jaw. It was like a brand searing her skin, and she cried out. "You listen and listen good." Her grip tightened. "You *know* what I'm capable of. I could've left this place, but *Abby* made me stay. I would kill for her, and I don't even know who she is. So don't think I won't kill you just 'cuz you're holding on to my memories. Open the Zoom and you get to live."

Tears burned in Hettie's eyes as a sick feeling swamped her. Was this who she was? Who she'd become? Hettie Alabama, the ruthless outlaw, a merciless murderer, a heartless tyrant who—

Who'd do anything to save Abby. The woman across from her *was* Hettie. Even without her memories, without love for her sister, without knowing entirely who she was... she'd stayed because she'd known something was missing. Something important.

And she—Ophelia—had taken that from her.

Hettie felt herself sinking, her vision graying, the sound growing more and more muted, as if she were drowning in a fog of silence. She was submerged in a world of gray. Vaguely, she heard the throaty murmuring of a familiar voice—her voice, she supposed. Or Ophelia's. She wasn't sure. It was all a blur and—

The rush of frost burned her skin. Hettie was clutching the cold brass staff planted firmly within the crystal. The dark aperture had spiraled open, leaving a carpet of icy crystals pooled around her feet. The other side was partially obscured by the moonless night. The scarred outlaw was already heading through.

"Come on!" she called.

Hettie started forward.

Agony ripped through her, and the ground rushed up to meet her. She cried out as she gripped her chest. Her hand came away hot and sticky and shaking.

"Stop right there or I'll kill her!"

Hettie's blood chilled.

Thomas Stubbs. The former Pinkerton agent who'd hunted her and Abby all over the country, terrorizing them. Black smoke wafted around him, the scent of machine oil strong. Hate surged through her, but the heat of it did not dispel the insidious cold creeping into her bones.

"Not before I'd kill you." The outlaw's voice was flat and deadly. "Best take your finger off that trigger, Stubbs, or I'll take it off for you."

"Hettie, please." Berkeley. Hettie turned her eyes toward the grandmaster, who was reaching out, pleading. "This is all a big misunderstanding. We'll start fresh again. You can go back to your work—"

A rush of green energy cut a swath at the man's feet. "I ain't a dress-up doll you can play with," the outlaw shouted.

"No, no, of course not. I can see no memory spell will get us the desired outcome, no matter what we try. But hear me out. No more spells. No more magic. No more tricks. Only the truth."

He inhaled deeply. "I really am your grandfather, Hettie. Your father really was born out of wedlock, and I've regretted letting him go since I learned he'd gone outlaw."

Even though the cold was overtaking her, Hettie felt something like a stone dropping in her chest. "Why the hell should I believe you?" the outlaw shouted.

"I told you. The best stories have roots in the truth. We're kin. Blood. Jack Farham was my son. And you, Hettie Alabama, are my granddaughter, and the one destined to inherit my legacy here at Berkeley Manor."

"Lies. All you want is Diablo."

The sorcerer spread his hands. "Don't you see? It was God's will that the very thing I've been hunting all these years is bonded to you. Your father's legacy is mine, too. We were meant to find each other. I was meant to be your protector."

"Protector? Is that what wiping my memory is about? *Protecting* me?"

"It was for both our protection. If Diablo became aware of me—"

"You mean if *I* became aware. If *I* knew what you really wanted. Diablo can't pull its own trigger. Frankly, I'm seeing less and less reason not to." The outlaw cocked the gun, making Berkeley flinch. "We don't owe each other a damned thing, old man."

"That's where you're wrong. Family means everything, Hettie. You're all I have left. You...and Abby." He took a step forward. "I can save her. I can save both of you."

She fired a shot just over his ear, and he cowered. "Tell me where she is, and you'll save yourself, too." She shifted her aim a hair to the left.

Berkeley remained calm. "I can't tell you that, but I know this much: they'll be done with your sister soon, and I can have her brought to the manor. The two of you can live your lives here peacefully. No one will ever hurt you again."

Hettie gasped. "What do you mean 'they'll be done with her'?"

Berkeley's eyes tracked to her, and the flesh between his brows crinkled. "Ophelia, just stay calm. You'll be all right—"

"Where's Abby?" She hauled herself up to her knees. "Tell me where my sister is."

Stubbs groaned. "Dammit all to hell, she took too many of her memories on. Didn't I tell you this would happen?" He gave a short bark of humorless laughter. "As if one of these harridans isn't enough, now we've got two."

The grandmaster closed his eyes. "I see. I'm sorry, Ophelia. It seems I overestimated your abilities."

"Quit yer stalling." The scarred woman fired a shot over his head that punched a hole through the back wall. "Abby's location. Now."

Berkeley held up his hands. "It's not that simple. The Division keeps a... a moving laboratory."

"Like on a train?"

"No. It's on a different plane of existence—a place between worlds, between realities. A magical pocket, hidden away..."

Hettie's vision was blurring, her hearing fading. Blood poured from the wound in her chest, and it was getting harder and harder to breathe. She coughed, and her spittle was bloody.

She could make out the Zoom, though. It was starting to close.

She struggled to warn the outlaw. From the corner of her eye, she could see Stubbs edging around, trying to flank the woman with the gun. He was going to stop her. Maim her. She knew his intentions by the malice glinting in his eye.

Something winked in her field of vision, and she focused. Marcus's pistol. It must have fallen out of her pocket when she'd been shot. She reached out for Claire. Or Luna. She'd never known which was which, or why there'd been two of the guns. But she knew with her dying breath that the only way to save Abby, to save them all, was for her to get that gun.

She dragged herself across the smooth, clean floor. She'd hand-polished this floor once, along with a few of the other maids, swirling big circles of wax on, then buffing them to a high gloss. She'd been so sore over the next few days... No, wait, those were Ophelia's memories. The sorcerer was surfacing, and Hettie's thoughts were sinking back.

She couldn't let Hettie—the real Hettie—get trapped here. She couldn't let her—them—get caught again.

Berkeley and Stubbs had the outlaw's attention, and the Zoom was spiraling closed. There wasn't any time left.

Hettie grabbed Marcus's mage gun just as Stubbs got a bead on her.

A flurry of golden fireflies took wing around her, exploding outward in a rush that blew through her mind and descended upon Stubbs. The man screamed, and Hettie sensed the moment of death—a locust army devouring the enemy's soul in a million simultaneous tiny gulps.

His body fell lifeless to the ground, the sick thud of flesh echoed by a rustle in her mind. There was a... void, as if she'd just awoken from a dream she couldn't recall. A lightness, like staring up through a tree canopy to realize the branches were bare and the sun was glaring directly down on her.

Memories, she thought shakily. The gun had claimed something of hers—or perhaps it was Ophelia's. She wouldn't even know what she'd lost unless confronted by it.

Berkeley gave an enraged cry. His hands clasped together, and a ball of light started to form as he spit out an incantation—

And then Pee Wee's big arm swiped him aside, flinging him across the room. The automaton's legs were gone, a hole blasted clear through his chest, his head caved on one side, and his glass orb eyes cracked. The metal man's arms gave out, and he collapsed.

The outlaw cried out, "No!" Her face contorted with rage, and she raised Diablo, primed to take out Berkeley.

The Zoom tunnel was closing. She couldn't afford to wait another second.

A calmness invaded Hettie.

"There's only one way," she whispered, her words not her own.

Ophelia nodded in her mind.

She locked eyes with the real Hettie Alabama. "Go. Save Abby."

She put the muzzle to her head and pulled the trigger.

CHAPTER TWENTY-ONE

The explosion of golden fireflies engulfed the woman named Ophelia, lighting her up like a lantern before her whole body slackened and collapsed to the ground.

In that flash, a deluge of images rushed through Hettie, filling her head until it felt as though it would pop—but then, like a dying wind carrying a whirl of leaves, the memories settled. The past couple of hours of getting into the collection were now overlaid with Ophelia's memories—the ones Hettie herself had shared trapped in the vessel of the maid's mind. It was like looking at overlapping images etched in glass.

And now Hettie remembered. Abby. Uncle. Ma, Pa, Paul, Cymon, Jezebel...the ranch, the Crowe gang, Diablo, Zavi...all of it.

She pivoted and dove through the Zoom, barely making it to the other side as it spiraled closed. She caught Berkeley's stony glare as the aperture winked out.

She raised Diablo, poised for the Zoom to reopen and the grandmaster to come through with a vengeance, but Ophelia had left her something in death: because Ophelia had opened the Zoom, Berkeley couldn't trace where Hettie had gone. The remote Zoom was tied to the sorcerer who'd cast it.

Hettie closed her eyes and sank back, relieved. *Thank you*, she thought. The woman who'd been her jailer had turned out to be an ally in the end.

And for reasons she didn't fully understand, she'd given up her life to save Hettie's.

She breathed deep, reciting her life in her mind, flashing through everything she knew, hoping nothing was missing. Well, *something* was missing—firing Marcus's gun had taken something from Ophelia, and it could have been one of Hettie's memories. The Pistols of Lethe did not discriminate.

Poor Marcus. Now she had a taste for what his life must have been like.

She reviewed her time at Berkeley's. Not all of the notes had dates, and the earliest one she had written down had been three months ago. But there had been a stretch of weeks—she was fairly certain of it, anyhow—during which she'd obediently sat in her grandfather's workshop, doing sketches of the items he'd put in front of her, making notes as he described them. Days and days of doing just that, and long, sleepless nights in which she continued her work in secret, copying what she'd learned the day before in the book she'd hidden in Pee Wee's chest.

Her heart went out to the automaton. His body had been metal, but his soul was human, and though he'd frightened her at first, it quickly became clear he only wanted to help. He seemed to grasp what was happening to her, only moving to communicate with her when Berkeley was nowhere near. She wondered if his body could be fixed—if his soul was still somehow bound to that shell. One day she'd return and free him from his captivity. Pee Wee should be more than a part of a collection.

And so should Rok.

"Rok?" she whispered, and waited. The raven didn't appear.

Heart heavy, she pushed to her feet. Despite the dark of night, Hettie knew exactly where she was.

She picked up the burlap sack and dropped into her time bubble, grateful for the silence and the safety it afforded her. She walked about a mile before she came upon the little cottage. The goat was lying across the threshold, making it impossible for Hettie to go in without nudging it.

The thing bleated and leaped away from her, kicking her in the knee and knocking its hooves against her hip as she tried unsuccessfully to dodge it. The time bubble dropped as the goat trotted away, bleating loudly.

A heartbeat and a half later, a cold blade pressed against her throat.

"Toward the moonrise, never ceasing," Hettie gurgled.

"Hettie?" Jemma's deadly grip eased. Her eyes searched her in the dark, and she gasped. "Dear Lord, we thought you were dead!"

"Jemma!" Sophie burst through the door, brandishing a shotgun. She had it pointed at Hettie's head. "Let her go, you—" Her breath stopped short. "Oh my God."

"Not quite, but I'll take it."

They ushered her inside, then hugged her tight. Hettie trembled, feeling safe at last among friends once more. "Where have you been? What happened to you?" They lit lanterns, stoked the fire, and peppered her with questions.

She answered them as she ate a hastily made meal of cheese, bread, and coffee with a splash of whiskey. Sophie, draped in a heavy nightgown, listened intently as Hettie related her time with Berkeley. "So... Grandmaster Wolverton Gray Berkeley is your grandfather?"

"Do you know him?"

"Only by reputation. Grandmère refused to serve any of the Division council members and rarely attended any of the galas they invited her to. Her silent involvement with the League made her suspect." She exhaled. "I do know that Berkeley was childless. Tragic story, actually. His wife miscarried at every attempt. She ended up a permanent resident at Kardec Hospital."

Meaning she'd been condemned to the asylum. Sophie continued, "That doesn't mean that what he said about fathering a child out of wedlock is a lie. Still, I'd be cautious about believing anything he said. He might have been using influence magic on you."

Hettie nodded, but she didn't tell her that Diablo had long been a safeguard against influence magic—it had been part of the reason why the inserted memories wouldn't stick. And now that she had her memories back, she *did* recall a man visiting the ranch after

Paul's death. It had been such a terrible time for her, she hadn't remembered much of anything…

"You said he knew where Abby was," Jemma prompted.

"He told me she was being kept in a moving laboratory. A magical pocket between realms. Maybe that was a lie too, but…" She rubbed the space between her eyes. She had no reason to believe him, but she did. Because of what he'd said about the best stories being partly true. "How long have I been away? I tried to keep track, but the memory wipes…"

"Nearly four months," Sophie said. "We got word from…" She trailed off.

Hettie's heart stopped. "What? What's happened?"

"Walker came to us, Hettie. He told us what happened in Junesfield. How you left with Mr. Tsang."

"He was none too happy," Jemma interjected, folding her arms across her chest. "You broke his heart."

Hettie pursed her lips. "How is he? When I left…"

"He's doing fine, last I checked. Horace is with him—they're safe for now. There was a story in the newspapers about the Blackthorn Rogues attacking Junesfield, and that a train engine explosion decimated the Rogues. The League knows the truth, of course. What's left of the gang is being run by Duke and Lena."

"What about Ling?" She'd told them about her travels to Montana, about the Division and the bomb that had created the dead zone around Newhaven. "He and Cymon were with me at Kilraven's Peak when Stubbs jumped me."

"I don't know." Sophie took her hands. "No one's heard from them."

Hettie swallowed past a lump. She'd just found her friend again, and to lose him so swiftly… She just hoped he and Cymon hadn't been hurt.

Jemma picked up the heavy burlap sack. "What is all this?"

Hettie waved a hand with a smirk. "Souvenirs. Over the past few weeks, I worked in Berkeley's collection and learned what these things were for. I thought they might help us if you or someone else could figure out how to use them."

Sophie's mouth fell open. "And you just stole them from a grandmaster's collection?"

"It wasn't as if he was *using* them."

Jemma snickered. Sophie blew out a breath as she focused on the bag's contents. "Well, I'm not detecting any tracking spells, so at least there's that. The League will be very interested in these."

"They can have whatever's there if they can help me find Abby. This pocket he mentioned… Is it real?"

"I've read papers postulating such a theory—that there are other realms separated by ether. Some believe magic is generated in these spaces. But the spells that have been developed to open them require an incredible amount of power." Which, thanks to the Fielding engines, they had now. Sophie's brow furrowed. "If the Division has figured out a way to access these places… well, there's no telling what else they can do."

Hettie's mind spun. She didn't understand everything about magic, but she knew that with that bomb device that had sucked all the magic out of Newhaven, plus Abby's indigo powers, the Division's reach and scope would be limitless.

"We need to talk to the League right away," Hettie said.

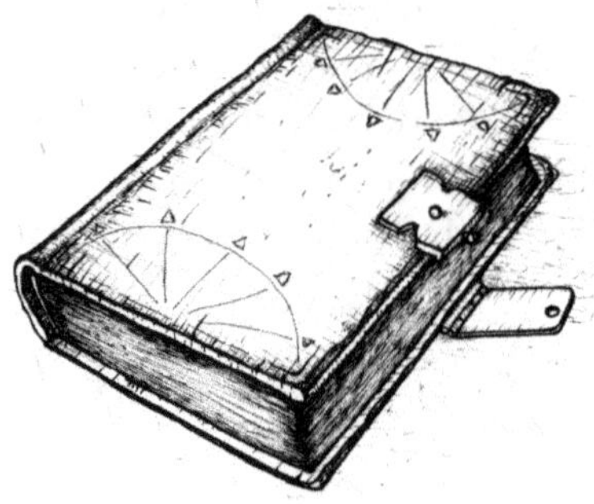

ALABAMA
1874

"Ain't nowhere left to go, son." Jeremiah Bassett trained his gun on the young man whose eyes darted left and right, seeking escape like a cornered rabbit. Jack Farham—or Elias Blackthorn, as Jeremiah preferred to think of him—had led him on one hell of a chase, from Wyoming Territory to middle-of-nowhere Alabama. Two years of near misses to finally corner him here, on the lip of a cliff with nothing but the sky to meet him. "Don't be a fool. This ain't no way to die."

"You bring me in and I hang." Jack glanced over his shoulder. "I ain't done nothing wrong, you know."

"You think leading the Blackthorn Rogues is nothing?" Jeremiah snorted. "Son, you've got a peculiar sense of morals."

"I ain't the leader. Diablo may be in my care, but I left that outfit the moment I could get away. Butch Crowe's the one you want."

"Listen. That revolver's all I want." Jeremiah's eyes stayed on the ivory grip. "You know the rules about mage guns and other enchanted objects. You need to register them with the Division."

"That why they sent you after me, Bassett? To make me fill out some paperwork?" A tremor warbled in his voice. Farham looked behind him longingly, fearfully.

"He's going to jump," Rok cawed overhead. The familiar, unseen and unremarked by most, wheeled through the sky, casting his

shadow over them with each pass like a lonely, morbid carousel. *"If he jumps, you'll lose Diablo."*

"And if I shoot him dead, I'll lose it," he murmured.

Rok gave another raspy cry. *"You can't let him escape again."*

"All you need to do is relinquish the Devil's Revolver to me," Jeremiah said evenly. "And then you can walk away from all this. Start a new life."

"You think I don't know that? It's all I *want* to do!" Jack's ruddy cheeks stood out against his pale face. "You don't understand. I'm not running from *you*. I'm running from *it*."

Seemed the sun had fried the boy's brains, Jeremiah thought. Farham was raving, but at least talking was better than jumping. "What's this *it* you're running from?"

"You don't believe me. You think I'm crazy." He shook his head. "The guardian—the true wielder. The one tied to this mage gun. He's after it—he's after *me*. He tries to find me in my dreams. He tortures me there."

Jeremiah set his teeth. There'd never been any mention of a guardian in the Division reports. But then, not many people survived an encounter with Elias and Diablo long enough to tell tales. And he knew the Division kept secrets, even from its own agents.

"Jed made me promise," Jack said despondently. "If I use this gun, the guardian will find me. I never got why the Blackthorns were always moving, but now I know. He's out there, looking. If he finds me..." He shuddered visibly.

Jeremiah shifted his grip, confused. The charm around his neck gave a low hum, letting him know Farham was telling the truth, or at least that he believed he was. And dammit all, Jeremiah believed him. This was no hardened criminal. He was just a scared boy. Slowly, he holstered his weapon and put his hands up. "All right, son. Look, whatever it is you're running from, I can help you. The Division can—"

"No." Jack brandished the gun. "I'm not going to the Division."

Jeremiah backed up. "All right then. No Division. Just you and me, okay? Let's talk about this guardian. Is it... Javier Punta?"

"He's…he's a…" He waved his hand absently, and a short bark of tortured laughter burst from him. "Angel? Demon? I don't even know. Only that he's coming for me."

Jeremiah frowned. "Rok? Is this your people?"

"Don't know, can't say," the raven called back, but Jeremiah wasn't convinced.

"*Won't* say, you mean." The demon familiar had his loyalties, and even though he was under Jeremiah's thrall and owed him his allegiance, he liked to play games. "What'll it cost me to get that gun out of his hands without hurting anyone?"

Rok wheeled silently above for three heartbeats, considering. *"A lot."*

"That ain't a price," he replied.

"A lot," the bird repeated stiffly.

Meaning the cost was more than Rok thought Jeremiah could afford. Of course, the bird had been wrong before. And it wasn't as if he could be in any *more* debt.

"Put it on my tab." He addressed Farham. "Listen, Jack, I ain't aiming to hurt you. I don't need another soul on my conscience. You come peacefully, and I swear on the lives of my kin, I'll do everything in my power to keep you safe."

Jack looked wild-eyed. He glanced over the lip of the cliff again.

"Maybe…this is supposed to end with me. Maybe this is for the best." He turned.

"Jack, no!" Jeremiah whipped out a seed pod and shouted an incantation. The bundle exploded in a tangle of green, snagging Jack around the waist and anchoring him to the ground as the tendrils took root in the earth.

Enraged, the young man pulled Diablo on him.

As Jeremiah stared down that black barrel, his life as a Division agent crystalized. All the men he'd hunted and killed, the lives he'd ruined, the people he'd supposedly brought to justice… What did he have to show for it? No legacy of his own; no widow to weep at his grave. Not a single person to mourn him beyond the paperwork some pencil pusher would file away once Jeremiah's shield was turned in.

He supposed he'd be settling up with Rok and his ilk a lot sooner than he'd—

Time turned to a slow drip as hell-green fire glowed from inside the mage gun's barrel. In an instinctual last-ditch effort to save himself, Jeremiah drew.

A flurry of black obscured his vision as Rok dove into Diablo's path at the same time Jeremiah pulled the trigger. The raven's dark eyes caught his in that final moment as the familiar's corporeal form absorbed Diablo's infernal magic like a sponge soaking up water.

Jeremiah didn't know what happened next. He was sitting on the ground, his face bruised as if there'd been an explosion. Jack was knocked out flat on the ground, the remnants of the seed pod scattered around him. Diablo smoked, just out of his grip. A shower of feathers drifted down. The raven's body lay between them, shockingly whole but clearly dead.

"Son of a..." Jeremiah got to his feet, collecting his gun and hurrying to Jack.

The young man looked as though he'd been punched hard, with purpling bruises darkening around a broken nose. He was still breathing, and no hell gate was opening nearby.

Jeremiah looked at Diablo, a shiver starting in his bones. Carefully he cast a containment spell, then withdrew the enchanted silk sack he needed to handle the gun.

He picked it up. A single tinny note vibrated through him, as if a bell had been rung too close to his ear. He inspected the weapon, feeling a touch ill as he shook it. Something rattled within, and he turned the gun over into his palm. The bullet Jeremiah had fired had gone straight up into the barrel and lodged there, somehow causing it to backfire.

But it wasn't just the bullet. On closer inspection, he found bits of Rok's feathers melded in the slug. His familiar had sacrificed his corporeal form to save Jeremiah...and Jack.

His throat burned as he knelt by the dead raven. "Dammit, Rok. It didn't cost *a lot*. It cost too much."

Wiping his tears away, he gathered the bird's remains and added Diablo to the enchanted sack. He was about to mount up when Jack groaned. "What...where am I?" His bleary gaze landed on Jeremiah. "Hello. I... Who are you?"

Jeremiah paused. Hell, what was he supposed to do with him? The law was looking for him, but really, what had the kid done except run scared? "My name's Jeremiah Bassett."

Jack looked confused. "Do you know who I am?"

Jeremiah stared. "You don't know?"

The young man ran his fingers through his hair, touching the broken bridge of his nose. "I'm…I'm bleeding." The blood drained from his face. He started shaking, and tears filled his eyes.

Aw, hell. "Take it easy now, son. You had a…a fall." In a manner of speaking. "You really don't remember?"

"Where is this place?" he asked again. Why was he so fixated on his location?

"Alabama. About ten miles from the nearest town that-a-way." He pointed northeast.

"Alabama." He said it like he was chewing on the word. "Alabama."

Jeremiah looked between the sack tied to the saddle and the dazed-looking Farham. Dammit, he couldn't leave the fool out here. "C'mon. You follow me. I'll take you to town to see a doctor." And shoot him in the back if he was trying to pull something. "There are good folks there. They'll take care of you. Seen 'em take in plenty of John Does."

"John." The man nodded slowly. "Alabama. That's my name. John Alabama." He said it decisively, as if he'd settled on a pair of boots.

Jeremiah looked over his shoulder to ask the raven what had happened to Jack's mind, but then remembered his familiar was gone. The sharp pang of grief skewered through him, and his throat constricted. For reasons he might never understand, Rok had sacrificed himself to save them; Jeremiah wouldn't let him die in vain.

"Well, then, John Alabama. How about you and me head to town and get ourselves a drink?"

John nodded. "John Alabama," he said with the vague, wonder-filled smile of an infant.

CHAPTER TWENTY-TWO

The League of Sorcerers for Free Magic was, according to the Division, a reckless group of dissenters and terrorists with dangerous ideas about the deregulation of magic. They'd existed in one form or another since before the Mayflower arrived, with branches all around the world wherever magic faced strict regulation.

Every arm of the organization had its own ideals and methods for protesting, of course. During the Revolutionary War, the League in America had split off from the British League, having their own magical mini war that had ended in a detente. But since the Division of Sorcery's crackdown on unregistered sorcerers, which had begun just after the Civil War ended, the League had become a united front against magical tyranny. Their methods had become more militant as the Division's policies grew stricter. It had been the mandatory enrollment of gifted children and the increasing number of mysterious deaths at the Academy that forced the League to resort to actual violence. Several Division outposts and offices were mobbed; a few were cursed with spells that crumbled buildings or made the people within them ill.

They were not precision attacks, but they got the message across. *We will not be manacled. Our children are not your soldiers.* But a lot of innocent bystanders were caught in the crossfire. As a result, the Mundane Movement gained a lot of followers—people who wanted to see the privileged gifted locked up or worse. As tensions rose, the Movement became more radical, more violent; the Division tried to placate their fears with more regulation; and the League responded with equal violence. And so the cycle went on and on.

Pa had had few dealings with the Division. He'd been registered, like most gifted in Newhaven had been, but he hadn't attended the Academy and rarely used magic except with regard to protection spells. Hettie knew now that Uncle had once been a Division agent himself, but he'd avoided most interactions with the government agency. Being a fugitive probably had something to do with that.

The journey to the League's headquarters was long and convoluted. Disguised as widows, Hettie, Sophie, and Jemma took a train north to a small town whose name Hettie couldn't remember, where they met up with a group of masked sorcerers who opened a remote Zoom to a location none of them could put a finger on. From there, they'd taken a cart to another site, where they stepped through yet another Zoom. Hettie supposed among the more powerful sorcerers not being caught was worth more than the magic they spent on keeping themselves safe.

On the other side of the Zoom, the wind bit through Hettie's coat, carrying the fresh scent of pine, and her boots crunched on the gravelly ground.

The portal spiraled closed quickly, disappearing against a pale blue sky. Hettie looked down from a hilltop plateau at the impenetrable thickets of evergreens surrounding them. The sun shone hot and bright against the spellground, taking some of the chill out of the air. About fifty tents and small wooden buildings, all of them painted with anti-Eye charms, lined the slope, arranged in a vaguely circular pattern. A giant protection circle, Hettie realized.

Farther below, men and women moved crates and barrels into a cave. There were maybe two hundred or so people here, along with their families, including small children. This wasn't a garrison; it was a refuge. It wasn't the magical stronghold Villa del Punta was, but then, walls weren't always the most effective defenses.

The twelve sorcerers arranged in a circle on the Zoom dais closed around them, murmuring a spell. Hettie tensed, but Sophie grabbed her wrist to stop her from drawing. "Don't. They need to check us for tracking and influence spells."

It took a moment before they were satisfied and shuffled off. "Where are we?" Hettie asked, looking around. She couldn't tell where they were in the country, if they were even in the States. With the magically open border to the north, it was conceivable they were in Canada.

"We call this place Root Hill, though you'd never find it on a map. All you need to know is we're safe here and have been for some time. The trees provide shelter and hide our presence from the Division. And there are no roads, no access points for mundanes. You can only get here via remote Zoom. Which means you need to know about this place first."

"Robin." A woman in a deep red dress greeted Sophie. She was in her thirties, if Hettie were to guess, with tightly bound black hair and wire-rimmed spectacles. The woman regarded "Robin's" companions warily. "I thought you were in seclusion."

"I was. But this couldn't wait." She gestured. "You know Magpie, of course."

"Lady Starling," Jemma greeted, and the woman in red nodded respectfully. Hettie realized they were addressing each other by code names, probably for their own protection.

"You and yours are always welcome here, Magpie. But I don't know this one, and I sense some powerful magics on her, though she is not gifted."

Sophie cleared her throat. "Lady Starling, I'd like to present Hettie Alabama."

The woman's already pale face went a shade whiter. "Hettie Alabama? The freedom fighter?"

Hettie raised an eyebrow. "I think you have me mixed up with someone else."

"Hettie, this is Lady Starling. She's the commander of the League of Sorcerers for Free Magic." Sophie's careful enunciation told Hettie to be cautious with her words. "Where are the others?"

"Jay and Hawk are out on a mission," Lady Starling replied. "They were due back this morning. There's no telling where they might be now. They could be dead." She was impossible to read. Hettie might have taken that as a grim joke, but there was a resignation to the woman's tone that told Hettie she was too practical and weary to be that wry.

She led them to a large wood structure beyond the dais. The walls were carved with runes and symbols for protection and festooned with all kinds of talismans. Hettie felt the slight repulsion of the place, but as Starling opened the door and beckoned them in, it faded. The interior was simple, with a swept wood floor, a potbellied stove, some chairs, and a large table. A meeting room of some kind was Hettie's guess. As Starling poured them each a cup of tea, she glanced toward Hettie, her lips lifting only a fraction in a loaded smile. "The stories of your crusade have spread far and wide, Miss Alabama. The League is honored by your alliance and welcomes you to the fight."

"That's not why I'm here." She set the bag down with a loud clatter. The sorcerer's eyes went to it questioningly. "Not exactly."

Sophie implored, "We need help, Starling. I've told you about Hettie's sister and her indigo powers…"

"Yes. I'm sorry about your loss, Miss Alabama. I lost two children to the Division myself. Both of them killed at the Academy due to 'accidents.' My husband was also arrested and taken to Swedenborg."

"They have a lot to answer for. But Abby's not dead, and I might know where she is."

It took her a long time to get Starling up to speed about the man-thing attacks in Junesfield, the bomb in Newhaven, and her imprisonment at Berkeley Manor. Sophie posited her theory about the pocket realm Abby could be trapped in. Starling listened intently, asking only a few questions for clarification, her expression giving nothing away. From her unblinking stare, Hettie got the sense the woman didn't need to be told anything twice.

"This is incredible," she finally said when Hettie's voice had gone hoarse from speaking. "We've been discussing the possibilities of a pocket realm for our own headquarters. Jay and Hawk are out now trying to recruit a metaphysical Mechanik who could help us."

"A meta…meta what?"

"A sorcerer who can build us a machine to help create the pocket realm," Sophie translated.

"I thought you said it was just a theory."

"A theory, yes, but one that has solid foundations. Zoom tunnels and portals exist within the same field of magic study—they open gaps in the magical ether that allow us to travel from point to point in our own reality. This pocket theory is the next step in that field: creating a real space in the ether and keeping it open."

"Ether...like Celestial ether magic?"

"That attribution was created to scare Westerners away from Eastern healers," Starling said pointedly. "According to the old masters in the Far East, their sorcerers get their magic from qi, which I believe roughly translates to 'lifeforce energy.' But because there's no English word for it, I think early magic scholars decided the Greek word *aether* was the closest they could get. That meaning slowly transformed as medical science advanced and doctors were looking for ways to keep their patients from visiting foreign healers.

"Not that this precludes a connection between Celestial magic and the theory behind Zooms and portals and pockets," she added. "We don't know how different magics work together, only that sometimes they do. How Eastern magics might be related to the Fielding engines is not something that's known."

"Except that Ling told me Chinese sorcerers in San Francisco were being drained by a different type of Fielding engine." Hettie went on to give them all the details she could remember. "So...doesn't that mean magic is all kind of the same?"

Starling shook her head. "I can't say for certain, since I don't know anything about this 'hog.' But it does suggest that qi is the same as other magics on some level. But you said these sorcerers were in long-term captivity?"

"That's what Ling said. They were trapped in that ship for months, attached to that engine, feeding it with their powers."

Sophie put a fist to her mouth. "How horrible."

"And yet informative. It means qi is not finite." Starling nodded. "Even the mundanes among the Eastern community speak of qi in their traditional medical practices."

Hettie blew out a breath. "So how are Abby's indigo powers related?"

"I have looked into these powers Sophie told me about. Indigo powers seem to work outside of all known existence, perhaps on a different plane, or on multiple planes. This pocket realm may be where Abby's powers are the most effective but the least damaging, if in fact the pocket does exist."

"It would make sense if that's where all the Fielding canisters are heading," Sophie said. "They would need a lot of sorcerers to open this pocket and keep it open. A lot more to keep Abby under control."

"To do what? Why hold her prisoner if she's so dangerous?" That argument had run laps around her brain night after night the past few years.

"That is the question." Starling gestured at the bag. "Let's see what you've brought us."

Hettie emptied the sack out onto a worktable, and Jemma carefully laid each item out. When Hettie eyeballed the other women who weren't moving in to help, Jemma explained her anti-influence scarring protected her against a lot of hexes.

Starling's lips moved soundlessly as she perused the assortment, her eyes widening. "This is an amazing and rather specific collection," she said breathily.

"Do you know what they are?"

"I have a good idea. The question is, how did *you* know?"

"I spent a lot of time pretending not to know I was missing my memories so I could study Berkeley's collection. He loved showing it off. I think he wanted someone to talk to about it."

"You mean he wanted someone to talk *at*," Jemma said with a snort. "Men love explaining things."

Hettie nodded. "When I learned about something I thought might be useful, I made a note of it in my book." Hettie handed her notebook to Starling, and she skimmed through it.

"This is... invaluable." Starling glanced up, her eyes shrewd. "But I sense you're looking for more than a simple payout in exchange for these artifacts."

"I need to find Abby. Berkeley said she's being held in this pocket realm. If you can get access to it, I want to be there."

She hesitated. "I don't know if that's possible. We're only just trying to figure it out for ourselves."

"That's why we came," Sophie said. "With Hettie's help and these talismans, maybe we can finally find the Division's stronghold and attack them where they'll be most vulnerable."

"Is that your intention? Violence?"

Hettie met the woman's intense gaze. "With all due respect, Mrs. Starling, my only goal is to get my sister back safe. If anyone tries to stop me"—she summoned Diablo—"I'm not likely to restrain myself."

The sorcerer regarded her steadily. "And you condone this, Robin?"

"Hettie is my friend," she said. "I trust her. The Division has taken too much from us already. If it hurts the Division, then she has my approval. Grandmère would back me up."

"Magpie, I've not heard anything from you," Starling addressed Jemma. "You are not one of us, but your insight is invaluable."

Jemma raised her chin. "I think it would be suicide to attack the Division."

Hettie glanced at her, surprised. Of all of them, she'd thought Sophie's bodyguard would be most supportive of an attack on the people who'd hurt them. Jemma went on, "They have the most powerful sorcerers on their side, Fielding engines and canisters stocked with power, and they're holding the loved ones of your own members in captivity. We can't attack them on their turf. Not without a plan."

"Or an army," Hettie muttered.

CHAPTER TWENTY-THREE

At that moment, the Zoom aperture spiraled open. Two men walked through, one tall and lanky wearing a dun-colored duster and a floppy hat. The other was a mountain of a man in buckskin pants and tunic. They halted at the sight of their guests.

"M-Miss R-Robin," the lanky man stuttered, tugging on his hat. He bowed awkwardly. His eyes grew wide as he looked at Hettie.

"Who's our *guest?*" the mountain man asked, one hand on the tomahawk on his belt.

"Hawk, don't you recognize her?" the lanky man whispered. "Look at the scar."

Starling said, "She's all right, Hawk. She's Robin and Magpie's friend."

"Hettie Alabama." Hettie stepped forward, holding out a hand. Pa had always said the best way to get the measure of a man was to see how he shook a lady's hand. "Murderer and outlaw, at your service."

The man called Hawk eyed her up and down. "You're shorter than I thought you'd be."

She dropped into her time bubble and snatched the tomahawk from his belt, then held it up to his face. "Hasn't slowed me down."

He snatched back his weapon, frowning. "And to what do we owe your humble appearance among us mere mortals?"

"Don't be rude, Hawk," Jay urged. To Starling, he said, "We couldn't recruit the Mechanik. He ran at the sight of this one." He jerked his chin toward Hawk.

"Ain't my fault he's afraid of real men."

"Real men, fake men, undead men... That man wanted nothing to do with us one way or another. Those zombies have him spooked."

"Another attack?" Starling asked wearily.

"A day or two ago. Not five miles from that town. People were preparing for a war."

"Excuse me... zom... *zombies*?" Hettie asked, confused.

Sophie interjected, "The creatures you call man-things have been attacking more towns. The papers have been calling them *zombies* after the Haitian legends. More and more of these drained sorcerers have been roaming the countryside."

"A few of us have been trying to stop the attacks," Jay added. "Doesn't help that a lot of towns are expelling their gifted. They've figured out the zombies are attracted to magic. They're bringing other diseases, as well, and poisoning the water where they die. Mundanes are afraid they'll spread the curse among their kind, too."

"There's something else, Starling." Jay cast his gaze around. "We touched base with one of our men on the inside. The Division has something planned. We're not sure what, but the Fielding expeditions are being recalled. They're bringing in all the canisters, whether they're full or not."

"The troops are rallying, too," Hawk said. "They have garrisons at all the major magical nodes and near the Zooms. Word is Division forces have commandeered the apertures from the Zoom Union."

Starling's brow furrowed in thought. "Have they traced where they're going?"

"No. All attempts to track them are lost the moment they pass through the Zoom. Not only that, Alastair Fielding himself was seen at Barney's Rock."

"Fielding's alive?" Hettie's fists clenched. "The last time I saw him, he was at Swedenborg. The Alabama gang, led by a warlock named Zavi"—she realized that would take a lot more time to explain—"had kidnapped him. They made him build the bomb that destroyed the prison. I'm pretty sure it's the same kind of bomb that was used in Newhaven."

"A bomb. Of course." Starling ground her jaw. "At Swedenborg, we'd detected traces of the same void the canisters give off, but the site is too toxic for sorcerers to get close to. You're certain it was him?"

"Yes. I watched him detonate it."

"And you say he—or someone—built another one of these bombs?" Hawk asked.

"And tested it. My hometown, Newhaven, in Montana." She repeated the story about the Division's experiment for Jay and Hawk's benefit. "The place is a magical void now. Not even Diablo worked there."

Sophie said, "The Division must have Fielding back. All these years he's been supposedly missing…he must have been working on this."

"A bomb to remove all the magic on a large scale," Jay said faintly. "But…why?"

"Why else?" Jemma said. "Only two things build weapons like this: fear and a desire for power."

Hawk grunted. "A device like that bomb could wipe us all out if we're gathered here in one place. Maybe we should scatter. Evacuate."

"No," Starling said. "That's exactly what they want. We're stronger together."

They argued back and forth about their course of action. But Hettie was preoccupied by a different train of thought.

The bomb. The recall of the Fielding expeditions. The pocket realm. Abby. They were pieces of a larger puzzle, but what was it?

Something Jemma had said was still niggling at her. *Only two things build weapons like this: fear and a desire for power.*

"Berkeley said the Division would be done with Abby soon," she said suddenly, and all eyes turned to her. "That can't mean anything good. They went through a lot of trouble to find my sister and bring her in. All her life, she's been watched. They sent hundreds of soldiers to Swedenborg, but not because they knew the Alabama gang was there, and not because they were trying to contain a jailbreak."

"Abigail," Sophie said. "Of course. I felt her power the moment her Zoom opened. I didn't know what it was at the time, but after you told me about it..."

Hettie nodded. There were pieces missing in this puzzle, but the picture was coming into focus. "What if we're missing the point? What if this isn't about draining all the sorcerers? If it were, why would they suddenly recall the Fielding expeditions and close the Zoom stations? Why have they been accelerating students through the Academy when so many of them aren't ready to serve? What is happening that would make Berkeley say they'd be done with my sister soon?"

He could have been lying, of course, but Hettie didn't get that sense. Everything she'd learned about the man told that he was confident in his status, had little at stake, and subsequently nothing to hide from her.

Everyone shuffled nervously as they contemplated the possibilities. No one had an answer, and they could speculate all day, but they all realized now *something* was going to happen, and that something was bad.

Starling braced her arms against the tabletop. "Miss Alabama is right. Whatever is coming, we need to safeguard our people, prepare for a battle, and strike first in this pocket realm if we can. Perhaps we can stop whatever they're planning before they realize we're onto them." Her lieutenants nodded in agreement. "First things first. We need a team to inspect the artifacts Miss Alabama brought and see what we can do with them..."

The sorcerers fell into a conversation that Hettie couldn't follow. It went on for some time, and Hettie's mind wandered.

Jemma appeared at her side. "I know how this bunch works. They'll be at this for hours while we sit around being useless."

Hettie raised a brow. "You have something else in mind?"

"I think *you* do. Division's rallying their troops; you should rally yours."

"I don't have any men left," she said flatly. "Most of them died in Junesfield..." She bit her lip. They hadn't died—she'd gotten them killed, and she hadn't done a thing to mourn them. Who knew how many of their ghosts were trailing after her... She went on relentlessly, "I abandoned them all to go after Abby."

"Are you regretting that now?"

Hettie pushed down a surge of irritation and bitter remorse. "I was doing what I thought was right at the time."

Jemma leaned against the wall. "It's all we can do. And I get it. I'd do anything for Sophie." She cast her longing gaze toward her. "If it were my choice, we'd run far away from here. Sail to France and let this world burn. But this kind of trouble will catch up to you eventually. Anyhow, she's committed to the cause and to finding Patrice. It's your fault, really." Jemma smiled lopsidedly. "I suspect Sophie's trying to be more like you. She admires your gumption. Marcus did speak highly of you. I think she was a bit jealous of that."

"I forgot to mention, one of Marcus's mage guns is in the bag. Berkeley had them. Sorry I couldn't save them both."

Jemma nodded. "We'll have it buried with him if the League doesn't need it."

She'd like to see the thing melted down. Having had her own memories played with, she couldn't understand why Marcus had continued to use Luna and Claire.

The answer was simple, of course: love. He'd loved Sophie and had sworn to protect her. What had his loyalty to Hettie earned him in the end? A cold plot in the ground in some ruined town?

Hettie supposed she was destined for the same ignoble end. In her years-long quest to find Abby, she'd maimed a lot of people, killed countless men and women, and brought pain and suffering to those closest to her.

"After everything I've done..." she said. "Getting all my people killed... I can't imagine anyone wanting to follow me anywhere."

"I know at least one man," Jemma said meaningfully.

Her heart caught. She meant Walker. Blind, magicless, gunless...he'd follow her straight into hell on his hands and knees if she asked him to. "I didn't do right by him, did I?"

"Walker's a good man. He'll forgive you again and again. That's what people who love you do." She skewered her with a look. "But he deserves better than to be cast aside whenever you find him inconvenient."

Hettie blew out a breath. "I just...don't want him to get hurt. He could've been killed in Junesfield, and it would've been my fault." Her fingers clenched tight. "Sometimes I think it would be better if he moved in with you two and married Sophie."

Jemma chuckled. "I'd be first to welcome him. He's a fine man, for all his rough edges. And he understands what's between Sophie and me." Jemma squeezed Hettie's shoulder. "But Walker chose *you*, Hettie Alabama, even when things were at their bleakest. That's got to mean something, even to you."

It did. Hettie finally had to admit that to herself. After everything she'd been through at Berkeley's—losing her memories of Walker, feeling utterly helpless, tetherless—she wanted to see him. Needed to know he was all right. To apologize. To seek comfort in his arms.

"I have to find him," she said resolutely. She'd left him behind...where would Lena and the others have gone? It might take weeks to track them down. Months, even...

Jemma smirked. "Good thing he's here."

Hettie's spine snapped straight. "What?"

"In the village below." She nodded downhill. "I didn't want to bring you to him till I knew your feelings."

It was on the tip of her tongue to shout at her for keeping them apart, but Jemma was only doing what she did best—protecting the people she cared about. Hettie wasn't sure she was any good at it herself. Maybe that was why she admired the bodyguard so much.

MONTANA
1895

Don't look back. Don't look back.

Jeremiah Bassett rode hard, his backside jouncing hard in the saddle, stomach churning, every muscle stiff. The box in the sack banged an angry tattoo of bruises against his leg. All his mistakes, all his failings would be forever branded on him.

I swore to help John. To protect his family…

"Failure! Failure!" Rok's ashy shadow resolved midflight next to him, the tips of his tail feathers brushing through his vision. *"Coward! Coward!"* The contempt in his call was unmistakable.

"Git your ass outta my way!" He swiped at the ghost bird ineffectually. The gray mustang gave a whinny of distress, and Jeremiah let him slow to a trot. He glanced back.

Above the ranch, plumes of smoke glowing the color of old blood blotted out the stars and stained the night sky.

His chest tightened. John. Grace. Hettie and Abby…

"All's lost! All's lost!" Rok soared in a tight circle above him.

"As long as Diablo stays out of that maniac's hands, we're fine." He shifted the bagged box to the other side of the saddle and rubbed his shin. "This gun's too much for one man. Blackthorn's legacy needs to die, and I'm the only person who can make that happen."

"Too much for one man," Rok hissed in disgust. *"You're* one *man."*

"The gun's safe in the box. John and his kin are the only ones who can open it."

"And if they die, there'll be no way to get to the gun…except for him." Rok's flight path dipped, and the bird slapped him with ashy wingtips. *"No little box can stop* him. He'll *figure it out.* He'll *come for you."*

Jeremiah balked. "You mean Butch Crowe?"

The raven gave a desiccated laugh. *"Too much for one man, but* he's *not one man.* He *knows you have it now.* He *senses your hunger.* He'll *come for you."*

Jeremiah's blood turned icy. "The guardian."

"Only Alabama blood should touch that gun. Diablo chose him."

Jeremiah spurred his horse forward, turning away from the red sky. "Hell, no. I won't let John or his girls anywhere near this thing. They're better off dead than cursed."

"Better off?" The outrage in the raven's cry did not give Jeremiah any warning. Rok dive-bombed his face.

His vision clouded with black ash, and he was suddenly breathing it, choking on it. He beat it away, waving his hands frantically.

When his sight cleared, he found himself at the ranch, fire raging around him. He heard a shot and a high-pitched scream. *Grace!* He bolted toward the noise.

A man with a horribly scarred face—Butch Crowe—stood over John. Blood blossomed on his friend's chest. He couldn't hear what he said, but then Butch raised his gun and put a bullet between Grace's eyes.

Jeremiah screamed. No. No, not Grace. She'd been the light of all their lives, the one who'd brought John back from the dark, given him something to live for. She'd forgiven them both their pasts and the sins they'd committed. She'd persevered through her difficult labor with Abby, mourned her firstborn's death…*survived.* She was the strongest woman he'd ever known…

"Whoops. Nearly forgot about this one." Butch stooped by the woodpile and grabbed something—

His heart leaped into his throat. "Hettie—!"

The sound of the bullet entering her skull point-blank was like a hammer blow against a tureen of stew. Her body dropped limply to the ground. Jeremiah dove for her, trying to catch her before she fell, but she passed straight through his arms.

Interpolation. Rok was projecting his consciousness to the ranch to be a firsthand witness.

"Rok!" he screamed. "Rok, goddamn you!"

"Failure! Failure!" The raven wheeled overhead.

Butch stooped over John, whose eyes were fixed on his daughter by the woodpile. His chest rose and fell in shallow, labored breaths.

"I ain't gonna kill you," Butch said. "I want you to live with this. You want revenge? You wanna save your girl?" He pointed toward a silent Abby. "You'll have to come after me, and bring Diablo. 'Cuz I won't be as charitable with her as I was with that one." He got up. "Don't disappoint me, Jack."

The gang melted into the shadows. A chorus of wolf yowls echoed through the night, their song in rhythm with John's rasping, labored breaths. He curled around his wife, cradling her head, and threw his own head back in a bloodcurdling howl of anguish.

"Enough," Jeremiah called raggedly. The interpolation spell faded, and he was back on his horse, miles away from the ranch. Rok perched on the horse's head and looked him in the eye.

"The wielder lives," he hissed. *"But not for long."*

Jeremiah kicked the horse into a gallop and aimed for the ranch.

CHAPTER TWENTY-FOUR

The League's "village" was lively and thriving, despite the feeling that, at any minute, they might have to pick up and leave. The tents were staked on muddy ground, with wood plank floors and waist-high siding applied to keep the rats out. Cooking fires were carefully arranged among the living areas. Several magicked wells had been drawn up through the ground, probably with the same water-drafting spell Uncle and Walker had used when they'd been traveling through the Arizona desert. Children ran through the muddy corridor, chasing stray chickens or playing at Blackthorn Rogues, though they didn't seem to realize what that name meant these days. A few of the kids tossed glow stones that shifted color as they changed hands.

Jemma had said Walker was down here, but she hadn't said which tent. Hettie scanned the bodies and faces, searching for those familiar broad shoulders, that crooked smile, those ice-blue eyes. Soon, returned stares and whispers told her the refugees recognized her. Knots of people parted hastily before her. A few women clutched their children closer. Several men took off their hats as she passed, wide-eyed and slack-jawed.

"That's her," she heard them whispering. "Elias Blackthorn's legacy. Hettie Alabama, the wielder of the Devil's Revolver." Her name raced through the camp like a snake with its tail on fire.

"They say she faced the zombie hordes and lived."

"I heard she killed ten Division sorcerers with one bullet."

"Stay away from her! She's a ghost now, a bride of the devil who walks in and out of life and death…"

She kept her shoulders squared, her look mean. If they were going to be afraid of her, she might as well look the part. She supposed she could've dropped into her time bubble to avoid the gossip, but then she'd only be feeding the rumors.

"What're you doin' here?"

Hettie froze. She knew that voice, and a surge of wary joy filled her as she faced the woman. "Daisy."

Daisy put her hands on her hips. The hem of her gown was caked with mud, but she looked otherwise hale and hardy. "Every time you and yours darken my doorstep, something else happens. You're a curse, Hettie Alabama."

"I'm here to see Walker," she said.

"I don't know any Walker." Daisy blocked her path, arms akimbo. "Now you go back to whatever hell you walked out of."

"Aw, let the po' girl in, Daze," Daisy's brother, Bear Brown, called from inside the tent, his voice as creaky as Hettie remembered it. "She's come a long way an' deserves a drink."

Daisy's glare cut through Hettie like a knife, but she threw back the tent flap and gestured her in.

The interior was cozier than she thought it would be, with a fine rug on the wood-slat floor, a large bed, and a small table with two chairs. Bear sat upright in an armchair, a blanket draped over his legs. He'd lost weight, though he wasn't as gaunt as he'd been when they'd first met.

"I promise I ain't no ghost," he said, beckoning her closer. "Not yet. Now you come give ol' Bear a hug."

Hettie did so. "I don't understand… How… Why are you here? I thought you were staying at Sophie's safehouse."

"We were there a good while," Bear said, "but them zombies found us just under a year ago, and the Division was right behind them. Jemma left us a remote Zoom beacon for a fast escape. We been here with the League ever since."

Daisy set a cup of coffee and a plate of biscuits on the table for Hettie with a glare. For all that Hettie had been unwelcome, it seemed Daisy couldn't help playing hostess. "I was told… That is…"

"Miss Hettie?" A dark face appeared between the tent flaps.

"Horace!" She leaped to her feet, and they hugged. Daisy complained loudly that people were tracking mud onto her nice clean floors, but only harrumphed when Horace apologized and offered to sweep up after himself.

"We thought you were dead." Horace held her back, inspecting her as a father might look over his child. "Why'd you leave us like that, huh?"

"I'm sorry, I really am. It's a long story." She glanced around hopefully.

"You want to see him." He knew. He led her out of the tent and farther along the main throughway.

A tremor began low in Hettie's belly. "How…how is he?" she asked tentatively, partly to stall the meeting.

"He's not angry with you," he said. "Sad, maybe. But not angry. Not really." He bowed his head. "Miss Lena took care of us. Got us safely out of Junesfield and away from the Division and the zombies."

Horace pointed at the ramshackle structure with an anti-Eye charm hung outside. "I'll give you two some privacy."

She hesitated, thinking of all the horrible things Walker could say or do. She imagined angrily thrown boots. It almost made her turn back.

Instead she took a deep breath and knocked.

"It's open." His deep voice sent tears to her eyes. Gods, she'd missed him. She entered.

Walker stood facing the rear of the tent. His broad shoulders stretched his white shirt across his back. His gun belt and black hat hung from one corner of the bed.

"You cut your hair," she said finally, her voice harsh and small, making scraping sounds like a worn key fumbling through a rusted lock.

Walker didn't turn. "Daisy insisted. Said I looked like an ugly woman."

Hettie couldn't help but chuckle, her stomach aquiver. By gods, she was nervous. "Walker…"

"Did you find her?"

Her heart squeezed tight, and a bubble of air went to her head so she lost focus a moment. "No. Not yet. But I'm close. Really close. That's why I'm here. Sophie brought me to see the League. They're helping me find this pocket realm…" She was babbling. She schooled the words threatening to spill from her. "I came here for *you*." She stepped forward.

"For me? Or for my help?"

Hettie halted, opened her mouth to protest, but no words came.

"They're not the same thing, if that's what you're wondering." He turned to face her then.

Everything inside her wanted to rush toward him, to have him hold her the way he used to. But the intensity in his ice-blue eyes wavered with pain—hurt she'd caused with every rejection, every moment she'd stepped back as he'd stepped forward.

She was forced then to admit that what she wanted more than Walker himself was his stability. His strength. She wanted him by her side again to help bring Abby home. She wanted him to be there for her, to pull her out of that hole just like that first time, when she'd collapsed the cave over Zavi's head and had been trapped at the bottom of a cavern with no way out. She wanted someone she could lean on, talk to, argue with. She'd wanted Walker for all the things he'd provided for her endlessly, thanklessly.

"I'm sorry," she said. "For leaving you and Lena and the others when you needed me. For putting you all in danger in the first place." She huffed. "I left because…it was my fault. Junesfield was a bad bet. I got the Rogues killed because of something that should've always been mine and mine alone to fight for."

"Like hell." He glowered. "You don't get to decide what's too dangerous for me. You don't get to set me aside because you think I can't handle it."

She watched his darting pupils. "You still can't see."

"I can see fine." He turned his face. "Better than I could four months ago, at any rate."

"But not perfectly."

His jaw worked.

Not well enough to shoot, she concluded at his silence. Hettie's heart sank, though she hated her selfishness. She should be happy he was alive.

"It'll get better. Lena's been helping me," he said. Lena had some healing powers, though they were nowhere near as powerful as Ling's.

"Where is she?"

"She comes every couple of weeks. She and Duke have been running what's left of the Rogues, doing what they can alongside the League to stop the zombie attacks. They check in with Sophie now and again."

So Duke had survived. Hettie was surprised they were all working together now. Duke wasn't much of a do-gooder, and she had a hard time imagining him sharing leadership with Lena. Frankly, she was surprised he'd even made it out of Junesfield alive, being mundane. But then, he was a survivor, like all of them. Things must have gotten pretty bad for Duke and the rest of the gang to turn to zombie hunting... unless, of course, it paid well.

"Is Ling with you?" Walker asked warily.

"No. We got separated in Newhaven. It's a long story."

"Is there any point in you telling it to me if you're just going to leave again?"

A pang went through her. "Walker..."

"I know why you came, Hettie. You wanted me and the rest of us back to help you save your sister. It's always about Abby."

"You want me to make it about you?" she asked, outrage rising in her.

"I want you to make it about *family*. Do you think you're the only one who cares for her? Dammit, Hettie! I left my mother behind in Mexico for you. I abandoned my people to go looking for you. And when I found you..." He forked his fingers through his hair. "You were catatonic for weeks. I took care of you. I kept you alive. I brought you back from the brink. And I didn't even get a thank-you." A tear dripped heavily from his watering eyes, and he swiped it away hastily.

Hettie pressed her palms together, trying to hold her own emotions in check. Anger was too strong a description. No, this was more like disappointment, but in whom? Herself for being so weak when traumatized? In Walker, for not accepting her choices? For being useless in her current crisis? That was a cold, unfeeling thought, and she hated herself, and Walker, for bringing the worst of her into the light.

And yet she desperately wanted to go to him. To have him forgive her again. She knew she didn't deserve it, had done nothing to earn his love. But she craved his arms around her like a dope fiend after the pipe.

"Walker, I didn't come here to fight. But you're right. I have chosen Abby again and again over everyone and everything else that matters to other people." She stiffened her shoulders. "I won't apologize for that. My sister means the world to me."

He flinched. He hadn't expected the truth. "You chose Ling over me," he said in a petulant rationalization to preserve his ego.

"I chose *Abby* over you. Ling had a lead. A good one, it turns out, even though it didn't pan out the way I thought it would." She sat down heavily in the tent's only chair, suddenly drained. "The place I ended up… The man I met… He broke me down, stripped away my memories until there was nothing left except who I was at that moment. And I didn't like her." The admission left her raw. That dual memory overlapped in her mind—seeing her own scarred face, feeling frightened of the woman she'd become… laid over the memory of the outlaw, staring hard back at Ophelia, trying to come up with the fastest way to get what she wanted, even if it was at the point of a gun. "The only thing that made her—me—someone I could live with was Abby."

She rubbed at the cuts carved into her arm. She'd used a wire from her corset to etch the words in, retracing the letters each time she rediscovered them and rubbing soot from the fireplace in to make sure the welt didn't heal over and disappear. "When I finally remembered her… it was like all the world made sense again. And then it was taken away from me, and all I had left were scars I didn't remember getting."

Walker's furious expression eased. He sat down on the bed and patted the space next to him. "If you're willing to stay… If you want to tell your story, I'll listen."

So she did. In some ways, she hated how easily he'd capitulated. Would she have been as forgiving had their roles been reversed?

Probably not, but Hettie had never been the forgiving sort. Not even of herself.

The story came out haltingly at first. It had been easier to tell Sophie and Jemma, for some reason, but then she realized she'd been holding back her feelings from them, protecting them from the hurt and fear swirling inside her after that prolonged captivity.

She told Walker about waking up every morning, feeling less and less a part of the world, not recalling much about the past or the place she came from until all she knew were the days behind her, in the study, talking with Berkeley, her life narrowed to the eccentric man and his lavish house and his fantastic collection of magical artifacts.

"The worst part," she said slowly, "was that at the height of it... I felt... like suddenly, everything was so much easier. If all I did was sit and do as he asked, be quiet and obedient and hardworking, I... I might have been happy."

"But you didn't."

"I couldn't. I knew something was wrong. It clawed at me from the inside. In some ways, I think I owe that to Uncle..." she said faintly. "I don't think I would've stayed sane for long, not knowing anything about my past... my childhood... who I was or who I'd been. Except that when Jeremiah traded my love for my parents in exchange for my life, it was like... a prelude. As if he knew he was preparing me for being anchorless in a storm."

Walker watched her steadily. "I didn't know you felt that way."

"Why did you think I was so obsessed with finding Abby?" She rubbed the inside of her arm. "She's my last link to my parents. My old life. I've protected her since... since Paul died. I was the reason he died, you know." She'd told him about it before.

"That's not true." He said it with quiet conviction.

"It is. I was the one who—"

"Your brother died because a man stabbed him. Nothing more." Walker gripped her arms. "You have enough ghosts haunting you, enough burdens to bear without hanging on to that."

Tears filled Hettie's eyes, and she trembled. Walker kissed her then, closing his arms tightly around her. She would never understand his capacity for forgiving her. But for now, in this moment, they had each other.

Robbed of his sight, Walker relearned her body by touch, and Hettie found a quiet peace in their coupling, departing the world briefly, blissfully, without forgetting about it.

Afterward, Hettie allowed herself to close her eyes, and for the first time in months she slept unafraid of the world threatening to steal what little she had left.

MONTANA 1895

You've got to do it."

"Shut up and save your strength." Jeremiah was shaking badly. He desperately needed a drink. His hands kept slipping from the cart's handles, though that might've been from the blood, or maybe the weight of the three bodies in the conveyance.

"I... can't..." John Alabama gave a pitiful sob, but his breathing was racked with wet coughs as blood filled his lungs. "Don't... don't let Butch..."

"I won't. I swore I wouldn't, and I won't." His promise was only a drop shy of a blood oath; he did not want to get caught up in the pact John had forged with Jed Crowe at his death.

"My girls... my girls..." John gave another tortured wail. Jeremiah's heart twisted into knots as he tried to hitch the cart to the gray mustang, but the damned horse hadn't been broken for it, and he shied and danced. Jeremiah didn't have the strength to do any kind of calming spell, though. His grief was tearing him apart, and he was barely holding on to what little protection magic he could.

"We'll get you to the doc. Get you patched up and out of here. We'll go after Abby and shoot Butch dead three times over. I swear—"

"I ain't long for this world, Jeremiah." It came out in a resigned half sigh, half moan. "These are my sins catching up to me. Diablo's blood price..." He dissolved into sobs again as he caressed his daughter's bloodied—

Hettie's head twitched, and her body spasmed. John gasped as garbled words flew from her mouth.

The box containing the revolver grew hot in the burlap sack. Suddenly it exploded in flames, and Jeremiah kicked it out of the driver's seat before it set fire to anything else.

"Hettie?" John's voice was small, fearful, hopeful. "Hettie, darling, wake up!"

Silence. Jeremiah held his breath; he'd seen bodies do strange things in death. But then the enchantment on the box John and Jeremiah had put in place so many years ago flared to life. The wood boiled as the grinning skull face meant to warn sorcerers away turned its ghastly visage up. Its eyes glowed green. And then its jaw moved.

"Releeeease meeee..."

Jeremiah yelped and kicked the thing as far as he could, preparing a protection spell. But the box arced through the air, doubled back on its trajectory, and whacked Jeremiah smartly in the head, bouncing back into the cart.

John barely managed to dodge it. The box landed on Hettie's unmoving lap.

"Releeeeease meeeee..."

"Jeremiah... The gun..." John reached out.

"Don't touch it!" He grabbed the box. It could only be opened by Alabama blood—Diablo must be trying to break the enchantment. Which meant...

John's death was imminent.

Rok burst into his sightline and landed at the edge of the cart, peering down at the girl's corpse. *"Chosen, chosen, black thorn's chosen!"* he cackled.

John stared at the spot where Rok sat. "He...he's real."

"You can see him?" No one but Jeremiah had after Rok's intervention in Alabama. No one, that is, except for the men dying at Jeremiah's feet, of which there'd been a few.

John licked his lips. "And hear him."

Rok snipped his beak. The damned bird was smiling. *"Crossing over, crossing through! Soon the reaper comes for you!"* His eyes flashed, and his feathers puffed up suddenly as if lightning had struck nearby. His demeanor settled. Instantly, Jeremiah recognized that Rok's true masters were speaking through him now.

"What did you mean about black thorn's chosen?" John asked steadily.

"You already know, son of Blackthorn." Rok still had the same voice; he was just more articulate. *"Your legacy, your curse, your burden, your birthright... It belongs to* her *now."*

"No. It's coming with me." John had relinquished the revolver a long time ago, but not to anyone specific. He and Jeremiah had simply locked it in that enchanted box.

"Don't lie to yourself. In her moment of death, you fairly shouted for me, offered up whatever it would take to save her. It wasn't in words, but it was in your heart."

Jeremiah gasped. "No— Dammit, Rok, no!"

"I will broker a deal," the raven went on, *"to save your daughter's life. In exchange, your soul, your allegiance, your promise."*

"To save Hettie?" John coughed blood.

"I forbid it!" Jeremiah shouted. "Let him die in peace! Let them all—"

"You will serve," Rok went on, ignoring him. Jeremiah hastily went through his pockets, seeking out Rok's bones. He'd crush them right now! He'd be damned if he let John—

"So...I go with you, and Hettie lives?"

The raven raised his wings, either in acknowledgment or a shrug.

"John, you don't understand what you're—"

"Do it."

Rok took off, his caws filling the air. All around them, it sounded like a thousand wings rushing up. The stars disappeared altogether.

Jeremiah cried out, unable to stop the transaction. John was a sorcerer, too, after all.

The flurry faded. John was still upright, staring up in wonder at the sky. Jeremiah held his breath. "John?"

The man didn't move. His mouth was slightly agape, but no breath could be heard. Not even a final gurgle as his spirit fled.

John Alabama was dead.

And Hettie was, too.

Grief and pain swamped him. Jeremiah stumbled back and landed on the cold ground, a cry wrenching from his throat. *Why, John?* He'd given up eternity for nothing…

*"Only one part of the bargain is done."*The raven stood before him, black eyes gleaming. *"A second still awaits."*

"You didn't even explain the terms to him." Jeremiah's rage made his palms glow with blue power. He didn't need a spell to unleash fury upon the bonded familiar, consequences be damned. "You didn't give him time to consider the cost—"

"The price is reasonable. Discounted, even, if you know what she can afford."

His breath stuttered in his lungs. He knew exactly what *they* would want…what Hettie had in abundance. And if he didn't facilitate the transaction, John's sacrifice truly would be for nothing. And Hettie would be forever trapped between life and death in that unknowable place in-between.

His eyes dried. He ground his teeth. They didn't have time to argue—a body still had its limits, and he needed to get Hettie to the doctor. A gunshot wound to the head did not get better with time alone.

"When this is done," he said scathingly, "you and I are going to have a reckoning."

"Won't we all?"

Jeremiah leaped into the cart and whipped the mustang into a gallop, pointed toward Newhaven.

CHAPTER TWENTY-FIVE

Over the next week, Hettie stayed with Walker in his tent in the village while the sorcerers did their work. She visited with Horace and the others, caught up, mended their friendships. Daisy complained long and loud about all the people tromping through her tent—it was the most spacious one—dirtying her floors, eating her food, and jabbering about nonsense. Bear quietly explained, "This is her way of saying she's happy for the company."

At the end of the week, Lena and Duke arrived at Root Hill.

"Don't see why you'd hug her after the way she abandoned us," the grizzled outlaw grumbled as Lena clutched her tight.

"Because she's my *friend*." Lena shot him a look. "She had her reasons for doing what she did."

"I'm glad to know you're alive and well, Duke," Hettie said with as much sincerity as she could muster. "I don't expect you to understand what I did, or even forgive me. I'm not responsible for your feelings. But you're here now, and from what I've been told, you're in pretty deep with the League now. We're allies. I can't expect any more than that from you, and I won't."

Duke looked as though he was going to argue, but he didn't. Hettie had given him what he wanted, after all—recognition and acknowledgment of his hurt feelings—disarming his indignation in the process. If he was spoiling for a fight, he wouldn't get it from her.

They got caught up. What was left of the Blackthorn Rogues—mostly sorcerers and a few mundanes who hadn't been at Junesfield—had banded together to help any towns or hamlets fight off the shambling hordes of zombies…for a fee, of course. It seemed mercenary work was more profitable than crime these days. The army was spread thin, the local authorities were inadequate to deal with this magical threat, and the Pinkertons gave the remote besieged towns a wide berth.

Worse still, the Division was proving useless in this fight. More and more, magic and the gifted were being blamed for the zombie attacks. Fearing for their lives, whole towns were purging themselves of anything that might attract the mindless hunger of the man-things.

"The government had an emergency session with the Division's council of elders," Lena explained to Hettie. "The president signed a document requiring all gifted, regardless of age, to report to the Division to help solve this crisis. And mundanes are being encouraged to report their gifted neighbors in case they don't comply."

Hettie swore. "I know the Division's always had that power over the gifted, but this…"

"Is nothing short of tyranny." Lena nodded. "If they were looking to unify gifted and mundanes in this crisis, they're failing miserably at it. I can't imagine they've come up with any kind of solution."

"It must be part of their end game," Hettie said.

"Only we still don't know exactly what that is," Walker added.

Hettie told Duke and Lena about the Division's pocket realm stronghold and how Abby was likely in it, and that the League was planning an assault. "We could really use you," she finished.

"Hold on a minute," Duke interrupted. "Far as I'm concerned, my men—"

"Our men," Lena corrected.

"—don't have to do anything you say. You left us, Hettie. You ain't no Elias Blackthorn."

"You're right. I'm not Elias Blackthorn. I'm just a girl with a magicked gun and a chip on her shoulder." She turned her gaze on him. "I never asked for loyalty, Duke. We're square, far as I'm concerned, and I'm not itching to dig up old grudges with you. But with these zombie attacks and all the gifted being corralled… I imagine it's only a matter of time before the rest of your sorcerers are rounded up." Her gaze canted toward Lena.

Duke's lips pursed.

Lena faced Duke. "I've been waiting for a chance to hurt the Division. And Hettie has saved and helped us more times than I can count. If you want to turn your back on her—on *us*—then you can go back to the hideout without me."

Duke growled. "Lena, we're a team."

"Yes, we are. But it's up to you to decide what you want to do. Wait for the Division or the zombies to pick you off one by one, or take your stand now, together." She drew herself up. "I follow Hettie Alabama," Lena declared with conviction. "To the pocket realm, to prison, to hell, if necessary."

Duke twitched. He looked between Lena and the rest of the crew. "By the Almighty." He placed his hands on his hips, stared up, and huffed. "You'll be the death of us all, woman."

"Probably." Hettie grinned. "Welcome to the cause."

A day later, everyone at Root Hill was called to a meeting on the plateau. Before the proceedings began, Sophie, Starling, and the League leaders summoned Hettie to the hilltop cabin. Walker, Horace, Lena, Duke, Daisy, and Bear all went with her. Hawk eyed them suspiciously as they filed in. "Quite a motley crew you've gathered."

"The motley crew ain't deaf, mountain man," Daisy snapped at Hawk. "An' she's got more manners than you."

"Bear and Daisy are friends and know more about the Division than I do. They've helped me before, and I trust them. I asked them to come along to consult. Have you figured out how to access the pocket realm?"

"Yes. You brought us artifacts of legend, Hettie. The Columbus Dial. The bowl of Io. The plume of Quetzalcoatl." Starling was nearly breathless. "Our people figured out a way to make them work together to unlock the pocket. Your notes were invaluable. But...how could you have known to gather these items specifically?"

"I didn't really figure out anything." She hesitated. "It was Rok."

"Rok?"

"Uncle's familiar. He passed him to me just before he died. He's a big black raven, and I'm the only one who can see or hear him. He's been with me, helping me these past three years."

The room shifted uneasily. "But...you're mundane," Lena said.

"She's missing part of her soul," Walker reminded them quietly. "Diablo's filled it nicely, but there's always room for...similar forces to influence her."

"You have a *demon* familiar?" Hawk shouted, taking a step back. The assembly gasped. Several of the sorcerers unknown to her made the sign against evil and began to pray.

"Twice touched," Bear mused, wickedly impressed. "Not one but *two* demons on your shoulders, eh? D'you even got room for an angel?"

Her face set in stern lines, Starling asked, "Hettie, do you *know* anything about this Rok? Who he is or where he hails from?"

"If Uncle gave him to me, I can only assume he's helpful." She continued, "Rok showed me what to read, pointed to things in the collection. I took notes and made sure Berkeley didn't know what I was up to."

Horace looked confused. "If this Rok wanted you to take these items, why didn't he just *tell* you which items to take instead of wasting all that time making you read?"

"Because he wanted her to take notes a sorcerer would understand," Starling said. "It's almost as if he's trying to help *us*."

"He's a spirit guide!" Jay exclaimed. At Hettie's confused look, he said, "In some traditions, there are entities who can lead voyagers between realms—between death and life, dream and awake, heaven, hell, purgatory...wherever. You see them in stories all over the world. Rok could be one of them. It would explain how he knew which items to pick—spirit guides are natural finders. Perhaps he could lead us to the pocket realm."

Hettie's heart sank. "He can't." She stuffed a hand in her empty pocket. "Berkeley took his bones from me, and I couldn't get him back. I had to leave him behind."

A collective sigh of frustration—or was that relief? "Perhaps that is best," Starling said soberly. "We can't entirely trust this Rok. He may have given us the means to access the pocket realm, but the question is, why, and at what cost? Demons always have their own agendas, *and* their price."

Jay said, "We still have Diablo. That's all we need. Come." He gestured for them to follow.

The people of Root Hill had congregated on the plateau where mesas had been magically raised to form a semicircular amphitheater. On the center dais, Jay unfurled a large… Hettie wanted to say map, but there were no recognizable land masses on it. The lines, shapes, and runes looked like a pile of scribbles, but the impression in her mind was of a physical space. It was like a giant version of the diagrams the elders used on those who'd come of age when testing for the gift: spelled so only the gifted could see. The gathering murmured.

Starling gave a short introduction, her voice ringing through an amplification spell that made her soft but articulated tone sound as though she were speaking directly to you. She got straight to the point. "Many of you came to Root Hill as refugees, hoping for nothing more than sanctuary, security, and respite from brutal, relentless harassment and violence. The League of Sorcerers for Free Magic has welcomed you here because we believe in a future where our children and loved ones won't have to live under the thumb of magical oppression.

"Unfortunately, the respite we've enjoyed here is coming to an end. The Division is readying to attack us."

The audience gave a collective cry, and panic rippled through the crowd. "We don't know when the attack will come," Starling said, "but we believe it is imminent. We're gathered today to offer you the chance to fight for your freedom and sovereignty, to stop the Division and their tyranny once and for all."

She gestured toward Hettie. "Thanks to the brave and valiant efforts of our greatest ally, the freedom fighter Hettie Alabama, we now have the means to strike at the Division's most vulnerable stronghold."

Arched eyebrows turned her way. She doubted anyone except Starling considered her a "freedom fighter." The sorcerer went on,

"Destroying this Division stronghold will cripple them, but we need sorcerers and soldiers to help us in the fight ahead. It will be dangerous. There will be casualties. But the alternative is hiding here, waiting for the day the Division or the zombies find us."

The acrid tang of fear tinged the air. Many of the refugees here had either escaped a zombie attack or had been turned out of their homes to keep from attracting them to their communities. There were stories that worse had been done to gifted in other areas.

Starling turned the proceedings over to Jay.

"Thanks to the artifacts Hettie Alabama has brought us, our people have been able to draw a map to the place where the pocket realm lies, as well as provide the conveyance to get us there." He drew a canvas sheet off a strange sculpture. The thing was as tall as Walker and looked like... well, no machine she had ever seen. It was a large spherical cage, the latitudinal and longitudinal lines made up of various elements—bent reeds, rope, loops of hair. Each hoop was its own protection circle. The talismans she'd taken from Berkeley Manor, from the compass to the bowl to that little figurine Hettie hadn't figured out, were woven into intersecting circles, along with other bits of bone and stone and feather.

Strange as it was, Hettie drew closer. It almost felt as though she knew this thing, as if she'd seen it in a dream.

"Jumpin' Jehoshaphat," Bear breathed, shying from it as if it were a small, radiant sun. "That's one hell of a talisman."

"We're calling it a multirealm globe," Jay said, and the sorcerers nodded along, "for obvious reasons."

"Not that obvious," Horace muttered, perplexed.

Lena asked, "How does it work? I thought pocket realms were..." She flattened her hands together, trying to articulate her meaning.

"Nondimensional? Theoretically, they are. They only become pockets when something exists in them." Jay gestured. "This globe catches energies and funnels them into our team of interpolation cartographers, who map out the signals they get back. The Division must have done something similar, but with what, I'm not sure."

"It's like getting through layers of a bunched-up lace tablecloth," Daisy explained for Hettie's benefit, though she said it loud enough for all to hear. "See, when you lay out a tablecloth, it's flat, but when you grab it up and bunch it together, there are layers upon layers with lots and lots of holes, and it doesn't look like anything but a big mess. Pocket realms are like all the spaces you can get to through these bunched-up holes. But finding the right one in that tangle? Impossible."

"That is a perfect analogy, Miss Brown. Thank you." Jay grinned and pointed to a cluster of lines on the map. "We're certain *this* is the pocket the Division is housing their headquarters in. The cartographers detected a high concentration of null energy—it must be coming from the Fielding canisters. This must be where they've taken all the magic they've stolen from the gifted."

Hettie's nerves ratcheted tight. That meant Abby had to be there, too.

Daisy indicated the map on the ground. "These ley lines lead to hundreds of realms. How are you going to get there without getting lost?"

"That's where Miss Alabama comes in." Starling addressed Hettie. "Diablo is a natural finder—the demon can sense these energies. You will lead us to the pocket realm. You'd be our dowsing rod."

"And how would we get out again?" one of the other sorcerers prompted. "If I'm reading this right, this is a one-way spell."

"That's the tricky part. This isn't like a remote Zoom we can reopen after a couple of hours for a rendezvous. The pocket realm is constantly shifting around. This key is good going in, but exiting is another matter," Jay explained.

Hawk piped up, "It's like a lobster trap. Critters can crawl in, but they can't crawl out."

"The Division will have a different spell to leave the pocket," Jay said. The assembled sorcerers murmured. "There'll be three teams. Hawk will lead the main fighting force. I will lead a separate team to find the exit spell. And Starling and Robin will be searching for any prisoners."

Including Abby. Hettie already knew which team she wanted to be on. "Any idea what we'll be facing once we get through?" she asked.

"No. This pocket realm is entirely new territory to us. We can safely assume magic works there in the same way it works in our realm, though."

"And how about guns?" Walker asked.

"If the Fielding canisters are being brought there, then we can assume the laws of Mechaniks and science apply there, too," Jay said.

"There is one way to find out exactly what's on the other side in case we're walking into a trap," Hettie suggested. "Send me in with Diablo first. I can use the time bubble to scout the place out."

Starling shook her head. "That's too dangerous. How would you get out?"

"I'd take two or three sorcerers with me. Assuming they can find the exit spells, we can all pop back out after we've had a look around. Then you'd have one less thing to worry about when we attack."

"Even with our most powerful sorcerers, there's no guarantee they can perform whatever spell you need to escape on their own. We're going to need our full force here."

"So send me ahead to clear the path," Hettie argued.

"We can't risk that, either. What if you damage what we need to facilitate the exit? You don't know what to look for."

"You can't risk Abby's freedom and safety, Hettie," Walker said gently. "I know you want to get out there, but this is the time to think and plan."

"There might be another way." Daisy pointed. "Save your finding force and put a wedge in the door. We can keep the portal open from this side."

"That would expose all of Root Hill. If the Division is rallying its troops, they could come through and kill everyone here. Plus, it'd mean we'd need a team of sorcerers to keep the door *open*, and this spell is a complicated one. I'm not sure we even have enough power among those of us capable of performing the spell."

Horace cleared his throat. "I think I might have a solution to your magic issue. Jemma, do you still have Fielding's portable engine?"

She crossed her arms. "I do."

"We don't juice here," Jay said, scandalized. "That is nonconsensual stolen magic. We don't use the enemy's means of oppression for our benefit."

Hettie sat on her itching palms.

"Hear me out. I've worked with the portable engine Alastair Fielding developed. Instead of juicing your people, why don't you use it to feed your globe?"

"The engine doesn't just *plug* into ancient artifacts," Hawk growled. "The engine's Mechanikal. The globe is magical. What d'you know of magic, anyhow?" He lifted his nose. "You ain't got the gift."

"Seeing as I worked *directly* with Dr. Fielding, I think I know quite a lot," Horace countered.

"Horace knows more about that machine than all of us put together," Hettie added. "And to his point, I *know* those canisters can feed a magicked portal device because Berkeley had a remote Zoom icon attached to one. He could open a portal all on his own with it."

Starling, Jay, and a few other sorcerers seemed to carry on a silent conversation among their exchanged looks. "That…that might be doable," Jay said hesitantly. "But we can't waste time if we can't figure it out."

"Give me a day," Horace said confidently.

The plan revised, the crowd was sent away to consider what their role in this battle would be. The cries of small children reminded her not everyone here could make that choice easily. Hettie rounded up Lena and Duke and formally introduced them to Starling.

"Hawk mentioned your people have been helping clear out a few zombie towns," Starling said. "I thank you for your service."

"Pays well enough," Duke said, and got an elbow from Lena.

"I can't speak for all our men, but we are invested in this endeavor and will recruit as many as possible. We have two Fielding canisters," Lena volunteered, "as well as an engine."

"We don't juice," Starling reiterated seriously. "It's an abomination to have stolen magic put into our bodies. It's unclean and amoral. We will have nothing to do with those machines."

"You'll wanna rethink that if you're facing off with the Division," Duke said gruffly. "I guarantee they ain't above juicing."

"If we give up our principles, then the Division wins. The line between right and wrong is a thin one. We're already compromising some of our values if your friend is right and we can feed the magic from the canisters into the globe."

"*Values* don't do much for the dead," Duke grumbled.

"Duke's right," Lena argued. "Our sorcerers will be most effective in this fight juiced."

Starling's flinty expression narrowed. "If they need to juice, perhaps they shouldn't be in this fight."

Lena's back stiffened. "Gifted is gifted, juiced or not. Are you implying otherwise?"

"The gift is exactly that. A gift. To take more than you were given speaks to greed and entitlement, and contravenes the laws of nature."

"You can make that argument until we're reduced to naked worms crawling through the muck." Lena pushed right into Starling's face. The League leader didn't budge. "That's Mundane Movement claptrap turned back on our own kind."

"We don't need to fight among ourselves. We've got enough enemies." Hettie inserted herself between the women. "A rain of bullets will do the job just as well as a spell. The Rogues are gunslingers first, hexslingers second. They'll get the job done, juiced or not. How many casualties we end up with is up to you and your principles, Starling."

The League leader set her jaw, but the fire in her eyes was banked for now. "Inviting a bunch of thieves and cutthroats into our community will do little to settle the people here." Her tone was once again even, matter-of-fact. Hettie respected her ability to keep a cool head. "How can I trust them?"

"The same way you trust me. No one who's followed me this far has been forced to do so. I've not given a single one of them reason to be within ten miles of me, but…" She looked toward Duke and Lena. "I'd trust them with my life." Admitting it out loud, despite her years of wariness and standoffishness, she knew it to be true. "Way I see it, if you want this mission to succeed, we're going to need all the bodies we can get. And the Rogues are good in a fight."

"Plus, they got no love for the Division," Duke added. "Especially after Junesfield. They'll be wanting their pound of flesh."

Starling considered carefully, assessing the Rogues' leaders with a probing look. Hettie wondered if she was using some kind of spell to suss out their motives. Coming to a decision, she exhaled. "I'll have the sorcerers prepare a remote Zoom for your men." She paused and flicked Lena a rueful glance. "And your canisters."

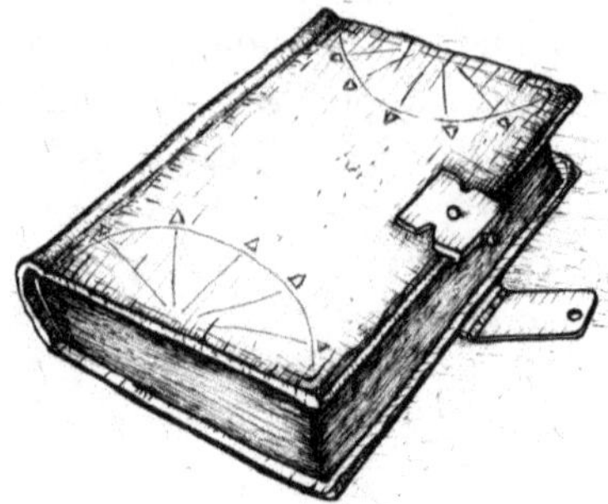

CHAPTER TWENTY-SIX

It wasn't as hard to integrate the Fielding engine into the globe as they'd all supposed. Once the portable engine had been brought to Root Hill from wherever Jemma had hidden it, Horace had shown the globe-building team everything he knew about it. With Hettie's detailed description of Berkeley's Zoom icon, the team got the canister—still partly filled with the magic they'd skimmed from the sorcerers from Quail's Hollow—to feed its magical contents into the globe.

"One little problem," Horace said. "We can't test the damned thing. Opening this gateway to the pocket realm could drain the canister faster than we think. That happens, and you could all get stuck on the other side."

"Well, Lena and Duke will be bringing their canisters, too. Once we juice our people—"

"We'll hook up the rest." Horace caught on and snapped his fingers. "It shouldn't be too hard to set up a chain."

Hettie beamed. "Horace, I'm telling you, you should leave the horseflesh business behind and become a Mechanik."

The hostler's face fell. He tipped his chin down and closed his eyes. A strange coldness seeped into Hettie's stomach then. "What's wrong?"

"It's been so hectic I forgot to tell you..." He cleared his throat and took off his hat. "I got word a couple of days ago. Jezebel passed."

At first she thought she hadn't heard right. A fist closed over her heart and dragged it into her gut.

"She went peacefully. Lay down in some clean, soft straw, and her heart just stopped." He rubbed tears from his cheeks. "I'm sorry I didn't tell you right away—with everything else happening..."

She nodded numbly in understanding.

"The old girl was a queen," he went on more firmly. "And we treated her like one. Jimmy O'Leary had her cremated, per your instructions. He'll keep the ashes safe till you're ready for them. I have his letter if you want to read it."

Hettie shook her head, though she hardly knew from the rushing in her ears deadening the rustle of her braided hair against her shoulders. Her father's horse, the mare who'd inspired fear in all who came upon her, who'd lived with Pa for most of his life since he'd become John Alabama, was gone.

She rubbed at the raw ache in the center of her chest. Abby would be devastated. Ornery as Jez had been, she'd always been careful around her sister, and Abby had seemed to know it, too. She'd bring her handfuls of sweet grass and say, "Good girl!"

Hettie palmed her tears away. There would be plenty enough time to grieve later. The mare's ashes would be put in the ground at her father's feet at the ranch. It was what Pa would've wanted.

A commotion outside the tent broke Hettie out of her daze. She and Horace looked up in alarm and hurried outside. Sorcerers with rifles took up positions, pointing down the hill toward the tree line.

Hawk marched past, and she grabbed his arm. "What's happening?"

"Perimeter spell went off. A remote Zoom opened barely half a mile from here. No one's supposed to be able to find us."

"Maybe it's Duke and Lena with the rest of the gang."

"No. They can only come through when the Zoom team opens the aperture. This is an unscheduled drop, one-way from the outside."

Diablo leaped into her sweat-slicked palm. "Who came through?"

"We're not sure. Whoever it was disabled the Eye spells we set up to watch the forest, and our scout hasn't reported back."

She gritted her teeth. "Horace, get to the stronghold. Keep an eye on Walker for me."

Hettie followed Hawk to where Starling and two other sorcerers were weaving their fingers in and out, muttering incantations. "We can't see anything," the commander said tersely. "Whatever—whoever is out there is practically invisible."

"If it was the Division, they'd have a whole army behind them," Hettie muttered, staring into the trees, watching for movement, listening for any sign of invasion.

"Terrain's too steep and uneven for horses or automobiles or cannons. They'd have to come on foot." Hawk checked the load in his rifle. "C'mon, wielder. I know the land if you'll lend me your time bubble."

Hettie dropped into her time bubble and touched Hawk's arm. He gave a cursory glance around him. "Damn," he chuckled, then led her down the steep, rocky hill.

"You know about Diablo's time bubble powers?"

"Only what I've heard through stories. Diablo's not the only talisman or spell out there that can manipulate time, though they are supremely rare." He smirked. "I don't know anyone who's so reckless about using it, though. Time's a tricky thing to play with."

"I don't *play* with it. It just slows everything down so I can get things done."

"Grays on your head tell me otherwise," he said. "Robin told us you're about her age. I'm guessing your advanced years are Diablo's blood price, but the rest?" He tsked. "It's a shame, really."

"My gray hairs are none of your damned business, and they sure as hell don't make my aim any worse," she snapped. "So how about you focus on your job instead of how I look?"

He said nothing more. The sharp rocks bit into the soles of her boots, but eventually the land smoothed to soft, springy loam. Hawk gestured silently, though he needn't have, and crept up to a copse of trees. "Sully should've been around here."

Hettie pointed at the scuff marks and broken foliage on the ground. "There."

They found Sully hogtied in the bottom of a ravine. Hettie dropped the time bubble, and they hurried to check on the man. He was unconscious, not dead.

"Sully. Sully, wake up!" Hawk hissed.

Hettie was about to bring the time bubble back up when she caught a flash of movement in her peripheral vision. Her grip tightened over Diablo, but curiously, it wasn't getting heavier in warning.

A few birds warbled in the distance.

"Hettie—"

She put her hand up and crept forward, staring hard into the forest.

A labored breath not her own stirred the underbrush.

Half a second too late, a mass of brown fur barreled out and pounced on Hettie. She cried out as she was slammed backward…and her face was bathed in slobber.

"Hettie!" The *cha-chack* of a shotgun round being chambered had her sitting up.

"Stop!" She threw her arms out.

The creature pivoted, putting his stinking hulk between her and the barrel of the gun. She grabbed his scruff and yanked him down. "Cymon, sit!"

The dog did so immediately, tail wagging, panting happily, waves of fetid dog breath stinging her cheek.

Hawk looked confused. Just behind him, the shrub rippled, and the mountain man yelped and stumbled back.

"This habit of disappearing on me is becoming a touch irksome, Miss Hettie," Ling said, a relieved smile creasing his face.

The fact that Ling had penetrated the League's defenses so easily made Starling and the others uneasy, to say the least. They checked him head to toe for suspicious spells and talismans, and despite Hettie vouching for him, Hawk, Jay, and a team of truthtellers interrogated him for nearly two hours before they released him.

As she and the others awaited Ling's release from "debriefing," Hettie noticed Walker grinding his jaw. Clearly he wasn't happy the sorcerer was back among them. Hettie had left Walker for Ling's lead on Abby, after all. She wanted to upbraid him for being jealous, but decided he wasn't likely to listen.

Ling entered, looking a bit ragged but otherwise unmolested. Hettie embraced him. Cymon, glued to her hip, wiggled between them to get some love. "I'm so glad you're all right," Hettie said. "What happened? How did you find us?"

"It's a long story," he said. "The gambler, Dugald Smedley, tried to kill me, but Cymon took him out before he could do anything." He grinned at the dog and rubbed his ears affectionately. "Smedley was working with Thomas Stubbs. When I couldn't find you, I...interrogated him." The cold glint in his eyes sent a shiver down Hettie's spine.

"It was all a setup. Stubbs knew you'd be looking for Abby, so he planted information about the Fielding hub all over the country and made sure to have it lead back to Smedley, who was waiting in Newhaven where folks would know your face, and where the void would make Diablo useless. Stubbs figured you'd find out about Smedley eventually and go after him. It was a trap."

"But...he would have been spreading that information around for..."

"Three years." Ling nodded gravely. "Stubbs was obsessed with Diablo, Hettie."

"Maybe he was smarter than I took him for. He got me in the end."

"'Was'?"

"Stubbs is dead." She pushed on, wanting to skip the details. "How did you find me *here*? This place is supposed to be a fortress, and you can't open a remote Zoom without knowing where you're going."

He grimaced. "You're not going to like this." He held up a stone wrapped in strands of dark gray hair. "I took the hairs off your bedroll and made a finding charm. I didn't want to risk you taking off on your own again."

She supposed she couldn't blame him for making the talisman without her permission. "And the remote Zoom?"

"After nearly three months of being unable to locate you, I thought you were dead. But then the talisman activated again. It kept swinging wildly. Eventually, it settled, so I followed it all the way to Kansas, but by the time I got there, you'd moved.

"I kept following the charm, hoping to catch up. Along the way, I encountered a group of rogue sorcerers fighting off those man-things, and I did my best to help them and heal those who'd been injured. In return, they opened a remote Zoom for me."

"These sorcerers—did they know of this location?"

"No, they mapped the ley lines from the talisman and opened a one-way, one-use aperture. They didn't know where I was heading or who I was after, only that I was looking for my friend. And they weren't entirely interested in following me, either. Truth was, I had no idea what I was walking into. I thought you'd been captured, that maybe *this* was the Division stronghold where Abby was. Thank the gods you're among friends."

Walker stepped forward. "Tsang." His brows were lowered, but he stuck out a hand for him to shake. Ling clasped it, and it seemed to Hettie some unspoken truce, or perhaps a warning, passed between them through that manful grip.

"I'm glad to see you well, Mr. Woodroffe." He met Walker's darting eye unflinchingly and asked more softly, "How is your vision?"

"Good enough," Walker growled.

"Liar," Horace scoffed. "This one's blind as a mole."

"But not entirely blind. That is good." Ling extended an upturned hand. "May I?"

Walker stooped slightly so Ling could put his palms over the sides of his face. He closed his eyes as soft light filled them. After a few seconds, Ling released Walker and exhaled.

"The damage isn't permanent. Your eyes are healing on their own, but you should keep them covered to avoid further damage."

Walker looked like he might argue, but he huffed instead. "I hate being useless."

"You're not useless," Hettie said. "We're going to need you here with whoever else is staying behind, preparing for wounded, protecting the camp, and readying for a quick getaway if things go south."

"So you've found Abby?" Ling asked earnestly.

Hope inflated the space around her hardened heart. "We think so." She explained how they'd found the pocket realm and their plan. "When Lena and Duke arrive with the others, we'll be ready to attack."

"I will join you in the search for Abby," he volunteered without hesitation. "She will likely need medical help when we find her."

"You're a Paladin," Walker pointed out. "I assume that means you don't do any battle magic."

"My code as both a healer and a Paladin forbids me from doing harm with my gift, yes. But I can still shoot a gun and help the wounded on the field."

"I never asked… What does being a Paladin even mean?" Hettie asked. "Why can't you just do harm?" It would likely be necessary in the coming fight.

Ling explained, "Paladins are one of the highest-ranking levels of sorcerers. They take binding oaths—blood oaths—that will strip them of their magic if they hurt or kill anyone with their magic. If I kill anyone with my powers, I will lose them."

"That even mean anything in Celestial qi?" Walker asked.

"An oath is an oath, Mr. Woodroffe. I take it seriously."

"Well, as long as you can still shoot a gun, you're welcome in the fight," Jemma declared. For all that she didn't trust him, the bodyguard seemed to respect the healer.

Ling nodded, acknowledging the pact between them.

"Mr. Tsang," Sophie ventured, "I know you've had a long journey, but there are some patients in the village who could use your healing touch, if you're up to it."

"Of course. I'll do what I can, Miss Favreau." He followed her out with a nod to everyone else.

Hettie could feel the waves of resentment wafting off Walker. The two things he'd once been feared for were gone now—marksmanship and magic. She could only begin to imagine how helpless he felt.

CHAPTER TWENTY-SEVEN

"Are you sure this is the right house?" Gallagher stared up at the tall gate—the main entrance to the sprawling grounds. Jane assumed it wasn't the elaborate wrought-iron sculpture of thorny rose vines that made him balk, but the subtle repulsion the whole property gave off. They'd driven by it twice without realizing they'd passed.

She gripped the letter she'd received and triple-checked. "Grandmaster Berkeley's invitation said we'd doubt it at every turn, so this must be it."

Since quitting the Pinkerton Detecting Agency, Jane and Hamish had crisscrossed the country, seeking out the components of Gallagher's spell. Uncle William had helped; he'd included a letter of introduction in her severance package that had opened a lot of doors. Of course, Jane would never tell him that letter might have been leveraged to scare some more reticent collectors and shopkeepers into donating their prized talismans and ingredients at a heavy discount.

Their quest was nearly at an end now. Soon they'd have a spell that might finally sever the link between Diablo and Hettie Alabama.

The moment the outlaw was powerless, Jane would arrest her.

She dismounted and went to the gate, gripping the letter. As she reached out, the doors swung wide.

"Miss Pinkerton. Professor Gallagher. I've been expecting you." The man's voice was amplified. Jane's ear was usually good at pinning down regional accents, but Berkeley's rang with markers from all across the country, his vowels drawn out as they were in the south but the consonants clipped as they were in the north, nasal to the east, throaty to the west. The voice was like the man himself—she couldn't pin down his origins.

She hopped back into the saddle, and they rode the long drive up to the mansion. Every foot closer to the house pushed her through layers upon layers of probing spells. Their horses shifted uneasily as the topiaries slowly turned to watch them. Farther along, three gardeners were pruning a bush that looked like an automaton; its metal torso was patched with tufts of greenery and bright blooms, and the outstretched limbs were made of twisted vines. Rust stained its joints and head. Not exactly the prettiest sculpture in the garden, Jane thought, but then Berkeley was a notorious collector of unique curios.

"Is it true what they say?" Gallagher asked quietly. "That he's the strongest influence sorcerer in the country?"

"I've yet to meet anyone as strong," Berkeley replied, startling the professor, "but we don't spell and tell."

Gallagher pursed his lips, and Jane gripped the anti-influence talisman at her throat a little tighter. She'd warned him not to say anything untoward on the property, but she understood his nervousness. Everything here felt... wrong, as if she'd stepped onto a swaying boat and was being told it was solid land.

The front doors opened. Berkeley wore a white linen suit, looking very much like a plantation owner from the South. White plaster dusted the toes of his boots.

He gestured grandiosely. "Welcome to you both. I've got refreshments in the library. My people will see to your horses. Please."

The suffocating feeling doubled as they walked into the house. The place was intimidating enough on its own, with polished wood floors and high, vaulted ceilings. She wondered how much of it was glamor; Berkeley was certainly rich enough that he didn't need to waste magic on hiding cobwebs or structural flaws, but he was also powerful enough to do exactly that. There was a reason he'd been conferred the title of grandmaster.

The sound of hammers and men shouting echoed through the lobby, and Jane craned her neck to peer down the south wing, where a scaffolding had been erected. Piles of debris littered the hall. "Doing some renovations?" she asked, though she could feel something else emanating from the area.

"It's a bit of a story," he said with a crooked smile, and gestured for them to follow, neatly sidestepping the issue.

The vast library made Jane itchy with excitement. She loved books, but this was not the time to go poking around. "We appreciate you seeing us. I know you're a busy man."

"Busier these days, what with everything going on." He waved a hand as if the latest government decrees giving the Division so much power were nothing. He eyed them. "I take it you two haven't yet checked in with your local Division agents to have your magic banked?"

"We have special dispensation to complete our mission," Jane said. It wasn't entirely a lie: waving Uncle's letter under the noses of the Division agents who stopped them had given them a pass. Jane didn't like what was going on, but she also understood why it was happening.

Berkeley nodded. "I understand you left the Pinkerton Agency in order to pursue the mage gun called Diablo."

"Not the gun. Its wielder."

"The elusive Hettie Alabama." He nodded slowly. "If you succeed, you'll do what hundreds of Division agents haven't." He turned his gaze toward Gallagher. "I've read your papers, professor. I'll admit that I dismissed them out of hand at first. With a few exceptions, Mechaniks has almost always let me down as glorified imbuement spells. But since the invention of Fielding's engine, well… it seems anything is possible these days."

"That's why we're here. We're close to having all the components for the spell to sever the bond between Diablo and its wielder. We can break the curse that ties that power to Hettie Alabama."

He nodded again, and Jane got the distinct impression he already knew all that. "We're here asking for your help in capturing a dangerous criminal and bringing justice to the families and loved ones affected by her reign of terror. We were told you are in possession of one of the only living Marriage Trap plants in the United States. We need to extract its nectar for the spell."

"It's also known colloquially as the Whore's Mouth," Gallagher added helpfully. "It's a kind of succulent that hails from—"

"Yes, yes, I do indeed have this plant." He waved them off.

"But…?"

"I'm wondering what you have for me in return." He sat back. "The Marriage Trap is very difficult to cultivate, and extracting the nectar could kill it."

Jane studied his expectant look and concluded the man was toying with them. "You have something in mind already."

He poured tea. "We're currently dealing with a crisis bigger than the problems Hettie Alabama's been creating."

"The zombies?" Jane asked. They'd heard rumors on the road, passed travelers who'd said their homes and villages had been attacked and overrun. Jane and Gallagher had no wish to reengage the creatures and had steered far away from those places.

He tilted his chin in thought. "If you were to ask me officially, I'd deny any such rumors of those creatures' existence. They are merely some rogue sorcerers playing with bedeviled magics." He glanced up. "However, I can see you're too smart to believe that. You were in Junesfield, weren't you?"

It didn't surprise her the grandmaster knew, and there was no sense lying to him. "We nearly caught Hettie Alabama there. She might even have been the cause of the canister explosion that killed all those people."

"The branch of the Division I've been working with knows otherwise. The explosion was caused by the League of Sorcerers for Free Magic."

Gallagher sputtered in his tea and coughed. "I thought they were just radicals with a penchant for vandalism," he said, wiping his mouth.

Violet-rimmed blue eyes touched him. "Not so, professor. They've become a deadly terrorist group full of socialists with dangerous ideas. They've done nothing but disrupt law and order, fueling the antisorcery Mundane Movement. And they've kidnapped children, claiming they're *saving* them when all they're doing is radicalizing them." His face had turned quite red.

"The Academy has been recruiting children for decades," Jane deadpanned. She knew. She'd been marched out of a hellhole orphanage and into an entirely new hellhole.

"The Academy educates and nurtures the gift. This witch who leads them, whom they call Starling, is turning these children into child soldiers to fight her war. The League is a pestilence. *They're* the ones who are creating the zombies."

Jane met his gaze, turning her unblinking look upon him. "How are they doing that, exactly?"

He elevated his chin, meeting her challenge. "We believe they've been capturing Fielding canisters and using hardworking sorcerers' banked magic to reanimate the dead. That's right," he said at Gallagher's gasp. "Reanimation. The most heinous of abominations."

Jane wasn't buying it. The man was too earnest, the light in his strange eyes manic. He sounded like he was preaching fiery damnation, almost gleeful in his condemnation. She'd bet he didn't believe a word out of his own mouth. She wasn't about to call him on it, though. They were only here for the Marriage Trap. "What is it you want from us?"

"We think the League is about to attack us at one of our strongholds. And we have it on good authority that Hettie Alabama has joined forces with them."

"And how do you know this?"

"We have a man on the inside." He leaned forward, paused as if considering, then said, "I will confess something to you. Those renovations in the south wing? They're actually repairs. You see, there was a violent robbery in my home some weeks ago in which a number of important magical artifacts were stolen by members of the League. These artifacts, put together, will form a deadly weapon that could end all of magickind. That is how I know they intend to attack our stronghold."

Jane hadn't read anything about such a robbery at Berkeley Manor in the local police blotter. "You didn't report this to the authorities."

"In matters relating to magic, I *am* the authorities." Berkeley sent her an arch look. "And I hardly believed anyone would dare attack me in my own home. It's more secure than Swedenborg."

Jane sifted through this information. The pieces didn't fit together. Apart from Berkeley's claim that Hettie Alabama was tied to the League of Sorcerers for Free Magic, what did any of this have to do with Gallagher's spell?

She glanced at the professor, who seemed to be considering the same. His brow wrinkled. "You don't think my spell will work, do you?"

Berkeley tilted his chin and grimaced. "Not in the way you hope it will. As I've mentioned, I've read all your work. In fact, I've been studying Diablo longer than you've been alive. I was the one who originally commissioned the Division to find the Devil's Revolver. When my resources there were exhausted and the organization shifted its focus from managing artifacts to managing the gifted, I gave the case over to the Pinkerton Agency and funded the search myself."

"*You* were the anonymous patron." It made sense time-wise. The file on Diablo had been open long before Jane had joined her adopted family's business.

Berkeley nodded. "I didn't want there to be any traceable connection to the Division, you see. There'd be too many questions from the government, wondering why we'd spend so much tracking down a magicked revolver. After the war, it was important the Division was seen as impartial, and that weapon in the wrong hands could have reignited the conflict between the North and the South."

"So... why did you want Diablo?" Gallagher asked tentatively.

"Officially, my job with the Division was to find a way to destroy it. Most mage guns aren't registered, you see, which leaves us a lot of rogue sorcerers with dangerous illegal weapons in their possession. Getting Diablo would have represented an opportunity to test some of the spells our people had come up with to unmake other such weapons."

"Like the wand purge of the Dark Ages," Gallagher said, a touch pale.

"And unofficially?" Jane prompted.

Berkeley grinned. "Who can resist the romance of the Devil's Revolver? I'm certain you understand, Professor Gallagher. I've read all your work regarding the subject. If there'd been anything to your research, I would have funded you a long time ago."

"But you didn't." Gallagher was working something out. "If you're so certain my spell won't work, why are we here now?"

"I didn't say it wouldn't work. It just won't work the way you think it will." He nodded to Gallagher. "Your spell requires a specific set of conditions that, quite frankly, you won't be able to replicate on this plane of existence. Recently, however, I've had some breakthroughs with my own research, and I believe that if we work together, we can make your spell viable. However, it will only sever Hettie Alabama's *magical* bond to the mage gun. Other bonds can never be severed."

Jane sat forward. All she needed to do to arrest the woman who'd killed her mentor was disarm her. "If Hettie Alabama can't use Diablo, that'll be sufficient to bring her in. But this takes me back to my first question: what are *you* getting out of an alliance with us?" It was no such thing, of course—all Berkeley had to do was say no, and they'd be stuck.

"The League, of course. When Diablo's link to Hettie Alabama is severed and you've arrested her, those rogues will be caught in our net, and we can end them once and for all."

Everything inside her warned her against the man's fantastic promise, but the need for revenge, for an end to this long, exhausting quest to bring Quentin and the others justice, clawed up from her heart and into her throat.

"Mr. Berkeley," the professor said, "would it be all right if Miss Pinkerton and I had a minute to confer in private?"

The grandmaster looked surprised. "Of course." He got up with a smile and left. They were in the man's house, so Jane doubted they'd get any privacy. The sorcerer could eavesdrop a dozen different ways, she was sure.

"What's there to discuss?" she said. "The Marriage Trap is the last thing on your list, and a grandmaster is offering to help us. By the sounds of it, your spell won't work otherwise."

"I'm just not sure about this deal. We have no quarrel with the League."

Jane lifted an eyebrow. "You don't sympathize with them, do you?"

"You don't?"

"They're terrorists who want magical anarchy. The League has grown increasingly violent in its attacks. They've killed dozens of people—"

"In retaliation for the thousands who've died and gone missing from the Academy and at Swedenborg," Gallagher argued forcefully. "You were there, Jane. Didn't you wonder where some of your classmates ended up? Why children were disappearing?"

"They flunked out or ran away, the way people do." It was a terrible situation, of course. But if she thought about it too hard . . . if she looked too closely at the establishment that had gotten her to this point in life from the nobody she'd been, she wasn't sure she could live with herself. She pinned him with a look. "Anyhow, that's all in the past."

"No, it's happening *now*, and has been for decades."

"The Division takes gifted children and trains them to ensure they don't hurt anyone if they lose control of their powers. Not teaching them is as bad as abusing them."

"You sound like you're trying to convince yourself," Gallagher said bitterly. "They brainwashed us to believe that. It's part of the propaganda."

She felt this like the sting of a whip. "If I hadn't gone to the Academy, I would've ended up on the street or worse."

"You didn't have that choice!" he shouted. "And neither did I!"

"You flunked out," she said without heat. "Don't you think your feelings for the Division are being colored by that experience?"

"No more than yours are." His tone was frosty. "All I know is that I don't condone Division policy, especially of late. I may not agree with the League's tactics, but at least they're doing something about everything's that's happening."

Jane huffed. "This argument is pointless. We're here for one reason: to separate Diablo from its wielder. The League has nothing to do with Diablo. Nothing to do with Hettie Alabama, except that Berkeley says they're affiliated. As far as we're concerned, the League is a fair price to pay to get Diablo out of the hands of a criminal like Hettie Alabama."

"Is that really what you believe? Or are you so close now that Hettie Alabama is all you care about?" He sighed. "Look at this rationally. Why would Berkeley need us if he has my research? As a grandmaster, he could requisition the ingredients for the spell much more easily and not involve us at all."

"A few of those ingredients were rare finds. Maybe it was just easier to involve us, knowing we'd made inroads. Maybe he's relying on your expertise. Have you considered that?"

It might have been a compliment, but he didn't look convinced. "When we started out together, you were adamant Hettie Alabama, the canisters, and the zombies were all connected. That's clearly the case, and the lynchpin holding them together is Berkeley. Don't you think it's a little too convenient that we're here now? That the only way we can get what we want is through him?"

Jane worked her jaw. It *was* too convenient, but she was so close now. "If we walk away from Berkeley, we're walking away from everything. And you and I will be done."

The ultimatum landed. Gallagher stiffened. Jane knew in her heart he wouldn't walk. Partly because he was enamored with her, partly because realizing his thesis mattered to him. It bothered her that she was leveraging the former.

Berkeley sauntered back in. "I hope you two have come to a decision." Jane had no doubt he'd been listening in.

Gallagher's jaw firmed. He blew out a short breath from his nose and gave a slight nod.

"We accept your offer of help on two conditions. One, Professor Gallagher gets to study Diablo to his heart's content. Two, I get to arrest Hettie Alabama myself."

Berkeley's answering grin didn't touch his eyes.

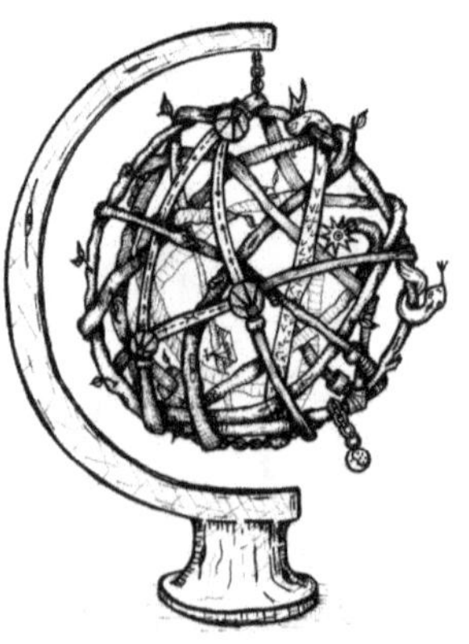

CHAPTER TWENTY-EIGHT

By the end of the week, Lena and Duke returned with a Fielding engine, two canisters, and thirteen Rogues in tow, five of them sorcerers. It was barely a fraction of the gang that had lived at Blackthorn's Hell, but Junesfield had killed most of the mundanes, and those who'd survived had hightailed it after their fearless leader disappeared.

The thirteen who'd come greeted her with relief and even a little awe. She knew their faces, though Hettie wasn't entirely sure about their names, and as she shook their hands Lena prompted her with a whisper in her ear.

"I hope you all came knowing what's at stake," she addressed them. "I don't want any of you being led on by promises of riches and glory."

"Ain't about either of those things," said Jerome, a sorcerer who'd had a hard time at the Academy as a young man and had grown to resent the Division. "We follow you, Blackthorn." The others murmured their agreement.

"It's just Hettie now," she insisted. "I ain't Blackthorn anymore. Never was, truth be told. Even with Diablo, that name needs to be put to rest."

The men exchanged looks, then Jerome shrugged. "A rose by any other name et cetera, et cetera, ain't that right?" He smirked. "Hettie it is."

The multirealm globe was hooked up to the canisters, and the globe team, which consisted of twelve middling sorcerers, prepared to open the pocket realm. Hettie still didn't know for sure how Diablo was going to lead them to the right realm, but she'd trusted the mage gun before.

You're sure you can do this? she asked silently. A pause, and then the grip ticked in her hand, a little thump like a baby's kick.

Sophie and Starling would be joined by Ling and Hettie on their mission to find Abby, along with Jay and a handful of others. Lena, Duke, and the Rogues would go with Hawk and Jemma and the rest of the League forces to battle the Division. Their goal was to create chaos and utterly defeat the Division on their home turf.

Walker, Horace, Cymon, and Bear would stay behind to help protect the camp and the families there. Daisy had volunteered to join the team opening the multirealm globe.

"This could be a trap," Walker said as he helped Hettie strap her blades and gun belt on. He'd done it so often he didn't need to see to know how tight to cinch them. His touch lingered, tracing the leather against her shirt. Hettie breathed deep, not wanting the distraction but relishing the moment.

"It's always a trap." Hettie had said that far too often. "But this time…this time, I've got a good feeling."

"I've got a bad one." His hands settled over her shoulders. "I hate that I can't be with you."

"You're needed here. Just in case. At the very least, I need you to watch Cymon."

"As if I can hold him back?" He chuckled. "With you and Ling both going, I don't know that I'll be able to stop him from following."

She squeezed his hand, a cold spike of fear suddenly impacting her gut. "Walker…if something happens, please take care of everyone."

He didn't reply. Didn't kiss her good-bye. That would be bad luck. He simply squeezed her hand back. It was enough.

The next stop was the Rogues' Fielding engine, where the sorcerers were juicing for battle. It had been over four months since Hettie's last hit. It would be stupid not to juice…

But she hesitated. She'd been magically clean all this time. Not going in juiced to this confrontation would be foolish. But she glanced at Walker, who watched her, unseeing, the lines around his mouth set in a deep frown.

"Something wrong, Miss Hettie?" Horace was helping with the engine. He held the clamps out to her.

"No. Nothing's wrong." She exhaled. "Save the juice for the others. We may need it."

"But Hettie—"

"I'll be all right, Horace." She hugged him. "Take care of everyone for me."

He squeezed her tight. "Don't do anything stupid. Please."

The forces gathered in unorganized clumps. The Rogues looked on from their horses, hard, imposing figures ready for battle, soldiers among scrappers. Starling, dressed in the sorcery battle armor of the Union Army, stood on top of a rock, shouting to be heard rather than wasting valuable magic on an amplification spell. A bracing wind cut across the dais, rippling her blue cloak like a standard.

"I see your faces," she shouted, "turned toward destiny and death and the unknown. We don't know what lies in the pocket realm, apart from our enemy. We can't be certain we will all return. But today, we avenge the loved ones we have lost. We will take this stronghold and give the Division a battle they will never forget."

A few men hooted, but uncertainty hung heavy over them.

Starling gestured at Hettie. "Hettie, this is your fight now as much as it is ours. Will you give us a rally cry?"

Hettie's tongue stuck to the roof of her mouth. Rally cry? She'd never been asked to do anything so…ceremonial as lead a battle. The Blackthorns simply did as she asked; she didn't need to give rousing speeches when she had Diablo to do the talking for her.

But now they were all staring at her, waiting. Cheeks burning, Hettie climbed up next to Starling and gazed at the men and women ready to die today. For their friends and families. For Abby.

"Give 'em hell," she shouted. "And don't die."

No one responded.

While the groups were arranged into lines, and weapons and spells were prepared, Starling led Hettie into the center of the dais where the multirealm globe sat. "The first stage of this journey is for you alone," she said. "You and Diablo will forge the path ahead of the rest of us. When you've made it to the other side, we'll be right behind you." She took Hettie's hand and placed her palm against the globe.

The globe team sorcerers, including Daisy, sat around the perimeter and began a chant. Hettie breathed deep, unsure of what to expect. It would have been nice to know what she was walking into. But instead of worrying she might get lost on myriad planes of existence, or blown to smithereens upon entering the pocket realm, Hettie thought of Abby and what they'd do this coming Christmas.

Hang on, Abby. I'm coming.

Power rippled across her skin. The hairs lifted on her arms, and her breaths came quicker, the air thinning. Her friends faded, sinking into an impenetrable silvery fog that swirled all around her. Diablo leaped into her hand and tugged, and her palm left the globe's surface.

Suddenly she was anchorless and floating freely in a world of gray that spun all around her. Her grip tightened, and the mage gun dragged her forward, skimming through a void of silver. It reminded her of the journey she'd gone on when Ling had plumbed her mind for memories of Abby—the darting, twisting, elliptical path of a murmuration of starlings or a school of panicked fish being pursued by predators.

The tugging became as inexorable as magnetism, and the path smoothed. *Are you all right?* she asked. Diablo distractedly replied as if too engrossed with guiding a pair of horses along a rain-slicked road in the night. *Mm-hmm.*

She was no longer being dragged now—she simply floated there as the world around them zipped to and fro, though in this featureless place, it was hard to tell. Diablo's lead became a mere ticking in her hand, and Hettie allowed it to guide her, trusting the demon in the gun would not betray her.

Something loomed ahead of them. It was a dark smudge at first, but it grew, until she could discern some shapes scattered below her, indistinct but clearly humanlike. *What is that?* she asked the mage gun.

Diablo hesitated, then drew her down, down, down. The ground rose to meet the soles of her feet. Unprepared, she collapsed to her knees.

The shadows around her resolved into clearer forms—heads, shoulders, arms, and legs. But they didn't become any more solid as they crowded around her, reaching out with pleading gestures.

She could hear nothing, but she got the bone-chilling sense that they were shouting, *screaming* at her. They reached out, but their hands passed through her like mist.

"I'm sorry..." she croaked. "I can't hear you... or understand..." Tears filled her eyes for some reason. These weren't malevolent spirits or poltergeists. They were people...

Diablo ticked at the same moment something caught her eye. She spun.

A little girl in a buckskin smock watched her placidly. Hettie knew her. "Crying Sparrow."

"We're in danger." Her voice was small but heavy with lifetimes of wisdom and sadness. She reached out. If Hettie took her hand, would she lose the way to Abby?

Diablo didn't reply, but it gave no warning ticks, no indication she was in immediate jeopardy from her spectral ally.

Hettie took the girl's hand. They glided through the misty shadows, then stopped. Crying Sparrow extended her hand to an approaching violet form.

Something about the shape, the way it raised a hand in greeting, had goose bumps breaking all over Hettie's body. The faint scent of roses drifted to her nose, and she gasped.

"Patrice?"

The violet shadow took the little girl's hand. Her form resolved, becoming a fuzzy version of the woman Hettie had known too briefly. She held back a cry. "This is... this is the place in-between. The place in all my dreams... my visions...?"

Those violet eyes grew wet, and she nodded. "We're trapped here." Her voice was faint. "Our power, our souls…everything that is us is here, and there's no escaping."

"Do you have any idea where your body is?" Hettie asked.

"No. I…I can't get back to it. Hettie…there's no return for those of us who are here, but there's no way to move on, either. We're being rounded up for the slaughter."

"Slaughter?" She turned in a slow circle. There had to be thousands of people here. "It's not just soothsayers, is it?"

"Souls of the lost. Souls of the damned." Crying Sparrow stared up at her. "This is because of Abigail."

Hettie's scalp prickled. "What does my sister have to do with this?"

"The beast feeds her, condemning more souls here to rot, to return to the mother stream, to become a part of the fodder for the ever-hungry beast." The dream walker's expression didn't change, but her censure was clear. "You must stop her. You must end her."

"No. No! I have to save Abby—"

"You can't," Patrice's breathless whisper stole the air from Hettie's lungs. "You can't save her, Hettie."

Hettie refused to believe that. Soothsayers and dream walkers be damned, Hettie had not gotten this far only to be told she *couldn't* do something.

Diablo kicked in her hand, as if in warning, and Hettie looked down. To the cloudy Patrice, she said, "I'm not giving up on her."

"No. You won't." Patrice's violet eyes shimmered, and she smiled sadly. "Tell Sophie I've always been proud of her, that she deserves to be happy. Tell her I love her, that she is loved, that she already has everything she needs to be happy."

Patrice released Crying Sparrow's hand and became a cloud of violet mist. The hazy form dissipated, melding into the cloud on a sigh. Hettie's heart clenched.

"What happened to her? Where did she go?"

"She is fodder for the beast, as we all will be if you do not stop Abigail." Crying Sparrow's look of bitter resignation was that of a thousand generations. "Magic is leaving the land, and this is the great river to which it flows. The beast seeks to dam it, flood the realms, throw the cycle out of balance. You must not let them do this, Hettie Alabama."

She set her teeth. "I'm not going to hurt Abby."

"That is your choice to make. But you cannot save her. You won't."

With that, she released her like a kite caught in the wind. Diablo tugged hard, and the phantoms rushed out of sight, becoming a faint mist as the world dropped away. Hettie tried to sort through what Patrice and the dream walker had told her, but she shook it off. No. She would save Abby. That was all there was to it.

Something new showed up on the horizon. A wall. Not just a wall but *the* Wall. Hettie could recognize that malevolent border even in this other place. Diablo rushed straight at it until it loomed large, and Hettie had a strange sense of déjà vu.

She inhaled sharply as she plowed straight into the black granite face. She might have been imagining the brush of cold grit over her skin, but she kept her hold on Diablo firm as it emerged into a cool, gray-white room with four walls, a ceiling, and a floor. Strangely, there were no right angles here: all the corners were rounded, as if the room had only been partially built from a fuzzy, out-of-focus dream of a room.

The ground solidified beneath her. The grayness melted away. Shapes and shadows materialized around her, coming into focus as if she were opening her eyes for the first time.

Suddenly, Hettie was *there*. Her limbs trembled. She felt as though she'd been walking for hours. The room had a black floor and white walls, all polished to a mirror gloss. Six men in white surgeons' uniforms and masks were bent over tables covered in Mechanikal contraptions. Brass armbands engraved with runes encircled their biceps. All of them were unarmed, and they hadn't noticed her yet.

Hettie inhaled and dropped into the time bubble. Starling said the others would be right behind her—she hoped her detour hadn't cost them anything. With Patrice's and Crying Sparrow's warnings, though, she couldn't take any risks. What if the League arrived and decided Abby couldn't be saved? Or, worse, if what the dream walker had said was true, what if they decided Abby had to be killed to save them all?

She couldn't take that chance. She'd scout out the place now and find Abby and see what else they'd be facing.

Diablo ticked in her hand, and she followed it out a door that pushed silently open and into a long hallway. Whatever this place was, she couldn't fathom how it had been built, or with what. The walls were whiter than fresh snow. The obsidian floors didn't sport a single seam, and they rang under her dusty, scuffed boots like a bell.

Hettie ran her hand along the wall, and her fingernails caught on a nearly invisible seam. She traced the seam upward—it was a door. Hettie pushed, the door's weight in the time bubble much heavier than in the real world. Jay had said magic should have the same effect in this pocket realm, but Hettie wasn't so sure. She regretted not juicing now.

The smell of rot and formaldehyde assailed her. The vast room was filled with narrow tables lined up like plots in a cemetery, each occupied by what was clearly a human body beneath a white sheet. Only...

She focused on a gray hand hanging limply from one table, peeking from beneath the sheet. It was entirely ruined, as if it had been dragged across the ground or gnawed on by some animal. Hettie held her breath and reached out to bring it into her time bubble.

The cold thing recoiled beneath the sheet, and Hettie stumbled back, knocking into the bed behind her. A moan rose up from the table, and she flung herself away. The two patients stirred. The smell of rotting flesh stung her nostrils. The sheets tugged and puffed up briefly, then settled with a resigned groan.

Hettie eased her clutched hand away from her hammering heart. She wasn't sure she wanted to lift the sheet away, but what if one of these hundreds of bodies was Abby's?

She wouldn't get through more than five beds before her time bubble collapsed. The weight of these two beds alone was straining her efforts. But the moment she dropped back into real time, the rest of the League would be here and begin its assault. And this sprawling complex seemed to go on forever.

Abby could be anywhere.

She left quickly, then found another door farther along the interminable hallway. She pushed in. The room was packed with tall metal racks lined with round glass flasks circled by bands of filigreed gold. The contents within glowed faintly. Hettie took another step in and was hit by a wave of nausea.

She grabbed one of the nearest flasks and stumbled out of the room. The sick feeling faded. She inspected the bottle: it was a Fielding canister, but in miniature, the same as the one Berkeley had shown her. *Rations*, she thought grimly. The Division had been harvesting magic, and this was how they'd distribute it. And those zombies or whatever they were in the other room…perhaps they were being drained the way the sorcerers in San Francisco had been. Or experimented on. Or—

Diablo nearly yanked her arm out of her socket dragging her away. "Slow down," she said, but the Devil's Revolver was like a hound on the scent now, pulling her down the long corridor.

Diablo jerked to a stop, and its weight doubled. Hettie's throat constricted. She was still safe in her pocket of time, but whatever lay beyond this door would hurt her.

And yet Diablo had brought her *here*. "Abby's here, isn't she?"

Danger. The warning was firm, and her trigger finger grazed the thorn.

"We should wait for the others." Saying it aloud didn't make the idea any better. What if this was her only chance to save her sister? If she needed help beyond these doors, she wouldn't get it. The League wouldn't know where she was, and they could spend forever searching this godforsaken place.

But if the League didn't make it here, she might lose Abby again. Maybe for good.

Resolved, she kicked the door open.

The weight of it in the bubble made her woozy, and without meaning to, she dropped back into real time. The world roared to life around her, and Hettie's heart rose into her throat as she looked up.

A massive Mechanikal engine towered above her in a room that seemed impossibly large. The machine was like a palace made of tarnished green bronze and oil-slicked steel, rusted iron and milky glass with twisted latticework spreading up the sides like sheets of veins. The whole grotesque mass throbbed like the churning bowels of a bloated beast, the sound a dull rumble mixed with the high-pitched squeal of gas escaping from some leaking pipe. Dirty light pulsed from distended, asymmetrical glass globes like bulging, inflamed organs.

The machine soared high above her, into the darkness, beyond sight. As she squinted, Diablo slapped her palm, and a pulse smacked between her eyes. She blinked and blinked again—no, the engine *did* end. But something about this place made her think it went on forever.

Glamor? But why? What was being hidden?

There was no one here, so Hettie holstered the gun and ventured farther in. She stepped around protruding structures of glass and brass that seemed to grow out of the ground, as if the machine were sprouting new branches. She stepped carefully around the "roots," not wanting to touch anything. Everything here made her feel as if she were waking up groggy in the summer's heat.

"Abby," she called out thickly. The low thrum gobbled the sound down, and she croaked out, "Abby? Are you here?"

A groan reverberated through the metal, making her skin crawl. It had emanated from deep inside the machine. Diablo jumped back into her hand, but it ticked again, urging her forward.

Hettie pulled on her gloves and clambered over a low wall surrounding the bulk of the engine. The groaning grew louder, and she bent low, ducking beneath a panel and slipping sideways into a narrow crevasse between two tarnished bulkheads that smelled like old blood.

She emerged in a nest of filaments glinting gold and silver, reaching up from the ground like spiky metal grass. They heaped together in a huge pile in the center of the space, and atop that... something stirred.

"Abby?" Hettie's heart raced. She found a foothold and started climbing the hummock, grateful for her gloves as the needles sliced across the leather and snagged her trousers. It was like scaling a haystack made of pins.

At the top, the filaments dipped down into a shallow basin filled with thick, crimson blood. In the center, the brass and iron and steel of the engine jutted up, twining to form razor-sharp barbed spikes skewering straight through the figure shuddering in the middle of the crimson pool. It wasn't Abby.

Hettie's grip tightened as a curtain of blood-crusted white-blond hair slipped to one side to reveal his face.

"Zavi."

CHAPTER TWENTY-NINE

The warlock stared at her with empty eyes. His chin wobbled as his cracked lips turned up. "Well…" He sputtered a desperate, humorless laugh. "Of course it would be you."

He'd been skewered by three large spikes, one through each shoulder, the third through one hip and protruding out the other, and they held him dangling just above the pool like a broken kite. His flesh was stretched and tented into little triangles of translucent skin on finer needles dangling from thin filaments that stretched into the ceiling. She'd seen pincushions with less wear. Trails of thick blood oozed from the larger wounds and into the pool below.

"What have you done with Abby?" she asked, voice strangled.

"D-do I look as if I'm in any p-position to have done anything with Ab-Ab-Ab…" He clenched his jaw and squeezed his eyes shut as a tremor racked his body. She wasn't sure what was happening, but she thought she saw an arc of blue lightning crawl across his skin. He gave a sob and then laughed. "You must enjoy this."

"Where's my sister?" she repeated.

He held her gaze with red-rimmed, bloodshot eyes. "Set me free and I'll tell you."

"You crawled your way out of molten rock." She lifted her chin. "You tellin' me you can't get out of *this*?"

"You have n-no idea what they've done to m-m-me. I-I-I..." He gave a pained cry and panted, and this time, blue light crackled over his skin, leaving sear marks that gradually faded. "The Division did something to me. Fielding set a trap. I knew he was smart..." He gave a humorless laugh. "I didn't know he was devious, too. This whole machine is an infernal engine..."

"An engine for what?"

"For keeping this pocket in reality open. For allowing all of *this* to exist. For running the beast." He rolled his chin around, the pierced skin of his neck stretching and oozing. "She built it all, you know. Her p-powers have grown beyond anything I could've possibly imagined. She is so much more...s-so m-much m-m-mo-more..."

"You mean...Abby made this?"

"Fielding's design, Abby's power, yes."

"Where is she?"

A loud boom echoed through the room, and the floor shuddered. Hettie gasped. The League! She'd left it too long—they were probably wondering where she was.

She reached for her time bubble—it didn't come. *C'mon, not now!*

Zavi laughed, his teeth stained with blood. "Not much use when you need it to be, is it?"

She scowled and raised the gun. The warlock's face blanched.

Hettie pulled the trigger. Green blazed through, cutting a swath across the bases of the spikes skewering him. They crumbled, and Zavi collapsed to his knees, released from the most tenacious arms of his crucifix.

Hettie waded into the ankle-deep pool. Zavi stared up at her. "No, wait—"

She grabbed a handful of the filaments and yanked. The warlock screamed as the needles were ripped out of him, leaving slick, oily blood trails. The pincushion holes closed up quickly, confirming Hettie's suspicions about the warlock's healing abilities. She grabbed another handful. "You're coming with me," she growled as she tore them out like the most stubborn of weeds. Zavi squealed and shrieked like a stuck pig. "You're gonna lead me to Abby, and then, if you're lucky, we'll all get out of here."

The warlock moaned as she removed the last of the filaments. She braced one foot on his chest and pulled out the spikes stuck through his torso with sick, wet sounds. She pretended not to enjoy bringing Zavi this much pain. She was doing him a favor, after all.

"Where's Abby?" She took a firm hold of his upper arm and dragged him out of the pool.

His breaths came in heaving gasps. "Farther in. There." He nodded.

Hettie didn't have much leverage over him—he was immune to Diablo—so she didn't trust his word. She pushed him ahead of her, kicking his feet out from under him and rolling him down the needle-spiked slope of the hummock. He landed at the bottom with an outraged yelp. She slipped down right behind him.

"I've been imprisoned in that thing for nearly three years," he exclaimed indignantly. "You don't need to treat me like an animal."

"Oh, I treat animals way better than that. It's no less than you deserve after everything you've put me and mine through. I wouldn't even be here if it weren't for you." She shoved him ahead.

Zavi staggered forward, glaring over his shoulder. She had no doubt that he was in pain, but his healing powers were not to be underestimated. He could turn on her any minute, and there was no telling what he'd do.

She'd let the tiger out of his cage. She only hoped he valued his freedom more than revenge on her. "Try anything," she warned, "and I will melt you to the floor ass up and use you like a shoe-shining stool."

Hettie kept him limping two steps ahead of her, wary of where he stepped. He walked gingerly, as if afraid to touch the latticework of iron that grew like lichen on the floor. "What is this all for?" she asked.

"The first part of the engine was designed to find and open this pocket," he said. "That's part of what Fielding's engine does. That sucking sensation? It's like a knife trembling on the edge of the spaces between realms. It's where magic has been leaking to and from since the beginning of time… if, that is, you believe in that kind of magic."

"What's that supposed to mean?"

Zavi laughed, though it didn't reach his eyes. "You mortal beings are so limited in your understanding of the powers you could wield."

"I never asked for powers, or this gun, or any of this," she growled.

He scoffed. "Everyone wants power. Money. Love. Peace. Change. Desire is the root of such power."

"Well, what I *desire* is for you to shut yer yap and take me to Abby." She shoved him toward a fork in the path. "Which way?"

He turned right. "You're not even curious about why the Division built all this?"

"I just want Abby. Once she's safe, the whole world can go to hell for all I care."

"Spoken like a true villain."

"I ain't no villain," she said. "Ain't no hero, neither, so don't think you have that over me."

"I claim nothing but a desire to return to my home. We have that in common."

"We have *nothing* in common," Hettie snapped.

He went on as if he hadn't heard her. "Single-minded purpose. A need to punish wrongdoers. A disdain for waste and inefficiency, and an inability to form human connections that don't serve your goals." He chuckled at her silence. "We're cut from the same cloth, you and I. Violently torn out of the comfort of our existence and pulled into a hell we can't handle. Of course, I've been at it at least a two hundred years longer than you…but in time, you'll understand. You'll see none of this matters."

Hettie set her jaw. A distant boom and the faint popping of gunfire reminded her that the League was probably on its way to find her.

The corridor sloped up as they climbed into the guts of the engine. The time bubble still wouldn't come, and she hadn't received any amplified messages to let her know the League was doing all right. She hoped they were okay, but she didn't dare turn back now.

It felt like a long time before they arrived at the uppermost section of the machine.

It had to be at least ten stories up. The ropes of filaments stretched all the way from Zavi's pool; the terminus connected them to a platter of glass. Hettie gasped at the figure lying atop. "Patrice!" Her body, anyhow, thin and draped in a white cloth.

"The far-seeing eyes of the great machine," Zavi said wryly. "Though she hasn't been very helpful in the past few months. She stopped being able to scry anything useful for us a long time ago."

She glowered. "You were the one who put her in a coma!"

"I didn't do anything of the sort," he protested. "I shooed her away as one might swat a fly. Her current state is thanks to the Division, not me."

Hettie bent and gave Sophie's grandmother a shake. She didn't stir. "What's wrong with her?"

"She's a vessel without a captain," Zavi said. "Adrift. The ship's sails might be whole, but without a crew, they can't be unfurled." He paused, and a tremulous, almost wistful smile crossed his lips. "She's dead."

Hettie's eyes threatened to fill with tears, but she couldn't afford them right now.

She glanced back down at Patrice, thinking about the violet vapor in the in-between. And she knew it was too late to save that part of the soothsayer, too.

"I'll come back for you," she said, gripping the soothsayer's hand. Even if it was only so that Sophie would have something to bury. "I swear it."

"Best not to make promises in this place. The reality of this realm is dictated entirely by Abigail. The Division has her under tight control, too. You start believing in things too much, they're likely to come true here."

If that was the case, the League would have found her by now, and they'd already be on their way out of this strange and horrible place.

They continued to climb, ascending the slope, then some stairs, then ladders into what felt like the attic of the engine palace. Something about the layout, the number of steps, the angles, and even the way it smelled—like leather and oil, lemon varnish overlaid with woodsmoke—pinged in her brain. *The ranch house*, she thought with wonder.

Hettie stuck her head up past one final floor just behind Zavi, and her breath caught.

Abby sat in a giant nest of colorful quilts, just like the ones Ma had made for them. A sheet was strung above her in a makeshift tent. Hettie clambered up into the space and found the floor was made of solid, rough-hewn wood made smooth from years of foot traffic.

A dark splotch shaped like a bird stained the floor, and she realized she knew exactly what it was; she'd tripped and broken a lantern in the kitchen when she was very young, right around the time Abby had been born, and the stain had never come out. That dark splotch always reminded her of her carelessness, and a profound sense of guilt spiked through her every time she stepped over it, even though her parents had just been glad it hadn't caused a fire and burned the house down.

"Abby…" Her voice was rough, strained.

Her sister looked up. Her face showed no expression, save the bland acknowledgment one might give an ant crawling near one's foot. Her violet eyes flickered, and then she turned her attention back to the dark-haired doll she coddled in her nest.

Hettie swallowed. It had been three long, desperate years, and Abby… She was no longer a little girl, but a young woman. The angles of her face were sharp, the hollows around her eyes dark and pronounced. Her blond hair fell past her shoulders, though it seemed to be clean and well-kept. She wore a simple dress of blue with an apron, and she even had socks and shoes, which surprised Hettie; Abby had detested footwear when they'd lived on the farm.

"Abby," Hettie said again, and stepped forward.

Zavi shouted, "Wait, stop—"

Hettie felt something close over her like a blanket, tightening over her skin, suffocating her. Diablo leaped into her hand, and she pulled the trigger blindly. Green fire roared from the muzzle, soaking the wood planks and consuming them instantly. But it wasn't enough to free her from the magic snare.

Nonsense words rang through her ears, drowning her in a rush of syllables and the shushing of her blood. They resonated inside her, reverberating through her guts like a gong until she thought she might vomit. She pulled the trigger again and again, panicked, scrabbling for the time bubble, anything to make the sensation tearing through her stop.

She stared around wildly, seeking the source of her torment. Faintly, she saw three people, and more emerging—a ring of sorcerers closing around her, chanting.

She'd stepped into a trap.

The first tug had her gasping, and she knew the sensation. They were trying to tear at her bond with Diablo. The mage gun curled up in her fist as she lashed out, firing over and over, but the sorcerers kept moving, blurring. They were entirely unaffected by Diablo's hellfire blasts.

Another tearing sensation, this time zipping from her throat to her nether. Breathless, Hettie wrenched around. She had to be in some kind of protection circle. If she could break it—

"Don't stop!" The voice was female. Hettie thought for a blinding moment she was hearing herself speak, but then she felt something lifting off her, peeling away, layer after layer, exposing deepening levels of pain. She thought briefly of that one time she'd been skinning a rabbit only to discover it had still been alive through the process, and she'd had to quickly stab it through the throat to its brain to make it stop thrashing so horrifically.

Suddenly she felt naked, except for a handful of filaments tying her to Diablo. *Pluck, pluck, pluck*—the fine threads popped, and through Diablo's one dark eye, she lived through every life she'd taken in a blink.

And then suddenly, horribly, the weight of the gun slipped from her fingers.

The Devil's Revolver landed with a thud at her feet.

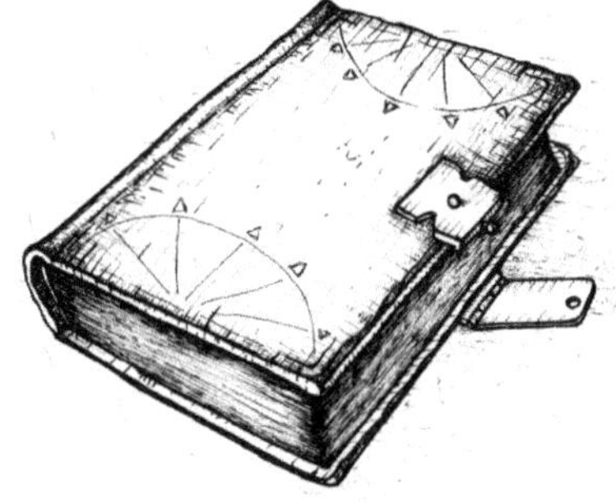

CHAPTER THIRTY

Hettie collapsed to her knees, gasping, the muscles in her chest and the cords in her throat raw, torn and stretched out like taffy. She stared up blearily in search of her sister, but Abby wasn't there.

Glamor, she thought with a curse.

She grabbed Diablo with trembling fingers and pushed shakily to her feet. Thirteen sorcerers formed a ring around her, watching her and the gun in her hand a touch fearfully.

"Did… did it work?" a small male voice asked.

"Now, now, Hettie, put the gun down. I know you better than you think. You don't want to hurt any of us, or yourself for that matter."

She whipped around, blood rushing through her. Berkeley. Next to him was a slight woman with brassy hair and a defiant glare. Her eyes reminded Hettie of the void of an empty grave, or the night sky framed within a hangman's noose. She met that hate-filled gaze, narrowing her own to dagger slits.

"Where's Abby?" She didn't care about the gun pointed at her heart by the woman with the death's head stare.

"She's here, of course," Berkeley said. "I told you she was alive and well. And I did promise we'd be done with her soon."

A tremor shook her arm, but she kept the gun pointed at the grandmaster and one eye on the woman next to him. "Bring me my sister or I'll kill you all."

He raised his chin. "Well, go on, then."

Hettie pulled the trigger. Nothing happened. She called out to the mage gun, but there was nothing. Not silence. Not a mental shrug or a struggle as if Diablo had been gagged. Just…nothing.

The gun in her hand was just that. A gun.

"Congratulations, Professor Gallagher," Berkeley called. "You've severed Miss Alabama's link to that infernal piece." To Hettie, he added, "Don't you see, Hettie? You're free of the curse of the Devil's Revolver. Isn't that what you've always wanted?"

Free? No, no, that couldn't be. She reached out again, trying to pull up the time bubble, trying for anything. But there was no magic in her touch. She impaled her trigger finger on the thorn, letting it sink in. *Click, click, click.* The grip was smeared with blood, but it was just a stain now. A mess. Not a bond.

Tears filled her eyes as the keen edge of loss sliced through her. She wanted to wipe that smug smile off Berkeley's face. Shoot that damned woman through each of her soulless eyes…

Then she remembered.

She pulled the hammer back and took aim.

"Look out!"

Hettie pulled the trigger as a body dove between them, toppling her target.

The gunshot came at the same time searing pain blossomed in her side. Hettie rolled out of the path of the bullets as they pinged off the floor, switching the gun to her left hand and drawing a knife from her boot. She sprang to her feet and stabbed the nearest sorcerer in the gut, wrenching him around by the knife handle to act as a human shield. Two more sorcerers came at her from either side, starting incantations for battle spells. She shot the first in the chest, the second in the head. Hot blood spattered her face.

The others scattered. The stabbed sorcerer in front of her slumped to his knees, and she crouched behind his bulk as she took aim at the armed woman. Paid throbbed through Hettie's side, and she grunted.

"This is a citizen's arrest, Hettie Alabama," the woman shouted. "You won't get away this time."

She didn't know who the woman was, nor did she care.

"You fool! You shot her! If she dies—"

"I won't let her escape justice that easily." The woman's conviction could cut rawhide.

Berkeley's nostrils flared. "Be that as it may, I've no clue what effect opening the hell gate will have in this pocket realm, and I won't have all my work here destroyed!"

Hettie thought hard. Her bond to Diablo had been severed, but somehow, killing her would still open the hell gate. She took shaky aim at Berkeley and fired. The bullet pinged harmlessly off the bulkhead behind him.

The grandmaster's head shot up, nostrils flaring indignantly. "Enough of this!" He pushed a hand toward her. Hettie flew back, and her head banged hard against the far wall. Stars winked in and out of her vision, and her stomach churned. "I'm sorry. I didn't want to do that, but I abhor gun violence." He nodded. "Now put that thing away, and we'll get you a healer before you bleed out."

She glared as she pushed up into a crouch. Blood poured from her side, spurting between her fingers. "I'm not going anywhere with you."

"Professor Gallagher's injured." The woman was bent over the man in the gray suit, her brow furrowed. "He jumped in front of me..."

Berkeley frowned and gestured sharply. Three sorcerers hurriedly carried Gallagher away. The woman watched him go, but her aim never strayed from Hettie.

Berkeley turned his attention back to Hettie and frowned. "Don't be foolish, Hettie. You won't get far with that wound. Drop your weapon and I'll get you all the help you need. I'll even let you go to Abby."

She looked for Zavi, for Abby, but saw neither. "Where is she?"

"In the next chamber. She can't see you in that state, though. What will she think after all this time?" He extended a hand, sounding reasonable, compassionate even. "Surrender Diablo. Let my healers take that bullet out. Have a meal and a bath. By then, Abby's work will be complete, and you can have your reunion."

She chewed on the inside of her cheek. The man's influence magic was *strong*, but Hettie was too stubborn to fall for it. "I'll see her *now*." Her aim wavered, but she zeroed in on the armed woman, who watched her like a hawk.

Berkeley compressed his lips and lifted a shoulder. "Follow me." He turned his back on her.

"You . . . you can't be serious!" the woman exclaimed.

"Miss Pinkerton, if there's one thing I've learned, it's to never come between a woman and her goals. Anyways, we have time." He beckoned as if he were the concierge at a hotel. "This way."

Hettie hobbled forward, gripping her wound, muzzle trained on Berkeley. The Pinkerton woman glared hard daggers at her, but her focus was divided, her eyes darting toward the exit the sorcerers had taken the injured man through.

With every step, pain shot through Hettie's side in a sickening wave that matched the throb of the machine. She didn't want the armed woman at her back, but she didn't have much choice if she was going to follow Berkeley.

They walked through an archway, and something shimmered over her skin. More glamor. She stopped in her tracks as her heart surged into her throat.

Abby, naked, floated three feet off the ground, suspended in midair, her body pierced through with needles that bobbed and wavered like silver porcupine quills. Fine threads of gold connected the needles to the rest of the machine above. Her sister looked peaceful, as if she were asleep.

A sob sawed through Hettie's tight throat. Three long years of cursing a pantheon of uncaring gods, of hoping Abby was alive but secretly wondering if she were better off dead. Three years in which Abby had endured gods knew what, in which she'd gone from little girl to young woman in the clutches of greedy, terrible men.

Her grip tightened around the gun. "What have you done to her?"

"It's all very scientific," Berkeley said. "But the short answer is that Abby's indigo powers have finally been harnessed, thanks to Dr. Fielding." The grandmaster glanced around. "Alastair? Where are you, doctor?"

From one dark corner, the shadow of a man crept out, trembling. "I h-heard g-gunfire and hid," he said shakily. His eyes lighted on Hettie and widened. "It's you."

Rage and pain and something like fear blew through her like a wave of heat from a furnace, prickling her skin. Hettie's glare must have skewered him, because he shrank away. This man had tried to take liberties with Hettie. If he'd laid one finger on her sister—

"Dr. Fielding, please explain to Miss Alabama how you managed this great feat with Abigail."

He cleared his throat. "In s-simple terms, I used the concepts that created the Fielding engines to develop this macro version, only I looped the raw power to filter through a"—he contracted like a snail into its shell, tucking his chin down—"magic proxy."

"Proxy?"

"The w-warlock," Fielding stuttered.

Zavi. The damned warlock she'd freed. He'd probably slunk off to lick his wounds and hightail it out of there. "What does this machine do?" Hettie asked Berkeley, hoping no one had noticed the absence of their "proxy."

"Up till now, it's been storing power. Augmented with what we've borrowed from other sorcerers, we're just about ready for the final procedure."

"*Borrowed.* You mean stolen."

Berkeley waved his hand. "It's a short-term loan for a long-term investment. The gifted will understand what this means once we've ended this magic drain and brought order once and for all."

"I thought you didn't believe in the magic drain."

"A *drain* implies it's not coming back. This is more of a drought. Magic will return, and thanks to these advances in science and sorcery, we have total control now." The corners of his mouth twisted upward.

"So you lied." Her gunshot wound throbbed. The taste of metal stained her tongue, and her hearing was coming in and out.

"Out of necessity. It's the Division's job to keep the masses from panicking. If we had acknowledged the shortage, we'd have rampant juicing; talisman forgeries ten times worse than what we see now; magic riots and power hoarding. Criminal enterprises would thrive among rogue sorcerers. Gifted children would be snatched from their homes. Why do you think enrollment in the Academy is mandatory?"

"Because the Division is trying to control all magic."

"We're trying to *protect* what's left of magic." A hard light filled his eyes. "The only way to preserve civilized magical traditions is to centralize all our gifted and their powers."

"And you took Abby for those purposes."

"I know it's hard for you to accept, but your sister was key to the salvation of magickind. With Abby, and Fielding's discovery, we finally have the means to not only preserve what magic is left—we can *restore* it."

"How?" This from the Pinkerton woman; Hettie had nearly forgotten she was there. It was hard to keep focus.

"It's long been theorized that the essence of magic comes from the heavens," Fielding explained, his shaky voice growing steadily more excited. "The Celestials believe it comes from their qi. The Kukulos believe it is a God-given destiny allotted to the superior race through their bloodlines. Some cultures have pantheons of spirits and gods they worship. But the scientific answer is that *all* of these things are true." He spread his arms wide, his expression manic as he turned his face upward. "Our strongest beliefs and traditions focus our energies and make manifest the ability to change reality, to manipulate what we collectively call *magic*. Only a small percentage of the population can actually do this, but the forces of magic permeate our reality, which must mean it comes from somewhere. That somewhere is the space common among all cultures and traditions that we must all be able to perceive to one degree or another, even if our names for it are different in every language."

"The place in-between." Hettie suddenly grew dizzy, and she staggered. She was losing blood fast. Her fingers tingled, and her vision was going gray.

A rumble like thunder echoed through the chamber, and fine dust rained down on them. "We discovered it by chance when we plumbed Miss Abigail's mind during one of her episodes. She travels to realms we can't begin to imagine along these corridors. We haven't been able to map them at all—they're infinite, twisting... and the magic there is nearly limitless." Fielding gestured helplessly. "Those pathways that link human experience—our stories, our myths, our very existence in this realm—we're all connected, don't you see? Gifted and mundane, dimcan or grandmaster..."

"The bottom line," Berkeley cut in sharply, "is that in a few moments, magic will be restored to its former glory, only now, the Division has the means to mine, harvest, and store it. Sorcerers can finally reclaim their rightful place as the inheritors to the earth. We can end the League and the Mundane Movement, and bring peace and order to the world. Our nation will become the greatest magical power on earth."

"Whaddya mean...?" Hettie's speech was slurred. The floor slid out from under her, and suddenly the world was on its side.

"Hettie!" Berkeley voice was sharp. "We can't let her die. Not here, not now, when we're so close."

"Don't worry. She won't."

Hettie turned over, and her heart beat hard. Sophie and Lady Starling were there, as well as Jay and several other sorcerers.

"Miss Sophie Favreau. What a pleasure it is to see you again." Berkeley gave a slight bow. "And... Lady Eden Prescott. Or shall I call you *Starling*?" He eyed her up and down in her battle armor. "I'd heard you kept some peculiar company, but I had no idea you'd fallen so far."

Starling watched him impassively. "It's over, Grandmaster Berkeley. My people are raiding your compound now. We found the drained sorcerers. I don't know what you're doing with them, but this ends today. We will expose you and the Division."

"Expose me? To whom?" He smirked. "You think an operation like this isn't sanctioned by the government? I work parallel to the president. I represent the interests of the gifted and all magickind. No one in Congress would listen to a fallen woman like you, or any of your ragtag band of miscreants. There's no one who could stop me."

"You're not exempt from the law." She pointed. "Kidnapping and assault is worth at least fifteen years in jail, by my accounting."

"Miss Hettie."

Hettie turned over and looked up blearily. "Ling?"

"Don't move. You're seriously injured." He pressed his palms to her blood-soaked side. Coolness swept through her, easing some of the pain.

"No...get Abby. Save Abby." Her sister could be rescued now, and Hettie didn't want to waste another second.

"Shh. It'll be all right." He grimaced down at her admonishingly. "It's a good thing I had that talisman. The moment you crossed over, I knew you wouldn't wait for us."

I know you better than you think.

Blood throbbed into her head, and her vision narrowed as the sound deadened in her ears. Berkeley was smiling, despite the sorcerers all around him, their spells at the ready. Fielding was hovering over a panel—

"It's a trap! It's a tra—"

"Doctor?" The grandmaster tipped his head.

Fielding pushed a button.

CHAPTER THIRTY-ONE

The world was washed in white light that seared a thousand starbursts of color into the back of Hettie's brain. Almost as quickly, it receded, like a riptide that dragged at her being. Whatever it was, though, couldn't seem to set its hooks in her, and the power withdrew, sloughing away like wet dough peeling off an improperly floured baking sheet.

Hettie blinked hard and gasped.

All her friends lay on the ground, writhing. Ling, Sophie, Starling, Jay, the other sorcerers, even the Pinkerton woman. Only Berkeley and Fielding remained standing.

Hettie pushed up, breathing heavily. "What did you do?"

"I've taken their powers. Fielding's ether engine is a marvelous creation. Not entirely practical in our realm, since it steals the power from everyone and everything in a given area, but it's the perfect targeted weapon here where Abigail controls magical reality. Were you aware of her selective blanket abilities? Marvelous."

Ether engine... It was what Zavi had called the bomb he'd used at Swedenborg. The same device the Division had tested in Newhaven.

Berkeley nodded toward the console, the walls now glowing brightly with the downed sorcerers' powers. "This was the last boost we needed for the final foray. We could've been sending

Fielding expeditions out for months, risking our men and their cargo, before we'd milked enough dimcans to power the engine. But instead I got you."

"I don't understand."

He smiled, eyes gleaming. "The Favreaus have long been suspected of collaborating with the League. When I learned about your connection to Miss Sophie Favreau, I knew you could lead me to the rest of the League. So I let you go, and sent you off with a few mementos to make sure their invitation to my trap was secured."

The notes. The artifacts that made up the multirealm globe. "You set me up. You made sure it'd be easy to bring everyone here."

"But not too easy. Thankfully, you take your smarts from my side of the family."

The Pinkerton woman was getting up slowly, groaning. "Wh-what's happening to me…"

"It's all right, dear. You'll be fine in a moment. You haven't been dosing as long as the good doctor and I have. It'll take a moment for the serum to run its course." He held out one of the small, round mini canister flasks. "Take a sip. Slowly, now."

"How are you not all affected by the bomb?" Hettie demanded.

Berkeley held up the glass flask. "Refined juice with a few other ingredients. Concocted it myself. It keeps all the sorcerers who work here immune to the effects of the engine and the bomb."

"That's…impossible…" the Pinkerton woman said faintly.

"It would be anywhere else. But here, in this reality our dearest Abigail constructed, our sorcerers can make anything happen. That, and her selective blanket ability, keep us safe. Do drink up, Miss Pinkerton, before you faint again."

"That's what this was all about. You needed Abby—a child with indigo powers—to make this pocket of reality for you." Uncle had warned her that her sister's powers were nearly limitless. "You needed her so you could break into the place in-between. And you wanted me for access to the League. And Diablo…"

"A curiosity for my collection," he pooh-poohed. "In the grand scheme of things, it is simply a trinket. A memento of my son's life."

"We ain't kin." Anger funneled through her at the mere suggestion.

"I don't know why you're so resistant to the idea. You have memories of me. People have built families on less." He tilted his chin up. "You've seen my home, the security I can provide. Why keep running and struggling when I can get you pardoned? The Alabama name will come to mean heroism. You'll be legends: the girls who saved magic. You'll be celebrities, bigger than Annie Oakley or Calamity Jane. Once Abby is done with her labors, she'll live in comfort for the rest of her life, and you…you can do anything you want."

"Not with you we won't." Hettie reflexively called to Diablo but got no response. The gun lay on the ground ten feet away.

The sorcerers began to stir. Sophie sat up first, trembling, her fingers curling into claws as she stared wide-eyed at them. "No…" She squeezed her eyes shut. "No…no, no, no!" Her lips were bloodless, her gold curls limp. Jay curled into a ball on the ground and shivered. Starling leaped to her feet and was looking around frantically, as if she'd dropped something. The others moaned and wailed and put their hands over their ears.

And Ling…

Her dear friend lay motionless on the ground, staring up at the ceiling with empty eyes.

"Ling?" She bent over him. His breaths were shallow, and his heart fluttered like a caught bird in his ribcage.

"H-Hettie…m-my qi…" His words dissolved into murmurs in his native tongue.

Qi. Ling had often referred to it as the source of his magic—his life force. She gripped his icy hands. "What do I do?"

But he didn't respond. It looked as though he were trying to hold himself together. Who knew how the other League members were faring?

Helplessness and fear morphed into rage. She glowered at Berkeley, standing triumphant above them, smirking down at Starling in particular.

A flame ignited in her chest. Hettie dove for Diablo—

—and bounced against a cushion of air. She gasped as she was lifted by an invisible fist closing around her torso. "I told you I hate gun violence." Berkeley held one hand up as if she were a goblet he was offering up in a toast. "When we're through here, I'll take you and Abby back to Berkeley Manor, and we'll have a civilized discussion. I won't tolerate disobedience. With your magical link to Diablo cut, I believe the memory wipes should work better now. A few sessions with my new memorist and you'll know everything you need to about life with me." To the far corner to the room, he said, "Dr. Fielding, if you wouldn't mind beginning the procedure…"

"Starting the drill now." Fielding moved swiftly, throwing switches and turning cranks. Hettie struggled, suspended midair, unable to do anything except watch. Power pulsated through the glowing walls, throbbing through the room.

The sorcerers writhed and moaned, and they started clawing at the ground, as if they could dig up magic from the uneven floor. Ling remained paralyzed, though his face looked waxy, his eyes wide and fixed.

Lightning crackled over the filaments wavering around Abby. Hettie's sister twitched, muscles spasming and jerking like an inexpert marionette. Her pinched and pincushioned flesh rippled as arcs of energy passed over her, the gold filaments undulating like a curtain.

All around her, a violet mist rose, drawing toward her, swirling into a vortex until Hettie couldn't see her sister at all.

"Abby!" Hettie had to wake her up, make her stop. All the sorcerers, all her friends, would soon become zombies slavering for magic. Their souls would get trapped in the place in-between… and the drill would take away or destroy anything that was left. Crying Sparrow had been telling the truth. "You have to stop this! We can't let them into the place in-between!"

The Pinkerton woman shouted, "Berkeley, this is madness. No one's ever done this. You can't be certain these theories will work. You're putting everyone here in danger!"

"Fortune favors the bold, Miss Pinkerton," Berkeley said above the roar of the magic "drill." His eyes gleamed with manic light. "We can't have advances in magic or science without sacrifice or risk. This will work because I *will* it to work. This realm was created for *me*, for this project. Failure is not an option."

A blood-curdling scream rent the air.

Fielding stumbled forward. Blood poured from the gaping, dripping hole in his throat. A metal latticework spike as long as an arm protruded from the Mechanik's chest. His eyes were huge and round, and blood bubbled from his lips.

Zavi twisted the makeshift lance, then ripped it out again, flinging a streak of crimson across one wall. Fielding dropped dead to the ground. The warlock turned pure black eyes on Berkeley, his chin dripping blood. He'd drunk the doctor to regain his strength. "I've been waiting for months to find out who the engineer of all this chaos was." He flashed red-stained teeth and pointed the lattice blade at the grandmaster. "I have to say I'm rather disappointed."

Berkeley dropped his raised hand, and Hettie crashed to the ground.

"Your quarrel's not with me," Berkeley said, eyeing Fielding's corpse. For the first time, he sounded a little uncertain, but then his wrinkled brow smoothed over. "In fact, I believe we can help each other. I can help you—"

The warlock laughed. "There's nothing you can offer me except enough blood to open a remote Zoom out of this place."

"I'd beg to differ." Berkeley held out a familiar little bag. The grandmaster emptied the contents onto the floor. The bits clattered across the hard surface like a heavy rain, but as Berkeley whispered his incantation, the bones rolled together, stacking up end to end as if held together by magnetism. As the form completed, it gave a shudder and flapped its wings.

"Rok!" He was just a skeleton, but Hettie would recognize the raven's cocky stance anywhere.

The bone bird rolled its shoulders back, canting from one foot to the other as it adjusted to its corporeal form. It tilted its head to one side as it regarded Zavi, then looked at Hettie with empty eyes. The familiar didn't say anything, though. Or maybe, since her bond with Diablo had been cut, she couldn't hear him.

"You want to go home, don't you? You'll need a guide—a finder to show you the way."

Zavi smirked. "I could just kill you and take what you're offering."

"He's a demon familiar. He won't go to just anyone, and especially not *you*... unless his master tells him to."

Zavi seemed to take that to heart. Berkeley went on. "I know your story, Abzavine, just as I know everything about Diablo. I know how you ended up in Villa del Punta, how the people there revered you, turned you into some kind of saint, and then cast you out of their hearts when you left them to pursue Diablo. I know everything you've done in your lifetime, gathered from thousands of accounts of the people whose lives you touched. They told me about the fallen angel of death, the greatest warlock of the Kukulos brotherhood, the savior of Santa Domina, the scourge of Los Lobos. You are this realm's greatest sorcerer. Your innovation, the ether engine you had Fielding build to destroy Swedenborg… That was foretold to me, too, by soothsayers who did not understand what you'd intended."

Rok snipped at the air and raised his bare bone wings ineffectually. He stared at the swirling mass of mist. In the center, where Abby was, light fought to blaze through breaks in the storm. With the others' attention diverted, Hettie slowly crept toward Diablo.

"You have the power to rule the country. The world. And yet…all you want is to go home." Berkeley softened. "Help me, Abzavine. You killed the only man who knows how to work the drill—but you're connected to the powers we're trying to tap. Only you can tell us how far to drill now. Any farther and we might break through all the realms."

"Maybe I should let it do just that." Zavi's eyes narrowed.

"And risk your realm, too?" Berkeley shook his head. "When the drill breaks through to the corridor of power—the place in-between, as it were—you'll have your way in. Your chance to go home. Do this one thing, and you can finally reclaim you place in the universe and rest."

Hettie reached Diablo and grabbed the mage gun. "Stop." She pointed the barrel at Berkeley. "Turn the machine off. Now."

Berkeley raised an eyebrow. "If I knew how to, I would have. As you can see, though, the process has already begun, and Dr. Fielding…" He gestured toward the Mechanik's body. "Believe me, it does me little good to get this wrong. If the drill goes too far, well, there's the distinct possibility that we could end all of existence."

"You don't sound terribly upset by that," she remarked, keeping one eye on Zavi. The warlock didn't say anything, as if he were waiting to see how this would play out.

Berkeley's smiling eyes were totally devoid of mirth. "The truth is, I take great comfort in the fact that no one would be any better off than me." His words bit into her like a nick from a razor. "But as I said, my future's been foretold. Abzavine will do as I asked. You'll turn your gun away. I really have no wish to harm you further, Hettie. After all you and your sister have endured, don't you think we *all* deserve a rest?"

Rok lifted his bone wings and hissed. But Hettie didn't need the familiar to tell her the man was lying.

She had two bullets left. Shooting Zavi wouldn't stop him. Killing Berkeley wouldn't help much, either. He was the only one who had any idea of how the machine worked, and possibly the only one who could disconnect Abby safely.

She turned to stare at the vortex surrounding Abby. From within, violet eyes opened, glowing, watching her, pleading with her…

Hettie. I can't… Please… Don't make me hurt anyone…

"Abby?"

The violet eyes blinked slowly. *Metal isn't affected by magic…*

Hettie's heart squeezed. No. No, she wouldn't! She *couldn't…*

The air throbbed, and the sorcerers moaned plaintively. Ling lay very still. Sophie was scratching at her arms, as if she might dig her missing magic from her veins. Starling was pulling at her hair while the others moaned and sobbed.

Filled with hatred, Hettie looked to Berkeley. There was only one way to save them all.

With a sick feeling in her stomach, Hettie holstered Diablo.

"There's a good girl." Berkeley addressed Zavi. "Now, Zavi, if you'll be so kind as to monitor the engine—"

"Kind?" Zavi turned his faraway gaze upon Berkeley. "You think I do anything out of *kindness*?"

Berkeley blinked and snickered. "I think we have an understanding—"

Zavi laughed. "You can't begin to conceive of what I *understand* about the universe. You think your power impresses me? That your access to soothsayers impresses me? That this precious paste realm Abby's slapped together impresses me?"

In a flash, the warlock materialized directly in front of the grandmaster and grabbed him by the throat, lifting him high into the air. Rok's bones tumbled and scattered at his feet. "The thing about soothsayers is that they can only predict the future in the realms they stand in. We are not in that realm now."

Horror filled Berkeley's face as his miscalculation sank in.

"I *am* Abzavine, the angel of Villa del Punta, grand warlock of the Kukulos brotherhood, the savior of Santa Domina, the scourge of Los Lobos, and keeper of the Devil's Revolver. And yet, despite all those titles, you treated me worse than a diseased plough horse." Ripples of power sparked and sputtered around Berkeley's hands. His face turned puce, and Zavi went on. "A man with twice your power once sought to control me, too." Zavi's eyes filled with hate. "But I am no one's servant."

"Zavi, no!"

There was a sickening snap, followed by wet popping sounds as Berkeley's trachea was crushed in the warlock's long-fingered hand. Blood gushed from the grandmaster's gaping mouth, his wide eyes bloodshot. The man's head flopped at a distressing angle as Zavi tossed him aside like a used rag.

Hettie bit back a scream. "What have you done?"

"What I was always meant to do. I'm ending this world and going home." He swung back to the control panel, pushed a lever to its fullest, and flipped some switches. A high-pitched whine sang through the walls, making the sorcerers put their hands over their ears and keen. As it reached a shrill whistle, Zavi raised his fists and smashed the console, sending up a shower of sparks and causing the machinery to pop and fizzle. The engine continued to throb and screech its warnings.

The clouds swirled around Abby in a torrent. Hettie's sister's glowing violet eyes disappeared, obscured in the vortex. Beneath her shadow form, a portal had opened, rimmed in violet and gold, and from it…

Hettie wasn't sure what she was seeing at first. It felt like a void, sucking in light but also emitting it, a sickening pulse that made Hettie's skin feel like it was burning off. Her vision grew hazy, and she felt a warm wetness soak her shirt anew. She looked down. Ling's healing magic that had sealed the gunshot wound had been sucked away. She bled freely once more.

Hettie's knees buckled. She grew cold and shaky as hope seeped from her as readily as her life's blood.

She had only one chance to save them, to stop this…but she wasn't going to shoot her sister. Not even to save the world.

She closed her eyes, the warning of her guide from the place in-between echoing in her ears. She couldn't save Abby. She was going to die here. They all were. Her family, her friends, all the people she'd met on her travels… Memories from her tumultuous life—her triumphs, her failures, her regrets—flashed through her mind like a high-speed lantern show. The regrets, especially. Three years of robbing, maiming, killing and more, and for what? Not redemption. Not even revenge.

Zavi appeared next to her, watching the portal beneath Abby expand, a gaping, gilded maw delicately eating up the world. He cradled the pile of Rok's bones against his chest, carefully gathered up off the ground like a posy. "Beautiful, isn't it? And far more efficient than the hell gate."

"What is it?" she asked, unsure why she bothered to ask. Maybe she just wanted to know how it would all end.

"In the crudest terms, it's a bore hole into the place in-between, as you call it. Far easier to navigate and certainly less torturous than the hell gate." He gave a giggle. "With Abby augmenting the power, this machine will drill indefinitely, piercing all the realms till they bleed into each other."

"Yours included?"

"I inspired this engine's design. I know how to protect my realm from it. I'll be welcomed home as a hero."

"Or you could just stop the drill now and go home anyway."

He glared. "You of all people should understand. The only way to ensure your own safety and security is to utterly destroy your enemies. No one will ever hurt me or my kind again."

She coughed a wad of blood. He looked down at Hettie and smiled. "You're dying, Hettie Alabama."

His words sank in like a dull knife. "No shit," she replied.

"I *could* save you." It was a taunt, of course. The warlock had never been an angel; he was simply a creature of utter spite now. "But why? Everything in this forsaken realm is about to be destroyed."

He raised his chin, contemplative. "I will spare Abby, though," he said decisively. "I will take her with me to my realm. She's an innocent in all this—the only one on this wretched plane—as used and abused as I have been." His lips spread in a cruel smile. "My people will enjoy studying her unique abilities."

He was making this personal. He was making sure she knew *this* was his revenge on her.

Hettie's heart hammered hard, beating against the leaden feeling slowly seeping into every muscle.

"The drill is almost through." Overjoyed tears filled Zavi's eyes. "I'm finally going home. Your world will end. And no one will ever hurt me again."

Hettie's hand closed over Diablo. The mage gun Javier Punta had made to protect his people. *Hubris*, she thought bitterly. It was utter foolishness to think any one person could wield this kind of power without sacrifices. Without consequences.

"You *do* deserve to go home," she whispered. She lifted Diablo. "But you're not taking Abby with you."

She put the gun to her own head and pulled the trigger.

CHAPTER THIRTY-TWO

Hettie tumbled through lily-scented blackness, her flesh flayed from her body in strips by a million tiny invisible razors. So, she thought wryly, hell hadn't changed since her last trip here. How comforting.

Barbs made of fire clung to her flesh and gouged out thimble-sized hunks. A fine rain of acid seared every inch of her. Soon, the outer layer would be gone to expose her innards, she supposed, and then the real fun would begin.

Hettie decided to make a game with herself: How long could she go without screaming? She'd have an eternity of this, after all. Might as well find ways to make infinite torment interesting.

When she was raw and divoted as a boiled potato, maggots descended to inveigle themselves into the braided ropes of wet, exposed muscle. Hettie watched them—she didn't have eyelids anymore, so she didn't have much choice—and stifled a giggle as they tickled her.

Hell didn't like that. A roar of flame, and the worms were evaporated. Shame. They would've made good company in her everlasting torment. Or maybe a secret snack for when the insatiable hunger hit.

The flames scorched her throat and lungs. Hettie gave a cough, contemplating the bloody sputum. How did hell work, exactly?

Did it use some kind of healing magic to regenerate her corporeal form so it could be forever dismantled, like some failed Mechanik's engine? Was this a torture of the mind alone?

She'd have eternity to come up with her theories. Maybe she'd even write some of them down, etch them into her flesh the way she'd...

She glanced at her inner arm.

SAVE ABBY.

Tears pricked her eyes, even as the gut instinct to get away, to move forward, bowed through her like a stiff wind catching her sail.

Save her how? I'm dead now, and this is my new existence—

No, it isn't.

Hope and a little horror rose inside her. *Is that you?*

We don't have time to waste here, Diablo said. *Abby's still in danger.*

Hettie's heart caught. *But...how do we get out of here?*

The demon held out a hand. For a brief moment, she thought she saw Paul smiling crookedly down at her. *Don't worry. I'll show you.*

With uneasy trust in her heart, she grasped his hand.

Paul pulled her up into the saddle in front of him. "There you go. Easy as pie."

Hettie shifted her weight as her brother and the horse adjusted to the new passenger. "You won't go too fast?"

He half turned. "*You* were the one who wanted to ride with me. I've gotta check the fences. If I don't ride fast enough..." He hesitated as she whimpered. "Aww...fine. I'll take it easy. But next time, you're riding on your own horse."

The filly took off at a trot. It was a while before Hettie was relaxed enough to ease her white-knuckled grip from the pommel and watch the long grasses rushing beneath the horse's hooves. Of course, she was too old to be riding with him like this, but for now she relished her brother's closeness, his chin resting on her head, his arms encircling her, keeping her from falling out of the saddle. She just didn't think she was ready to ride on her own.

The horse slowed and gave a low nicker. "What's wrong, girl?" Paul bent in the saddle to check her hooves. "I think she has a stone in her shoe—"

The man came out of nowhere, rising from the grass like a sea monster from the ocean. He rushed at the horse and yanked Paul out of the saddle. A flash of metal, and Paul cried out. Her brother landed hard on his side.

Then the man came for Hettie.

The nervous filly danced back, hind end swerving. Hettie screamed and kicked out at the attacker as he grabbed the reins. She clipped him in the chin. He gave a feral growl, and his grip closed around her ankle. The world spun, and she hit the ground hard. She let out a piercing cry of pain, of fear. The man and his knife staggered toward her.

"Hettie!" Paul, bright crimson staining his shirt, tackled their attacker, but while her brother was tall for his age, he was maybe half of the other man's weight. They rolled across the dirt, but the rustler overpowered him easily.

The man's rusty knife flashed—

Hettie screamed and squeezed her eyes shut. *I don't want to see this part.* Of course. *This* was her hell. She could think of no worse torment than reliving the worst day of her life over and over again.

Her lungs shrank as screams and sobs washed over her. She kept her eyes closed, but the scene played out. She knew the exact moment the knife made its fatal plunge in Paul's soft body; the sound of Paul's shocked exhalation had never left her. The horse squealed as the murdering rustler mounted and kicked his prize. Hoofbeats juddered through her bones, fading.

"Paul…" Little Hettie's voice was high, thin, choked with tears.

"I'm okay, Hettie…I just… I need to rest." His voice rasped as blood filled his lungs.

Hettie's shaking hands grew slick and sticky as she tried to stop the flow, but her hands were too small, too weak, too incapable to stop the bleeding. She couldn't even tear strips out of her dress; the fabric was too thickly woven.

Paul grabbed her hands and held them still. "You…you gotta take care of Abby now, Hettie," he whispered.

"No! I don't want to! I can't! I don't know how…"

But he didn't respond. His eyes had softened beyond dreamy, a small, reassuring smile on his face—a benediction.

"Paul, please, no! Don't…don't leave me! I promise, I promise I'll take care of Abby, but please, don't leave me…"

Hettie pressed her palms against her tear-streaked face. No, no, no. She'd rather have her flesh peeled away and her teeth yanked out for eternity. Anything but *this*.

"I'm so sorry, Paul," she whispered. "I failed you. I couldn't protect you…or Ma or Pa or Uncle or…or…" She couldn't bring herself to admit her failure.

"You did your best."

She looked up in surprise. Her brother stood over her, whole, almost…shining. "You did everything you could, but you couldn't save Abby in the end."

"I can," she protested, fire filling her belly. "I will!"

Paul chuckled. "You'll try. But there's only one person now who can save her." He extended a hand. Hettie took it.

The familiar weight of the Devil's Revolver rested in her palm.

The ranch was gone. A night-dark field engulfed her, the smell of cordite and lilies heavy in the air, the grass wet beneath her booted feet. A full moon shone high above, a milky eye peering blindly down at her from an inky sky. The breeze caught her hair, bringing with it the faint scent of wood smoke and tobacco.

"Hey, girlie."

She spun, and her heart caught. His shirt was neat, clean, his scruff trimmed, his boots polished. She'd only seen him this spiffed up once, and it had been in Patrice Favreau's home. "Uncle." She rushed toward him, arms outstretched. But he held his hands out and stepped back.

"No, Hettie. Don't touch me. I… We can't." He stuffed his hands in his pockets. "Not without consequences."

Her heart sank. She hadn't realized how much she needed to hug the old coot, but now that she couldn't… "Consequences? What are you talking about?" She glanced around. "Where are we?"

"It's a bit hard to explain. Let's just say it comes with the office." He took off his hat and slapped it over his knee, despite there being no dust on it. Old habits died hard, apparently. "Didn't expect to see you here so soon." The lines on his face deepened. "Didn't expect to see you here at all."

"I don't understand what's happening. Is…is this hell?"

"Of a kind. But not yours."

"But…I shot myself in the head." She looked down at the gun, checking the chambers as if she could prove she wasn't wrong. The wheel was fully loaded. She touched her temple, still feeling the ghostly graze of Diablo's barrel. "I didn't miss. I have to be dead…"

"It's complicated." He wiped a hand down his face. "C'mon. There's something I need you to see."

He took three steps, and suddenly they were in front of a pretty cabin with a porch and a rocking chair. He opened the door and beckoned her to follow.

The one-room cottage was bigger, cleaner, and prettier than the one Uncle had inhabited on the Alabama ranch. It was simply furnished with a bed, a little table, and a stool. A cheerful fire burned in a small potbellied stove, and a pot of coffee brewed on top, filling the room with its rich aroma. A round, plush wool rug in vivid shades of green and yellow lay in the center of the room. And on it, a pale figure cowered.

Diablo leaped into her hand and swung her arm up. "Zavi."

The warlock didn't acknowledge her. He stared into the far corner, eyes wide, trembling.

"Easy now." Jeremiah pushed her hand down gently. "Rok brought him here." In the corner of the room, the raven, fully formed, his feathers glossy black and his eyes gleaming, preened on his perch. "The hell gate opened and sucked Zavi in. Lucky for him, he had my familiar…or at least, his bones. You were supposed to hang on to those, y'know."

She frowned at the mage gun confusedly. "I had other concerns."

"This place is steeped in the power that made Diablo. That's why it still works here," Uncle explained.

"So what's wrong with him?" She indicated Zavi, who hugged his knees.

"The magical bond between you and Diablo was severed; that spell also cut the tether that kept Zavi linked to Diablo. When he went through the hell gate, he didn't have his anchor in the world anymore. His mind and spirit drifted through hell like a ship lost at sea." He looked upon the warlock with pity. "He's in shock."

Hettie's lip curled. "After all the people he killed—the children he stole and the lives he ruined—he deserves worse. Rok should've left him there."

"Maybe so, but it ain't that simple, Hettie." Uncle turned sad blue eyes on Zavi and beckoned her to the window. "C'mere and have a look." He handed her a spyglass.

She looked through the eyepiece and gasped.

Abby stood spread-eagle in what appeared to be a doorway, clenching her fingers around the doorjamb as a gale-force wind tried to dislodge her, her gold hair rippling like a shredded flag in a hurricane. In the next moment, she was deluged by water, a foamy torrent of blue-green ocean rushing past her. And still she clung. Then there was fire, and then a sandstorm—it was as if all the elements had banded together to try and flick her tiny body out of the way, but she was stubbornly hanging on.

"What's happening to her?" Hettie cried.

"When you opened the hell gate inside the pocket realm, the space in-between cracked wide open. The dam's broken, and all that magic is trying to rush into our world and all the worlds connected to it. Abby's the only thing keeping that from happening now. She's absorbing all that magic into her pocket realm, keeping it from rushing into your realm."

"It's hurting her. Why doesn't she let go?" Hettie put the spyglass down. "I need to get to her!"

"You can't. Not from here."

"Then how?" she shouted.

"Hold your horses, I'm gettin' to that." He blew out a breath. "All the realms are like a bunch of eggs floating in a pot of water. Abby's pocket realm is like a yolk in your egg, and the powers that created it are as thin as the skin that keeps the yellow from leaking into the white. That drill of Fielding's was meant to tap through the shell and into the water. When you opened the hell gate, though, it was like shooting a gun into the pot."

"But…my world…"

"Abby's the only thing holding everything together right now, keeping the other realms from spilling out into each other. The problem is that the pocket realm is a product of her imagination, her power, and it's swelling with the magic from the place in-between.

It's a rattler's egg in a nest full of chicken eggs, and it's growing, infinitely, as far as we know. The snake inside will eventually break out of its shell and consume the rest of the eggs." He wiped a hand over his mouth. "Whatever reality she thinks to shape is being fed by more power than we've ever known."

"What does that mean?"

"It means everything we know will cease to exist. *Every* realm. As the pocket fills with magic, it will overtake everything—heaven, hell, the in-between... and Abby could remake all of reality, or she could destroy it."

Hettie's mind raced. "Why aren't we affected *here*?" She gestured around the cottage.

"This place exists in the place Diablo's bubble does. It's on another plane—a different layer of reality, like a lantern show on a canvas. That's where you go when you freeze time around you. But this place will eventually be consumed, too. Before we can help Abby, you need to travel across this plane to take Zavi back to his home."

She bristled. "Why? What does he have to do with this?"

"He doesn't belong here, Hettie. He's a loose thread that's unraveling the fabric of the universe, just like Diablo. This is where it all began, or at least one of the many reasons why magic was draining out of the world. Javier Punta punched a hole through the realms to get the demon that inhabits Diablo, and he accidentally snagged and dragged Zavi through with it. He compromised the skin keeping the realms separate. Ever since then, magic's been leaking out of our world faster and faster. It wasn't just him, though. Tons of spells have been doing this for centuries. Transmogrification. Alchemy. Magic was never meant to be abused the way some people have, and all those spells poked holes all through the membranes. But the worst hole of them all is the one that Javier made. Until we return Zavi and Diablo and repair those holes, we can't ensure the safety of our realm. It'd be like trying to inflate a balloon with pinholes in it. The whole thing could burst."

"Eggs, balloons, fabric... You're making it sound awfully complicated."

"I told you it would be." He snorted.

"What about the soothsayers? Patrice and the others… Their souls or whatever are trapped in the place in-between. I saw them when we used the multirealm globe to get to the pocket realm. They were faint…"

"Because you were traveling on a different plane from where they are. It's like…" He halted and made a frustrated noise. "It's like climbing through silk hosiery soaking in a bathtub. You're there but separate. I'm sorry, I don't know how else to explain it so you'd understand." He rubbed his temples.

"Okay. How do I help them?"

"Shut down the drill. But before that, Diablo and Zavi must be returned to their rightful places. Until those holes are plugged up, we can't close the breaches and save Abby."

"But why *me*?" Her voice grew rough with exhaustion and helplessness. "I'm not even a sorcerer. Why can't *you* do it?"

"I've got my own burdens to bear. Besides, you're the only one who can traverse this plane. You've been on it before, had practice. And you have Diablo, which can lead you along the way."

"What if I refuse?" It was a sudden, mean, but singularly simple and unfeeling thought. End it all. The world was unjust and full of cruelty, and Hettie was tired of getting kicked around and made to suffer for its continuance. Berkeley had been onto something when he'd said he took comfort in the fact that no one would be better off than him if the world suddenly ended. And in Hettie's experience, no good deed went unpunished. Why not let the world burn? Either way, she was damned.

Jeremiah's shocked expression slackened, dissolving into resignation. The night sky reached down and enveloped them. The cheery room disappeared, and cold seeped into her bones. Zavi curled up even tighter, trembling like a child.

Out of the liquid shadows stepped her father and mother.

No. Not her parents. They wore their faces, but it wasn't John and Grace Alabama.

"You owe us a debt, wielder," mother-woman said. "We've come to collect."

Hettie notched her chin up in defiance, facing her parental doppelgangers. She was tired of being pushed around. "Ain't nothing I've got you can make me give up," she returned sharply. "You learned that the first time I came 'round these parts."

"We warned you the price for your sister's life would be high," father-man said. "If you have no intention of honoring our agreement, we will take back what we gave."

Hettie stilled. They meant Abby. They'd take her life back.

"No. She lives. Take my life instead."

"Your life is not worth as much," they proclaimed coldly.

Hettie firmed her stance. "What is it you two bargainers really want? Why'd you go through all of this? For Abby? For Diablo?"

"Our role is to balance the books," the father-man said. "Pay off the first debt, accrue interest…"

"And *invest*," mother-woman finished.

"Invest in what?"

"Continuance," they replied. Rok shook his feathers, shuddering.

Hettie considered this a moment. "I take it continuance isn't a thing if that pocket realm eats us all."

"You owe us a debt, wielder," they said again.

Not a lot of help there. She deflected. "Why is my uncle here?" Or was he a doppelganger serving her shadow parents?

"He has his own debts to pay," father-man said.

"Leave it, Hettie," Jeremiah said. "I made this deal on my own. Ain't nothing you can do to get me out of it."

"You don't belong here," she said fervently, and realized for all the times she'd cursed him, she meant it. "This can't be where you end up."

"Girlie, I've done some terrible things, but they were all the *right* things to do at the time. I made my choices, and I don't regret them." Conviction burned hot in his narrowed gaze. "But now I've got to pay for my actions, my choices, same as you—as any of us. That's all there is to it. We all got bills to settle."

Tears burned in the backs of her eyes, but she swallowed them and turned her glare on the creatures wearing her parents' skins. "If you take Abby's life, the magic will pour into all the realms and destroy everything, including you."

"If you do not help us, the same will happen." Her shadow parents watched her steadily. "Which odds do you prefer?"

She hated conceding, but she wouldn't put Abby in harm's way. "So I'm supposed to take Zavi and Diablo back to their respective homes. One problem: I was already *in* hell. Diablo wouldn't leave me. Can't I just drop Diablo off here with you?"

The mother-woman and father-man laughed, the sound like the warble of a band saw as it sliced through bone. "This is not hell. Not *your* hell, and not Diablo's home."

"This is neutral territory," Uncle explained. "The place where bargains are struck."

"Funny. I must've gone the long way 'round through hell that time I followed Abby here."

"*We* rescued you," the shadow parents corrected sharply. "The hell gate is the painful doorway to many worlds, and only a fool would enter through there." Their eyes flicked to the cowering Zavi. "When you, Abby, and Diablo were first sucked in, you were supposed to be sorted to your individual fates. But *you* were too stubborn, too determined to release your sister and Diablo. That's when *we* intervened, to make sure you didn't do any more damage."

"Me?"

"You had your foot in the door and let the elements in," Uncle said wryly. "All that magic swirling through what you call hell and all the other places was wreaking havoc. That's how Diablo got that patina. It was fighting a bunch of other demons to keep you from letting go." He nodded to the shadow parents. "They had to convince you to get out of the doorway."

"You owe us for more than your sister's life," they said.

She scoffed. "I don't owe you any more than what we agreed on, so you can just strike that from your ledger." She paused. "But for Abby's sake, I'll do this thing you asked and take Zavi home. It'd help if I knew where I was headed, though. It's not as if I know how to get to wherever *he's* from." She waved at Zavi.

Uncle smirked. "You've grown quite a pair, there, girlie." He gave an ear-piercing whistle.

The wind stirred, and the inkiness lifted to reveal the grassy slope once more. A pale dawn light painted the sky in silver, and from the horizon streaked a shining star…

Hettie blinked back tears as the figure resolved, mane gleaming, muscles firm and strong. Her hoofbeats shook the ground like an avalanche. Jezebel gave a whinnied greeting as she high-stepped next to her.

Hettie grabbed her bridle and buried her tear-streaked face against the mare's neck. It took her a long time to regain her composure before she could croak out, "How…?"

"Horses don't live by any of our rules," Uncle replied, almost wistfully. "In this place, they're free spirits. They go where they want…including any realm or plane they damn well please."

"And you came to help *me*?" She rubbed the mare's velvety nose. Jezebel nuzzled her and blew softly into her neck.

"Rok will lead you to the edge of Zavi's realm," Uncle said. The raven perched on his shoulder. "Diablo's good, but a second guide can't hurt. Anyhow, we don't have any more time to waste. Jezebel will take you where you need to go. But you'll have to convince the gatekeeper to let Zavi back in."

"And then?"

He hesitated. "You'll need to ride to the heart of actual hell, where the demon inside Diablo was born. And you'll have to convince it to leave you and go home for good. You do this right, and you'll save Abby."

"What about the soothsayers?" A pang went through her remembering Patrice was well and truly dead.

"When the magic deluge ends, things'll be calm enough that you can use that multirealm globe to plumb the souls out of there. Lead the way back to your realm."

"And my friends and all the other sorcerers?"

"They'll be flooded with magic, but they should be all right. Go on, then. Time's a-wastin'."

She hesitated, glancing back at the silent shadow parents. Uncle's eyes were the color of a sky on the verge of clouding over, the promise of either sun or rain ambiguous in their stormy depths.

He was lying about something. About her friends, the soothsayers…was he lying about saving Abby, too?

"Are you sure about this?" she asked, but she wasn't questioning his confidence in the plan.

"Dammit, girlie, you're *still* questioning everything I'm telling you?" he asked incredulously.

She shrugged her hopes away. "Can't be too paranoid. Guess I learned that from you."

Jeremiah Bassett puckered his lips sourly as if trying to suppress a smile…or maybe tears. He nodded sharply and looked away. "Well…guess I did some good in life, then. Better be off."

She looked down at Zavi, a pitiful creature staring wide-eyed at nothing. Gently, she tugged at him, and he came willingly to his feet. She managed to maneuver him into Jezebel's saddle. She mounted in front of him, because otherwise she wouldn't be able to see past his tall, lean form. He clung to her waist as if she were a life raft.

"Hettie," Uncle called as she turned Jezebel toward the sun. She looked into his lined, grizzled face, taking in every detail and searing it into her memory. Her heart called out to him: *Come with me. Ride with me one last time.* "At the end of all this…you and I will have some words. Real words."

She nodded stiffly. "I suspect we will, old man. I ain't plannin' on that conversation anytime soon, though, so don't wait up."

His eyes were sad. "You never asked what would happen to you once Diablo was returned and everything's put back to rights."

She smirked. "Yup."

Hettie kicked Jezebel into a run, Rok taking wing, leading them into the unknown.

CHAPTER THIRTY-THREE

They might have traveled for weeks. Months. Hettie didn't know, since it was, as Uncle had explained it, basically Diablo's time bubble but stretched out. The thing was, night and day came and went on a whim. The moon was full one night, then a mere sliver the next. The sun rose from every direction, and at a moment's notice sometimes, rising and setting across her shoulders as quickly as a spider would skitter, or resting on the back of her neck until she thought her shadow was a permanent part of her. This plane, with its fields of gilded grass and lazy slopes that rolled like sea waves, spread on forever. If she'd tried to travel here on her own, she would have lost her mind.

Thankfully, Jezebel never tired, never stopped for food or water. She ran without limits here, exalting in absolute freedom from bodily needs, borders, or terrain. She flew across the ground as if it meant nothing and yet everything to run. Oh, to be so free! Her boundlessness was one of the few things that gave Hettie a sense of peace. All she needed was a reliable steed in this strange land.

The rolling hills became sand dunes, and Jezebel negotiated their shifting spines as gracefully as a ballet dancer. The desert went from silky to serrated, with jagged peaks rising like knives from a cracked and parched ground. They journeyed through red rock arroyos that began as parched skin and deepened into canyons that swallowed the skies. Gradually, the ground went from the color of old blood to milk white as they emerged into a snow-crusted valley.

Jezebel forded tirelessly through snow so deep it brushed Hettie's boots. The cold didn't touch any of them, but neither had the sun nor the wind nor the rains, nor hunger, thirst, or the need to rest. They simply rode on, pursued by the gnawing edge of anxiety, a restless sense of impending doom that dogged Hettie with every step.

The valley thickened with pines bowed under the weight of snow. The forest thinned, turned green, then gold once more until the tree line came into sight. The great plain they'd started on stretched ahead of them, and Hettie's heart sank. "We didn't go in a circle, did we?" she asked Rok, whose shadow had stayed ahead of them the entire journey.

The raven sent her a withering look. *"Circle? Yes. It is all a circle. Ring around the rosy, pocket realm full of posies! One edge to the next. Fastest way is through. No time to circle, circle, circle..."* He flapped on.

Jezebel forged ahead. They came across a herd of buffalo running across the plains. Her father's horse gave a whinny in greeting, and the herd acknowledged her with guttural lows. The herd parted, surrounding Hettie, their thick, shaggy hides a carpet insulating them on all sides. Suddenly, it was as if Jezebel were sprinting, the landscape rushing beneath her hooves, carried along the tide of the buffalo.

"Hurry, hurry," Rok said, urgency in his tone. *"No time left to waste."*

Eventually, the buffalo broke off, and the world stopped streaking around them. Jezebel galloped on, energized, but her breaths were becoming more labored. The roaming sun settled in one place and became a fiery wall, a looming golden mural that curved up as if painted on the concave inside of an enormous dome. Rok squawked and wheeled around to perch on Zavi's shoulder.

Jezebel pulled up, lungs heaving, and came to a standstill.

They'd arrived at Zavi's realm.

Hettie unlocked the angel warlock's arms from around her waist and dismounted. She stared up at the surface of the golden sun. The shifting, gleaming flames danced, and Hettie got the sense that they were *alive*.

She prodded Zavi, who sat staring blindly in the saddle. "Hey. Wake up." He hadn't said a word on the entire journey, except to occasionally whimper. "Wherever you are in your head, it's time to come out. You're home." When he didn't stir, she grabbed his leg and yanked him off. He slid down and hit the ground with a groan. She reminded herself that Abby was still in trouble; she didn't have time for games.

"You gotta front door key or something?" she asked him as he sat up. If there were a barrier spell, she wasn't about to test it and get knocked back to where she'd started.

Zavi turned pale eyes up to her, looking entirely lost. Frustrated, she snapped her fingers in front of him. "Anyone there?"

But he wasn't looking at her. She glanced over her shoulder. The flames were gathering on the mural, forming a vaguely human shape about three stories tall that wavered and danced.

"Who approaches the threshold of the Ones Above?" The deep voice boomed in her ears, shuddered through her bones. Her flesh felt as if it might jump right off her skeleton, and she clenched her jaw.

Hettie swallowed down a bolt of fear and steeled her nerves. "I'm Hettie Alabama. I'm here escorting Abzavine back to his realm."

The fire figure came closer, its large, amorphous outline tightening and resolving, becoming the shape of a very large man as it approached. The flames went from orange-gold to nearly white. It was like the reverse of a shadow.

The fiery gatekeeper considered Zavi, who crouched on the ground. "We do not recognize this creature." He'd lowered his volume slightly, perhaps in consideration for her discomfort.

Hettie glanced back at Rok. Had the familiar brought them to the wrong realm border? "Well, by my reckoning, it's been over two hundred years, so maybe he's just different from what you—"

"We do not recognize him because Abzavine is no longer welcome here," the gatekeeper clarified, voice rising and making her eyeballs hurt. "The Ones Above have watched him in your world, seen the things he's done. He is tainted and broken."

Zavi stiffened. The warlock wasn't entirely catatonic after all.

Hettie set her jaw. "Well, that ain't my problem. If you 'Ones Above' have been paying any attention, we need to get him back where he belongs so that we can stop magic from totally destroying all the realms."

"Your destruction does not concern the Ones Above." The figure stepped away from the wall, his flaming body expanding as he walked away.

"Doesn't concern— You'll be destroyed, too. This one"—she indicated Zavi—"told me he knew how to save y'all."

"The Ones Above are beyond the reach of such mundane magics. The Ones Above—"

"Like hell you are. And from where I'm standing, seems we're on equal ground, so you listen and listen good. I've crossed the whole damned country and a few other realms, nearly died a dozen times, dragged myself through hell, and gotten killed twice to get to this point. I ain't letting some fancy-talking, highfalutin' doorman stop me from saving my sister."

The gatekeeper roared, and the wall erupted in an inferno. Hettie scrambled back as he burst through the threshold in a fireball. He towered over her, two overlong appendages swinging at her head.

She ducked and rolled out of the way as the gatekeeper slammed a fist down, gouging a blazing crater where her head had been a second ago.

Diablo leaped into her hand, and Hettie unleashed the mage gun's hellfire, engulfing the gatekeeper in a furnace blast of roaring green flames. The creature barely got out a shriek as he was snuffed out, a matchstick flame swallowed by an inferno.

The threshold flared, then suddenly went dark. Zavi gave a wretched cry as the curved gold wall crumbled and dissolved in a burst of ash. Above them, the sky was a starless black void.

"You fool!" Zavi screamed, fingers clenched. "You killed the gatekeeper! Now we have no way to get into my realm!"

She regarded him with a scowl. "I don't think he was going to let you in one way or another." She sucked air between her teeth. "Anyhow, it's not like you were helping."

"You expect me to attack my own people?"

"What, you suddenly have a conscience because they're your own kind?" She scoffed. "I've seen what you're capable of. I've seen the things you've done to people—to children! You might have powers beyond anything most have seen, but you haven't done a thing to prove you're worth two bits against the lowest of criminals. For all the fancy powers and righteous words you have, you're no better than any of us. You think we're just insects crawling through the dirt for you to watch? Well, guess what? You're stuck down here with us now, and there ain't no one who cares if they step on you."

Zavi looked taken aback to have been spoken to in this way. He said, "I am one of the Ones Above. I am stuck here because of *your* kind. What I have wrought has been of your doing. I have suffered loss you can't imagine—"

She barked out a sharp, humorless laugh. "Loss? You think you know loss? Or grief? You don't know what that even means. You've never loved anything in this world. Nothing matters to you because there's nothing you care about."

Then, she suddenly understood. Zavi had no one, nothing. He was immortal, and pain did little to thwart him; he had no kin here, no one he loved or cared about. *That* was what made him so angry and bitter and reckless. He was taking his unhappiness and utter desolation out on the world. He played games with humanity under the guise of noninterference, probably in some misguided belief that he was following the righteous code of his people.

And she and Zavi were exactly the same.

Traumatized. Hurt. Bereft. Walker and everyone else had warned her that she had been going down a dark road since Abby's capture. She'd lost everyone and everything that had mattered, closed herself off from the people who'd been reaching out to her to prevent any more pain, loss, or suffering. That was not who she was. It was not who she'd been since...since...

Hettie thought hard. She didn't know herself anymore. Four years ago, she'd begun the most difficult journey of her life, banking loss after loss...for what?

To have the Pearly Gates locked on her, that was what. And even though she knew she'd never enter that place...even if she hadn't been sure she believed in it...hadn't she hoped for redemption? For approval? For some last-minute reprieve that would allow her to reunite with the people torn from her life?

Hadn't she suffered enough to earn that privilege?

Zavi sat down hard in the dirt and crossed his arms, his face a study in malicious petulance. Seeing him so utterly defeated and still angry about it, she knew now that suffering hadn't earned her anything, just as his hatred would never get him what he wanted.

She couldn't bank pain. She couldn't forfeit hope and expect to be paid in miracles. She'd spent the past three years convinced she was bound for hell for all her misdeeds, but instead of trying to redeem herself and live a better life, she'd used her sins as an excuse to stew in hatred and self-loathing, to wallow in blood and bullet casings and dispense her form of gruesome justice upon people whom she had no right to judge. She'd built her own hell, all in Abby's name.

Patrice and Crying Sparrow had been right. She could never have saved Abby: not the way she'd dreamed, Diablo blazing a path through a forest of bodies. She'd been too willing to kill for her sister. To die for her. She'd *wanted* to die for her.

She'd killed herself for her.

What would Abby say to that? Or Ma or Pa or Uncle?

You gotta take care of Abby now.

She couldn't do that when she was dead. But she'd made her choice. And now it would all end.

She couldn't seal the holes Diablo and Zavi had punched through the realms. She couldn't get back to Uncle in time to even come up with another solution. She had no way to save Abby, or Walker, or Ling, or Patrice, or Sophie, or Jemma, or anyone else…

Defeat weighing her down, she folded her legs beneath her, easing herself to sit on the grass. She wondered what came next. Would she feel the end of reality? Would it hurt? Would she even get to glimpse her parents or her brother or any of her friends in those final moments? She wasn't certain she wasn't dead now. Could something worse be waiting for her?

Sensing her surrender, Rok gave a disgusted caw, took wing, and circled overhead like a buzzard. The dumb bird would be caught up in the end, too, she realized. Nothing would survive.

Jezebel took a few tentative steps forward and nudged her shoulder.

"Sorry, girl." She rubbed the horse's muzzle. Her father's horse would also see an end to her happy, carefree running. "I've got nothing left in me. I can't save any of us."

Diablo ticked in her hand. She glanced at the gun. The demon peered at her in her mind's eye. *Home?*

She blinked down. *You...still want to go?*

It projected a sense of peace, serenity. *Home*, it thought, to be with its kind, its...family.

Not that *family* was the word it used, but the concept was there. Kin, not by blood. Like the chupacabra, Diablo had infernal brethren, packmates, beings it had been raised with and guardians who'd fostered it right up to the day it had been snatched from its realm and imprisoned unjustly within the mage gun...

She glanced over at Zavi. *Family*, Diablo said with more confidence.

Suddenly, it all made sense. Diablo and Zavi, Abby, Ling, Uncle, Sophie, Jemma, Walker... She sprang to her feet. "Get up. Get up, get up!"

Zavi glowered. "Why? What's the point?"

She climbed into Jezebel's saddle. "I reckon you and Diablo are kin. Adopted brothers, half brothers, stepbrothers... kin, though, through magic—through your link, severed or otherwise. You can't go home, so it's time you found a new home. New family." She held out her hand. "There's a place for you still. Come with me now, and we can save the realms."

"And if I refuse?" He stuck his chin out defiantly.

She ground her jaw, realizing she'd said the exact same thing to Uncle. "I can't convince you to do anything. I'm not even going to bother telling you that what you'd do is right or just or noble. I've got my own selfish reasons for wanting the realms to continue existing. So ask yourself what it is you *actually* want to do: Stay here and let it all end while you pout? Or get your ass off the grass and do something that actually means something?"

Zavi hesitated. Silently, he stood and mounted behind her.

Rok gave a cry. He flapped down and landed on the pommel. *"I cannot go with you,"* the bird said. *"This is Rok's realm. The other place...too dark."*

"I understand." The familiar had only been tasked with taking her across this plane, after all. She could not ask him for more, and besides, she had Diablo to guide them. "Be well, Rok. Thank you for everything."

He tapped her hand sharply with his beak, but she couldn't decide if he was kissing it farewell or biting it in retaliation for all her abuse. Then he took flight, spiraling up into the sky, dropping a single long, glossy black tail feather, which she caught midair and tucked into her headband. It was a gift, she knew. One she would treasure for as long as she had it.

Hettie rubbed Jezebel's withers. "Jezebel, can you take us to hell?"

The mare stomped her foot. She turned sharply, as if trying to catch her own tail. Three sharp spins that nearly knocked them out of the saddle.

The sky darkened. The ground disappeared beneath their feet.

They fell.

CHAPTER THIRTY-FOUR

Jezebel stumbled but regained her footing quickly, as if she'd only tripped. She gave a fretful, almost apologetic neigh and trotted more carefully forward. Hettie supposed that even freed, a creature like her father's magicked mare wouldn't want to venture into hell, or wherever this place was.

She'd expected the nightmare tunnel of blades and fire that seemed to be her customary entrance into Diablo's realm, but now she understood that had just been the hell gate, her private entrance to the bad place Diablo supposedly hailed from. This place was dark and cool and close. Hettie's skin crawled, and a feeling of restless anxiety invaded her.

"So... which way?" she asked out loud.

"No need to travel any farther." The man who emerged from the darkness had Hettie gasping.

It was her father. Not a proxy wearing his face. Not a demon doppelganger. Every fiber of her being knew this was John Alabama. He was dressed as she'd always known him to dress, with black boots and a black hat, light shirt and worn trousers, a brown vest over top of that. It was what he'd been wearing when he'd died.

"Pa." She held her breath, waited for grief to strike. But there was nothing. She sagged, disappointed she didn't feel something more than vague surprise. With a heaviness that hurt, she dismounted and approached tentatively. "You ended up in hell?"

He dipped his chin. "*Hell* is not the word I'd use. It's more complex than the scriptures make it out to be." He stuffed his hands in his pockets. "The hell people think of… It only exists for those who believe in it, who truly think that is where they have to spend eternity. Truth is, we all have our own private hells where we contemplate our mistakes."

"I'm starting to see that," she admitted. "What about Uncle? I met him on the way…"

"Uncle's serving his time. Paying his debts. And he'll be doing that for a good long while yet. You don't need to worry about him or me."

Jezebel nickered in greeting, and John smiled as he cupped her hairy chin and nuzzled her, murmuring sweet words into her neck the way he used to.

He hesitated. "Remember how I stopped going to church? It was right around when I started remembering who I'd been… Jack Farham, a Blackthorn Rogue. Elias Blackthorn himself after that. That pastor was always haranguing us, saying we were either sinners or saints and holding us to impossible standards. And there I was, a murderer, a thief, and a liar, and bound for damnation." He wiped a hand over his mouth. "Believe me, Hettie, when I say I struggled not to tell you the truth about my past and the legacy I was trapped with. I thought I'd spare you all the pain, but in the end…" He sighed.

"This is the way it was meant to be," a softer voice interjected.

Hettie turned and gasped. "Ma…"

Grace Alabama wrapped her arms around Hettie. Her mother smelled exactly as she remembered, like baking bread and lavender. And yet, despite the memories she associated with them, there was that peculiar sense of numbness. Uncle's bargain had cost her so much… but she supposed everything came with a price.

"Let up, Grace, you're making the girl uncomfortable," John said.

"A woman needs her mother's arms around her now and again. I don't care if she can't love us anymore. I'm her mother and always will be." She held Hettie at arm's length and smiled.

Hettie's eyes grew wet. It was true. All she really wanted was a pair of strong arms around her, and someone to tell her it'd all be okay. "How are you, Ma?" she asked stiltedly.

"Like your father, I've got my own life to think on. Mainly about what we kept from you." She glanced up at her husband. "We thought we were protecting you… We were wrong."

Hettie let out a breath. "It doesn't matter now."

"Yes, it does," her father insisted. "We argued about it. Your Ma thought you were ready to hear the whole story. You were seventeen and had already suffered so much pain with Paul… I thought I could protect you from my own mistakes if I just kept you in the dark."

"I forgive you," she said, and realized she meant it. "Both of you. I don't blame you for what's happened. I can't. You did what you thought you had to do. What anyone in your position would do."

"Not anyone," John said grimly. He glanced toward his wife. "I should've listened to your ma. You are so strong, Hettie."

Something inside her cracked. Her chest hurt. She didn't feel strong. Suddenly, a crippling weakness made her limbs tremble, her stomach turn. She realized what she'd lost, how much she'd missed her parents.

Love poured into her in a deluge, and she gave a great, racking sob and flew into their arms. They held her tight and let her cry.

Of course her love for her parents had been restored to her here and now. *Her own personal hell.* The shadow parents had manipulated her like this once, too, trying to get her to relinquish Diablo to them.

But this was the devil's work. *This* was hell because love inevitably meant loss.

Her shoulders and chest heaved with great racking sobs she thought might tear her asunder. It hurt so much, and every fresh thought about the people she'd lost…the people she'd killed…brought another wave of grief crashing down on her.

If the world ended here, she would be grateful. Content, even.

But she couldn't let it end here because Abby was still out there. And she had to save her.

Thunder rolled through the sky. Hettie wiped her tears and steadied herself. "We're here to bring Diablo back to its home, and

Zavi—" She gestured at Jezebel, where the warlock sat, silently observing.

John held out his hand to stop her. "We can't take him." He nodded at Zavi. "He doesn't belong here. There isn't a realm for him. The Ones Above, as they call themselves, aren't compatible with this place."

"Well... you have to take Diablo at least. Here." She held the mage gun out. "Take it. It's yours."

He didn't reach for it. "It's not going to leave you, Hettie."

"What do you mean? It asked me to bring him and Zavi to this place. Here, I relinquish Diablo to you." When he didn't take it, she offered it to her mother. "Ma?"

"I'm sorry, Hettie. It doesn't work like that."

"Then tell me what I'm supposed to do! Abby's still out there, and I don't know if she'll last much longer!"

Frustrated, she flung the mage gun into the darkness, but it burst back into her hand with a stinging slap, making her hiss.

She turned to Zavi. "What if I gave it to you?" She held it out to him, and he stared at the grip warily. "Take it."

The warlock bit his lip. "I—I..." He looked up at her helplessly. "I can't."

"What do you mean *you can't*? This is all you wanted before!"

"It's not..." He shook his head. "It was a means to an end. Diablo can do me no good here in this place, not now. Besides... it won't come to me."

She stood in shock. She turned back to her father. "What's happening?"

Her father let out a long breath. "Hettie, listen. Even if you put Zavi and Diablo back, there's no saving your sister or your friends."

Her stomach bottomed out. She stared into her mother's eyes, looking for some hint of deception, but why would she lie? "But... Uncle said—"

"Abby is standing in the doorway between realms, holding back the tide of magic that will sweep everything we know away." Grace nodded. "Hettie... there's no stopping that tide now. The rift is open. The pocket realm is saturated. Abby can't hold the door forever."

"It'll be Abby's time soon," her father said sadly. "It was always going to be this way. You have to let her go, Hettie."

"No! I won't accept that!" Hettie paced. "There has to be something we can do. I promised to protect her. I swore on Paul's blood as he died in my arms."

Her parents were silent in that way only parents could be in the face of catastrophe—helpless, resigned. Anger boiled through Hettie's veins. In that moment, she wanted to scream at them for not helping, for not providing the solution. She was on her own, had been for a long time, and there was absolutely no one to help her now.

"You swore on your brother's death?" Zavi's voice was so low and quiet, Hettie thought she'd misheard.

She said over her shoulder, "He died protecting me. He died right after I promised to take care of Abby."

"That explains it. I don't know how I missed it before…" Zavi gave a low chuckle. "You made a blood oath with your brother, and it was witnessed at the threshold of death, notarized by the gatekeepers, no less. A blood oath supersedes all others made afterward. Blood you share with your brother, with your sister, with your family…it is the strongest bond of all. And you share it with Diablo. The reason you can't send Diablo back is that it's part of your family now, too. Part of the contract you made at your brother's death. Part of *you*. Your need to protect Abby is based on more than just some flimsy emotion you call love. It's the blood bond. Diablo can't leave you because it's committed to protecting Abby, just like you are. The bond can never be severed, not by magic, nor anything in your realm."

Hettie's heart clutched. That was what Diablo had meant when he'd told her he wanted to go back to his family. He meant the Alabamas. He wanted her last moments of existence to be with their loved ones.

"Wait…blood oath?" She shook her head. "But…Paul wasn't a sorcerer."

Her parents exchanged looks. "Hettie…he *was* gifted. We hid his powers from the elders when they tested him. We didn't want him going to the Academy. Don't you remember how we told you never to say anything? How careful we always were around other gifted who might sense his powers? Hettie...we told you to ride with Paul that day he was killed because Elder Sanderson was visiting, and we didn't want him putting a truthtelling spell on you in case he made you tell him anything you weren't supposed to."

She remembered none of that. She'd been the one to insist on riding with him. His death had been her fault. Her brother hadn't been gifted. She'd caused his death...

And then she remembered that Ophelia had fired Marcus's mage gun and killed Stubbs while still holding on to Hettie's memories. The Pistols of Lethe used memories as ammunition...

She closed her eyes as the truth swept through her. Zavi was right. Paul had been gifted. The blood oath...she'd sworn on his death to protect Abby, and she always had. But it hadn't been all magic, had it? She loved Abby. She'd do anything for her...

A choked sound sputtered from her tightly clenched teeth. This was all too much to take in. But it didn't matter. The only thing that did matter was Abby.

"How do we help my sister?" she demanded of the group, conviction renewed.

Zavi thought a moment. "You need to use your link to your sister, communicate with her what's happening."

"But...what am I supposed to tell her? And how do I even reach her?"

"I can help you. I've contacted her through those links, too, after all." The warlock smirked. "As to what we tell her..."

"Trust her." This from her mother. "Trust her, Hettie. Abby has always been stronger and smarter and more powerful than any of us could understand."

"But...trust her with what?"

"With our lives. With the fate of the realms." He gave a short laugh. "With all of reality. Trust her to save us."

Hettie stared. Trust her with her life. But...*Hettie* was the one who was supposed to save *Abby*. Her sister had sacrificed too much already for them. She couldn't risk letting Abby sacrifice herself again. Not for Hettie.

Then she remembered what Paul—or was it Diablo?—had said: there was only one person who could save Abby now. He'd meant Abby. Hettie had trusted her sister once to be on her own with

Ling, to learn how to control her indigo powers. Abby had saved Hettie's life in exchange for her own because it had been the only choice she could make.

And now Hettie had to let go and allow Abby to make the right choice again.

Sucking in a lip, she nodded. "All right. But what about you and Diablo? The whole point of us being here was to plug up those holes."

"This is the trickier part," Zavi said. "The only way to plug up the holes in the fabric of the realms and keep magic from leaking out any further is to send me and Diablo back. I have no realm to go home to now... unless I'm reborn into one."

"What does *that* mean?"

"I have to take on a different form. A mortal one, so that when I die, I'm sent back to my own realm, like the ones your parents inhabit." He locked gazes with her. "In order for me to rejoin a realm, I'll need *you* to give birth to me."

Her insides quavered, and she automatically put a hand over her abdomen. "But..." She gestured helplessly. "I'm dead. I shot myself in the head."

"Didn't kill you the first two times, did it?" her father said with a dry chuckle. Grace smacked him in the arm lightly.

"Diablo's powers are greater than you will ever know. The demon, as you call it, is a being of life and death, of creation and destruction. You're the only wielder I've known who has ever even broached any understanding of it that is deeper than a gun whose aim is sure." Zavi sounded almost impressed by her.

"You knew this was possible?"

"It's not something I *want* to do," he growled. "This form... Everything you see that is me will cease to exist." He looked uncomfortable. "But the alternative is no better. This is the only chance I can see of ever returning to the realm of the Ones Above. If Diablo's in agreement, you will live to bear me... if that is Abby's will, too."

Hettie bit her lip. Was there any choice? "Fine. I'll... *bear* you. But... I mean..." Her cheeks grew hot, aware her parents were standing right there. Even if they were dead, this was not something she wanted to be discussing in front of them. She knew the mechanics of making children, of course, but she was not going to… Not with Zavi!

He rolled his eyes and tossed his blond hair. "Don't flatter yourself, wielder. The procedure doesn't require anything quite so crude. But understand this: I will not be *me* when I am born. I will be born to die, to save the world. To save *your* world."

"Yeah, I get it."

Grace's eyes softened. "I'm not sure you do. This isn't going to be easy, Hettie. There's no going back from here."

"I'd die a thousand more times to save Abby," she said staunchly.

"I know. But this is going to be different. It's going to be…difficult."

She exhaled slowly. "Just do it."

Zavi reached out. "Draw Diablo and take my hand."

Hettie glanced back at her parents, and her stomach torqued. There wasn't time to say good-bye or make promises about seeing them again. She didn't know where she'd end up, if not heaven, hell, or whatever lay in-between. If she still existed after all this to die again, this special hell might welcome her and provide never-ending torment in the form of frequent, too-short visits with her parents.

She supposed that was the most she could hope for.

She slipped her hand in Zavi's.

CHAPTER THIRTY-FIVE

Hell rushed away, the darkness lifting as the world zoomed past. They flew straight and true along an invisible road that cut through the skies of the realm in-between.

Zavi's gaze stayed glued to the horizon, which roiled with storm clouds the color of a bruise. Lightning flashed through them, illuminating horrific scenes of violence in the briefest flashes. Hettie saw wolves and fire, a dark cave filled with whimpers and strange smells. And then there were shouts and large men with needles and knives, manacles and chains and all manner of restraints rattling and clanking around them. Hettie flinched as phantom hands clawed at her hair.

"Don't look too closely," Zavi warned. "Abby's memories are manifesting to protect her. If you start believing what you see, they'll have power over you."

She turned away from the nightmare show.

They flew directly into the eye of the storm, and the deep purple clouds crowded them, the gusts of wind buffeting Hettie this way and that. Thunder cracked and rolled loud in her ears. Zavi's grip on her hand tightened. "Don't get distracted. This path is far more treacherous than a regular interpolation. It lies directly in Abby's consciousness on a plane of existence she shapes with a mere thought. If we die here, that's it. There's nowhere else for our souls to go."

The thunderheads thinned as they neared the center. They emerged in the center of the storm, a clearing bathed in golden light and ringed by a wall of dense white cloud. And in the middle of it all…

"Abby!" Hettie dropped Zavi's hand and rushed toward the same blanket tent she'd seen earlier in the pocket realm. Her sister peeked out as she approached, her violet eyes wide.

"The storm's loud," she said, ducking her head as thunder clapped overhead. Abby's gaze went from her sister to Zavi, and she frowned accusingly. "*You* made it this way."

"I'm afraid I didn't." The warlock glanced nervously at Hettie, and then she remembered that Abby had all the power here. She could blink the warlock out of existence altogether if she wanted to. "Abigail, think back to what you were doing before you came here. Do you remember the men who were trying to hurt you? I was there, too."

She blinked slowly. "You and Patrice tried to stop them."

He nodded. "I'm sorry we couldn't. They hurt all of us."

Her frown deepened. "They should be punished." The clouds around them boiled with lightning. Zavi's eyes darted around warily.

"Abby, stop," Hettie said. "Those men aren't here. They did bad things, and I know you're mad at them, but… you can't hurt them, or anyone else."

"Why not?" Abby demanded.

Hettie exhaled. "Because it's not our place to make those choices. There are rules we need to… to follow."

Abby studied her, and Hettie felt her probing magics delve through her. She thought about the past three years and knew her sister was rifling through those memories, inspecting them, reading her thoughts and feelings. Her sister's pointed chin lifted.

"The Division hurt all those people. Took those children. Killed thousands… And the Pinkertons. And those zombies. And the army…" Her violet eyes turned pitch-black. "I could stop them all now."

Hettie's skin lifted in goose bumps. "I know. But you don't need to."

"They hurt you. They hurt so many people." Her voice was tight and small, a clenched fist in the back of her throat. Hettie had seen Abby petulant and pouting; she'd seen her throw tantrums. But she'd never seen her *angry* like this. "They hurt Ma and Pa and Uncle and…" She gasped, and her eyes went violet once more. "Cymon!"

The cloud wall began to whirl. A bolt of lightning cracked across the space. Zavi backed toward the tent. "What's she doing?" Hettie cried.

"Nothing good," the warlock said.

Abby lifted the flap of the tent. She was hastily wiping tears from her eyes. "It's going to rain real bad, Hettie. Come in here. You'll be safe."

Hettie thought quickly. "I want to, Abby, but I need you to stop all this first."

"Don't you want to play? We haven't played in so long." She hung her head. "I don't have anyone to play with anymore. All my friends are gone. They got…lost." She looked away, toward the maelstrom closing around them. "I'm afraid I might get lost, too."

Hettie was about to assure her that she wouldn't let her get lost, but then she remembered why they were there.

"Wielder…" Zavi warned as the wall of cloud shrank rapidly.

"Abby, listen. I know things are hard. But…" Hettie swallowed thickly as her sister turned her eyes up to her. "If you get lost, I know you'll find your way back to me. You always do. Every time we've been separated, you've been the one who's found *me*. You're smart and you're strong. Stronger than I ever was."

"But…I can't." Tears formed in her confused eyes. "I'm just a little girl."

"You're a little girl who's done more than most grown-ups do in their whole lives. You traveled across the country a bunch of times. You know all kinds of spells and stuff about magic. You can do things I never could."

The wind howled, and the blanket tent billowed and flapped dangerously. Abby clung to it. "Hettie, come inside!"

"No, Abby." She stood her ground. "You have to let go and trust yourself. It'll be okay."

"Just take my hand! Please!" Tears flowed from Abby's eyes, caught in the high winds and sparkling like diamonds as they were whipped off her cheeks.

Hettie dug her heels in, fighting the punishing squalls and the wrenching need to wrap herself around her sister and hold on. "Abby..." Her voice broke. "I can't save you. You know what you need to do. We're all counting on you now."

Abby shook her head. "What if I make a mistake? What if I end up hurting a lot of people?"

"Then you live with your choices. You can only do your best. It's up to you now. I believe in you."

Abby bowed her head. The wind howled.

Clinging to the ground as if a tornado were on top of them, Zavi shouted, "The pocket realm is expanding! The rift is feeding it too fast. This interpolation is going to collapse!"

Hettie looked beseechingly at her sister. "Please, Abby. I can't do anything to save us. I need you to be the brave one now. I'm...I'm scared."

Abby's face fell. The calm that overtook her was almost frightening, the steadiness with which she held herself reminding Hettie of their pa, just before he'd shot Shadow Frank between the eyes. Her sister already knew what she had to do. And it would be terrible.

Abby stood and threw off the quilt, and the maelstrom ripped it away. Brilliant golden light like a summer's day in the orchard haloed her. The storm pressed closer. Abby smiled tentatively. "You really trust me?"

"With everything in me." And Hettie meant it.

Abby closed her eyes and tilted her chin. "Okay."

She lifted her hand, and Hettie's arm jerked up, Diablo primed and ready. The mage gun squeaked in shock and protest as Hettie's finger slid over the trigger thorn.

Green hellfire poured from the muzzle, engulfing the space, splashing up against the storm wall...through Abby.

Hettie's scream stuck and stopped up her throat as her sister's form evaporated. Every muscle in her body was locked tight as a vise. She struggled to breathe. To shout. To do anything—

This couldn't be happening. This was an interpolation. It wasn't real. No one was alive here, not really—it was just their spirits or souls or…

The green flames finally dissipated. Abby and all evidence she'd been there were gone.

The storm closed around them.

"Hettie!" Zavi grabbed hold of her shoulders and spun her around. "There's…there's nothing we can do…" A manic look between despair and loathing filled him. He clamped his hands on either side of her head. She thought he might snap her neck—

He planted his mouth over hers.

The darkness swallowed them.

CHAPTER THIRTY-SIX

Hettie heaved a torrent of blood, and she turned over and retched. Her ears rang, her vision blurred. Every muscle screamed with pins and needles.

She pushed up blearily. The world around her rushed in a cloud of light and swirling smoke. The fissure beneath her sister dimmed, closing until she could see Abby once more, floating within the vortex.

Shut down the drill. The directive came from deep, deep down. Nothing would matter unless she did that.

She raised her gun with a shaking, mangled hand, her vision graying out. She had one bullet left. But what to shoot? She didn't know what part of the Mechanikal engine would cause a fatal breakdown…

It's all right, she heard a voice. Voices. So many of them…and then she felt hands soft as water gently guiding her aim…

Her muscles tensed, and she pulled the trigger. The recoil snapped her wrist and she collapsed to the floor, moaning. She couldn't even see what she'd hit, though she'd heard a ping, a crack, and then a hiss as pressure released.

A blast of heat and light rolled over her. Her eyelids stung. Hettie kept her face down, letting the fire roar across her back, waiting for the end.

Gradually, the wind died down. When she glanced up again, the world was awash in smoke and fire, ashes and chaos.

Hettie couldn't see Abby. She tried to crawl toward where her body had lain, but she only got a few inches before everything inside her gave up. She blacked out.

ᛉ

A deep, dreamless sleep ensnared her. *Heaven*, she thought, but it lasted only a moment, and then her senses blinked back to agonizing life, tasting blood, smelling foulness, hearing her own sluggish heartbeat and the rush of blood through her ears. She couldn't see anything, though. Maybe she didn't want to see how bad the damage was. Except…

"Abby?" It came out a croak.

"She's alive!" A familiar woman's voice, but it sounded…changed. Weaker. She couldn't put a name to it.

Blackness claimed her again. There were flashes of sensation, voices and bits of low conversation swirling around her. She might have liked to stay there, only she kept climbing out of that void, bent on making sure her sister was safe.

Something else was going on, too. A small voice within whispered reassurances, hummed, nodded along to the rhythm of her pulse. She became aware of it the way she was aware of Diablo. And in those moments of dark bliss, she spoke to it.

You are not alone, it said. Or was that her speaking? Or Diablo?

At one point, she awoke to a clammy something enclosing her hand. She flexed her fingers—a spasm, really—but whoever was at her bedside gripped her hard, and she heard Walker's distinct voice above her. "Oh, God, Hettie, please, please, wake up…"

She tried to climb out of the abyss, but her limbs were leaden, her eyes weary. Despite her best efforts, the darkness dragged her back. The little life inside her asked about the voice, and she found herself telling it about the bounty hunter and all they'd been through together.

You miss him? it asked.

Hettie hesitated. *I don't know. I want to say yes, but I can't trust my feelings. I've been lied to and manipulated. Had my memories played with.*

What if what I feel isn't real? I've done terrible things to people, things I should never be forgiven for. He shouldn't love me. What if I hurt him?

You've already hurt him many times, the voice offered. *But he always comes back. That's what love is.*

They'd all be better off without me.

Do you really believe that?

The darkest dark, the coldest cold, opened up beneath her. She felt herself being drawn toward it. Panicking, she scrambled away. Abby. She couldn't go until she knew her sister was safe...

Open your eyes. Open your eyes.

I'm trying.

"Open your eyes, Hettie. Wake up. You need to wake up!"

She struggled to surface. The first thing she tried moving was her mangled trigger finger. Everything about it ached. Was it broken? It felt so stiff.

Finally, as if they'd been glued shut, her eyes cracked open, the eyeballs rolling back behind heavy eyelids. She repeated this horrible exercise several times more, trying to ignore the voice encouraging her to "Stay awake, y'hear? I'm sick of sitting by this bedside!"

Uncle?

Her eyes snapped open.

It was Walker, hand tightly clasping hers, eyes red-rimmed and stubble thick. "Hettie?"

She moved her lips, but no sound came out. Walker shouted for people to come, and then it was a flurry of activity as healers put liquids to her lips, rubbed her stiff muscles, asked her an unending series of questions and generally made a fuss.

The whole time, she thought she sensed Uncle standing by, watching from the corner of the room, possibly swigging something foul from a bottle and grunting about how tough she was.

"Where's Abby?" Hettie finally managed when she had the strength. But no one would answer her.

In time—how long, she couldn't say—Hettie figured out she was in the Favreau mansion in New Orleans. It had seen better days, especially after the Pinkerton siege, but it was four walls and a roof, with beds and clean linen, and it was mostly quiet.

Hettie's body was a wreck. Coming out of the hell gate a second time had taken its toll on top of the injuries she'd sustained in the battle in the pocket realm.

On top of checking her stitches and various injuries—a gunshot wound to the head, a gunshot to her side, a fractured arm, a broken leg, four fractured ribs, and eight of her ten fingers also broken—Ling stuck her with needles to stimulate the atrophied muscles. It reminded her a little too much of the beast Abby had been strapped into, but Hettie didn't have much choice in the matter, and the treatment did seem to be working. Soon, she was strong enough to go to the chamber pot without Walker's help.

Ling didn't say much beyond reporting her progress to her, and oddly, he wasn't using his healing gift. Maybe it was because Walker was always at her bedside when Ling visited. Maybe it was because Ling was mad at her for...well, who knew anymore? She'd done so much wrong. Unfortunately, even he wouldn't tell her where Abby was. All he ever said was "Rest" and then left the room, pale and tight-lipped.

Eventually, Sophie and Jemma visited. Something about the debutante seemed...different, but then Hettie supposed the battle had scarred them all. Jemma looked plain tired.

"Sophie, please." Hettie met her eyes. "No one is telling me anything. Where is my sister? Where is Abby?"

Sophie took her hand and squeezed. "I'm sorry, Hettie. I...I don't know. No one does. Alive or dead... We never found her. But you need to listen to what I have to tell you first."

Sophie gathered herself, Jemma holding her hand for reassurance. "We thought you were dead the moment the hell gate opened. We saw you shoot yourself in the head—" Sophie bit her lip. "The hell gate dragged you and a few other sorcerers in, including that Zavi. But Abby... She plunged in headfirst after you.

"The moment Abby was sucked in, the pocket realm collapsed. The rift that had opened beneath her split, and..." She waved helplessly. "The next thing we knew, you were here and she wasn't."

"That can't be. I saw her body. She must still be trapped in the pocket realm—"

"No, Hettie… Magic… All the magic everywhere… It's gone."

She gasped. "Gone?" Her stomach bottomed out. "Diablo?" She reached out for the gun, but there was nothing. No presence. No voice. It hadn't even occurred to her until now to summon it.

Jemma brought her a lidded box from a side table. On the plain black velvet within lay a twisted lump of metal, something that had the vague shape of an old pistol, only it looked as though it had been thrown into a fire.

When Hettie didn't reach for it, Sophie scooped the mage gun off the velvet and pressed it into her hands.

"None of our powers work anymore. Not without a lot of effort." She rubbed her hands in a nervous washing motion. "In the past four weeks, the entire length of the Wall crumbled and sank into the earth. All the natural Zooms collapsed. Protection spells, contract spells, healing and anti-vermin charms and talismans… Everything's stopped working."

"The zombies?"

"Some died. Some survived. Many are in hospitals all over the country."

"Meanwhile, the president had the council of elders and all the grandmasters jailed for treason," Jemma interjected. "Apparently, they found evidence that the Division was planning a coup, with spies in the White House weaving influence spells to keep the government out of magic affairs. That's why they were collecting all that magic—they were readying for a war on mundanes. At least, that's the word from the White House. It might be more antisorcery propaganda, but I don't see why they'd need it now."

Hettie swallowed tightly. "What about…the soothsayers…?

Sophie bit her lip. "They didn't make it. We found Grandmère…" She put a fist to her mouth and turned her face away.

"I'm so sorry, Sophie." Hettie's gaze dropped. "I failed her."

Sophie shook her head. "You did everything you could have, everything that was asked of you. This…this all happened the way she said it would. At least now we can lay her to rest."

Stoic as a soldier, Jemma went on. "Magic didn't leave all at once. With the pocket realm collapsing, we retreated to Root Hill, got all the dead and wounded out. What we didn't know was that the Division had launched an attack there the moment the multirealm globe opened the gateway to the pocket realm. It was a trap. They'd traced the globe's magical signature and opened a remote Zoom on us." She blew out a breath in frustration. "I knew it was too good to be true."

Hettie closed her eyes. Berkeley had told her as much.

"Horace, Bear, and Walker were ready, though," Jemma continued. "They defended the people, saved a lot of lives, sending the people into the trees where they'd be safe. Bear…he juiced and cast a hide spell that kept them safe while we rallied and drove back the Division." She blew out a breath. "He didn't survive. And we lost a lot of people."

The knife between Hettie's ribs twisted as Jemma recited the names and numbers. All their sorcerers had been caught by the bomb, and many had turned against each other in the ensuing hunger madness. Six of the thirteen Rogues Lena had rallied had been killed. Duke had been badly injured, taking a bullet to the shoulder and a rotting hex to his leg. Jay and Hawk had both been killed.

She sat up, suddenly realizing one presence she'd missed. "What about Cymon? Where's my dog?"

Jemma pursed her lips. "I'm sorry, Hettie, but…Cymon was shot in the battle, defending a little boy." She swiped at the wetness running down her cheek. "For all that he stank…he was a very good dog."

Hettie's heart wrenched hard. Tears poured from her eyes. Sophie and Jemma left her alone to grieve.

When she awoke, eyes puffy and head aching from crying, she found Ling by her bedside. He sagged as if some of the air had been let out of him, and his complexion was gray.

"How are you?" she croaked, understanding now why he'd been so quiet.

"How I am doesn't matter." He hung his head. "I'm sorry, Hettie. I failed you. I failed Abby."

"Don't blame yourself. I went against orders. I'm the one who…" She trailed off. There was nothing she could say to rectify any of this. "I'm sorry about Cymon." He'd spent more time in Ling's company than hers these past few years.

He nodded, his eyes wet. "How are you feeling?" Businesslike, he placed a hand over her forehead. "You're still running a temperature."

When she didn't reply, he frowned. "You can't die, Hettie. Everyone here needs you."

She stared up at the ceiling. "For what? Abby's gone. Patrice is dead. Diablo's stopped working now that there's no magic left in the world. If I get better... well, it'll just be a matter of time before the authorities or a mob catches up with me. I'm still a wanted woman. And now I'm also the reason magic's gone and the world's in chaos."

"I may not have my healing abilities, but I'm still bound by my oath to heal and do no harm. That includes making sure you don't die by self-neglect. Besides..." He trailed off, jaw firming, then got to work putting together a batch of some horrible smelling tea with the ingredients on the dresser.

"Besides, what?" she prompted.

His face was a blank mask as his hands paused over the mortar and pestle. He asked over his shoulder, "Do you remember when your last courses were?"

Her cheeks heated. "I... I don't know. They were never regular to start with..."

And then she realized what he was saying. "I'm with child."

"I'd wondered if you already knew or not when I arrived in Root Hill. I'd sensed... something. But I wasn't sure. These things are not always certain. You could just as easily have had fleas or some other parasite."

Hettie put one hand over her belly. She glanced around, looking for Walker. No wonder Ling had been so quiet. He'd wanted to consult her before he said anything else. "How far along?"

"I don't know for certain. Only you can confirm it. But if I were guessing, maybe three months. Unless you've been spending time in Diablo's bubble and I'm not aware of it."

A flurry of thoughts scuttled through her brain. A baby. Walker's baby. And not only that...

I will not be me when I am born. I will be born to die, to save the world. To save your world.

Zavi.

"Congratulations," Ling said with a wry smile. "You'll make a fine mother."

She tipped her head back and let out a long breath. Hettie, a mother…to a reincarnated divine being turned evil warlock who'd kidnapped her sister and tortured and nearly killed Hettie any number of times. But *she'd* made that bargain, and it had to be fulfilled.

What would be the point, though? Did such a contract even hold in this magicless world?

A flutter in her abdomen had her sitting up. Her heart beat wildly at the sensation. She swallowed thickly. "This baby… Ling, I need to tell you something."

She told him about the bargain she'd struck with Zavi to give birth to him in order to save the world. She thought she would've held this strange and awful secret close, but Ling was all the family she had left, and she needed someone to know.

"I don't know what to expect next," she said, excited and anxious at once. "I mean…did I just imagine all this? Will this baby even survive?" Her fingers convulsed over her abdomen, icy fear suddenly sluicing through her veins.

"I don't have the answers to those questions," Ling said. "But if everything you told me is true, I would not discount any bargain made in the other realms. Magic isn't just the power that the gifted can manipulate. It's in everything… My qi…I don't feel it as prominently as I once did, but it's still there, buried, like a seed in the earth, dormant but filled with all the potential of a great tree. With some training and healing and meditation, I think I may coax it back."

"So…magic isn't entirely gone?"

"There is always magic, always hope. It just takes work to find it, and faith to foster it. That has always been the true source of magic." He let out a breath. "I imagine there are others who may have retained some of their abilities, however faint." He paused. "Considering Abby's powers, she may have found a way to survive going through the hell gate. She could be out there somewhere."

Hettie stared up at the ceiling. She desperately wanted that to be true. To have some little shred of hope to cling to. But the thought of even trying to push out of that bed…of mounting her horse and pointing it toward the unknown, on some wild chase after a sister whose body might not even exist anymore…

She inhaled shakily. "That kind of hope's like a mirage in the desert I could chase forever," she whispered. "For all the salvation it promises, it's nothing but a figment of my imagination. And I'm so tired of chasing shadows." Tears filled her eyes. "I…I just can't anymore. I've failed her too many times now, died twice for her, for nothing. I've got nothing left in me to give. I'm sorry."

Ling smiled sadly and placed a hand over hers. "You have one thing."

Born to die…

Hettie clutched her stomach fearfully.

CHAPTER THIRTY-SEVEN

Walker took the news of the baby quite well. Actually, he'd been jubilant. She'd never seen him so happy, then terrified, all at once. But then he'd sobered. "You... you are asking me to help you raise the baby, aren't you? You're not going to... give it up?" His Adam's apple bobbed. His sight had mostly returned with the disappearance of magic—it seemed it was more curse than ailment—and his eyes pinned her now.

She shook her head. "You're the father, Walker."

Her reassurance didn't wipe the doubt from his eyes—doubt *she'd* instilled in him. Guilt was like a bullet festering inside her. She'd done so many people wrong, and all for nothing in the end. She had to make things right. "Marry me," she said.

He blinked. "Are you telling me, or asking?"

Her cheeks heated, and she scoffed. "You gonna make me say it again?"

He laughed and kissed her gently so as not to disturb her injuries. Then, more purposefully, infusing her with a promise, branding her with his devotion... filling her with hope, even.

They had a small, private ceremony in the Favreau mansion, and because Hettie was still recovering, they spent their honeymoon there, too.

As she got stronger, Hettie learned about the fates of the rest of her allies. No charges had been laid against members of the League of Sorcerers for Free Magic who'd purportedly attacked Division agents, but Sophie and the others were still working on exonerating members who had been convicted of crimes against the state.

When Hettie's recovery was well underway, Ling joined Starling in helping the drained sorcerers who'd formerly been zombies. Scattered across the country, they were in need of medical care and a way home. In addition, about a hundred young people were found crowded together at the base of the Wall at the border, as if they'd emerged from the rubble of the collapsing monolith that had once divided nations. Among them were many of the missing children from the Division's Academy. Apparently they'd been taken and used in magical experiments—Hettie mentioned the zombies she'd found in the pocket realm to Starling, and the League's leader wrote a letter positing that theory to the new liaison with the formerly gifted before rounding up her team and heading south. With as much medical attention and succor as they could provide, the children would eventually be reunited with their families. And so, with the government's blessing, the new Coalition of the Gifted was born.

Horace went with them.

"They'll be needing supplies, contacts, carts, horses . . . and I can get them at a good rate," he said, one eye on the wagons being loaded. "Miss Sophie says she'll handle all the financials and make sure we get what we need."

"What about your shop?"

"Business can always wait. People who need help can't." He tipped his chin up and chuckled. "Never thought I'd go from businessman to outlaw to philanthropist in a single lifetime."

"Ain't what you call yourself that's important. It's what you do."

They hugged, and he vowed to see her again soon. Daisy called to him, "You hurry yourself up, Mr. Washington! I'm not fixin' to wait in this godforsaken swampland for some jacked-up horse trader!"

Hettie waved at Daisy, who rolled her eyes and turned away. "Is she okay?"

"Grieving her brother, no doubt. Don't worry. I'll watch over her." He flashed his teeth, but there was genuine feeling there, too. Hettie had no doubt Daisy would be in good company.

When most everyone had cleared out, Sophie made sure to write reference letters for every last one of the mansion's displaced servants and then put her grandmother's home up for sale. Patrice had left everything to her granddaughter in her will, which had incensed her estranged father. Instead of keeping it all, though, Sophie and Jemma liquidated Sophie's beloved grandmother's possessions and put the funds into helping Starling with magical recovery efforts. "Grandmère always said we had more than anyone would need for ten lifetimes." Sophie stared up at the family portraits hanging in the gallery. Patrice smiled serenely down at her, a twinkle in her all-knowing eyes.

"What will you and Jemma do?"

Sophie chuckled. "We might do some traveling—to the Caribbean, perhaps. Somewhere we can just enjoy the sunshine." Light filled her eyes. "It doesn't matter where we end up, though. All I really need is her."

Jemma had different ideas. "Paris. I'll fatten you up on croissants, and we'll go hat shopping. I want you to have so many hats, we can't go anywhere without you feeling bad about leaving your collection behind."

Sophie took her hand and kissed it. "Yes, ma'am."

They had Marcus's body brought to New Orleans for burial in the family plot in St. Louis Cemetery, one of his two mage guns—Luna? Claire?—buried with him. Hettie wondered if Lena and Duke would find the other in Berkeley Manor; she'd sent them a detailed letter about the grandmaster's opulent home, and with magic gone, she imagined the place was exposed and ripe for robbing. Of course, the Rogues had suffered enough losses, and would be licking their wounds for a while. If Hettie had her druthers, she'd go to Kansas herself and raze that palace of false memories to the ground.

Perhaps she would one day. She felt it was her duty to return what belonged to Marcus. She owed him this, at least. He'd been the only person to understand her curse, her burden.

When all was settled, Sophie handed an embarrassing amount of cash to Hettie in recognition of her services to the Favreau family.

"A little money is hardly enough to thank you for saving the world," she said when Hettie tried to refuse, "especially one that wants you dead."

"Thanks for that reminder," Hettie said.

Sophie chuckled. "If I've learned anything in my time knowing you, Hettie Alabama, it's that you could stare death down and win."

And then Sophie and Jemma packed up and left.

Hettie was just starting to show when she and Walker drove a cart out of New Orleans and took a train north. Fortunately, no one looked too closely at them. Everyone was still dazed by the disappearance of magic and distracted as they tried to navigate a new world where protection talismans were replaced by guns, and personal safety and security became a question of whether you knew how to use one.

Mundanes who'd never had ready access to magic were smug at first; this was the reckoning the Mundane Movement had said was a long time coming, and the people reveled in watching the mighty fall. But professionals whose skills were magic-based found themselves without employment. The government cut the Division's funds severely, and thousands of agents and enforcers had to find other work. The country went into a recession. And then everyone realized they were surrounded by fearful, jobless former sorcerers looking for reassurance in a world where they no longer had power, and now kept it in the form of irons at their sides.

By the time Hettie and Walker crossed the border into Manitoba, Canada, the leaves were just starting to change color. They bought a cabin in the woods just far enough from town that they wouldn't be disturbed, on a parcel of land rich with game. Hettie picked up a Winchester for the first time in nearly five years. She bull's-eyed five squirrels on her first hunting trip out.

Winter came fast and hard. Hettie grew big and irritable. And then, one clear, cold night when the moon stared down unblinking upon the snow-laden land, she gave birth to a little girl.

Hannah Abigail Woodroffe had her mother's looks and her father's temperament. As she nursed, hungry for life and her mother's milk, Hettie remembered holding Abby for the first time, tiny and purple and eerily subdued. A changeling, some had whispered, but her ma had refused to listen when they suggested she end the baby's life before it became a tragic one filled with pain and suffering.

Now, Hettie had brought a changeling into the world in order to save it.

Winter turned to spring. Hettie's injuries never fully healed. She developed a tremor in her left leg, and random bouts of dizziness incapacitated her. Her magically advanced years had taken their toll, too: she was always tired now, and having a young daughter didn't help with her fatigue. Despite all that, she slowly grew to relish this new peaceful life. Her days as an outlaw seemed like a distant nightmare. Still, the ghosts of the past haunted her, and there were days when she'd glance over her shoulder, afraid the authorities would find her and break up their little family.

I understand now, Pa, she thought one night as she cleaned the Winchester, one eye on the dark woods. She thought she'd seen wolves out there.

CHAPTER THIRTY-EIGHT

Hannah grew up, sensing her mother's fear, knowing she felt hunted, but never understanding why. She wondered why her mother kept a twisted lump of metal locked in a box set high on the mantel where Hannah couldn't reach, yet had two shotguns, her Winchester, and a brace of pistols hanging by the door, as well as wearing a Colt everywhere she went. Instead of telling her the truth, Ma and Pa told her wild stories about outlaws and sorcerers and evil warlocks. Hannah was not impressed. She only wanted the facts.

It wouldn't have been so bad if it weren't for her mother's nightmares. She'd wake up screaming and sobbing and had run out of the house a few times, grabbing her guns on the way and staring hard into the night, poised for a fight. Hannah knew that Aunt Abigail, for whom she was named, featured in those dreams. But when she asked about it, Ma only shook her head, looking pained. So Hannah shut her ears when her mother cried out in the night and pretended Ma was all right.

Once a year, Uncle Ling, who was not her uncle, would visit. He always brought her fascinating toys and puzzles imported from his homeland to play with. He was a polished and wealthy man, as well as a physician, and had married a girl in San Francisco, where he spent most of the year. He called Hannah his "goddaughter," though he was not Christian, and they practiced no faith in the house apart from the oaths her mother and father sometimes let slip. As far as Hannah was concerned, though, "goddaughter" meant she got a lot of very nice gifts, and she was all right with that. When she asked him in private about her mother's nightmares, he told her, "Your mother has demons of her own to deal with."

In Hannah's seventh year, Ma got very sick. Her voice had gone soft and ragged, and her coughs were dry and wheezy. She struggled to breathe.

Hannah went to her mother's bedside, intent on helping her get better. "What can I do, Mama? Do you need medicine? Magic? Maybe I can write Uncle Ling..."

Hettie shook her head. "Sometimes people just get sick."

But this wasn't a regular sickness. Hannah could feel it, like a shadow in the cabin. She knew time was running out for her mother, and she would do anything to help her.

"Maybe...maybe if I found Auntie Abigail, she could help you."

Ma's eyes widened. "What did you say?"

"Aunt Abby. In your sleep, you sometimes talk to her...and you say stuff about her healing you. Sometimes you cry. But sometimes...you smile and laugh." Hannah reached out and took her hand. "Would it help if I went to look for Abby?"

Hettie searched Hannah's dark eyes, glimmering with burning conviction too intense to be a child's. She wondered if Abzavine, twisted by fate and a cruel and vindictive world, was finally surfacing in this mania.

I will not be me when I am born.

She studied her daughter's raven-black eyes and hair, wondering if Rok had had any hand in her daughter's looks...whether the proxies were trying to send her a message through Hannah. She was still delicate in her features but well on her way to becoming the spitting image of her ma. Hettie pondered whether Hannah—Zavi—was meant to continue the search she'd abandoned. If that was a torch, a burden, she was born to bear.

A swell of memories overtook her. Faces, names...the smell of cordite and gun smoke searing her nostrils; the bitter tang in her mouth after a battle; the singing of a blade as it sliced through flesh and sinew, hacked at bone; the ache in her hands as she choked the life out of men twice her size... She could not give her daughter that legacy. Diablo was gone. Elias Blackthorn had to die, too, and she had to be the one to kill him.

But Abby... Hettie had given up looking, but Ling had thought she might still be alive. What if Hannah were her only chance to save Abby?

She closed her eyes. And then Hettie remembered what her parents had told her. She'd always known how to find Abby. Their bond was stronger than any other. It was the bond of blood. Of sisters. Of family.

Hettie *would* find her.

"There is something I think would help," she told her daughter. "I'd like a bath."

Hannah grinned, happy she could finally do something to assist her mother. She raced off, yelling for her pa.

It took a long time to fill the tub with enough hot water, and then Hettie asked Walker to take Hannah for a walk in the woods so she could have some peace.

"Are you sure can get in and out yourself?" he asked worriedly.

"I'll be fine. The warm water's helping my breathing. I'm feeling stronger already." She gripped his hands and kissed him gently on the cheek. "Thank you, my love."

Walker smiled, kissed her forehead, and left.

Hettie waited for his footsteps to fade before wedging a chair beneath the doorknob. She unlocked the box on the mantel and picked up the charred, twisted lump of slag that had once been Diablo. It felt warm to her. It was no longer magicked, but it had led her all over hell and the realms in-between, till she'd arrived here. Maybe, if she believed enough, it would lead her where she wanted to go.

She stepped into the tub, her nightgown billowing and soaking up to her waist, then sat down in the water. A lifetime ago, she'd climbed out of bed to seek her sister among the reeds in the stream on the ranch.

She'd said she could hear her friends better there. And now, standing in the water, Hettie could hear their whispers, too.

She sank chest deep, chin deep, dipping her ears back. The whispers grew louder.

Hettie.

Her heart raced, squeezed, ballooning till it felt ready to burst. "I'm coming, Abby."

She sank beneath the surface.

The pressure in Hettie's head built. Darkness closed over her, and the aches and pain and heaviness lifted as she floated away.

Before she could drift off into oblivion, though, someone grabbed her hand. It was a firm, sure grip, and it drew her down till her bare feet met the ground.

Abby beamed at her. Her violet eyes shone, a ring of gold circling her irises.

"I did it, Hettie!" Abby's gold curls bounced as she grabbed her around the waist and squeezed. "I found you!"

"Abby." She hugged her sister tight, shaking with sobs. Silky curls tickled her arms. A slight dampness soaked her nightgown.

Real. This was real.

It had been seven long years of doubt, of hope, of relentless grief and guilt. Tears filled her eyes, clogged her throat. "I thought I'd killed you."

"Killed me?" Abby laughed. "How could you have? Last time we talked, it was through interpolation."

"But Zavi said if we died… I shot you with Diablo and…"

"No, I borrowed some of its powers. I just needed a boost for what I had to do. Plus, it helped me find you again."

Hettie blinked confusedly. "You mean…this isn't the end?"

"The end?" Abby chortled, a sound so sweet Hettie's teeth ached. "This is just the beginning for you, for me, for all of this." She spread her arm out. Hettie stared around.

The haze around her was gradually resolving into a golden landscape with rolling hills. "Where are we?"

"Don't you know? You've been here before. Well, before, it was kind of shapeless and"—she wrinkled her nose—"boring. But I made it better. You helped me make it better."

"The place in-between." She turned in a circle. "But I thought it was destroyed."

"Well, it was. Kind of. But I fixed it." Abby laughed again, then tapped her temple. "I remembered it, so I put it back together."

"But how?"

Abby screwed up her face. "Well...it's like how you know how to clean a gun. Take it apart and put it back together. Practice." She shrugged. "It's just the way things go together. Only I made it better. I needed Diablo's power to erase what was left in that realm so I could create a new pocket realm."

"Wait...I don't understand. We were already in a pocket realm."

"I made a *new* pocket realm *inside* that realm." She explained it with a roll of her eyes. "The first one expanded, just like Uncle said it would, like a tide rushing in and then pulling back everything. The only way I could save all of you was to make a second pocket realm that I could go into. I didn't want to hurt anyone. So I took the magic flooding that first pocket and put it all in the second one. See?" She held out a hand, and a ball of fire coalesced in her palm, bright as a small sun.

Hettie's mind boggled. "So...all the magic that's gone from my realm..."

"It's here." She grinned. "One day, I might release it back into the world a little at a time. But for now, everyone's safe."

"Abby...this is incredible. But..." She hesitated. "But now what? Am I dead?"

"It's complicated." The corner of Abby's mouth twisted up. "I'll explain it to you later." Abby put her fingers in her mouth and gave a piercing whistle.

The thunder of hoofbeats and a deep, resounding bark echoed around them. Hettie's heart soared as Jezebel and Cymon crested the hill and bounded toward them. The big mutt reached them first, bowled her over, tail wagging. He circled the sisters as if he could draw a protection circle around them for all time.

"C'mon." Abby hauled her sister to her feet. "I want you to meet the others."

“Others?”

“My friends. Patrice is eager to see you, too. And Ma and Pa and Paul are waiting.”

Her heart stuttered. Ma. Pa. Paul.

“But…” Hettie turned to look back at the plains stretching around her, gleaming with decadent golden sunlight. She thought about Walker and Hannah, her friends and life above the shimmering surface of the water in the tub.

“Don’t worry,” Abby assured her confidently. “I’ll get you home in time for dinner.”

Hettie gave a startled laugh. She didn’t ask how Abby would do it, or even if she was telling the truth: she simply trusted she would and was.

Jezebel nickered as they mounted. Hettie wrapped her arms around her sister as she took the reins. Her chin didn’t rest on the top of Abby’s head anymore.

She flicked the reins, knowing Jezebel wouldn’t need the prod but unable to stop herself from shouting, “Giddy up!”

The big gray mare took off at a gallop across a field of gold that stretched beyond infinity. The setting sun burnished Abby’s hair till it shone bright as day. Hettie’s heart lightened. And then they were flying.

EPILOGUE

EXCERPT FROM THE DIARY OF JANE PINKERTON, NÉE JANE DOE

COURTESY OF THE MUSEUM OF MAGICAL WONDERS, BOSTON, MA

June 14, 1901

Quentin used to say that if you dig too deeply, eventually, you hit the center of the earth and everything starts going topsy-turvy. Down becomes up, and you don't know which way right is anymore. That's the only way I can describe what happened in the days after we lost magic.

I won't go into the specifics, as I'm sure anyone who is currently reading my personal journal will also have read the news clippings of the era, as well as my court testimony against the actions of various members of the Division of Sorcery. What those records won't show are what happened to me and Professor Hamish Gallagher directly after the blast I witnessed. Hamish thought that, having a unique perspective on the situation, I should put pen to paper for posterity, and as a counter to the Erasurists trying to rewrite history.

After the "bomb"—we learned later Dr. Alastair Fielding actually called this the Fielding Ether Engine—sucked away my magic, the warlock whom they'd called Zavi murdered Dr. Fielding and Wolverton Grey Berkeley with his bare hands. Still incapacitated, I wasn't able to stop him from increasing the power to the device they called the "drill." From what I gathered, the machine was designed to bore through the metaphysical layers between realms. Caught up by the chaos and in a weakened state, I was unable to stop the outlaw Hettie Alabama from shooting herself and opening the gate to hell.

I'm not sure what I was expecting. I think part of me always thought it was a metaphor, or some kind of urban myth. But I will never forget the sight of that threshold to damnation. I have never felt so powerless and fearful as I have looking into that portal. Viscous appendages flailed from it, grabbing whatever they could and pulling it in, like a hasty harvest before a sudden snowstorm. As much rational thought as I've applied to this experience…having survived that ordeal…I can only say that I am less reluctant to believe in the afterlife and am perhaps a little more receptive to the occasional sermon on good and evil. That place could only have been a province of the latter.

I can't claim to understand everything that occurred. Berkeley had brought us to that strange pocket realm with only the minimum of explanations. I thought—or made myself believe—that the place was glamored. But after thinking about what I'd heard, piecing together the clues gathered for evidence, here's what I believe happened.

With the portals to the corridor of power—the place referred to by parties as the "in-between"—and the hell gate open, it was like two giant-mouthed monsters battling for dominance, one spewing fire, the other consuming it, but neither seeming to enjoy the process. The inky hell appendages grasped for the power flooding from that other place of light, but they were boiled away in the process. The light sought to invade the shadows, but failed at the brim of the gate. Equal and opposites in power…yet I'm sure, given enough time, one might dominate the other and plunge the world into unrelenting chaos.

The hell gate could not have been open more than ten seconds, but it was the longest in my life as I clawed my way to safety. I didn't know it, but a shock of my hair had gone white in the process. (Hamish thinks it's rather becoming. I think I look like a damned skunk.) Suddenly, the hell gate slammed shut, and the portal to the corridor narrowed. I'm not certain what I saw next: I was aware there was a young woman caught in that maelstrom. I think she was Abigail Alabama, the rumored sister Hettie had been searching for. But in a flash, she disappeared like smoke, and then the portals were gone, and the pocket realm Berkeley had ferried us to began to crumble.

Here, I will confide something. I had little feeling for Hettie Alabama after she'd killed Quentin, and I would still see her hanged for her crimes. But she cried out for her sister like a wounded, grieving animal, and it plucked at my heart. Bloodied, broken, a hole in her head… I thought her on death's door, and yet grief and loss resurrected her.

She collapsed, but I could not get to her to see that she yet lived for the hangman's noose. Someone whom I believe was with the League of Sorcerers picked me up and carried me out of that strange engine room as it fell apart like a wobbling castle made of jellied milk.

When next I awoke, I was in a Division hospital, Hamish at my side. The bullet had been successfully extracted, his wounds healed. My injuries were superficial, but my powers were almost all gone, my reservoir of strength diminished to a shallow pool.

I was not the only one. Soon, the Division hospital was filled with patients suffering from symptoms similar to withdrawal. Shakes, pain, nausea, vomiting, itchiness, restlessness… And Hamish and I were both subject to it, too.

It took me a lot longer to recover than him; the healers believed it was because the stronger of the gifted had much more to lose, relied on that power more. As the hospital was already overflowing, I vacated my sick bed and went home to Chicago for the remainder of my convalescence.

Uncle William was not entirely pleased by my return; a good portion of his workforce had been put on medical leave, and it was uncertain whether they would come back to work. Still, he seemed relieved I was all right. Father wrote and suggested I go to New York to take up a job as his secretary. I had other plans.

The thing was, during those long days alone (well, mostly alone, as Hamish insisted on staying by my side, the poor man), I'd had a lot of time to think over my actions, my part in the collapse of magic.

Be assured, dear reader, I do not blame myself. But I am aware of my choices. I was hunting Hettie Alabama—not her fantastical gun, not her mysterious sister, not even the secret the Division had held so closely. But that was my failure, because it was a secret that, had I been paying more attention, would have led me to Grandmaster Berkeley's doorstep much sooner with an arrest warrant in hand.

My need for vengeance against the woman who'd killed my friend and mentor blinded me to the cruel, immoral, evil, and clandestine dealings of the Division. We should have recognized its lengthening, deepening reach, the powers it had finagled out of our administration, starting with its corruption of Uncle William's ethics. He blames influence magic, and it isn't a theory without merit, but I have some reservations. I'm sure he has regrets, too.

What we can both agree on is that we should have acted much sooner when the "accidental" deaths at the Academy didn't stop; when sorcerers were required to register; when the Division started snatching children out of their parents' arms. Children! But a strange kind of trust, indifference, and complacency has settled over us since the War.

How often had I heard, or myself said, that the Division was doing its job? Keeping people safe? Securing the nation's resources? I was no fan of the Academy, but I understood it was a necessity. When their interference didn't affect me directly, I did not care. I was an orphan who, by circumstances out of my control, managed to climb out of the dust to the top in every way imaginable. I would never have had gifted children to worry over, or been subject to the "banking" of magic, because of my adopted family name. But if my father hadn't seen me in the Academy that day, I might have ended in far worse circumstances, had a different opinion of the Division's policies.

I'm sure that when historians look back, they will judge us harshly for our inaction, our smug indifference, and wonder whether that black hell gate should not have been wedged open. I do.

The truth is, we got lucky. The only thing the world lost that black day was magic. Yes, there were many deaths—many of the "zombies" perished in the days following those events. A few juicers and sorcerers sadly ended their lives. And now we live in a frightening new world. But it wasn't those dueling portals that had killed them. It was the Division.

There are still efforts by the new Coalition to restore magic, but let us not be too optimistic. Calling an apple a pear does not change the fact it's full of worms. Even if some of the League of Sorcerers for Free Magic are involved, I am suspicious. I believe these erstwhile sorcerers are simply trying to regain favor among the politicians and the public, but it will be a long time before anyone forgets what happened or trusts anyone who ever had magic. Already, people are saying too many public resources are being used on those who are suffering the worst from magic withdrawal, that "real" citizens are starving all over the country. I can't say I agree with them. I was never empathetic to the plight of juicers, but now that I understand their suffering, I find myself reevaluating my views.

To help stave off the cravings and restlessness, Hamish keeps me busy. I think he's afraid if I'm idle too long, I'll go haring off into danger. We're planning a trip to England to study the history of the magic drain there, and to bring back any learnings that might help.

As for my quest for justice... Well, I cannot say I am satisfied. Hettie Alabama remains at large. Though I would not hesitate to turn her over to the proper authorities should our paths ever cross, my role in this debacle, in the disappearance of magic, was due in part to my obsession with her. But I never asked the right questions. Never asked what justice actually meant.

Quentin once told me that magic required faith, truth required resolve, love required patience, and that the answers to the universe required all six. I don't think I will ever have all the answers to my questions now. Not unless I ask Hettie Alabama herself.

I think I am content not to know.

AUTHOR'S NOTE

The magical Wild West of *The Devil's Revolver* grew out of a long tradition of Western stories, fantasy-land tropes, and timeless tales told of questers, searchers, outlaws, villains, champions, and more. It is a setting I have described as "history as it happened...but with magic," including all the injustices, horrors, erasures, and wonders the traditional Western genre frequently glosses over.

Any adjustments to timelines, dates, names, facts, and so forth may be chalked up to the existence (and limitations) of magic in this universe. All other historical inaccuracies are my own. (But also...*waving hands*...magic!)

Of course, there is no way one story about one girl in a fictional magical universe can tell all the stories in history. America is a land of many immigrants and indigenous peoples from all walks of life. I encourage you not only to find their stories but also to learn about the history of the places you live, to find out where your people came from and what they lived through and endured so you could be here today.

AUTHOR'S ACKNOWLEDGMENTS

The Devil's Revolver series would not have been possible without the patient, loving support of my husband, John Michael McGrath, who always gave me space and time to write, an ear when I wanted to bounce ideas off him, home-cooked meals, child care for the Irrational Biped, and thorough explainers about everything from U.S. history to urban planning. John made it possible for me to live out this dream.

Of course, my agent, Courtney Miller-Callihan, was the first one to love Hettie. She found her a home at Brain Mill Press after many years roaming across the publishing landscape. Courtney, you are my compass.

The mapmakers were the dedicated and hardworking Mary Ann Hudson and Ruth Homrighaus. As my editor, Mary Ann steered Hettie and her cabal on the right course, while Ruth flagged the path ahead of us. This metaphor is getting tortured, so let's just say they did all the difficult stuff. They also commissioned the amazing artwork and design for the series, including the custom cover font. Y'all should be checking out the wonderful books they publish at www.brainmillpress.com.

Cassandre Bolan is the fantabulous artist who painted the book covers and made Hettie flesh and blood in my mind's eye.

Cassandre, you are a goddess. Check out all her amazing works of art at www.cassandrebolan.com.

The interior drawings are by the fabulous Ann O'Connell. Every time I see Rok, I laugh.

Special mention goes to the ever-patient Trisha Tobias, copyeditor, who put together the style guide I couldn't, despite my training as a proofreader. I am thankful for all her hard work.

To some special people who've graciously praised and promoted my book: Donna Thorland, Deanna Raybourn, Christine D'Abo, KJ Charles, Melissa Leong, and my #1 fan, Tina Hahn. Thank you all for your cheerleading and support!

To the fine people at Rockstar Games who made the video games *Red Dead Redemption* and *Red Dead Redemption 2*, which inspired this series—thank you for hundreds of hours of entertainment, beauty, and wonder.

I'd like to acknowledge the funding support from the Ontario Arts Council, an agency of the Government of Ontario, for the grant that allowed me to complete this series.

To all my friends, family, and colleagues who've bought and pushed my books—thank you.

To the Fancy Pals: we'll ride the Bone Carousel together one day, I promise.

To my mom and dad—I love you both.

To my sisters, Fiona and Jenny—you guys mean the world to me.

To the Irrational Biped—thank you for being patient with mommy while she works. I love you so much.

And finally, to the fans—thank you for going on this journey with me and Hettie.

ABOUT THE AUTHOR

V. S. McGrath is a published romance author (as Vicki Essex) and has six books with Harlequin Superromance: *Her Son's Hero* (July 2011); *Back to the Good Fortune Diner* (January 2013), which was picked for the Smart Bitches Trashy Books Sizzling Book Club; *In Her Corner* (March 2014); *A Recipe for Reunion* (March 2015); *Red Carpet Arrangement* (January 2016); and *Matinees with Miriam* (November 2016). She has been featured in the *Globe and Mail*, *Metro Toronto*, *Torontoist*, *Inside Toronto*, and Canada.com. *The Devil's Revolver* is her debut young adult fantasy. You can find her on Facebook, Twitter, or her websites: vsmcgrath.com and vickiessex.com. She lives in Toronto, Canada.

www.ingramcontent.com/pod-product-compliance
Lightning Source LLC
Chambersburg PA
CBHW050959180726
48291CB00006B/1893

* 9 7 8 1 9 4 8 5 5 9 3 3 1 *